VITAL FOUND

The Evelyn Maynard Trilogy
Part Two

KAYDENCE SNOW

Cover design by Mila Book Covers
Book design by Inkstain Design Studio
Editing by Kirstin Andrews

www.kaydencesnow.com

For you, the readers.

You make it possible for me to live my dream.

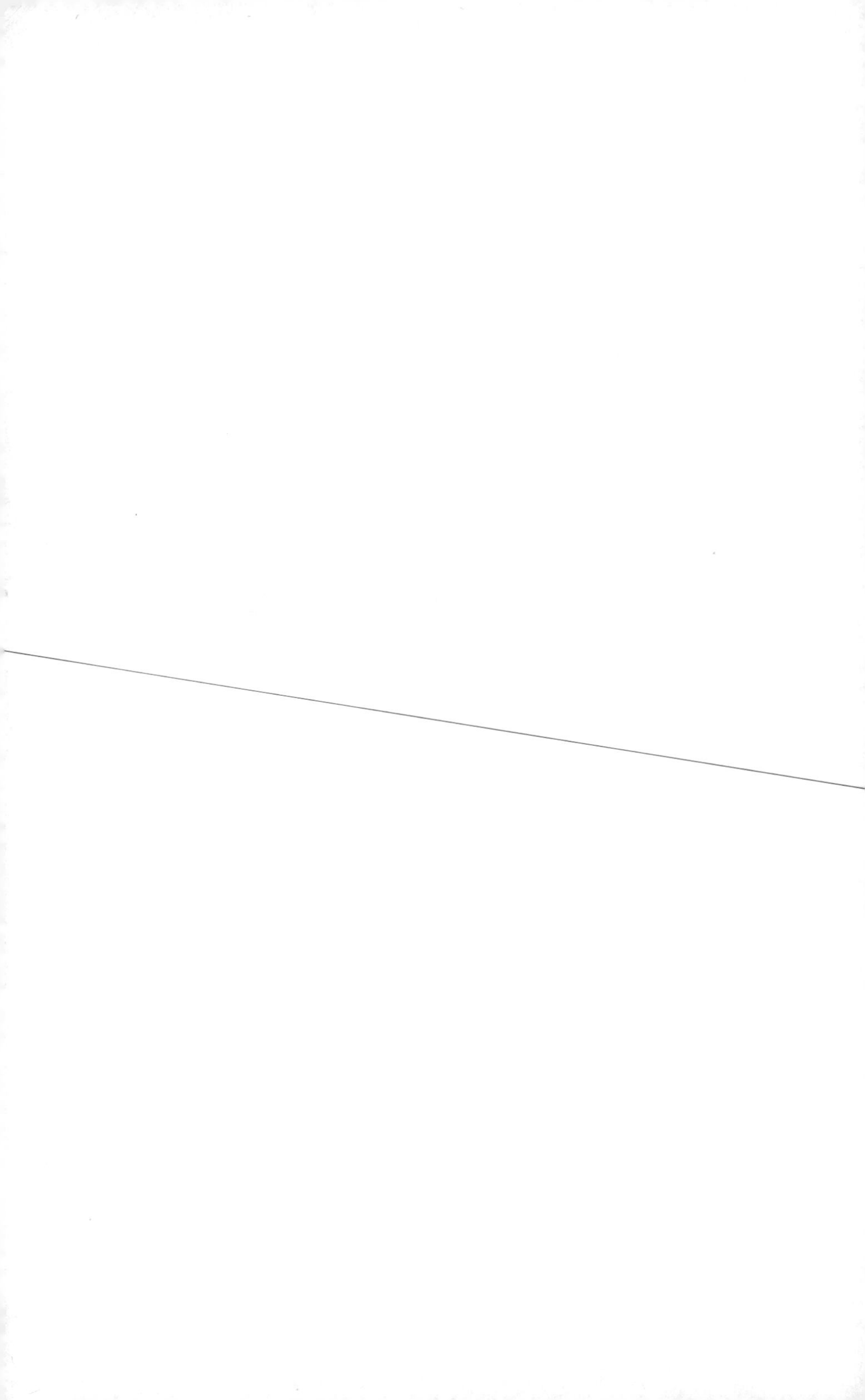

VITAL FOUND

PROLOGUE

At the sound of three excited little voices coming up the drive, Joyce smiled, set down her book, and checked her watch. With the others here, Evie and Ethan wouldn't stay asleep much longer. They'd gone down for their nap a little later than usual, but one hour was still good.

Tyler was the first to let himself into the house, Alec hot on his heels.

"Hey, Auntie Joyce!" they yelled in unison, making a beeline for the fridge. At ten and eleven years old, they had more energy than they knew what to do with and needed unbelievable amounts of food to fuel it.

"There's cookies next to the stove," she called after them, coming around the couch.

Amanda came in a few moments later, a five-year-old Josh holding on to her hand.

"Can I have a cookie, Mom?" He looked up, tugging on her arm. It made the Thomas the Tank Engine backpack on her shoulder come loose.

Joyce caught it before it hit the top of little Joshy's head. She took the bulky handbag off her friend's other shoulder and set both down by the door.

"Yes. Go. Eat the cookies." Amanda heaved a massive sigh and then collapsed into a hug with Joyce, who patted her on the back.

"Long day?"

But before they could start their conversation, three-year-old Evie interrupted from the hallway, shuffling from one chubby foot to the other, her chocolate-brown hair a mess. "Mommy, I need to pee."

Joyce took her to the bathroom and put some shorts on her, then headed back to the living room.

Ethan was up too, rubbing his eye by the kitchen island, his favorite stuffed bunny hanging from his other hand; he always took a while to wake up properly. Joyce patted him on the head as she passed, grabbing a yogurt from the fridge for Evie.

"Enough." Amanda lifted the now half-empty plate of cookies high over her head as the two older boys groaned. "You have to eat something other than cookies or your parents will kill us!" She set it down on the island before pouring two mugs of coffee.

Joyce grabbed a cookie, but she paused with it halfway to her mouth and looked down. Ethan was hugging her leg, the bunny still clutched in his hand. He blinked his almost too-big eyes at the cookie, then looked at her and grinned. With those adorable dimples, how could she refuse? She sighed and handed it over.

He dropped the bunny and wrapped both hands around the sweet treat, devouring it.

"You spoil them," Amanda grumbled, perching on one of the stools and taking a long sip of coffee.

Joyce took a sip of her own, keeping an eye on the kids. "I know, but I love it."

After their snack, the children all piled out into the backyard to play. Joyce watched through the kitchen window as the boys broke into a run. Evie lagged behind, her little legs unable to keep up, but Alec shouted for the others to wait and turned around to take her hand in his.

Joyce smiled and pressed a hand to her chest. These kids were so precious, and she knew, she *just knew*, they would be friends for life. Just as all their parents were.

These people were her family—the family she had chosen—and they meant the world to her. She loved the chaos and laughter that came with having a bunch of kids around all the time. She loved how they all took turns watching them, picking them up from school and day care, feeding them, and having sleepovers. She loved Sundays, when they all got together, and it was the best kind of craziness.

And when she was with them, she could almost ignore the awful memories of that night . . .

Not a day went by that she didn't think about what she'd done. Guilt was a permanent part of her life now, choking her as she brushed her teeth in the morning, tightening around her lungs as she played with the kids, casting a dark shadow over joyful meals with close friends. Staying silent was killing her, but what other choice did she have?

All it took to strengthen her resolve was looking into Evelyn's dark blue eyes, so like her own. Joyce couldn't leave her little girl, couldn't stand the thought of her alone in the world. And maybe it was selfish, but she couldn't leave *him* either.

Motherhood had changed her—put things in perspective. Nothing was more important than Evie, and Joyce would protect her—here, beside the people who were her home.

After everything that had happened a few years back, she was finally finding true happiness in the simple pleasures of life.

ONE

I waded into the pool slowly, letting the sparkling water cool my skin and soothe my sore muscles. The midmorning summer sun was already scorching, and I ducked my head under, wading around for a few minutes before settling into a shady corner of the pool and leaning back.

The Zacarias mansion looked even more impressive from this angle. I'd been spending a lot of time there since the end of last school year—since the invasion and Charlie's abduction.

I couldn't quite believe it had been over two months.

It made sense the time had flown—we'd all kept busy. I'd taken a few extra classes to lighten my load for the coming year, and Ethan, Josh, and I had also been getting some additional training, as the guys had decided I needed to learn to defend myself.

With all the Vital abductions and the invasion of Bradford Hills Institute—an icon of the Variant community—I couldn't disagree. No one other than Zara, Dot, Charlie, and the guys' uncle Lucian knew I was a Vital and that Alec, Tyler, Josh, and Ethan were in my Bond. But with the appearance of new technology that could identify a Vital, I was definitely at risk.

Resting my elbows on the edge of the pool, I kicked my legs lazily through the water, wondering how long the large bruise on my left thigh would take to heal. I understood the need to learn self-defense—I just wished the process wasn't so brutal.

Tyler had arranged for an ex-Melior Group operative named Kane to come out several times per week and train us in the fully equipped gym in the basement. He was a Kane by name and a cane by nature, with a stocky build and light brown hair. I wasn't entirely sure how old he was or what color his eyes were, as I was too afraid to make eye contact long enough to find out.

Kane was told Josh and Ethan wanted to train in preparation for joining Melior Group in a few short years. That couldn't have been further from the truth; one of the reasons we'd kept our Bond a secret was that none of us wanted to become superspies, or whatever the hell Alec did. Melior Group's recruitment tactics for Variants with impressive abilities, and Vitals to enhance them, could be very persuasive. Kane didn't seem to care about that though, or the fact that he was also there to train me, stating, "All the recent tension between Variants and humans is making me nervous."

He didn't blink an eye when Dot joined us either.

She had spent a solid two weeks in bed, crying and hardly eating, after Charlie was taken. If being punished in the gym with us provided a distraction, none of us were going to say no.

The only other thing that had managed to take her mind off Charlie, if only for a few minutes, was finding out I was Evelyn Maynard.

Dot hadn't put two and two together until a few weeks after she'd gotten out of the hospital. Even though Dot's family had never met my mom, she'd heard the guys talk over the years about their missing childhood friend who was likely Alec's Vital. When she finally made the connection, she had a million questions. I didn't have many answers, but I did my best to keep her talking, keep her engaged, keep that vacant look out of her eyes for as long as I could.

Ever since then, she'd treated me like the sister neither one of us ever had.

Ethan, Josh, Dot, and I had just finished another murderous session with Kane, and I'd made a beeline for the pool while the others had gone to shower or do whatever they needed to recover.

At least the training made me feel as if I was doing *something*, as if I was strong—even though it always left my limbs feeling like jelly. The bruises from the sparring sessions always healed quickly—our Variant DNA allowed us to take harder hits and heal faster than a human—but it still hurt like a bitch

Thinking about the aches only made them worse though. Instead, I took a deep breath and dipped below the surface again.

I swam to the other side under the water, emerging at the deep end and gripping the edge. A big pair of black boots sat on the ground nearby. Just past them, in the farthest corner, was a body in the lounger, partially obscured by the shade of a tree.

The boots and the pile of black clothing were Alec's. He was facedown, his head turned away from me, his tattoos prominent on his naked back, which rose and fell rhythmically in his sleep.

I frowned. He was in the sun, and if he'd been too tired to go upstairs when he got back at some obscenely late hour, I was pretty sure he hadn't worried about putting on sunscreen.

We'd hardly spoken since our encounter in Tyler's study the night of the invasion. Dot had dubbed the incident "Studygate," and it annoyingly caught on. Both Alec and I were refusing to speak about it, but it had created even more tension between us, so the others were constantly trying to pry it out of us.

Regardless of my messed-up personal relationship with Alec, I saw how hard he was working to find Charlie. Family—including Tyler and Josh, even though they weren't related by blood—was incredibly important to him, and that I could understand, even grudgingly admire.

He was an ass to me most of the time, but he'd probably spent all night out on some dangerous mission. I didn't want him to get sunburned on top of it.

Deciding to blame it on the Light that tethered me to each member of my Bond, I lifted myself out of the pool and found the sunscreen near a basket of towels at the pool house, then made my way back to Alec. From this angle, standing over him, I could see the side of his face. His mouth was open slightly, his lips smooshed against the lounger.

I bit my bottom lip and fiddled with the lid of the sunscreen bottle. *Maybe I should just wake him up and tell him to go inside. Maybe I should just let him get burned. It would serve him right after the way he treated me.*

Trying not to think about it too hard, I squeezed some of the white gloop into my hand and spread it between my palms. As gently as I could, I rested one knee next to his hip for balance and leaned over his broad back. Starting at the tops of his shoulders, I spread the sunscreen in two big streaks down the length of his back with slow, gentle movements. When I made a pass back up and over his shoulders, he sighed.

I checked to make sure he was still asleep and smiled despite myself. Some part of me got satisfaction from the fact that he felt pleasure from something I was doing to him.

I'd moved on to his arms when he woke up.

He froze, the muscles in his back going rigid, his breathing halting completely for a beat.

He raised himself up onto his elbows, turning his head to fix me with a hard stare, his ice-blue eyes narrowed. I jolted away and back to my feet as soon as he moved.

"What are you doing?" His voice was low and gravelly from sleep.

"Umm . . ." I fidgeted with the strap of my bikini bottoms, suddenly feeling like a naughty kid caught with my hand in the cookie jar. "The sun is strong and . . . uh . . . sunscreen?"

He looked at me as if I were crazy, then lifted himself into a sitting position, giving me his back, and started rubbing his closely cropped hair with both hands.

"I didn't want you to burn in the sun, and I didn't want to wake you." I managed to complete a sentence. I was on the verge of saying "sorry" but managed to hold it back. His reaction made me feel guilty, but I hadn't done anything wrong. In fact, I was doing him a favor. Asshole.

He sat up straighter, ignoring my explanation, and stretched one arm over his head, holding his side with the other. The muscles in his defined back danced under skin riddled with scars and ink, drawing my eyes to the curve of his spine.

In a bold, clean font, the words "With pain comes strength" ran across the top of his back. Underneath that, some tattoos were jagged and warped by scars, and some scars were partially obscured by the black or gray ink. I ran my gaze over the box jellyfish and some kind of snake entwined in either a dance or a battle, a striking female face licking the sharp side of a knife, and a skyline that looked familiar with angry-looking lightning above it.

He stood up slowly, and I snapped my eyes up, not wanting to get caught staring. When he turned around, I gasped, my hand flying to my mouth.

Angry, mottled bruising covered his ribs on his left side. He'd obviously had a rough night, but I knew better than to ask what had happened.

He scooped his boots and clothes up, wincing in pain, and I winced with him. As he walked past me toward the house, he muttered, "Thanks" without looking at me, but I was so distracted by the evidence of how dangerous his job was that I didn't even register it until he was halfway to the house.

My chest was aching a little bit in a familiar way—the way it had the night of the invasion, when Alec had overused his ability to incapacitate all those people; the way it had the night when Ethan had overused his ability, and an inexplicable force had drawn me to him. I shuddered to think what that meant for whoever had been on the receiving end of Alec's ability last night.

He hadn't truly overused it though. The pain in my chest wasn't as urgent or overwhelming. He hadn't depleted himself to the point of putting his own life in danger.

That's why it had seemed like a good idea to rub him down while he was asleep instead of just waking him up. I hadn't even realized I was transferring Light to him while I rubbed sunscreen on his back—tiny, unnoticeable amounts, as though it knew it had to be careful not to gush out of me too fast.

I considered going after him—the pull was still there, faint as it was—but I knew he would flat out refuse, and it would probably end in a fight. A good sleep would get him back on track.

With a sigh, I flopped down onto the lounger, trying to focus on the feel of the warm sun on my skin and the sweet smell of summer in the air. Trying *not* to think about the feel of Alec's back under my hands and the way he'd sighed in satisfaction.

Ethan and Josh ran past my chair, one on either side, and cannonballed into the pool. I chuckled at their antics. Dot walked up a little more calmly, wearing a black one-piece with bold cutouts that looked perfect on her petite frame.

"You already been in?" She took the seat next to me, gesturing to my wet hair.

"Yeah. I had a quick dip to cool off."

A shadow fell over me, and I turned, shielding my eyes from the sun.

Tyler was in gray pants and a teal shirt, the sleeves rolled up in his signature way. The sun was directly behind his head, making his messy brown hair look like a glowing halo.

"Just came to check if you needed to do a Light transfer." He sat across from me, swiping back the messy bit of hair that seemed to always flop over his forehead. His gray eyes looked bloodshot and tired.

"I'm all good. Thanks." I smiled. He was working as tirelessly as Alec, spending many hours at Melior Group headquarters or cooped up in his study—even disappearing with Alec from time to time.

"Good." He smiled back, leaning his elbows on his knees, drawing my attention to the corded muscle of his forearms. Why did he always have to roll his shirtsleeves up like that? It made me want to run my hand up from the expensive watch at his wrist to the fabric of the shirt, feeling the hair on his arm. "Let's do one later, just in case."

I nodded and made myself look at his eyes. "I'll come find you after lunch."

Even though I was getting better at controlling my Light flow, and Ethan and Josh were getting better at managing the extra Light and using it to develop their abilities safely, I was still mainly going to Tyler if I needed to expel excess Light.

"Great. I'll be in my study."

"Nope." I shook my head emphatically. I'd refused to step foot in that room since the night of the invasion.

Tyler and Dot both groaned. In the pool, the splashing and laughing stopped.

"Are you ready to tell us about Studygate yet?" Josh asked, treading water near the edge of the pool.

"Nope." I popped the *p* and crossed my arms over my chest.

Tyler had already shifted his attention to his phone, tapping away, his brows pulled together. He finished what he was typing and stood up. "I have to go debrief with Alec."

"Maybe let him sleep for a bit," I said quickly before he could disappear.

He turned back to me, one eyebrow arched in surprise. I was the last person to know what Alec needed and certainly not one to advocate for him, but the faint tightness in my chest was still there, a pull toward a certain room on the third floor. Tyler's eyes narrowed in on my hand lightly rubbing my breastbone.

"He's OK," I reassured him before he could ask. "I found him asleep out here. He was a bit banged up, had some bruising on his ribs." I winced as I said it. "I'm pretty sure he abused his ability a little too. I woke him and he went inside, but he's fine. Just let him sleep for a while." I left out the awkwardness with the sunscreen. No one needed to know about that.

"He'll recover faster if he lets you transfer the Light he clearly needs," Tyler huffed.

I didn't say anything. What was there to say? I was lucky I'd managed to transfer some before he woke up, but I wasn't about to share that with the group either.

"All right, I'll deal with him later." He turned to leave, then paused, running his eyes over me quickly. "Did you put sunscreen on? Don't get sunburned."

"Yes, Dad." I rolled my eyes, then scrunched my face up in disgust. I was pretty certain Tyler wasn't attracted to me like that, and I was still trying to sort through my feelings for him, but referring to him as "Dad," even jokingly, had left a bad taste in my mouth. I looked at him, and he was wearing the same expression.

He shook it off and walked away without another word.

I turned back around to find Dot holding back laughter.

"Oh, don't start with me." I groaned. Teasing me about my complicated relationship with the four Variant men in my Bond had become her new hobby.

She must have seen something serious in my eyes, because she took a deep breath and changed the subject. "Have you heard from Zara?"

"Yeah." I frowned as I squeezed some sunscreen into my palm and passed the bottle to her. "She's coming back tomorrow."

Zara had been spending the summer with her family in California. She'd been released from the hospital a few days after the invasion, just in time for Beth's funeral. Her parents had whisked her home straight after. We'd stayed in touch, sending each other messages while doggedly avoiding mentioning Beth or anything that had happened that day. It felt wrong to talk about it through a screen, but it meant our conversations felt superficial. Hollow. We hadn't spoken at all for the past week, and when I'd asked when she was due back, all I'd gotten in response was a date and a rough time.

It made my stomach clench—I was equally looking forward to and dreading seeing her again.

"She's cutting it close," Dot said. Classes were due to start the day after her return.

I shrugged. "I can't imagine she's too keen to come back to the res hall."

Dot just nodded, rubbing sunscreen into her shoulders.

Tomorrow would be Zara's first night sleeping in our shared suite since it all happened. Her first night back in the rooms she'd shared with Beth for three years. I'd known Beth for only a few short months before she was killed, and I felt the loss keenly. I couldn't imagine how people who had known her longer felt.

I'd been reluctant to stay there myself. It felt barren and sad without the Reds around. The guys refused to let me out of their sight anyway, so I spent most of my nights at the mansion in one of the many spare rooms. I still stayed at the res hall when I had an early class, but one of them would always insist on dropping me off, and someone would always be there in the morning to walk me to class. Between that and the Melior Group agents posted at all the gates for extra security, I was never far from a protective force.

Yet I never quite felt safe. I wasn't sure if I'd ever be able to walk the grounds of campus without reliving the horrors I'd witnessed there.

Josh stopped my dark thoughts from spiraling by using his ability to flick the corner of my towel into my face. It brought my attention to his cheeky grin, his head disappearing under the water.

Just as I realized Ethan wasn't in the pool anymore, he grabbed me under the knees and behind my back and lifted me off my seat as though I weighed nothing.

I yelled and tried to wriggle out of his arms, but he just laughed, flashing me a wide grin that made his dimples appear, his amber eyes sparkling with mischief. One second we were standing at the edge of the pool, and the next we were flying through the air and hitting the water with a massive splash. He released his hold once we were in the water, but as my head broke the surface, I held on, twining my arms around his thick neck. I couldn't reach the bottom at this end of the pool, but he could.

"You are in so much trouble!" I laughed despite myself, pushing wet hair off my face.

"Oh yeah? What're you gonna to do about it?" Ethan was a hopeless flirt, turning every situation into an opportunity to make a double entendre, smirking with his full mouth and smoldering with his sexy eyes. Not that it worked on me. I was way too astute to let a little obvious flirting affect me.

"I'll . . . um . . ." I laughed again. Naturally my brain supplied the least helpful words possible. "I'll kiss you." Maybe I wasn't as immune to the flirting as I thought.

He started to walk us toward the shallow end, and I wrapped my legs loosely around his middle, trailing behind him in the cool water. He was tall, broad, and muscular, but his big hands were always gentle with me.

He didn't reply to my last statement. Instead he just watched me intently as he moved, keeping my gaze captive with his eyes.

He pressed his lips to mine as he continued to walk me backward, and I sighed, completely lost in his touch. I ran one hand through his wet black hair, but before the kiss could intensify, we came to an abrupt stop as my back hit something hard and warm and slick. Josh.

Josh was the shortest of the four, his physique lithe and athletic. But all the training with Kane was resulting in extra definition. His shoulders were looking a little broader, his crisp collared shirts straining a little more over his chest, and there was a six-pack becoming more noticeable every time he took his shirt off.

"That's not much of a punishment, Eve." Josh's voice was low, but it sounded semiserious. I pulled away from Ethan as Josh's hands found my waist. He tugged, and I leaned back into his chest, my legs still around Ethan's middle, not ready to let go but eager to have contact with Josh at the same time.

"Are you jealous, Joshy?" I teased, covering his hands with mine and turning toward him. His green eyes bored into mine, the lashes stuck together. His dirty-blond hair looked much darker when wet.

"Yes," he whispered, his breath washing over me. There was no hint of teasing in his voice.

My immediate instinct was to kiss him. The Light and I were in agreement when it came to wanting to even the score. I closed the small distance, pressing my lips to his. He sighed into the kiss, not hesitating to tease my lips with his tongue, but this kiss was cut short too.

A loud battle cry cut through the relative silence, followed by a huge splash as Dot launched herself into the pool, literally throwing water onto our heated moment. All three of us startled, and the boys released me. My feet found the bottom of the pool, and I stood between Ethan and Josh as Dot broke the surface.

"Did you three dickheads forget you had company?" Her voice was teasing. She wasn't actually upset, but I did feel bad that I'd forgotten she was there. "Save that ménage shit for when other people aren't around."

My eyes widened at her casual mention of threesomes. I stared at her, my lips pressed together, silently trying to communicate that she should stop speaking immediately. I mean, technically I had been in an embrace with both of them. So it was *technically* a threesome kind of situation. I just hadn't thought about it in any tangible way before, and we certainly hadn't talked about it.

I cleared my throat and chanced a look at Josh and Ethan. They were having their own silent conversation, their eyes locked on each other. Ethan was smirking, the dimple only just visible in his cheek, and Josh's eyes were narrowed, but there was a twitch pulling the corners of his lips up too. They turned to look at me as one, and I quickly averted my gaze, suddenly incredibly self-conscious.

I didn't want to examine too closely the thrill of excitement that jolted through me, settling somewhere low in my belly, at the charged energy between the three of us. I lifted my head to find Dot's smiling face. She was casually leaning on the edge of the pool, her elbows propped up behind her, looking satisfied.

I moved toward her as fast as I could in the water and splashed her viciously. She screamed and tried to get away, laughing and spluttering before changing tactics and trying to splash me back. The boys joined in, and the rest of the morning went by without any more awkward moments or teasing from Dot.

That moment in the pool was the first time I'd heard her laugh freely since Charlie had been taken. I knew by the way she retreated into herself for the next half hour—pretending to read a magazine on her lounger while not once turning a page—that she felt guilty about having fun when we had no idea what kind of awful situation Charlie was in or if he was even alive.

We gave her space, and not long after, she made an effort to join in the joking and fun. We all knew it was what her brother would want—for Dot to be happy.

TWO

That evening I sat on the edge of the kitchen island while Ethan cooked dinner. He moved around with ease, his posture relaxed, his smile coming easily as we chatted.

We talked about coursework, what he was cooking, how Dot was doing—and about our parents. Now that we knew we'd known each other since childhood, conversation turned to our parents a lot easier than it used to. We never reminisced for long or in much detail—it was too painful—but it felt good to talk about my mother in a context that didn't involve rehashing her death. It was nice to be able to ask them what she was like.

Ethan and Josh weren't much older than me, so they didn't remember much, but Tyler made an effort to describe in great detail whatever he could remember. Like how she used to bake cookies for us as after-school snacks, or how all of our families would get together on Sundays for these chaotic, joyful meals.

Alec was avoiding speaking to me at all, so I had no idea what he remembered of my mother or of me as a child.

We also never spoke about the day of the invasion outside the context of looking for Charlie. We had come so close to losing each other again . . .

"My power is so destructive." Ethan spoke low; we'd all become accustomed to lowering our voices when we talked about our Bond. He moved his chopping board closer so we could hear each other. "I just want to be able to do something positive with it, you know?"

"Ethan, it's not about the nature of the ability. It's how you use it."

He gave me a devious look, twisting my innocent statement into a double entendre. I rolled my eyes but couldn't help chuckling. Dirty jokes were now a daily occurrence.

"I know what you mean." He turned serious again, checking the pot on the stove before giving me his full attention. "But I still want to figure out how to put them *out*."

Ethan was trying to develop a new level to his ability.

Tyler had discovered he could not only tell when someone was lying; with enough Light from me, he could also glean the basic truth behind their words. It was proving to be a handy yet slightly annoying development. He'd taken to constantly calling us out on our bullshit. Like when I asked if anyone wanted to watch *Cosmos* with me and they all said "yes," Tyler was quick to point out Ethan actually did not.

He respected our privacy when it came to serious things—he still hadn't asked about what had happened between Alec and I when his ability was enhanced with extra Light—but he was pushing us all to be more honest.

Josh, too, had noticed a new development. After he'd accidentally made Ethan float during one of our training sessions, we realized he could levitate not only inanimate objects but also people, even the members of his own Bond—as long as the intention to harm wasn't there. Recently he'd set his mind to making *himself* float. He was trying to learn to fly—and actually beginning to succeed. With extra Light from me and deep focus, he'd managed to get himself about ten inches off the ground.

Ethan's control had improved too, and the fire he wielded was becoming more powerful. But unlike Tyler and Josh, Ethan hadn't been able to discover a new aspect to his ability; he was just improving on what he already had.

A little frown formed above his bright eyes, and I sighed. He was beating himself up instead of acknowledging all he had achieved.

Putting fire out sounded deceptively simple. Ethan could make *his* fire disappear easily, but it was tinged with the Light that flowed through him to create it. He described it as pulling a limb back against his body. It was an extension of him.

What he couldn't do, and was trying his hardest to work out, was putting out regular fires. Fires started by someone else with non-supernatural means were beyond his reach.

"I know, hot stuff." I squeezed his shoulder, trying to distract him by starting up our nickname game. "You'll get there. Focus on the positives."

"I know, I know. Just imagine all the good I could do."

A slow grin spread across my face. It was fueled in part by how softhearted my big guy was—he just wanted to make the world a better place—but also by his not noticing my nickname. We'd become so used to calling each other increasingly ridiculous things that it was expected, and that, in turn, had given rise to a whole new game. We were now trying to slip them in so the other person wouldn't notice.

He smiled back but with some confusion. I plastered an innocent look on my face but couldn't wipe away the grin.

It didn't take him long to catch on. He pushed back from the bench and groaned in frustration even as he laughed. Playing every sport imaginable,

Ethan certainly had a competitive streak. He loved these little games.

He checked the pot again, added the cilantro he'd been chopping, and quickly switched the burners off while I waited for him to concede defeat. With his latest culinary masterpiece no longer in danger, he placed one hand on either side of where I sat on the island, his big arms boxing me in, and fixed me with one of his dimpled smiles.

"You better hope Josh doesn't notice the cilantro in that stew—you know he hates it—and I don't know why you're smiling. You just lost a round," I teased, leaning back on my hands.

"Josh can suck it. And I may have lost"—he leaned forward, following me—"but you think I'm hot, so I figure I won as well."

I laughed softly, no longer trying to get away, maybe even tilting toward him a little. "Well, yeah, you do have a fire ability." My voice was almost a whisper.

"Whatever. You think I'm hot." His lips were inches from mine. "You want to hug me and kiss me and . . ."

I closed the miniscule distance between us and pressed my lips to his. We both sighed into the soft kiss.

Kissing Ethan felt as natural as it did exciting. With our continued training, my control of the Light and my guys' control of their abilities were getting better, which made it easier to be more intimate. Ethan and Josh were stealing more kisses, and so was I. It was only when things started to intensify that I'd lose control of my Light and we'd have to stop.

It was driving us all crazy. The three of us, that is. Tyler had maintained his platonic barrier.

He'd given me a hint of thawing out the night of the gala. The way he'd told me I looked beautiful as he dragged his fingers down the length of my exposed spine still gave me shivers to think about. It had felt like the beginning of something more between us.

But then he'd reestablished the boundaries. Despite his newfound fondness for calling out the cold hard truth at every corner, this was one thing he was keeping his mouth shut about. I knew if I asked him, he would tell me the truth, but I was afraid of the answer.

Alec had gone back to ignoring me as if we weren't even connected.

I may have been avoiding talking about intimacy with half my Variant Bond, but I was trying my best to make it past the make-out stage with the other half. So I did a mental check of my Light flow before deepening the kiss with Ethan.

Just as I scooted forward, opening my legs wider and pressing up against the hard planes of Ethan's body, the sound of the fridge opening interrupted the moment, and we pulled apart. The clang of bottles and jars in the fridge door rang through the kitchen as Alec slammed it closed.

We both turned to look at Ethan's obnoxious cousin. Alec was in sweatpants, shirtless and barefoot, breathing a little heavy, a light sheen of sweat covering his toned, tattooed body. He'd obviously just come up from the gym, and in our distracted state, we hadn't heard him.

He opened a bottle of sparkling water, the top making a distinctive hiss, and looked between us before taking a deep drink.

"Ah!" Keeping his eyes locked on us, he sighed exaggeratedly before wiping his mouth with the back of his hand, which, when it came away, revealed a crooked grin. He knew exactly what he was doing. He wouldn't even talk to me, let alone touch me in the way he had in Tyler's study, but he was determined none of the rest of my Bond would either.

Ethan dropped his arms and stepped away, sighing. He shot Alec a dirty look and got back to cooking.

Grinding my teeth, I jumped off the island and walked toward him. His eyes tracked me as he raised the bottle back to his lips, the eyebrow with the scar lifting slightly.

I stopped next to him and leaned in. "You are such a cockblocker." I spoke low, but my voice carried in the quiet kitchen.

His eyes widened, and he choked on his sip of mineral water, some of the liquid spurting past his lips and dripping down his tattooed chest.

It took physical effort to stop my eyes from following the droplets as they made their way down. I knew what it felt like to run my hands down that chest . . . But I refused to give him the satisfaction. I made myself look away and left the room.

Ethan's booming laugh echoed behind me, and I finally let a grin cross my face. Alec had tried to get to me, and he may have succeeded, but I'd gotten to him too.

Tyler and I had ended up skipping our Light transfer because he'd gotten tied up with work, and I woke up feeling a little itchy around the forearms.

The time between how often I needed Light transfers was getting longer the more I practiced mindfulness and control of the flow, but it still got away from me sometimes. The state Alec was in when I found him by the pool probably had something to do with it; the Light was pushing into me in an effort to get to him.

I went for a run with Ethan to try to work some of it off, careful not to touch him. When the Light was uncontrolled like that, the transfer could be sudden and violent, and that's when *he* would have to practice perfect control not to accidentally set something on fire.

After the run, which helped only slightly, I grabbed a quick breakfast and went searching for Tyler. I ran through the obvious areas of the house first—

kitchen, living room, patio, even knocking on his bedroom door—before dragging my feet downstairs to his study.

The door was ajar, and I nudged it open while rapping on the frame. My feet stayed firmly planted on the outside of the room.

"Hey, got a minute?"

"Hey, Eve." He looked up from the pile of folders and newspapers on his desk before dropping his gaze again. "What's up?"

"We never got around to doing that transfer yesterday."

"Oh, yeah. The debrief with Alec went longer than I thought it would." At the mention of his name, we both looked over to the leather couch in the corner—the spot where he had lifted me to the highest peak of pleasure and then torn me down to the lowest point in the space of five minutes.

"I'll put the TV in the living room on." With one last glare at the couch, I left to wait for him.

He joined me after only a few minutes. "One of you is eventually going to have to tell us what happened on the night of the invasion." He sighed but sounded resigned. He knew I wouldn't tell him anything.

"Let's just focus, OK?"

He turned to face me, but I kept my eyes glued to the TV as he gently extracted the remote from my fingers and flipped to CNN. When he extended his hand, I grabbed it without hesitation, and immediately the Light poured out of me. Tyler grunted, and I worked at steadying the flow.

"Haven't felt it that strong in a while."

"Yeah, I think it might be because of Alec yesterday."

"Makes sense."

We turned our attention back to the news.

After the invasion, the media had reported on it almost around the clock for a full week. It had been the first large-scale, outwardly violent attack by an extremist human group—the Human Empowerment Network—against a Variant institution and Variant civilians in a very long time.

After the first week, the reports about the invasion became more sporadic, but almost every day contained a new report of a Variant business owner refusing to serve a human, or a gang of humans beating up a Variant with a passive ability. Variants were becoming less shy about calling humans *Dimes*—the derogatory term that had been so offensive a few months ago it was almost never heard in public. Humans were picketing Variant businesses and institutions all over the world. People were scared.

Today, we were staring at a story about how some senator was running for president. I sighed, exasperated, and tried to pull my hand away from Tyler's, but he held on tight. He was watching the screen intently, his eyes flying from side to side.

I got excited and wrapped my other hand around his, pushing more Light through our connection. If he was onto something, I wanted to make sure he had all the juice he needed.

Absently, I registered the sound of a commercial break, and Tyler gently pulled his hand away, moving backward until his legs hit the couch. He was staring into space, his brow furrowed.

Alec walked into the room in shorts and a sweat-soaked tank top, moving to the kitchen and rummaging in the fridge. After a few moments, he looked over, abandoned his snack on the bench, and came to stand in front of Tyler. "What did you see?"

In need of something to do, I grabbed the remote and turned the TV off. That seemed to snap Tyler out of his stare.

"Senator Anderson," he said, as if that explained anything.

When it looked as though he wasn't going to elaborate, Alec asked, "Christine Anderson? The Variant senator? What about her?"

Tyler had started to stare into space again, so I tried to keep the information flowing. "There was a news report about her running for president just now. Isn't she the one who gave the speech the night of the gala?"

Alec cleared his throat before answering, "Yes."

That was the night he'd first kissed me. The night he'd made me think I betrayed my Bond by kissing him back. I crossed my arms and refused to look at him.

Tyler shook himself out of his stupor. "Sorry. I was trying to make sense of it all. Anderson mentioned the invasion in her speech just then. She's running on a platform of unifying the humans and the Variants. I think . . . My ability doesn't work nearly as well when the subject is not physically right in front of me, but I think she knows more than she's letting on about the invasion, which means she may know . . ."

"Something about Charlie," Alec finished for him. "It's a lead."

"Yeah, but we're talking about government level . . ."

I didn't hear the rest of what Tyler was saying. They rushed out, talking over each other.

I was left standing in the middle of the room, my hands by my sides, stunned. "I'll just . . . stay here," I said to no one.

"Hey, petal pie!" Ethan beamed at me, emerging from the gym and looking as sweaty as Alec.

"Hey, snookums. Did you do *more* exercise after our exercise this morning?"

"Hells yeah!" He went straight to the kitchen, picking up where Alec had left off. "Takes serious commitment to look this good." He flashed me his dimples as he exaggeratedly flexed his arms.

"Modest as always." I perched on a stool across from him.

"How was your thing with Tyler?"

"Make me one of those sandwiches"—only Ethan could make a sandwich taste like fine dining—"and I'll tell you all about it."

"Way ahead of you." He slid a plate to me, and I told him what little I knew.

After our brief chat, he took two very large sandwiches into Tyler's study, and I went upstairs to grab my stuff. I would be staying in my res hall that evening. Zara was due back that afternoon.

Backpack slung over my shoulder, I made my way downstairs, but I knew better than to leave without telling anyone. The campus may have been teeming with Melior Group agents, but the three blocks between the Zacarias mansion and the front gates were completely unprotected. One of them would either drive or walk me there. Overprotective, maybe, but I didn't mind.

Thinking about why the extra precautions were needed made me feel sick, but I didn't want to end up like Charlie.

As predicted, Josh and Ethan were both waiting for me in the foyer.

"It's not too hot. Do you wanna walk it?" Josh asked. He was dressed in shorts and an AC/DC T-shirt. I looked pointedly at it, my eyebrows raised. He loved his band tees when relaxing at home but wouldn't be caught dead out in public without a collared shirt and pressed pants. He was preppy on the outside and wild rock on the inside.

He rolled his eyes. "It's not like anyone will see us. It's three blocks."

"Yeah, let's walk."

We all moved to leave just as the door to Tyler's study flew open. Alec poked his head out.

"You going?" he asked, looking right at me.

I stared back, trying to remember the last time he'd spoken directly to me. No one had been around to hear yesterday morning's "thanks" by the pool, and I wasn't entirely convinced it had happened.

"Eve's staying on campus tonight," Josh answered for me when I remained silent.

Alec came to stand right in front of me, digging his hand in his pocket. In the office behind him, Tyler had his phone to his ear, but he was watching us.

After a moment, Alec pulled a small item out of his pocket and let it hang on a chain between us.

We both opened our mouths to speak, but my words rushed out first. "You're giving me jewelry?"

Was I dreaming? Was this some kind of nightmare? Was he about to give me a necklace, and then when I tried to give one to him, he would throw it at me, declare he "doesn't want anything from me," and walk out?

"What?" His brows creased, and his lip turned up in a grimace. "It's a tracking device and distress beacon."

"What?" The item in question was still swinging in front of my face on a simple silver chain. It looked like a solid silver rod, a little thicker than a pencil and about half the length. The top third of it was matte black.

Alec rolled his eyes and sighed. "It allows us to know where you are at all times, and if you get in trouble, you can activate the distress signal." He delivered the speech as if he'd already explained it a thousand times.

"Wow. The stalking has gone to another level." I crossed my arms. "I'm not wearing that."

"Dammit! Tyler, talk to her." He let the little device flop to his side.

Tyler finished his call and came out to join us. "I thought you were going to give it to these two to give her."

I turned on him. "You knew about this?"

Alec spoke at the same time. "I didn't have a chance to give it to them, and they were about to leave, so . . ."

"Yeah." Tyler sighed but had the decency to look a little sheepish. "We came up with the idea together."

I looked at them all one by one. "Idiots." I rolled my eyes.

"Eve." Tyler had his serious face on. "Vitals are disappearing every day. With those machines, it doesn't matter that we're keeping you a secret. If they track you down, they will take you. We want you to have the freedom to go on with your life, go to class, stay on campus—but we need to take precautions. Please—"

"It's either this or a subdermal implant," Alec cut across him, apparently done with civilized conversation. He stepped in front of me again, blocking my view of the others and holding the necklace up.

"No way in hell are you putting anything under my skin! That is so creepy."

He looked smug and shoved the necklace farther into my face.

Grumbling, I took it and slipped it over my head, giving him a "there, it's done" look—my eyes wide, my head cocked to the side. "Happy?"

He didn't answer, instead reaching out to grab the pendant in his hand. His knuckles brushed against my sternum where the long chain ended, and I gasped, surprised at the casual contact. He saw my reaction, his eyes boring into mine for the briefest of seconds.

"It's constantly transmitting your location," he explained. "But if you're in any kind of trouble, you just pull these two bits apart"—he yanked, and the bigger silver bit of the rod came away from the smaller matte black part—"and it will send an alert to us."

As if to illustrate his point, their phones went off, a high-pitched alarm bouncing off the marble. All four of them extracted their phones and turned the sound off quickly. Alec kept speaking: "If none of us responds with a password, an automatic message will be sent to Melior Group."

He joined the two parts together again.

"You try it." He dropped the heavy little bar, and it bounced on my chest. I picked it up, yanked the two bits apart, and braced myself for the alarm. It didn't disappoint, filling the foyer with its wail again.

I reconnected the two bits as the guys shut off the alarms.

"OK, got it." I sounded bored even to myself.

"Take this seriously, Evelyn," Alec growled at me. "This is not a toy. If that alarm goes off, I'm assuming your life is in danger, and we are coming in hot."

His intensity took me aback. "OK," I whispered, then cleared my throat. "OK, I get it. I'm not a child." A bit of frustration crept in at the end.

"Aren't you?" The question wasn't mocking. It was delivered with a completely straight face. An incomprehensible expression crossed his features, and then he disappeared into Tyler's study.

Tyler took his place in front of me, looking apologetic. "Sorry about Alec. He's just not used to . . ."

"Having normal conversations with actual people?" I finished for him.

"Something like that. Look, all we want to do is protect you, OK? This is the least invasive, least overbearing way we could think of."

I nodded. "I wish you'd included me in the conversation, but I get it." We had been isolated for the past few months, cocooned in the safety of the mansion's sprawling grounds. The escalating violence out in the world may have felt removed, but the threat was real. I just had to look into Dot's broken face to be reminded of it.

"Good." Tyler smiled warmly. "Now, it goes without saying that you can't take this off. You sleep with it, shower with it. It stays around your neck at all times, got it?"

"Yes, sir," I said a little playfully.

"And don't tell anyone about it either. It's inconspicuous enough that it should go unnoticed, but if anyone asks, tell them it was a gift from Ethan."

"Yes, sir."

He gave me an exasperated look, his eyes narrowing. Behind me, Ethan and Josh laughed quietly at some private joke. With one last lingering look at the unassuming pendant, Tyler waved goodbye and followed Alec.

Ethan, Josh, and I took off, walking most of the way back to campus in silence. I was lost in thought, trying to reconcile Alec's volatile treatment of me with his obvious desire to keep me safe. The boys mostly just watched me surreptitiously. As we passed the security checkpoint at the gate and moved away from the guards, I began to get exasperated with them.

"Stop it," I snapped.

Ethan stepped into my path and wrapped his big arms around my waist, leaning down to look at me. It was always Ethan in public. Josh couldn't touch me like this where someone might see. I glanced at him. He appeared casual, his hands in his pockets, his shoulders loose, but there was a tightness to his mouth. He was struggling with this more and more. I was too.

"We're just trying to keep you safe." Ethan's amber eyes were unusually serious.

"I know. Thank you." I hugged him, but I watched Josh as I did, putting as much warmth and meaning into my look as I put into Ethan's hug. He quirked his lips and nodded his head almost imperceptibly.

We said our goodbyes, and I headed to my res hall. As I approached the entrance, I kept my gaze fixed on the door, refusing to look at the building next to ours—the spot in the alcove where I'd last seen Charlie. My heart hammered in my chest every time I walked past there, remembering . . .

I ran up the stairs, the burn in my legs giving me a distraction, and made myself think about Zara. I'd sent her a few messages that morning—wishing her a safe flight, asking if she needed a lift from the airport, asking when she'd be back on campus—but she hadn't answered any of them.

THREE

The breeze drifting in through my window still carried the warmth of a summer morning. It was only a matter of time before it became too cold to have the window open at all, so I enjoyed the sweet smell of fresh air, the sound of early birds.

I sat on my bed in my PJ top, a heavy book on my lap: *Vital Myths in Medieval Texts*. The book wasn't as old as the parchment and vellum tomes it referenced—it was published in the late nineties—but it did have pictures of early texts depicting Variant life hundreds of years ago.

As I leaned back on my pillows, I stared at a depiction of a Vital found in a monk's tome from 1508. The Vital man stood in the middle of five women. Precious gold leaf had been painstakingly applied to the sections of the drawing that were supposed to be his skin, and a yellowish-white color had been drawn in all around him. Gold-leaf arrows pointed to each of the women, his Variants.

It was clearly representing what I'd experienced on the train platform, and again with Alec, yet the book was dismissing it as the overactive imagination and religious devotion of a person from a time before science. This was just how they saw Vitals at that time—sent from God and therefore glowing in the light of his divinity. It theorized that our modern terminology for the Light came from this idea.

Interesting, but completely useless. I sighed and let the heavy book flop onto my lap, abandoning it halfway through a sentence. I'd been almost obsessive in my research over the summer, trying to find any information I could about Vitals glowing—what it was, why it happened, if it was dangerous. But after two months, all I had were vague references in history books and a few conspiracy theories online about the government experimenting on Vitals with exceptional levels of Light. I had nothing.

At the sound of movement on the other side of my door, I set the book aside and swung my legs over the edge of the bed, then paused. Zara was up, but I wasn't entirely sure she wanted to see me.

When the guys dropped me off the day before, she still wasn't back. She hadn't arrived until after I'd eaten dinner, tidied up my room, and read half the latest issue of *Astronomy & Astrophysics* waiting for her. She'd let herself in quietly, pulling her suitcase inside as she backed through the door.

"Oh." She straightened when she saw me on the couch. "Didn't think you'd still be up."

"Of course I'm up." I went straight to her, giving her a tight hug. She stiffened for a moment, then returned it.

When we separated, I saw her eyes were as misty as mine, her jaw clenched. She didn't make eye contact, fidgeting with the handle of her suitcase and letting her silky red hair fall over her face.

"So"—I cleared my throat, trying to speak around the lump in my throat—"how was your flight?"

"Fine. Delayed." She rolled her eyes, then dragged the suitcase into her room, hefting it onto the bed and opening it to rummage inside. "I'm actually really tired. I think I'll just have a shower and go to bed. Can we catch up tomorrow?"

She gave me a tired smile as she held up her toiletries bag.

"Of course." I smiled back, and she shut herself in the bathroom. The sound of the shower starting reminded me I was still standing in the middle of the room, staring at the bathroom door.

I wished Beth were there.

I'd gone to bed, telling myself Zara needed space. Losing her best friend, having her own life put in danger—it was a lot to handle. Coming back to where it had all happened couldn't have been easy.

Which is why I was now hesitating, unsure if she wanted to walk to breakfast together.

I got dressed in jeans and a loose T-shirt, and as I was braiding my hair, she let herself into my room.

"Hey, ready for breakfast? I'm starving." She leaned on the edge of my desk.

I smiled, relief and longing fighting for strongest emotion. She and Beth used to both barge into my room like that. Beth would have been flipping through the clothes in my wardrobe by now, second-guessing her own outfit.

Zara was looking at the same spot.

"Yeah, let me just brush my teeth."

She gave me a weak smile before leading the way out of my bedroom.

Fifteen minutes later, Zara and I were walking toward the cafeteria. We enjoyed the lightness of our bags while we could; in a few weeks, we'd be buried in so many assignments that all the books we needed wouldn't fit inside them.

It was obvious things had changed, both with Zara and on campus.

With the beginning of the semester, the bulk of the student body—those who had not hung around for summer classes—had arrived at Bradford Hills Institute, and at a quarter to nine on the first Monday, everyone was on their way somewhere. Several people had their faces in giant campus maps, looking a little overwhelmed, and I smiled to myself, remembering my own attachment to my map only a few months ago.

In a few weeks, the new students would be obsessing over the results of their Variant DNA tests, but for now, everyone's focus was on the heavily armed men making their presence known all over campus. Bradford Hills had always had its own campus security, posted at the gates and occasionally patrolling, like any other college in the country, but the new black-clad groups of hard-looking men were impossible to miss.

Melior Group had descended on Bradford Hills in the days following the invasion, and they hadn't left. The Variant community didn't take the safety of their best and brightest lightly. It had been officially announced that Melior Group would be handling increased security on campus for the foreseeable future. With Bradford Hills Institute offering free counseling to all staff and students, the two organizations were working closely to make sure their people were supported through this tough time.

I knew the frowning men and big guns were meant to make us all feel safe, but all it did was painfully remind me of why they were necessary.

Doing our best to ignore them, Zara and I took our time walking the curving paths of Bradford Hills, enjoying the morning sunshine peeking through the trees lining the laneways while we chatted about anything *other* than Beth. Now wasn't the time. I asked Zara about her summer, but she didn't give me much; she'd probably spent most of it grieving and closed off to the world.

"We should swap schedules," Zara suggested as we rounded the corner to the square containing the cafeteria building, "so we know when the other one is free."

"Yeah, sure." I smiled widely, happy she wanted to hang out with me. I'd been so worried about our friendship fizzling out, unable to withstand the pressure of losing Beth and two months of distance.

I was watching Zara's profile, so I saw the exact moment her eyes narrowed, her jaw clenched. My own body tensed in response, and I turned to see what she was looking at.

Sitting on a picnic bench facing us was Rick. The man who'd killed Beth was leaning his elbows on his knees and staring at the ground as people went about their morning around him.

"Why the fuck is he here?" Zara hissed between clenched teeth.

"I don't know. Come on." I pulled her by the elbow, trying to move toward the cafeteria. I didn't want to see him, didn't want to speak to him, didn't want to be reminded of his existence at all. But Zara was frozen to the spot, and Rick looked up and spotted us.

He sat up straight, eyes widening, and rubbed his hands down the length of his thighs a few times. When he rose and started walking in our direction, I gave up trying to drag Zara away and threaded my arm through hers. If we had to face him, I was glad neither of us was doing it alone.

The investigation into what had happened on the day of the invasion was still ongoing. With so many casualties and no surveillance footage, it would take a long time to unravel—to figure out who died by which gun, which Variants killed which humans in self-defense. Tyler was helping as much as he could with questioning the assailants they had captured. Alec was helping with the interrogations too. I tried not to think too hard about the kind of interrogating his particular skill set would be used for.

But Beth's death had been solved early. Zara's account of what happened, coupled with the electric burns on Beth's body, painted a clear picture. Plus, Rick had handed himself in almost immediately.

Had he walked up to the investigators looking as disheveled and tired as he did walking over the green grass now?

He came to a stop before us.

No one said anything.

Rick gazed intently at the ground, his shoulders tight, his breathing ragged. My eyes couldn't seem to settle on one thing; they flitted from Zara's profile to Rick's furrowed brow to the treetops swaying in the warm breeze to the people around us starting to slow down and take notice.

But Zara's eyes were glued to Rick. Her rigid body pressed up against mine as she watched him, not saying anything, her gaze almost daring him to.

"I want you to know that . . ." His voice broke. He swallowed, cleared his throat, and finally looked up. "That I am sorry. If I could go back and take her place, I would. I am so, so sorry."

He took a shaky inhale, his wide shoulders trembling as his eyes filled with tears.

Zara's voice didn't tremble. She lifted her chin and spoke with finality. "Fuck. You." She extracted herself from my hold and walked away.

"Zara . . ." I tried to call after her, go after her, but my knees were weak, and she was so fast.

"Eve . . ." My name sounded like a plea as Rick gave in to the tears completely.

I swatted at my own tears before turning away. I didn't have the strength to move, so I hugged my chest, breathing heavily, feeling cold and alone in the warm morning sun.

I missed her so much. I knew, logically, his intention hadn't been to kill her, but he was still the reason she was gone, and I couldn't look at him.

A hand touched my shoulder, but I didn't recoil from it; I knew the touch of one of my Variants. The loafers peeking out under neat trousers and the smell of expensive aftershave told me it was Josh.

I leaned into him, pressing my forehead to his shoulder, and his arms wrapped around me. We shouldn't have been hugging in public like this, but I needed him.

"Rick." Josh's voice reverberated through his chest. It was a comforting thing to focus on, and I tucked my face farther into him, circling my arms around his waist. "Maybe now's not the best time, yeah?"

Rick sniffled and coughed, trying to get himself together. He didn't say anything, but I heard footsteps retreating.

For a beat, Josh just held me, crushing me to his chest. Too soon, his grip on me loosened, and my knee-jerk reaction was to tighten my hold on his waist, telling him wordlessly I wasn't ready to let go.

"People are looking, baby," he whispered, sounding pained. "I want nothing more than to just hold you, carry you away from here, but . . ."

But I was supposed to be Ethan's girlfriend—not all of their Vital. That was a secret we still had to keep. I pulled away, nodded, and wiped my tears with the tissues he handed me.

Josh stuffed his hands into his pockets—something he was doing more and more when we were together in public—and we walked the rest of the way to the cafeteria in silence. He sat me down at a table in the corner, and while I rested my head on my hands and tried to get my emotions under control, he got me some breakfast.

I was halfway through the eggs when Ethan bounded up, loudly greeted us, and plonked himself in the chair next to mine, stealing a bite of my toast. When neither of us returned his greeting as enthusiastically, the bright look on his face fell.

"What happened?" He lowered his voice, draping a protective arm over the back of my chair.

As Josh explained, I leaned into Ethan's warm, strong body until I was practically in his lap. I took long breaths of his smoky smell and focused on the pressure of his hands holding me close.

Having some contact, even if we were still careful to avoid skin contact, helped clear the dark clouds Rick had brought with him.

The boys walked me to class and reluctantly left my side. Most of the early classes consisted of introductions and get-to-know-yous, the professors answering questions and going over the coursework. I was already ahead in most of it, so I tuned out to check in on Zara.

I sent her a message in our "roomies" group chat—the one Beth was in too. It made me feel closer to her, as if at any moment the little round icon with her smiling freckled face would zoom to the bottom, indicating she'd caught up on all the messages.

Zara said she was fine, that she only had a few classes that day, and since they were introductory ones, she was going to go catch up with a friend instead, get away from campus for a bit.

I hoped I wasn't one of those things she needed to get away from. I hoped our friendship wouldn't fall apart without Beth there to keep us together.

Summer was holding on, and the mornings were still hot, but I didn't have time to lie in bed and enjoy it. My first class started at nine.

I dressed in jean shorts and a loose tank top with a photo of Einstein sticking his tongue out on the front. I tried to be as quiet as possible, not wanting to disturb Zara; since our run-in with Rick a few days ago, she'd been especially withdrawn.

But when I tiptoed out of my room, she was already gone. Pushing the sadness aside, I rushed through my bathroom routine and pulled my hair up into a messy ponytail so it wouldn't stick to my neck. Then I grabbed an apple to tide me over until I could go to the cafeteria.

Slinging my light backpack over my shoulder, I opened the door and came face-to-face with Ethan, his fist raised and ready to knock.

"Hey, sugar." Ethan smiled with his whole being. Most people would pull their lips up at the corners, maybe show some teeth. When Ethan smiled, his face lit up, his dimples appeared, his amber eyes sparkled, his shoulders rolled back. It was like a breath of fresh air you couldn't help inhaling, making you smile back whether you wanted to or not.

"Hey, sunshine." I leaned in for a quick peck on the lips.

"Hey, snookums," Dot cooed in a high-pitched voice, popping her head around Ethan's frame.

"Hey, you weirdo." I laughed, giving her a hug. "What are you guys doing here? I have to get to class."

"Yeah. Biology. I have the same class." Dot leaned on the doorframe. She'd put her black hair in pigtails and was wearing what looked like a basketball jersey sewn up at the sides so my petite friend could wear it as a dress. Paired with the heeled Chuck Taylors (where did she even get those?), it looked perfect on her.

It was the first crazy, uniquely Dot outfit I'd seen her wear since Charlie was taken. There was still sadness in her heavily made-up eyes, but I was happy to see her doing something to make herself feel better—to feel more like herself.

"We went to the bookshop yesterday. Picked yours up too." Ethan held up a bulky-looking bag, then leaned around me to dump it just inside the door.

"Here's the biology textbook."

I shoved the heavy book Dot handed me into my bag while taking a bite of my apple. "Fanx," I said around the tart fruit in my mouth. "Les go."

Ethan slammed my door shut, then frowned at it.

"Is that the only lock that thing has?" he asked as we moved toward the elevator.

"Yeah . . ." It was a simple round door handle with a self-locking mechanism. It was basic, but if someone could make it past the armed, trained men downstairs, no door was going to keep them back.

"Hmm. Not very safe," he mumbled, pulling his phone out, probably to message my other overprotective boyfriend to complain about my door. I rolled my eyes at him.

Our walk to biology took us past the admin building, where Melior Group had set up a base of operations in the back rooms of the ground floor, much to the ire of the busy receptionists. One of the frowning, hard men clad in black was Alec. You could even say the asshole was the frowniest and hardest of them all, and he happened to come down the stairs just as we passed. Three identically dressed men followed close behind him.

I tried to pick up the pace, but Alec came straight for us, avoiding my gaze but waving Ethan down.

"Hey, Kid," he called out, "what do you mean her door is not safe?"

I turned to Ethan, shocked. I thought he was texting Josh about my "unsafe" door. I never would have guessed it was Alec on the other side of the message.

"Just has one standard entry handle, and the door isn't reinforced. Dunno." He shrugged. "Just seems flimsy. You're the security expert."

"My door is not flimsy." This was getting out of hand. "And anyway, with all the heavily armed men around campus . . ." I gestured to the men who had caught up with Alec and were listening in on our conversation, but Alec ignored me.

"Nah, good call, man. I'll make sure Gabe gets someone out today to deal with it."

I turned my shocked expression on Alec. I couldn't believe he was buying into Ethan's paranoia and even getting Tyler involved.

"Holy shit, it's Hawaii girl!" one of the men standing behind Alec called out, slapping one of his companions lightly on the chest.

Alec reacted immediately, speaking a little too fast as he turned to his Melior Group friends. "We should get to our post, guys."

But the one who'd spoken walked right past Alec to stand in front of me. He was of average height with straight black hair, cut very short—the standard among Melior Group employees. He reminded me a little of a teacher I'd had when my mother and I lived in Japan, only about ten years younger.

"You look much better than the last time I saw you." He smiled warmly, his intelligent eyes challenging me to remember.

I frowned. "Thanks? Have we met?"

"Well, you weren't really conscious, so technically we didn't really meet."

"OK. Well, that's creepy." I laughed nervously, taking an exaggerated step back. Neither Alec nor Ethan was going into protective Variant mode, so I was pretty sure this guy wasn't an actual threat, but not being able to figure him out was bugging me.

"Don't blame you for not remembering. It was dark and cold and wet. And you wouldn't have seen my face." He smiled again, raising his eyebrows expectantly.

"Uh, getting creepier by the . . ." Then realization dawned. I looked from the smiling man in front of me to Alec, who was frowning at us with his arms crossed, to the two other men behind them.

Images of water lapping at my face and the sensation of stabbing cold in my limbs came back to me as I finally understood: I was standing in front of Alec's team.

These were the men who had saved my life.

I inhaled sharply as my hands flew to my mouth.

"I think she remembers us." The man chuckled, turning to his teammates.

I rushed forward, regaining the distance I'd put between us only a moment ago, and threw my arms around one of my saviors, holding him tight around his middle.

He froze in surprise, but then his arms gently tightened around my shoulders.

"Thank you." I kept it simple but made sure to say it fast. The last time I'd tried to thank someone for saving my life, he'd made it outrageously difficult. "Thank you so much." I squeezed again to punctuate my statement.

"You're welcome. It's all part of the job, kitten." He was still holding on to me but letting me take charge and decide when the hug ended. I liked him already.

"Kitten?" Alec huffed, clearly bothered by my display yet unable to do anything about it. "You going to let another man hold your girl like that and call her 'kitten'?"

"He saved her life." Ethan's voice held a hint of teasing. "Our relationship is solid, bro. She can hug whoever she wants."

"Don't mean to be disrespectful." The man I was still wrapped around spoke to me, not my boyfriend. I released him and leaned back. "It's how I thought of you when I pulled you out of the water. You were soaked, shivering, and felt so light and fragile—like a drowned kitten."

"You're the one who pulled me out of the water?" I knew Alec had pulled me into the helicopter and stayed with me for the ride after.

He nodded, smiling again. I remembered the feel of his arms holding me firmly as my body lifted into the air, and another surge of thankfulness came over me. I placed a gentle, chaste kiss on his cheek.

Behind me Ethan let loose a full-bellied, mirthful laugh. I chanced a glance at Alec, and he was staring daggers at us. I hadn't intended to piss him off, but I put it down to a happy bonus.

I raised my eyebrows pointedly at him, hoping he would get the hint to get his shit together. Then I stepped around the man who had braved the freezing waters of the Pacific Ocean for me and quickly hugged the other two members of Alec's team, delivering my sincere thanks.

By the time I was done doling out hugs, Alec had managed to calm himself and was once again watching everything with a passive expression.

"I'm Kyo," the recipient of my kiss introduced himself, "and that's Marcus and Jamie."

"Eve. It's nice to meet you."

"So you're with Kid now. Gotta say, I'm surprised. And I'd love to know how you ended up in Bradford in the arms of Alec's cousin. When he went AWOL to stay with you in the hospital, we thought you might be his Vital. He was a little obsessive about it."

"Yeah, and that was a frightening thought for anyone who doesn't like excruciating pain," Jamie, the redhead who was nearly as tall as Alec, piped in, and they all chuckled. Alec just frowned more.

"You know we're just teasing, Ace," Marcus added, using a nickname I hadn't heard before. "You're terrifying even without a Vital." Marcus was bald with a dark complexion and the same height as Kyo. His full lips curved into a smile.

"Playtime is over. We're on duty. Time to get to our post." Alec's calm, even voice didn't give anything away, but it had a visible effect on his team. They all straightened a little, their shoulders pulled back, their expressions more serious.

"Yeah, and we really need to get to biology," Dot added. "And I'm Dot. Not that anyone cares."

"Oh, I care." Kyo flashed her a wide grin, dropping his serious soldier face for just a second.

"Mmhmm," Dot grumbled, turning to walk toward our lecture, but I caught the little smile before she fully turned away, and I caught the way Kyo's eyes lingered on her ass.

"Nice to meet you all. Bye," I called over my shoulder, jogging to catch up to her.

FOUR

The first week of classes had been hectic with everyone trying to settle into a new routine. I was way ahead on the reading, so by the time the weekend arrived, I wasn't stressed about schoolwork, but I was a little apprehensive about our next session with Kane.

Ethan picked me up from my res hall, and we walked to his house slowly, holding hands in companionable silence as the sun came and went behind fat clouds. The air had an edge of chill to it; fall was on its way.

At the gates to the property, one of the ground staff flagged us down, wanting to chat with Ethan specifically—because he treated them all like family rather than an army of servants paid very well to attend to his every need.

I gave Ethan's hand a squeeze and kept going up the tree-lined drive to the main house. Dot would be there, and I hadn't seen her in days. Other than that biology class on Wednesday, our schedules didn't overlap.

Lost in my worries for the little black-haired demon, I let myself in through the front door as usual but pulled up short, an embarrassing squeak escaping my lips.

Wandering out of Tyler's office, half-distracted by a stack of papers in his hand, was Lucian Zacarias. He was dressed casually in tan pants and a collared T-shirt and, for a second, looked as startled to see me barge into his house as I was to see him. He was never home.

A smile quickly replaced the surprise on his face, and for the first time I saw a hint of Ethan there. The resemblance to his other nephew, Alec, was evident in the strong jaw and intelligent, calculating eyes, but I could see only Ethan when he smiled.

"I'm so sorry, Mr. Zacarias. I should have knocked."

He chuckled, turning to face me fully and dropping the hand with the papers to his side. "Nonsense. My nephews have all told you to treat this as your own home. And please, Evelyn, call me Lucian. Or Loulou, if you prefer."

His eyes sparkled a little, clearly amused at some joke that had gone over my head.

"I'm sorry. What?"

"Loulou. It's what you used to call me when you were little."

"Oh . . ." I wasn't sure what to say to that. A strange kind of nostalgia for something I couldn't even remember swept over me, reminding me once again I wasn't a newcomer here. These people had known me since I was born.

As I mulled that over, Lucian watched me with kind eyes. Right then, he reminded me most of Tyler. I knew they weren't related, but it hadn't escaped my attention that he'd referred to them all as his nephews; they were obviously all close to Uncle Lucian.

"I think I'll stick with Lucian, if that's OK."

He smiled and nodded in approval, but before he could make another move, I blurted out another question. "Did you know my mother? I mean, I know you knew her . . . you all knew her, but . . . did you know her well? Do you remember her?"

"Yes. I knew her well." The sadness in his eyes was so similar to mine whenever I thought of her that it was simultaneously disconcerting and comforting.

A weight I hadn't realized I was holding lifted slightly. I wasn't the only one who remembered her. Keeping her memory alive was no longer my solitary burden to bear.

My mother had rarely spoken about her life before it was just the two of us, running all over the world under a cloak of anonymity, and here was a person who had known her well, who seemed open to talking about it. With a firm nod, I opened my mouth to ask Lucian more, but then Ethan burst through the door.

"Hey, Uncle Luce!" he boomed, grabbing me by the hand and dragging me toward the stairs.

"Hey, Kid. Try to get some studying done as well. Don't just slack off all day."

"Yeah, yeah!" he called back, already halfway up the stairs.

I looked back toward the first person I'd met who knew my mother before she was a mother, but the spot where he'd been standing was empty.

As Ethan and I barreled into Josh's room, I was distracted by the music coming from the high-quality speakers and the sight of my other boyfriend sprawled on the couch, so absorbed in a book he didn't even look up. He was in sweats and a Misfits T-shirt, listening to Muse and reading Orwell's *1984*.

I dropped Ethan's hand and leaned over the couch, pressing my face to the back of his book. Then I slowly peeked over the top of it. On cue, the corner of his lip twitched.

"Do you have any idea how distracting that is?" His green eyes danced with amusement as they finally looked into mine.

"Yes. That's why I'm doing it." I tried to keep a straight face but laughed.

With an over-the-top sigh, Josh dropped the book onto the coffee table just in time for Ethan to come up behind me and surprise us both. In one swift move, he swept my feet out from under me and flipped my legs over the back of the couch, making me land hard on top of Josh.

I screamed, but it ended in hysterical laughter.

"Oof!" Josh had the air knocked out of him, but he wrapped his arms around me. "Kid! A little warning!"

"Hey, is it because of your uncle that everyone calls you Kid?" I asked. My back was to Josh's front, and I made myself comfortable.

"Yeah, I guess so." The big guy shrugged, planting himself on the couch at our feet.

"He used to hate it when he was little." Josh chuckled, his breath tickling my neck.

"I'm the youngest, and after . . ." He still couldn't bring himself to say the words. "When we all started living with him, it would always be 'take the kid with you,' 'make sure the kid eats,' 'has the kid done his homework?' Tyler and Alec looked out for me and Josh, but Josh was always mature for his age, and it left me feeling like I wanted to be older all the time. Constantly being referred to as 'kid' definitely grated."

"But it stuck," Josh added.

"It stuck. I got used to it. I don't even notice it anymore. But I do notice that you don't call me that. You only ever say Ethan now, if it's not one of our nicknames." He smiled, flashing me his dimples.

He was giving me an out from a potentially heavy conversation, but I had a feeling he needed some reassurance. "After that night when I ran here like a crazy person because you'd overused your ability"—the smile left Ethan's face, and Josh held me a little tighter—"I just couldn't think of you as Kid anymore.

It felt too casual. There is nothing casual about what you are to me, Ethan."

The smile slowly crept back, but it wasn't a playful one. He leaned forward, keeping himself suspended above us, and kissed me, unbothered by the fact that I was still in Josh's arms. The kiss was sweet and ended quickly, but it made me melt.

Ethan joked and laughed all the time, but he had a real vulnerable side that needed to be nurtured. Sometimes the big booming laugh and inappropriate jokes were just a cover for the scared little kid inside. And if he could be my protector, I could be his support.

Dot arrived just minutes before Kane, and we sweated and grunted through a heavy sparring session. After recovering, we spent the next few hours studying and practicing Light transfer. Dot floated in and out of Josh's room for a while, joining our study and conversations, but she ended up keeping mostly to herself in her usual room at the mansion. She was having a down day, her usual vibrant personality dulled by worry for her brother and Vital. I wanted to go be with her, but Josh stopped me, suggesting she needed some time to herself.

At lunch we wandered down to the kitchen, and Ethan made pizza—with handmade crust and Italian prosciutto and mozzarella. The incredible aroma brought Tyler, Alec, and Lucian out of the study. The men all sat around the big dining table stuffing their faces, and conversation turned to the search for Charlie and the other missing Vitals.

I finished my pizza but couldn't stop thinking about Dot, all alone in her room, so I put a few pieces on a plate and went back upstairs.

No movement or music was coming from her room, but the door was open. Thinking she might be taking a nap, I approached quietly, avoiding the creaky floorboard in the hall.

I stopped just outside her door, and my brows furrowed. Dot was kneeling in front of the bed, her butt resting on her heels and her hands on top of the mattress. For a moment I thought she might be praying, and I nearly backed away to give her privacy.

But something about the posture didn't fit that explanation, and a tiny movement in front of Dot's head caught my attention. Lying on her belly inches in front of Dot's face was Squiggles. The gray ferret seemed to be staring as intently at Dot as Dot was at her, both their heads resting on their folded hands/paws.

My usually feisty friend was trying to communicate with her ferret.

My heart sank. Dot was *really* struggling today. I hadn't, until that moment, realized how far-reaching the effects of losing her Vital were. She'd lost not only her brother but her access to the Light and, with it, the ability to communicate with animals that had been such a massive part of her since childhood.

Dot sighed deeply. Squiggles lifted her head and reached a tiny paw out, resting it gently on her human friend's cheek, her beady little eyes darting all over Dot's face.

"I know," Dot ground out between gritted teeth, her voice almost too quiet for me to hear. "I'm trying. I'm trying *so hard*." A soft sob escaped her and pushed me into action.

I walked into the room, setting the plate with the pizza on the bedside table and kneeling next to my friend.

She looked up at me with wet eyes. I pulled her into a tight hug, and she let her tears flow freely while I rocked us back and forth.

After a few minutes her crying calmed down, and she pulled away, leaning her side against the bed. "I'm losing Squiggles, Eve. Within a few weeks of him being gone, I started to lose the ability to connect to any animal within range remotely. But I've had Squiggles for years, and our bond is strong, so I could always reach her if I needed her. But in the last few days . . . I'm losing her too. I can only hear her clearly if we're touching."

"Oh, Dot . . ." I didn't know what to say. I'd never had an ability or a brother. I didn't know what it was like to lose either one, but I knew pain when I saw it.

"I've had this since I was, like, five, you know. With sibling Bonds, sometimes the abilities and the Light access manifest sooner, so it was just, like, a normal part of our childhood. Now all of a sudden I'm finding out how little I'm capable of without him, and it's like losing a limb."

My heart was breaking clean in half for her.

We both got lost in our own thoughts for a few minutes, staring into space. Hearing Dot talk about how much Charlie's Light made a difference to her abilities got me thinking about my own Bond and the nature of the Light in general. My mind randomly remembered some of the tutoring sessions I'd had with Tyler, specifically the very first one—before either of us knew he was mine.

I sat up straighter, an idea forming in my mind.

"Dot." I placed a gentle hand on her shoulder.

"Hmm?" She looked up, distracted.

"I want to try something."

"What?"

"The Bond is instinctual, right? And the Light flows easily between Bonded Vitals and Variants."

"Right . . ." She frowned at me. This was common knowledge.

"But it's possible for a Vital to transfer Light to any Variant—not just the ones in their Bond."

"Not as easy or natural but, yeah, entirely possible." The frown lifted as she caught on to what I was suggesting.

I gave her a little smile.

"You would do that for me?" She sounded unsure, but a little hope had brightened her red-rimmed eyes.

I'd never transferred Light to anyone outside my Bond, but I couldn't think of a person more deserving or more in need than the one sitting in front of me. If I could do anything to ease the pain Dot had been living with for months, then of course I was going to try.

"I'm just sorry I didn't think of it earlier."

"Eve . . ." She looked so touched by the mere suggestion that it was already worth it.

"I don't know if I can do it," I added quickly, "but I'm willing to try. If you are."

"Fuck yes! Let's do this." Her enthusiasm was infectious.

"OK." I took a deep breath and sat up straighter, crossing my legs. Dot mirrored my pose and waited patiently.

I shook my hands out, not really sure why—it just seemed like a good preparatory action—and took another deep breath. I was getting a little nervous. What if I couldn't do it and she was disappointed? What if it hurt?

"OK, um . . ." I tentatively reached out in Dot's direction, then pulled my hand back. "Shit! I don't know how to do this."

Instead of looking crestfallen, Dot chuckled. "Just relax, Eve. Pretend I'm Josh or something."

I snorted. "I don't think you want me pretending you're Josh. Unless you want to make out with me, I'd better pretend you're Tyler."

We both laughed at that, which eased some of my nerves.

"Wait. Don't you want to make out with Tyler?" Dot looked a little puzzled. "I thought the Light pushed you to have the same level of intimacy with all your Variants. Isn't that a thing in non-sibling Bonds—if you're getting it on with one of them, you're getting it on with all of them?"

"According to all my research, yeah. But you try telling Tyler that—I'm not the one that doesn't want to make out. And other stuff." I couldn't believe I'd said that much out loud, but Dot didn't make me feel any more awkward about it. That's why I loved her.

"According to your research? What about the practical application, Eve? You have the perfect test subjects!"

"Yes, I know. And by all observable accounts, the Light is indeed pushing me to strengthen the Bond with all my Variants. Like I said—I'm pretty sure *he's* the one who's not interested."

"Interesting. I wonder why he's holding back."

"Maybe I'm just not his type."

"Pfft," she scoffed. "Please. You're his Vital—trust me, you're his type. There must be another reason. Got to admire his willpower though. Can't be easy. What about Alec, then? You said the Light was pushing you to all of them . . ."

"Stop distracting me. I'm trying to do something important here." I couldn't deny I was attracted to Alec, but he'd been such a colossal jerk to me I couldn't wrap my mind around my attraction. Plus, this conversation was sure to lead to Studygate, and I was definitely *not* talking about that.

Talk of Tyler, however, had reminded me once again of our first Light transfer and the way he'd held his hands out for me to take. It seemed to flow the easiest through my hands. Without letting Dot get another comment in, I held my hands out to her with more confidence, palms up.

She took a deep breath and placed her hands in mine.

I closed my eyes.

Using some of my mindfulness techniques, I located the barrier I'd carefully built up over time and lowered it a fraction, allowing the Light access. With the Light flow open, I drew a small amount into myself and then carefully restored the barrier. I didn't want to take in too much and have to run to Tyler if I couldn't expel it into Dot. It was like testing any new substance—you spot test in a discreet area first to see if it leaves a mark.

The pure power within me hummed faintly, and I tightened my grip on Dot's hands, putting all my focus on sending the Light to where we touched. With any one of my Variants, it didn't need to be directed. As soon as we had skin contact, it poured out of me and into them. I'd spent months learning how to *stop* the Light.

I'd never had to *push* it into someone. It was easy enough to get it to come to my hands, ready to release, but once it realized it wasn't one of my guys on the other side of the contact, it slammed the brakes on. It felt as if I were trying to push a toddler through the door to the dentist's office, and it had a death grip on the doorframe.

I focused on my breathing and reminded myself that I was in control here. Yes, the Light was pure, unadulterated power, but it was at my mercy. I got to choose when it flowed into me, and I got to choose when and how much of it flowed out. Most importantly, I got to choose *whom* it went to.

I was choosing Dot.

Slowly, reluctantly, the Light bent to my will.

Dot gasped, and her hold on my hands tightened, but she didn't say anything. She was controlling herself like a champ so I could focus. I smiled a little and put my full concentration back into what I was doing.

Thankfully, though, it didn't require much more hard work from me. The Light flowed just fine now that I'd established the connection. With my guys, it would gush out of me like a dam breaking anytime I let it; with Dot it was more like the flow of a shower in a cheap motel room with really bad water pressure—underwhelming but dribbling through steadily.

After a few minutes, we released each other's hands, and I opened my eyes. Dot was beaming. It was so good to see a genuine smile on her face that I couldn't have stopped returning it if I'd wanted to.

She launched herself at me, almost knocking me flat on my back, and squeezed with all the might her delicate arms could muster.

"Thank you, thank you, thank you!" she fired off, then shot up and ran to the window. Throwing it open with more than a little dramatic flair, she leaned out and shouted, "I'm back, baby!"

I laughed and lifted myself onto the bed next to Squiggles. The little ferret was bobbing up and down on her hind legs in excitement. Dot rushed back to the bed and leaned down.

"I'm back," she whispered before planting a kiss on Squiggles' head. The furry noodle did a weird excited turn on the spot, and Dot laughed. "I know, right?" she replied to whatever it was Squiggles had communicated to her.

Before I could jokingly ask if they were talking about me, Dot rushed back to the window and held her arms straight out. What followed was like a scene from a Disney movie.

All manner of woodland creatures—squirrels, mice, a racoon, and various brightly colored little birds—streamed in through the window. The birds perched on Dot's arms, and the furry friends crowded around her feet.

I sat on the bed, frozen, my mouth hanging open. Apparently Squiggles wasn't as impressed as me though, because she didn't rush forward to join the fun. When an actual *bald eagle* landed with a big flap of its impressive wings, Squiggles rushed up my arm and perched on my shoulder, giving me a very humanlike "are you going to do anything about this?" look.

"Let her enjoy it," I stage-whispered to the ferret. "I'll protect you from the . . . eagle."

When I looked back to the window, however, a snake was slithering its way in. I shot up and scrambled backward until my back hit the wall. One hand held on to Squiggles—who was trying to hide her face in my hair now that there were *two* potential predators at the window.

"Dot!" I said as firmly as I could, but my voice still wavered as I kept my eyes glued to the snake that was now halfway into the room.

She ignored me.

"Dorothy, cut it out!" I knew the use of her full name would annoy her enough to get her attention, and she looked at me over her shoulder, amusement written all over her face. "Squiggles is scared," I finished lamely, putting my attention back on the snake.

With a roll of her eyes, Dot turned back to the window and dropped her arms. Almost immediately the eagle flew off, the snake began to slither back out, and all the other creatures scurried off.

I took a breath, letting the tension in my shoulders release, and gave Squiggles a soothing stroke down her back.

"I don't know what the big deal is. We were just catching up." Dot waved casually in my direction as she wandered over to sit on the bed, enthusiastically biting into the cold pizza.

Squiggles untangled herself from my hair, scampered down my leg, and went to stand in front of Dot, making a sound that was something between the squeak of a mouse and the purr of a cat.

"You're being dramatic." Dot rolled her eyes as she answered whatever Squiggles had said.

Squiggles ran to the adjoining bathroom, let herself in through the crack in the door, and somehow managed to slam it.

I chuckled and, after checking that the snake really had slithered back out, pushed away from the safety of the wall. "How you feeling?"

Dot was stuffing pizza into her mouth so fast she was on her last slice already. "Arrazing!" she said around a giant mouthful, then paused, her eyes suddenly going sad. She swallowed slowly, staring very hard at the floor in front of her.

"Hey?" My brows furrowed. "What's going on?"

"I feel amazing," she repeated, but her tone suggested the complete opposite. "It feels so good to have my full ability again after all this time, but . . . Charlie."

She looked up at me, her eyes wide.

"Oh, Dot." I sat next to her and wrapped an arm around her shoulders. "Charlie wouldn't begrudge you this. You know he wouldn't. He might give you shit all the time, but really, all he wants is for you to be safe and happy. Wherever he is, he knows we're doing all we can to find him."

"I know. I just feel bad that for a moment there, I forgot about him. I felt so good and full of Light that it was all I could think about. I'm a shit sister."

"No, you're not!"

"Yes, I am!" She was on the verge of tears again.

Arguing with her wasn't going to get me anywhere. Dot was a proactive, energetic kind of person. She was a doer. So I would give her something to do. "You know what? No. I'm not going to let you wallow."

"But . . ."

"No!" I cut her off sharply. "We just had a win. I mastered a new part of my Vital powers, and you're fully juiced up for the first time in months. You might be feeling guilty, but I'm not going to let you dwell on it. Now, the boys are all gathered around the dining table downstairs discussing strategy again. So if you want to do something about Charlie, let's go down there and help."

By the time I finished my tirade, her tears had stopped, and she was sitting up a little straighter, so I threw in a joke to lighten the mood. "Help or get in the way and annoy them. Whatever."

She giggled softly, nodding, then stood up and took off, finishing the rest of her pizza as she walked.

FIVE

The guys were sitting where I'd left them, empty plates and napkins the only remaining evidence of the several pizzas. Lucian leaned back in his seat at the head of the table, arms lightly folded over his chest, his intelligent eyes observing the heated conversation Alec and Tyler were locked into.

They were on opposite sides of the table, both leaning on their forearms. They weren't yelling, but their shoulders were tense as they fired arguments at each other. As I walked past Tyler's chair, my fingers actually *twitched*—that's how strong the urge was to rub some of that tension out. But I held myself back. We didn't have that kind of relationship.

Why didn't we have that kind of relationship again? Why was it that one of my Bond members didn't want to touch me unless it was completely necessary? I shook my head, trying to sweep those thoughts away—now wasn't the time.

I plonked myself down next to Josh, and his hand immediately landed on my knee, giving it a gentle squeeze. He met my eyes with one of his knowing half smiles, and I wondered how obvious my thoughts were.

I returned his smile and, making sure my Light was locked down, placed my hand over his, reveling in the moment of intimacy.

"Alec, we've tried everything else." I'd so rarely heard frustration in Tyler's voice that he immediately had may attention.

"No, we haven't," Alec was quick to reply. "We're still waiting on intel to come in. Uncle Luce is pressing some of his other high-up contacts, and we're working on setting up an exchange of intel with some of the European governments. This shit takes time. We need to give it *more time.*"

"It's been months." Now Tyler just sounded defeated. Again, I ached to soothe him in some way, but I threaded my fingers through Josh's instead.

"I can't believe you're even suggesting this, Gabe. Aren't you supposed to be the logical one?"

"We've explored all other avenues. And I appreciate that new info may come in anytime but . . ."

"But Charlie may not have time," Dot finished for him, making our presence known to everyone who'd been too absorbed in the argument to notice.

"Dot." Alec turned to his little cousin, the hard expression on his face softening considerably. "I know this is hard for you to listen to. Maybe you should—"

"We're not leaving," I interrupted. "We need to feel like we're helping too. Dot needs this."

Alec didn't look in my direction, but a muscle in his cheek twitched. I'd be lying if I said it didn't hurt that he'd been soft and caring toward Dot but the mere sound of my voice had him looking as if he wanted to hit something. There was only so much rejection a girl could handle, especially when it came from people who were literally made for me, supernaturally tethered to me.

"Do we even know where to find a Lighthunter?" Ethan's booming voice cut in, preventing an argument before it started. "I thought they were, like, a fairytale or something."

"Is this what it's come to?" Dot dropped her head into her hands. "Gabe, the most logical person I know, suggesting we use a *Lighthunter*. Fuck . . ." She started muttering to herself about Charlie being doomed and everyone losing their minds.

"There is some historical evidence suggesting they weren't just myth and legend," Josh explained. "I've been doing a little research since Gabe first floated the idea the other day, but there isn't much available from reliable sources and not much that's recent. The historical texts all point to them being real though."

"But even if they were, Josh," Alec argued, "you're talking in the past tense. There's nothing to suggest they're legit in this day and age."

Tyler crossed his arms. "That's not entirely true."

"Hold up!" I had to raise my voice to get everyone's attention. "What's a Lighthunter? I was raised as a Dime, remember?"

"Evelyn, please don't use that word," Lucian objected.

"Sorry," I whispered, appropriately chastised. Still, it made me smile a little. It had been so long since I'd had a parental figure in my life.

Lucian cocked his head at me, and his lips twitched too. Apparently he had some of Josh's talents for deciphering my feelings.

"The concept of the Lighthunter has been part of Variant culture and lore for thousands of years." Tyler stepped into his tutor role seamlessly, explaining everything in the same patient, calm voice he used during our study sessions. "In the last hundred years or so, it has fallen into the realm of myth."

"OK . . ." I nodded for him to keep going.

"According to legend, Lighthunters are Variants who have a special connection to the Light."

"Isn't that just what a Vital is?"

"Not like a Vital. Vitals have access to the Light and can channel it, passing it to Variants. Lighthunters don't do that. Their connection is less direct in some ways and more . . . informative in others."

I was fine with complex mathematical concepts and scientific theories. Those things were based in logic. This sounded more like fantasy.

At the confused look on my face, Tyler quickly continued. "Think of it like this: You, a Vital, can feel the Light as it flows through you. A Lighthunter can see it and sense it. They can take one look at a Variant and be able to tell who their Vital is and vice versa. Some of the texts suggest that with a deeper understanding of a particular Variant or Vital and their ability or Light access, respectively, they can locate members of the person's Bond."

As the implications began to sink in, I looked at Dot. She still had her head in her hands.

"For centuries Lighthunters were a revered part of Variant society," Josh jumped in. "They were instrumental in helping Variants and Vitals find each other. In a time when travel was limited to horse and cart, it was much more difficult for people to leave their village and 'network' in an effort to find their Bond. Having someone to point you in the right direction was incredibly useful, and Lighthunters were paid handsomely for their services."

"How exactly did they do that? Were some of them better at it than others? Was there a limit on the distance?" I fired off, my curiosity piqued. Tyler gave me an indulgent smile; I often did this in our sessions when something interested me.

"The historic texts aren't too clear on the specifics," Josh said, "and I've yet to find a text dedicated to the subject. So far it's been just obscure mentions here and there. Around the turn of the century, any mention of Lighthunters seems to just vanish. Until the forties. Some World War II books mention them being used to identify Variants in Germany. And we all know what the Nazis did to known Variants in the thirties and forties." Josh's beautiful green eyes turned sad, and I gave his hand a squeeze.

Now that I had a basic understanding of what we were talking about, I tried to bring the conversation back to the present. "So, how can this help us with finding Charlie?"

At the mention of her brother's name, Dot sat up straighter. She looked very skeptical but at least a little curious too.

"There are people who claim to be Lighthunters still," Josh went on. "They're hard to—"

"Yeah, but they're all nutcases! Carnies and fraudsters," Ethan interrupted. His deep voice sounded serious, rare for him, and I was reminded once again how much Charlie's disappearance was affecting everyone.

"Exactly!" Alec sounded as if he'd been bursting to interrupt the history lesson. "The scum who call themselves Lighthunters these days are no different from their human equivalent—psychics, clairvoyants, and mediums. They dress like hippies and prey on desperate young Variants, giving them some vague bullshit that's enough to give them hope while taking all their money. I don't even know why we're still talking about this!" He threw his hands up and leaned back in his seat.

Lucian gave him a weird look. "Calm down, Alec. We're only having a hypothetical discussion." He looked baffled by his nephew's behavior, although I was under the impression this was just Alec's default setting. I did my best to ignore him and focus on what Tyler was saying.

"We're talking about it because it's time to think outside the box, and I believe there's enough historical evidence to suggest Lighthunters were real. We don't know why they disappeared some hundred years ago, but I do think it's possible a few remain who are authentic. Also, I've already reached out to some contacts who can put me onto an individual who I believe could be the real thing." He delivered the last part in a slight rush, as if trying to get the words out before someone interrupted him, but his voice was still confident and sure.

There was a moment of silence.

Lucian's brows rose in surprise. Alec stood from his chair slowly, the muscles in his neck bunching, his jaw tight. Something in me was pulled to him in the same way I'd been pulled to soothe Tyler, and I squeezed Josh's hand again.

"You didn't. Please tell me you didn't." His intense blue-eyed stare was fixed on Tyler, who remained in his seat.

"I did. I think it's worth a try." I was impressed by Tyler's calm reply; I'd been on the other end of Alec's icy stare.

"You're a fool."

"Alec." Lucian winced as Dot sucked in a breath on the other side of the table, her hands flying to her head.

Alec looked between them, his eyes widening momentarily before he swore profusely and walked out of the room. Apparently he took the pain with him, because the only two people in the room affected by it visibly relaxed.

"Tyler, I think you'd better explain." Lucian had his serious, director-of-an-international-security-firm face on.

"Some years ago, through some contacts at The Hole"—he sighed and Lucian frowned, apparently not liking where this was going—"Alec and I made contact with a person claiming to be a Lighthunter. It was through underground channels, and it was not easy. This was not some hack at a carnival with a table you could just walk up to. That, combined with the fact that she couldn't help us—and said so instead of taking our money—makes me believe she may be the real deal."

Everyone at the table was quiet, their expressions thoughtful and a little sad. No one was looking at me except Tyler, who seemed expectant—as if he knew I would ask a question. Of course I had many, but one was at the forefront of my mind.

"Why were you two even looking for a Lighthunter?"

"He was trying to find you," Tyler said in a quiet voice.

I frowned and looked at the table. It didn't make sense. Why had Alec been looking for me? He hated having me around, hated the fact that I amplified his ability. So much hate . . .

"He never told me about this," Lucian said quietly.

"Probably because it was a bust. Like I said, she couldn't help us. She took one look at him and said no. He was convinced it was because of his ability—that she was keeping him away from his Vital so his 'curse' wouldn't be allowed to grow." He did air quotes around the word *curse*. "She explained it was because the Bond wasn't fully formed yet. She could indicate a general direction but couldn't pinpoint a specific location. The signal was just too weak. You know what he was like—he stormed out of there before we could even have a proper conversation, and that was the end of it."

"You really think she's the real deal?" Josh asked.

"I don't know. At the time I was only trying to be there for Alec. Had I known the Vital he was looking for was also *my* Vital, I would have insisted on staying." He gave me a warm smile before continuing. "That's why I've reached out to her again. I think it's worth looking into. Dot and Charlie's Bond has been building since birth. It's as strong as it can get. If she's legit, she might be able to lead us straight to him."

Dot was leaning forward and listening intently to everything. For the first time in months, her wide eyes had hope in them.

"Or she might lead us straight into a trap," Lucian added. The hope drained right out of Dot's face. "I appreciate the out-of-the-box thinking and the initiative, but this might not be worth the risk."

"Which is why I'm not doing it as an official part of Melior Group operations. At this stage it's just talking to some old shady friends. They may not even be able to find her. And if they do, what's the harm in just speaking with her?"

"All right, but this is strictly intel-only at this stage. The minute you need to use Melior Group resources to verify anything, you come straight to me. We'll need to be as by-the-book on this as possible."

"Yes, sir." Tyler's easy tone suggested what Lucian was saying went *without* saying.

Ethan stood to clean up the mess he'd made while cooking lunch. With a resigned sigh, Dot went to help him. Tyler planted his hands on the table as if to get up, but an idea was forming in my mind, and I had more questions.

"Ty?"

He paused at the sound of my new nickname for him. I was trying not to use it too much—it felt too intimate when he was trying so hard to keep me at arm's length—but it slipped through sometimes. "What's the litmus test?"

"I've been thinking about that too. We would need to verify she can indeed detect a Bond, and then we would need some way to test how accurate the locating portion of the ability is. We have no idea where Charlie is, so we'd need to know she can track him to potentially the other side of the world. Unfortunately, so much of the psychic-like stuff can be faked, and with today's technology, it's possible to find almost anyone if you know enough about them."

"But wouldn't you be able to tell if she was lying?" Surely Tyler's ability would provide all the information we needed, especially with extra Light from me.

He smiled sadly. "Unfortunately, no. I couldn't pick anything up from her, not even a hint. And when Alec lost his shit and stormed out, several other people in the room doubled over in pain, but she didn't even flinch. Lighthunters are immune to all other abilities. Josh's research suggests the same."

"A double-blind test would be ideal, then." I was thinking out loud.

"Yes." He smiled in that way he always did when I understood a complex issue. "Having her try to track someone she doesn't know and who doesn't know they're being tracked would be ideal, but it's impossible. There are too many variables we couldn't control. And Lucian's profile is too public. With enough research she could find some of the Vitals he knows in other parts of the world. That's the other problem. Vitals are so precious in our circles and Variants are so proud when they're located that you'd be hard pressed to find one who hasn't been interviewed by local media or bragged about on social media."

"Right." But we did have a Vital like that. *I* was a Vital like that. I was about 99.8 percent sure the idea I had brewing would not be received well by my overprotective Bond, so I quickly asked another question to prevent Tyler's ability from raising a red flag. "So how might this lead into a trap?"

Lucian answered this time. "The circle of people we can truly trust is dwindling. The tensions between the Human Empowerment Network and Variant Valor are increasing by the day, which means the tensions between humans and Variants are too. People do crazy things when they're scared. We have to consider the possibility that whoever is behind this might plant someone to pretend to be a Lighthunter and lead us into a trap to weaken Melior Group's combative forces."

It sounded pretty paranoid—planting people to pretend to be other people and setting elaborate traps. But then, he was the director of an international security agency, so what the hell did I know?

"I've got to get back to work." Tyler sighed, finally standing from the table and stretching his arms over his head.

"Let's do some training," Josh suggested. "Focus on something productive. I think I might have this flying thing down soon." He flashed me a playful smile and tugged on my hand as he got up.

As everyone dispersed, I excused myself to the bathroom, telling Josh and Ethan I would meet them upstairs.

On my way there, I came face-to-face with the last person I wanted to see. For someone who hated me so much, he certainly popped up an awful lot.

Alec was leaning on the elaborate end of the banister at the bottom of the stairs. He straightened as I approached, his ice-blue eyes looking right at me.

"What?" I demanded with a juvenile eye-roll.

He scowled. "I want to make sure you're not getting any stupid ideas with this Lighthunter shit. It's not going to happen."

"Don't call me stupid, you asshole."

"I wasn't calling you stupid," he ground out between clenched teeth, looking as if it took all his self-control not to yell the words in my face. Then he sighed, and his tense shoulders slumped. "I'm just trying to protect you," he said softly to my feet.

But I was over his attitude. "Are you? Well, that's hard to believe, because the only person who's really hurt me since I came to Bradford Hills is *you*."

His head snapped up. So much confusion crossed his face that for a split second I questioned if I'd hallucinated the shitty way he'd treated me and all the awful things he'd done and said.

"What are you . . . Is this about Dana? Just because you happen to own my fucking soul doesn't mean you get to dictate who I sleep with." His voice was hard, defensive.

"You think I'm jealous? Get over yourself." I crossed my arms and scoffed.

I was jealous, but I wasn't ready to admit that to even myself, let alone him. "This isn't about what disgusting things you do with some slut."

"Then what the fuck is it about?" He raised his voice a little, his eyes bugging out as he leaned into me.

"You told me you hate me, you dumbass!" I replied before I could think, my voice rising to meet his.

"What . . ." Confusion clouded his face once again. The idea that I'd been feeling like shit about something so insignificant to him he didn't even remember it just turned the knife, but it was out now, so I might as well complete the humiliation.

"None of the shitty things you've done and said before and since that night even come close." The temptation to look down was strong, but I forced myself to keep eye contact. It may have been petty, but I wanted him to see the hurt in my eyes so he might feel some of it along with me. "You and I might not like that the Light has tethered us to each other, but it has, and I'm as powerless to do anything about it as you are. Do you have any idea how much it hurt to hear one of my Bond members tell me he *hates* me?"

Tears began to well in my eyes, and I only just managed to get the words out without my voice breaking. But I refused to give him the satisfaction of seeing the tears spill over.

"Fuck!" I yelled up to the ceiling and brushed past him, storming up the stairs.

"Fuck!" I heard him yell behind me and then the sound of a door slamming.

SIX

The sunlight filtering through the treetops jittered across the pages of the book in my lap, and I leaned my head back against the thick trunk of the oak tree. The leaves were changing, yellows and oranges dancing with the greens in the soft breeze. It would soon be too cold to sit outside, so Dot, Zara, and I were making the most of the warm October day.

We were supposed to be studying. One month in, we all had assignments and reading to work on, so we'd laid out a big picnic blanket in a quiet part of Bradford Hills' grounds. The spot was away from most of the academic buildings—it hadn't seen any violence on the day of the invasion; it was not soaked in the blood of the fallen.

We'd hoped the sunshine and fresh air would be motivating. And it was for about an hour, but I smashed through my chemistry homework and abandoned the textbook for another heavy old book from a dusty part of one of the campus's three libraries. My unwavering hunt for information about why

I'd glowed had been reduced to a tome containing Eastern European folktales.

Next to me, Zara sat with her legs crossed, her elbows resting on her knees, her face in her phone. She'd been the first one to give up any semblance of study.

Dot was sprawled out on her belly facing us, still kind of reading her biology textbook, but her eyes were drawn more and more to Squiggles. The ferret was having the time of her life, chasing squirrels and darting in and out of piles of dead autumnal foliage.

I set my book aside and reached into Dot's tote for snacks, finding myself rewarded with the telltale crinkle of a chip bag. I opened it and set it in the middle, grabbing a handful for myself.

"Good idea," Dot mumbled before stuffing some into her mouth.

Zara barely spared us a glance before returning her attention to her screen.

"Who have you been talking to, Zee?" Apparently food had perked Dot up, and she was ready to break the comfortable silence.

"No one" was Zara's distracted reply.

Dot and I shared a look, a devious smile pulling at her delicate features. I was positive she was thinking the same thing: Zara was seeing someone.

I'd noticed her face in her phone more and more, her fingers flying over the screen. At first I thought she was just using technology to distract herself, but every time I asked her about it, she became cagey, hiding the phone away and changing the topic.

"No one?" Dot's voice was dangerously innocent. I narrowed my eyes at her in warning. Zara had been a bit more distant, but she'd also been quicker to anger than ever, snapping at little things and taking her frustration out on inanimate objects. It wasn't a good idea to push her.

Apparently Dot had a different opinion. She pushed herself up and nearly snatched the phone out of Zara's grip, but Zara pulled it back out of her reach.

"What the fuck?" she snapped, as predicted. "I said it was no one. Respect my fucking privacy."

A few people walking on a nearby track turned to look in our direction. Dot sat up, her eyes wide, her hands held out in front of her. "Sorry. Geez." She frowned at Zara and sat back on her heels, watching her warily.

"Let's all just take a deep breath." I channeled Beth, trying to defuse the situation as Zara breathed heavily through her anger and Dot remained silent.

I could understand why Dot had done it. After moving to Bradford Hills, Zara and Beth had both barged into my life in the most unassuming yet forceful way—invading my personal space, borrowing my clothes, reading my messages, entering my room without preamble. Dot had been just as quick to insert herself into my private business. It wasn't a stretch to assume that before their falling out, Dot and Zara had had the same easy closeness that allowed them to touch each other's stuff without asking.

But I could also understand Zara's reaction. None of us liked to be startled anymore.

My eyes drifted to a Melior Group guard walking past, clearly on patrol.

Zara closed her eyes and took a deep breath. "Sorry," she said softly. I knew it wasn't easy for her to say, and I was glad when Dot immediately accepted her apology.

I reached for the bag of chips, and the loud crinkle helped break the uncomfortable mood.

Zara left her phone sitting on the picnic blanket between us, and I caught a glimpse of the time as I leaned back.

"Shit." I swallowed my bite of chips as I hurried to gather my books. "I'm going to be late for my session with Ty."

"Have you noticed how she calls him Ty?" Dot whispered conspiratorially to Zara, a grin spreading over her face.

"Mmhmm." Zara nodded, eyebrows raised, a smile pulling at her own mouth. "No one calls him that. How sickeningly fucking adorable."

I rolled my eyes but didn't have time to come up with a witty retort. With a heavy pile of books in my arms, because I'd stupidly forgotten to bring a bag, I rushed off, only letting my smile through after I'd turned away. I was glad they weren't holding on to the earlier tension, even if it had been broken at my expense.

The admin building was a good ten minutes from our quiet picnic spot. I set a steady pace, hefting the books onto my hip.

I wasn't the only distracted one lately. Tyler had been as attentive as always during our tutoring sessions and training, but in the moments between, when our conversation would have turned naturally to more casual topics, he seemed more reserved. Our conversation didn't flow as easily. He didn't smile as warmly. He didn't even look at me with quite as much affection in his eyes.

I tried to tell myself he was withdrawn because of all the things everyone was dealing with—the invasion, the deaths, the search for Charlie—but the insecure girl-with-a-crush part of me couldn't help worrying that it had something to do with *me*.

"Need a hand with those?" The appearance of a black-clad man at my side startled me.

"Holy Copernicus!" My hand flew to my chest, and one of my books slipped and thudded to the ground. "Kyo, you scared the crap out of me!"

"Sorry, kitten." He chuckled, picking up the fallen book and taking a few more off my hands while I caught my breath. "It becomes second nature to move silently after a while. Didn't mean to scare you."

"Kitten? Really? That's happening? We're making that a thing?" I gave him a withering look.

"I like it." He shrugged, breaking into a grin.

I sighed. "OK, whatever. You did save my life, so I guess I'll let it slide."

"Yes, yes, I did! Where you off to?"

"I have a meeting with Tyler," I answered, resuming my walk.

"I'm headed that way too. You know, it's funny, with all this extra Melior Group presence, he's had to pull back on his Bradford Hills duties, but he still hasn't canceled any of his sessions with you."

"What happened that night? The night you saved me?" I deflected like a pro.

"Uh, what?" He looked a little taken aback, his eyes searching my face, but thankfully he didn't press the issue.

"I mean, I know the plane crashed. I was there. But I still don't really know what caused it or even why you guys were able to get there so fast."

"Right." He rubbed the back of his neck awkwardly, most likely calculating how much I already knew, how much I'd learned from my close proximity to the guys through my relationship with Ethan. But he had a precarious line to walk. He was bound by my least favorite word: *classified*.

"I've tried asking Alec about it, but for the longest time he refused to even accept my thanks, and he's just so frustrating to talk to." I frowned at the ground.

"Yeah, he can be hard to get close to. A lot of people are intimidated by him, so he's developed a shell."

Kyo was looking straight ahead, his brows furrowed. He'd nailed Alec and one of his many, many issues perfectly. He had to be pretty close to him—not an easy feat to achieve. I was equally happy Alec had support in his team members and frustrated he was capable of opening up to people outside his family—just not me.

"Yeah, I learned that the hard way." My baffling feelings about Alec weren't going to derail this conversation. We were nearly at the admin building's front entrance, and Kyo seemed to genuinely like me. I might actually have a chance of getting some info out of him. "My mother died in that crash."

His gaze flew to mine. "I'm so sorry. I had no idea."

"It's OK." I smiled reassuringly. "I just want to know what happened, you know? I still feel like I have no closure."

I was being more open about this with Kyo than I had been with most people. He was just super easy to talk to; it was probably a massive advantage in intelligence gathering situations.

"I can understand that. And I'd like to help as much as I can, but some things are . . ."

"Classified," I finished for him, with a tight smile. We'd reached the bottom of the steps leading up to the admin building. Several black-clad and suited-up people nodded to Kyo in greeting as they passed. "I hate that word," I mumbled, taking my books back. "Thanks for your help."

"I'll tell you what, kitten." His bright smile had me turning back to him, pausing with one foot on the steps. I was going to be late for Tyler, but he was probably still wrapped up in some important meeting that was going over time anyway.

"How about an exchange of intel?" Kyo leaned forward, lowering his voice conspiratorially.

I narrowed my eyes. What information could I possibly have that a Melior Group special agent couldn't get? "I'm listening."

"I'll tell you all I can without breaking the classification and losing my job."

"And in exchange?"

"You tell me some things about your friend Dot."

He smiled wide, not even a little embarrassed. I laughed; he might just be the kind of guy she needed.

"Deal." We shook hands, and then I hurried on my way.

Upstairs, I passed several people in the hallway outside Tyler's office. Melior Group people and Bradford Hills staff all ignored me as they filed out.

He stood at the door, speaking to Stacey from admissions, who always wore her hair in a neat bun and was always nearby, ready to give Tyler a helping hand. I swallowed the bitter taste of envy in my mouth but couldn't seem to look away from how their heads bent toward each other, how she nodded and smiled before touching him on the arm and strutting past me without even looking in my direction.

But Stacey was completely forgotten once I reached Tyler—chased out of my mind by the way his shirt stretched over the muscles in his forearm as he pushed the messy brown locks off his forehead.

"Hey." He gave me a tired smile.

Our session was shorter than usual, Tyler flying through the topics we needed to cover without pause, his shoulders slumped, his beautiful gray eyes almost never meeting mine.

We were interrupted by one of the admin staff coming in to ask Tyler a question. I packed up my books and excused myself, letting him get back to work. He barely spared me a wave goodbye as he rummaged through the pile of papers on his desk.

On the elevator ride down, I bit my lip and told myself yet again he was just busy, preoccupied, that his wavering attention wasn't personal.

It still hurt.

Outside, I patted myself on the back for not letting the tears overflow. Kyo spotted me at the same time I saw him and provided the perfect distraction, smiling widely from across the square and waving me over.

We found a picnic table near the cafeteria and sat down across from each other, both of us eager to get into our mutually beneficial exchange of information.

Kyo had a warm, relaxed manner that kept the conversation flowing naturally, despite my sometimes awkwardness and the way I asked a million questions without pausing. Unfortunately, he couldn't tell me much about the plane crash that I didn't already know. But he did help me get the pieces straight in my head, confirming what I'd managed to get out of Tyler and Alec.

Over the course of the past few months, I hadn't abandoned my quest for answers. The search for Charlie and the work to solve the mystery of who was behind it all was taking up most of everyone's time, but I'd still found a few opportunities to ask Tyler about the plane crash. Even Alec had answered some questions for me once, when he'd been in a good mood.

They told me the crash was not accidental; I'd suspected as much based on the crash investigators being so cagey about their findings. It was deliberately brought down by a targeted missile. They suspected it was an assassination attempt on the life of Senator Christine Anderson. She was supposed to have been on the flight but had ended up on a different one at the last second.

Kyo spoke about the crash not being accidental but didn't elaborate on the specifics, which told me Tyler had crossed the "classified" line by filling that detail in for me. They all remained tight-lipped about who they suspected was behind it though.

Knowing Ty had put my need for answers above his work made me feel better about his recent distance. I dug one nail into a groove in the timber tabletop, letting a smile cross my features. Maybe he really was just run down.

"So, the fact that the plane crash was deliberate is a good thing?" Kyo's laughter contained a hint of apprehension.

I lifted my head and laughed. "No! Sorry, I got lost on a tangent in my head. I do that sometimes."

"Care to share who was making you smile like that?"

I smiled again—I couldn't help it—and cleared my throat, looking away.

"Ah, so *not* Ethan, then." Kyo leaned forward on his elbows, grinning mischievously.

My face fell. *Shit*! I'd gotten so relaxed with this charming, friendly man I'd inadvertently clued him in to the fact that my boyfriend was not the only man in my life.

"I didn't say that." Remembering that deflection had worked so well earlier, I decided to try it again. "One of the other things I've been thinking about is why you guys were able to make it to the crash site so fast. It's like you knew it was going to happen . . ." I let the implications hang in the air between us.

Kyo watched me for a few moments, a challenge in his eyes, then chose to drop it and answer my unasked question. "That was pure coincidence. We were in Hawaii wrapping up another job. We were simply the closest team."

"What job?"

He grinned. "Classified," we both said at the same time, and I rolled my eyes.

Kyo chuckled. "It's my turn to ask questions."

I folded my arms on the table. "Shoot. But I have to warn you, I'm limited in what I can tell you due to the strict policies of girl code. Some things are *classified*."

He laughed, launching right in. "Is Dorothy single?"

"Yes, but don't ever call her that—she hates it. Call her Dot."

"Noted. Anything else I should avoid?"

"Leather. Foods containing palm oil. And anything tested on animals. Oh, and don't ever bring up dog breeders." I winced. Anything to do with animal welfare set her off.

Kyo fired off questions almost as fast as I had. I answered some and remained cagey about others.

As he was trying to squeeze info out of me about Dot's exes—and refusing to believe I didn't know anything, as she'd been single the whole time I'd known her—Jamie and Marcus walked up. They seated themselves at the table, and both greeted me warmly.

"Dude, you know this assignment isn't to embed yourself with the natives, right?" Marcus teased, pointing at the cafeteria nearby. "You embracing campus life? Gonna eat here?"

"Hey, the food here is actually not that bad." I defended my beloved source of sustenance.

"I say why not!" Jamie piped in, his red hair looking more orange in the midday sun. "This assignment is the easiest one we've had in ages."

"Shits all over the three months we spent in that hovel in Uzbekistan," Kyo agreed, and they all laughed at the inside joke. I smiled and tried not to be awkward.

"He means that literally," Marcus smiled at me, making me feel at ease once more. "We were in an actual hovel, gathering intel."

Kyo coughed and gave him a pointed look.

"I get the feeling that's classified." I raised my brows at him but let a teasing smile pull at my lips.

They all laughed, and Jamie pulled his phone out of one of the many pockets in his cargo pants, typing something into it quickly.

Despite joking about divulging restricted information, they were clearly very serious about their work. But I marveled at how easygoing and fun they all were. They shared things about their personal lives, their families, their hometowns. How in the hell did Alec fit with them? They were so warm and friendly, and he was so . . . not.

Kyo stretched his arms over his head and groaned, rubbing his belly. "I actually am pretty hungry. Wanna go into town?"

"Ace is on his way." Jamie whipped his phone out again to check it. I guess that's who he was texting. And that was my cue to bail.

Just as I moved to gather my books, Alec arrived at our table, an easy smile on his face. The sight of him looking relaxed was so shocking I abandoned my retreat and stared at him.

The smile fell as soon as he saw me.

"Wanna go into town for lunch?" Kyo asked as they all got up from their seats. "The Indian place looks good."

"Sure" was Alec's clipped answer as he avoided looking at me. Kyo frowned.

"You coming, Eve?" Marcus asked as I got up, holding my books close to my chest.

"I don't know . . ."

"Yeah, come with." Jamie smiled, his invitation genuine. "Don't worry, you'll be safe with us."

He was half joking, but clearly he thought my hesitation was because I felt unsafe off campus.

I smiled back but it felt forced. "Thanks, but it's not that. I . . . uh . . ." I couldn't help glancing in Alec's direction. I had no idea how to end the sentence; I couldn't think of a lie quick enough.

Alec's eyes met mine, and he made a visible effort to relax his posture. "You should come, Eve. I'm . . . I'd like you to come."

I stared at him, stunned. I would have assumed he was just putting it on for his team—trying to look casual so they wouldn't get suspicious—but his voice had that honey quality in it that told me he was being honest, genuine. *He actually wants me to come to lunch?* I couldn't quite believe it.

He'd been acting strange ever since I told him how much he'd hurt me. He no longer immediately left any room I entered and had been joining us for meals more often. Whenever I glanced in his direction, I would catch him staring at me as if he were trying to do algebra. It was creeping me out, but at least he wasn't looking at me as if I'd just kicked his puppy anymore.

The invitation to lunch—actively attempting to spend time with me—was another new development.

I blinked slowly, still gaping at him. The determined expression on his face was melting more and more into worry the longer I didn't reply. His eyes darted around, not focusing on anything, and he cleared his throat.

"Eve!" Zara waved to me from near the entrance to the cafeteria, snapping me out of my shock and providing the perfect excuse.

"Sorry! Gotta go! Enjoy your lunch!" The words rushed out, too loud and high-pitched, and I hurried away without waiting for a response.

Halfway across the grass, I couldn't resist looking over my shoulder. The four black-clad men were walking away in the opposite direction, heading for the main gate.

Alec was lagging behind as the others chatted, his hands in his pockets, his broad back rigid. He turned a split second after I did, and our eyes met. We both faltered in our steps. I had a strong urge to catch up to him, say I'd changed my mind. I wanted so badly for us to have that kind of easy relationship—one where every single interaction wasn't fraught with tension and hurt. But that wasn't our reality. I squeezed the books tighter to my chest, hoping to alleviate the heaviness I suddenly felt there.

Alec was the first to turn away. I was expecting him to be angry, frustrated, but more than anything, he looked . . . sad.

SEVEN

The distinctive rumble of Ethan's voice on the other side of my res hall door made me move to open it, but the seriousness of his tone pulled me up short.

". . . sure about this. I don't like it."

I stared intently at the closed door, leaning forward to hear better.

"I don't like it either, man, but Alec needs us." Josh sounded just as somber. The mention of Alec immediately raised my suspicions. I glanced at the multitude of locks; they were all unlocked. I could get busted listening in at any second.

"I know. It's just . . . if something happens, we'll all be at least an hour away . . ." Ethan sounded torn.

"Trust me, I know how you're feeling. But she said she was staying in. I even sussed Dot out, and she went on about how we weren't invited to the girls' night in. Eve will be safe in her res hall all night. And Tyler has ordered a whole unit of Melior meatheads to monitor the building."

Ethan just grunted. He didn't sound convinced.

I knew I shouldn't be eavesdropping, but they were standing right outside the door and talking about me. I couldn't help myself. The talk of stalking me by Melior proxy wasn't all that surprising. Them being away from me, however . . . I burned to know what it had to do with Alec.

I leaned a little closer, careful not to make any sounds.

"Maybe one of us should stay behind," Ethan offered. "Dana will be there."

"And what? Crash the girls' night? I don't think that would go down well." Josh sounded amused. "Plus, you know they don't let Dana in until after the match. And anyway, could you really stay back in Bradford Hills knowing what Alec is putting himself through?"

"No," Ethan growled. "Dammit. He's such an idiot. Why is he doing this?"

"I don't know, man. That's why I want to be there. That's why Tyler is using major Melior Group resources to keep Eve safe so he can be there too. Maybe he's not doing as well as—"

A warm body pressed up against my back, and since I was being sneaky as fuck, it startled the living daylights out of me.

"Whatcha doin'?" Zara whispered into my hair, and I jumped—literally jumped into the air—my heart flying into my throat as I gave a strangled shriek.

Zara threw her head back and laughed, thoroughly amused, just as the boys burst into the room.

"What's going on?" Ethan boomed as Zara's laughter quieted to giggles.

"Nothing!" I burst out before she could narc on me, giving them my best reassuring smile. "Nothing," I repeated, throwing Zara a warning look that I'm sure had a hint of panic in it. Thankfully she kept her mouth shut. "Let's get going."

I grabbed my bag and herded everyone out, even as Ethan started protesting, demanding to know what was going on. He really was on edge.

Zara locked the door behind us and managed to distract him with chitchat. That bitch was sneaky, catching me off guard like that, but she was loyal too.

As we walked to class, I worked at calming my breathing. Of course, Josh noticed something was off. He cocked his head and raised a blond brow.

In answer, I rolled my eyes and nodded toward Zara just ahead of us, chatting with Ethan. His brows furrowed; he wasn't convinced my mood was just about Zara. I gave him a warm smile and twined my arm around his, leaning my head on his shoulder for a second before walking ahead into the lecture hall.

He was starting to rub off on me. His uncanny ability to notice things most people didn't, coupled with our always having to pretend there was nothing between us in public, had made us both excellent silent communicators.

He wasn't likely to let it go, but the busy day ahead wouldn't leave any chance to talk.

The little bit of information I'd overheard plagued me all day, my brain naturally filling in the gaps with the worst possible explanations. I was distracted in all my classes, wondering what Alec was up to, *with Dana*, that had the guys so worried. I couldn't just come out and ask them; that would mean admitting I'd eavesdropped.

So, naturally, I did the most mature thing possible—I obsessed over it until I'd whipped myself up into being pissed off at them for not telling me about it.

By the time our girls' night in rolled around, I was in a foul mood. I was flicking through channels and trying to take my mind off the situation while Zara studied in her room. When Dot knocked on the door, I stayed firmly planted on the couch.

She knocked again. "Open up, bitches! I have snacks!"

"I'll get it." Zara gave me a pointed look as she passed me, and I stuck my tongue out at her once her back was turned.

She undid the multiple locks, and Dot came into the room in a flurry of bags, pillows, and silky black hair, Squiggles darting madly in and out of the pile of stuff she deposited in the middle of the floor.

"Jesus, Dot. Are you moving in?" Zara started relocking the bolts.

"Whatever. I like to be prepared." Dot smiled sweetly, and I snorted.

They both turned to me, and I gave Dot an unenthusiastic "hey," pulling the blanket I'd draped over myself closer to my neck.

They exchanged confused looks. Dot gestured to me with her head, raising her eyebrow in silent question. Zara shrugged and crossed her arms over her chest.

I couldn't believe it. A couple of months ago these two weren't even speaking. Now they were having silent conversations?

"Don't look at each other about me! I'm right here, dammit!" I sat up straight, my hands in tight fists.

"What?" Dot laughed, but Zara had had enough.

"What's up your ass?" she demanded.

Her delivery left much to be desired, but she got straight to the point. That's why I loved her.

I groaned and flopped back against the couch, the fight draining out of me. It wasn't fair to take things out on them.

"What's going on, sweetness?" Dot sat beside me, and Zara lowered herself to the ground on the other side of the coffee table, rummaging through Dot's bags.

"I overheard Ethan and Josh talking earlier, and I shouldn't have eavesdropped, but I heard something, and I don't have the full story, and it's driving me mental."

"Aww. Did you have a fight with your harem? Is that why Alec's team are camped outside your building instead of one of your guys being here?"

"Don't call them that!" I whacked her lightly with the back of my hand, but I couldn't help laughing a little.

"Who's outside our building?" Zara walked over to the window as she devoured a bag of chips. After a few seconds, she whistled low. "Wow. They're not even being subtle about it. They just checked Pete's ID and frisked him." She chuckled. Pete was doing his honors in Variant studies and lived one floor above us; we'd exchanged polite chitchat in the elevator.

I finally peeled myself off the couch to stand next to her. In the waning evening light, I could clearly see Kyo and Marcus, fully armed, on the ground below us. I would've bet money Jamie was at the rear of the building.

"What did you do?" Zara asked around a mouthful of chips.

I sighed and sat back down. I told them everything I'd heard the guys say, hoping Dot and Zara could shed some light on what they were talking about.

"They won't let Dana in until after the match? That's what he said?" Dot asked.

"Yup."

She looked over at Zara, who was leaning against the window, frowning.

I looked between them. The fact that they weren't teasing me about eavesdropping on a conversation between my boyfriends and getting all worked up about it was making me nervous. This was exactly the kind of thing Dot liked to give me shit about.

"Guys, what am I missing here?"

They exchanged a wary look.

"The Hole?" Zara asked.

"Yeah, I'm thinkin' The Hole." Dot ran her hands through her hair.

"What's The Hole? Do I even want to know?"

"Probably not," Dot mumbled.

"It's a kind of underground club for Variants," Zara explained. "If Black Cherry is *the* exclusive place to be seen, The Hole is *the* shady, disgusting *literal* hole to be avoided."

I'd never been near it, but I knew Black Cherry by reputation; it was a VIP club in Manhattan, frequented by high-profile Variants, and often popped up in magazines like *Modern Variant*. This other place, The Hole, I'd never even heard of.

"OK . . . I don't get it. What's with the secrecy? It's just a shitty bar. Right?"

"Not exactly. The main form of entertainment is cage fighting—unregulated and completely illegal—and you have to be a Variant to get in. They have scanners at the door."

"Wait, does that mean that Alec . . ." I groaned. I didn't need to finish the question. *Of course* this was the kind of thing he would be involved with.

"Sounds like it," said Zara. "Yeah. I mean, I've only been once or twice, and I've never seen him there, but that doesn't mean . . ."

"Yeah. Alec will be fighting tonight for sure." Dot shook off her worried stare. "I've never been, but I know he used to go a lot. He and Tyler used to fight regularly."

"What?" Zara and I asked at the same time, incredulous. I could imagine Alec doing something stupid and destructive, but Tyler?

"Yeah. They went through some pretty hard times after their parents died. All the guys did. Alec and Tyler were angry young men with no outlet for their rage. This place was perfect for them. But then they started hanging out with a rough crowd, and Ethan and Josh got dragged into it. That's when they both joined Melior Group and sorted themselves out. Alec would still go back occasionally, but only to fight. He couldn't seem to walk away completely."

"Why?" I was slightly horrified, but I wanted to know more.

"Look I don't really know the full story, OK? Charlie would go with them sometimes, so I only know what he's told me and what I've gleaned from Ethan and Josh talking about it. And maybe a little from what Squiggles happened to see . . ."

"Dot . . ." She wasn't telling me something.

"Spit it out, tiny." Zara had my back.

"Fine." With a sigh and an eye-roll, she gave in. "The rules of the fight are simple. One on one. No gloves and no abilities. The first one to use an ability, tap out, pass out, or die loses."

"That's why they won't let Dana in," I mumbled, chewing on the corner of a nail.

"Yeah," Zara confirmed, "with Dana around, blocking everyone's abilities, it would be just a boring cage fight. You might as well go watch humans doing it. The whole point is to have enough control to keep your ability back while having enough skill to beat your opponent."

I chuckled darkly and shook my head. That was right up Alec's alley. I'd never met anyone with worse control issues than Alec. "Wait. So then why would Dana even be there?"

My two friends both shrugged.

I moved back to the window and crossed my arms, frowning down at the guards below without really seeing them. My mind was going wild with images of the only times I'd seen Alec and Dana interact—in the limo the night of the gala, her hands all over him; at his bedroom door when he was in nothing but a towel; at Ethan's party.

I ground my teeth, my breaths coming faster and shallower at the thought of her touching him after the way I'd touched him in Tyler's study that night.

What the fuck is wrong with me? He'd made it perfectly clear he didn't want me like that, or in any other way. Maybe his unattainability made me want him more? That probably had something to do with my never knowing my dad—what's more unattainable than nonexistent?—but I couldn't go down that train of thought. Not yet. That rabbit hole would take way too long to crawl out of, and I'd probably need the help of a mental health professional.

No, I needed to deal with the present situation, and I couldn't do that by seething silently in my room. There was no way I was going to sit around watching movies and braiding our hair while Alec did something so stupid. *Shit,* he was an asshole.

Clenching my hands into fists, I turned around. "We need to go there."

Dot and Zara wore matching looks of worry.

"How did I know you were going to say that?" Dot gave a small eye-roll, but her mouth quirked into a smile.

"Because she has a savior complex," Zara answered for me, crossing her own arms and looking as though she was about to try to talk me out of it.

"What? I do not have . . . whatever. Look, you guys don't have to come. Just tell me where this place is. I need to do something. He's not just hurting himself. It's not fair on the other guys, and it's . . . it's not fair on me."

I finished firmly with a little nod. The more I thought about it, the more I was convinced Alec was pulling a *really* dick move. Whatever messed-up shit he had going on inside his own head that made him want to get pummeled, or pummel someone else, was unfortunate. But he couldn't just go around doing stupid shit that hurt his family. Ethan and Josh were worried about him, and Tyler would certainly be stretching himself to take charge of the situation and make it easier on everyone.

"Relax." Zara's eye-roll was much more sarcastic than Dot's had been. "We'll take you to the dodgiest place in the tri-state area. What're friends for?"

"Really?" I was a little surprised it was that easy.

"Yeah." Dot shrugged. "He's your Variant. We know it would be impossible to sit here and do nothing when you know he might be getting hurt."

"But how do we get past the goon squad down there?" Zara pointed out the main problem.

"Yeah . . ." Dot dug through the pile of bags she'd brought, already figuring out an outfit. "Let's start by figuring out what we're dealing with first."

Squiggles ran over to the window and looked at me expectantly. I opened it for her, and she disappeared to do what she did best—reconnaissance.

"No." Zara's laughter dragged my attention back to my friends. "You can't wear a buttercup-yellow poodle skirt to The Hole."

Dot was holding the item up in front of her, frowning as if to ask why not.

We spent the next ten minutes getting dressed in dark, simple clothing at Zara's insistence. She was adamant we would be spotted within seconds if we went in outrageous outfits, if they let us in at all.

Riding down in the elevator, we were almost in matching outfits—all of us in black jeans and tops with dark jackets. Dot's jacket was some high-fashion mesh thing that probably cost a fortune, Zara's was her favorite leather jacket, and I'd just thrown on a dark gray hoodie. I really couldn't care less; I just *needed* to get to my guys before something bad happened.

Squiggles was waiting in front of the elevator when the doors opened. She and Dot stared at each other for a moment; then the little ferret ran off.

"Thanks, Squiggles!" Dot turned to us. "OK, so the good news is that it's just Alec's team out there. The bad news is that Squiggles overheard them talking about their orders, and they're specifically to guard the three of us—not the building."

"Shit." Zara groaned.

"What if I distract them somehow?" Dot suggested. "Maybe a flock of birds . . ."

Zara looked at her as if she were crazy. "I think an elite unit of trained fighters can deal with some birds, Dot."

"Yeah? Think they could deal with a bear?" Dot threw back defiantly.

"Yeah. They have guns."

Instead of listening to another bickering match, I marched past them to the front entrance, looking out the door's narrow window.

They followed me but didn't say any more.

"You said their orders were to 'guard' us, right?" I kept my eyes on Kyo as he slowly paced the stretch in front of the stairs, his arm resting casually on the butt of his automatic weapon.

"Yeah." Dot's voice was almost a whisper. "What are you thinking?"

"Not sure yet," I mumbled as I pushed the door open and stepped outside, my friends right on my heels. I was taking a bit of a gamble, but it was the most direct way of achieving what I needed. Get to the city; get to Alec. I just hoped there wasn't more to the orders than what Squiggles had overheard.

At the sound of the door opening, Kyo turned in my direction.

"Hey, girls. What's up?" He smiled casually, but his body language was no longer as relaxed.

"Hey, Kyo." I tried to keep the burning desperation out of my smile. "Whatcha doin'?"

"Working." His eyes narrowed. "What are you three doing?"

"Heading out." I held his gaze, my chin lifting a little in challenge.

"Are you?"

"Yep." I nodded firmly. As Marcus and Jamie emerged from the shadows, my friends stepped up next to me. They had no idea what I was planning, but they had my back. "What's it to you?"

Kyo's eyes narrowed, but his smile remained in place. He didn't say anything, so with a determined set to my shoulders, I walked down the stairs heading for the parking lot and Zara's car.

"I can't let you do that," he finally said on a sigh.

"Oh?" I kept walking, all five of them following behind. "Why's that?"

"Kitten, come on. I have orders."

"Do you?" I turned, making them all stop, our weird little group congregating in the light of an ornate street lamp. Marcus and Jamie hung back a little, keeping an eye on the darkness beyond. "And what are they exactly?"

"Can't say. Classified."

"I hate that fucking word. Look, I know it would be easier for you all if we just stayed in like good girls, but we all know your orders are to protect, not detain. Even Alec isn't stupid enough to order you to use physical force to keep me somewhere."

Kyo sighed and looked up, as if praying for patience.

"Either come with or fail your mission. It's up to you." Zara shrugged, unlocking the car and moving toward the driver's side.

"Come on. Could be fun." Dot smiled at him mischievously, and I could almost see his resolve breaking. Almost.

"No. I'm sorry, but this is the safest place for you. My orders are to keep you safe, but how I do that is up to me, and I will use force if I must." He wrapped his hand tighter around the butt of his gun. I didn't think it was meant to be threatening, just a subconscious reaction.

Zara whistled under her breath and propped her arms up on the roof of her car. Dot's eyes narrowed, and Kyo refused to look at her. He had an assault weapon and years of elite combat training, but I was pretty sure he was scared of my dangerously cute friend.

I decided to take a gamble. "Do you know where he is? Do you know where they all are? Why you're here guarding us?" I stepped into him, trying not to let the giant gun freak me out, and allowed the anger and frustration to finally enter my voice. "He's at The Hole right now, pummeling some poor asshole because he doesn't know how to deal with his own emotional shit. And Tyler, Josh, and Ethan are all there because they don't know how to stop him from doing it."

His brow creased in confusion, and he looked between the three of us, registering our serious faces, my desperate voice. "Why do you care?"

He wasn't stupid. My reaction to Alec being in danger was too strong for someone who was just his cousin's girlfriend. I hesitated only a second, weighing the risk of letting one more person in on the secret.

Dot tried to save me. "She's just worried about Ethan—"

"He's mine," I cut her off before I could change my mind. Alec didn't have many people in his life who truly cared about him, but I'd seen him with his team. They were more than just work colleagues. These guys genuinely cared about him. I hoped. "They're all mine. I'm their Vital."

I spoke low, but my voice was firm and sure.

Kyo took an involuntary step away, his wide eyes darting across the ground as he processed the implications. Then he looked at me again, a hopeful smile crossing his face.

"Fuck!" He huffed in frustration, and I knew I had him.

"Kyo? What's going on?" Marcus cut in. They couldn't hear what we were saying.

I ignored him, focusing on Kyo, pleading. "We need to go."

He nodded, finally realizing how serious the situation was for me. For Alec. For all of us.

"Change of plans, boys." He turned to his teammates, slinging his weapon off his shoulder. "We're heading into the city. Civilian clothes and concealed weapons only. We need to leave now, so we'll change in the car."

Everyone looked at Zara's purple Mini Cooper; it would fit maybe four people if we squished up. Zara just stared back, unflappable as ever.

Kyo rolled his eyes, walking over to a monstrous all-terrain vehicle with blacked-out windows and chrome wheels. "Obviously we're taking the company car."

EIGHT

About a half-hour drive past Manhattan, we pulled into a parking area in an industrial part of town. It looked like a massive lot for a giant factory, but the only building around was a brick structure that couldn't have been bigger than a four-bedroom house.

As we came up to a door recessed in the building, a very large man stepped out of the shadows, scowling. Kyo took the lead, and the bouncer's face relaxed measurably when he saw him.

"Kyo! Hey, man!" They did one of those manly handshake-hug things with lots of thumping on the back. "All the old crew is here. Should have known when I saw Ace slip in the back with his fight face on."

"Yeah, good to see you, man." Kyo launched into a catch-up session, keeping the focus off the rest of us.

I bit my tongue to keep from fidgeting impatiently.

"Anyway, better get in there." Kyo brought the chat to an end. "Don't want to miss anything."

"Cool, cool. It's gonna be an epic night." The bouncer gave him another slap on the shoulder and then turned to the rest of our group. "Bit young . . ." he remarked, eyeing me and Dot.

Kyo laughed.

"Since when have you guys bothered with legal drinking age?" Marcus asked. "Or legal anything?" He ended on a wicked little grin, slinging one of his arms around my shoulders. I leaned into him and smiled at the bouncer, doing my best to look relaxed.

"They're cool." Kyo drove the point home. Apparently that was all the convincing the "security" man needed to let three eighteen-year-old girls into possibly the seediest establishment in the city. He swung the metal door wide open for us.

The structure appeared to be completely empty, and I frowned, but everyone kept moving. Kyo made his way to a second door farther inside, opening it dramatically to reveal a stairway leading down and a pounding, heavy beat of music trailing up.

"Welcome to The Hole," he announced, resigned. "Remember what we talked about in the car. Stick to our sides and don't talk to anyone."

He took a deep breath and thumped down the narrow stairs, muttering about how crazy this was.

The Hole was quite literally a hole in the ground. The space spanned an area much larger than the brick structure above, and it was teeming with people. At least two scuffles broke out in the time it took me to reach the bottom of the stairs. My eyes struggled to adjust to the dim light; at first only the bar was clear, stretching along the left wall under the naked light bulbs hanging from the high exposed ceiling.

As "Can't Go to Hell" by Sin Shake Sin started playing, I stepped closer to a dark corner behind the stairs, tilting my head. There were two people back there, a woman and a man. I couldn't quite see what they were doing, but something about it didn't look right. The woman was leaning back into the man, her eyes closed and lips parted, while the man pressed one hand to her throat and one to the exposed skin under her crop top. If not for the look of bliss on her face, I would've thought he was hurting her.

Curious, I inched closer. Just as the woman's eyes opened, Kyo's firm grip on my elbow dragged me away.

"Stay the fuck away from the Lightwhores," he growled close to my ear. My eyes widened, and I looked back just in time to see the woman walking away as the man stuffed some cash into his pocket.

Not all Variants had Vitals, but the Light was craved by all, so some Vitals chose to sell their Light. The Bond was sacred for Variants; a Vital's Light was something precious and usually reserved only for his or her Bonded Variants. Selling Light as if it were a street drug was considered outrageous and dirty.

I let Kyo pull me along, taking in the rest of The Hole. The bar was on the highest and widest level—the one we'd emerged onto. The middle level had high tables and chairs. The only other well-lit area was on the lowest level, in the very center: a hexagonal chain-link cage raised on a platform. Bright floodlights illuminated disturbing stains on the cage's bare floor.

Zara leaned over my shoulder.

"Charming, isn't it?" she deadpanned. I just grunted in response. "The sides of the cage come off, so sometimes it's just a stage for live bands. But mostly people come here for the fights."

As if to illustrate her point, the next fight began. The music lowered, and the lights trained on the cage intensified as two people entered through a gap in the fence. A palpable buzz of excitement spread through the crowd. Several people shouted over everyone, openly taking bets on the outcome.

I moved over to the first-level railing to get a better look.

The two people in the cage were warming up. One was a bald man with a wiry physique, wearing a pair of shorts. The other was a woman with tied-back black hair, wearing shorts and a sports bra. They were both barefoot; neither one had any kind of protective gear.

My heart rate sped up. *Was it such a good idea to come here?* I wasn't so sure I wanted to watch a bare-knuckled fight, but I couldn't look away. I wrapped my sweaty palms around the steel barrier and braced myself.

"Keep an eye on the light above the ring, in the center there." Zara pointed at a flat, unassuming light—the kind of thing you might see in a garage—low wattage with a crappy plastic cover. "If it comes on, you know someone's used their ability. Although it's often plain enough to see anyway."

I nodded. I'd seen similar items before. Even though science didn't truly understand the Light or how it worked, we'd figured out how to detect its distinct energetic signature.

"What happens if someone in the crowd uses an ability?" I asked. "Won't that set it off?"

"Nah." She shrugged. "The sensors are placed around the top of the cage, and they point in. It's rudimentary but it works."

I didn't have a chance to ask any more questions; the fight was underway. A loud clanging bell was the only indicator it had begun—no presenter to get the crowd going, no introductions of the fighters.

The two people in the cage circled each other, and then the man lunged, throwing punches at the woman's head and torso. She shielded herself, then went from defensive to offensive in a heartbeat. She pummeled the man, giving as good as she'd got. Even from as far away as we were, the look on her face was visibly feral, blood already trickling from the corner of her mouth.

When she landed a particularly savage blow with her elbow to the side of his head, many people in the room gasped, me included, but more cheered, their bloodlust only intensifying the more violent the spectacle became. The woman pushed the man into a corner. He had his arms up, trying to find a way to push out.

The man's guttural growl of frustration could be heard even over the music; the woman wasn't easing up. Was I about to see a man die?

In the next instant, though, the woman sprang back, clutching her middle. She was facing the other side of the room, so I couldn't see her face, but I did see the light on top of the cage flick on.

The man remained slumped against the corner of the cage, but his hands were no longer hands—they were claws, something between bear and human. The woman turned toward the opening in the fence, where three bouncers were letting themselves in. She dropped her hands to reveal four jagged, parallel gashes oozing blood on her abdomen. Her hands and forearms glistened red, and she swayed as she exited the ring with the assistance of one of the bouncers, trailing blood behind her.

Her cuts were fresh, but I could guess what they would look like when healed. Alec had the same ones around his side. I could remember their texture from that night in Tyler's study. Right before he told me he hated me. Right before we . . .

"That was disgusting," Dot announced from my other side. I glanced behind us. Kyo, Marcus, and Jamie were standing close by, keeping a watch on us and the room.

"I told you not to watch." Kyo smirked at her.

"Yeah, I wish I hadn't. I need a drink." Dot's face held pure disgust. In contrast, Zara looked amused, even a little excited. Sadistic bitch.

"That asshole always ends up scratching someone. Like a petulant kitten. I've never seen him win. Don't know why he keeps fighting." She started toward the bar.

"Those didn't look like kitten claws," I grumbled, following her. If that was supposed to be the minor fight, I shuddered to think what kind of monster Alec would be pitted against. Or maybe Alec was the monster in this scenario . . .

Jamie stayed close to my side, while Kyo placed a gentle hand on Dot's lower back, guiding her forward. Marcus was glued to Zara. I guess they'd each assigned themselves one of us.

I needed a drink too. Alec wouldn't be happy to see me, and his shit would be easier to deal with if I had a little liquid courage.

"What do you want?" Kyo asked Dot, his hand still lingering on her back even though we'd reached the bar.

She arched a perfect brow. "You're allowed to drink while on duty?"

"Keep your voice down." Kyo leaned into her but made it look casual—as if he was flirting. Maybe that wasn't so far from the truth. "We're all just here to have some fun, have a few drinks."

He gave us all pointed looks. Clearly authority figures were not welcome here. Having a drink at the bar would help us blend in.

Dot looked worried for a split second, her eyes flying about the room, but she plastered a smile on her face. "Something refreshing to cleanse the foul taste that left in my mouth. Maybe a mojito?"

Zara and the guys all laughed. I wasn't in on the joke. I wasn't in on anything tonight. I crossed my arms, not feeling very jovial.

"*Mojito*. Oh, you crack me up." Zara wiped a tear from the corner of her eye. "They don't do cocktails, princess."

Dot gave her the middle finger. "Fine, then what do they do?"

"The core four and maybe vodka and OJ?"

"The core four?"

Zara counted off on her fingers. "Jim, Jack, Johnny, and Jose."

"Jose! I'll have tequila," I piped in loudly, and they all turned to me. "What? Might as well embrace the ambience."

Marcus ordered six shots of the amber liquid, and we slammed them back without salt or lemon.

Dot and Kyo started a private conversation, leaning into each other as if they were on a date, while I scanned the crowd for any of my guys.

Two women sauntered up to the bar next to us, chatting as they waited to order.

"Oh, by the way"—one of them raised her voice—"I heard that Gabe is here."

"Really?" The other one perked up.

"Yep. Apparently Ace is fighting tonight. Didn't the two of you have a thing a while back?"

I tuned in more closely to the conversation, making sure my gaze stayed trained on the crowd.

"Yeah, kind of. I only slept with him a few times, but god, it was hands down the best sex I ever had."

The two snickered, and I chanced a glance. They looked as if they fit right in. They were both brunettes, but one had some blonde highlights, and they both were wearing dark, tight clothing—cool, edgy, and a bit rough around the edges.

Zara noticed me looking and stepped closer, gripping my hand and asking me a silent question with her eyes. It was either "Are you OK?" or "Want me to punch her?" The options were equally likely.

I gave her a tight smile and squeezed her hand, turning away from the chicks at the bar as they resumed their conversation.

"Yeah, I remember. What was so good about it?"

I'd be lying if I said I didn't want to know the same thing. As much as hearing another woman talk about having sex with one of my Bonded Variants pissed me off, morbid curiosity had me glued to the spot.

"I think it was his ability honestly," the one with the highlights answered.

"What do you mean?"

Yes, what did she mean? It was painful for anyone to touch Alec. He had control over it most of the time, but if it was his ability this woman liked so much, what kind of kinky shit was he into?

"Well, he kept asking me questions." I frowned and nearly turned to look at them. "Do you like that? Does that feel good? That kind of thing. And while the dirty talk was hot, his ability meant he knew the answer every time and was able to . . . adjust accordingly. He knew exactly what I wanted, and he was more than happy to provide it. It was mind-blowing." They giggled, and it dawned on me.

They weren't talking about Alec. They were talking about *Tyler.*

My eyes widened. The extent of his ability always surprised me—how many and varied its applications were. This was just another one I hadn't yet considered. Another one I may never get to experience for myself . . .

The women were finally served, and their conversation came to an end. Dot appeared at my other side.

"Something to look forward to?" She winked, proving she'd heard the entire thing too and hadn't been as wrapped up in Kyo as I thought. They'd probably all heard.

"Not likely." I snorted, dropping Zara's hand and crossing my arms.

"Don't you like him like that?" Zara asked.

"Of course she does," Dot answered for me.

"I'm not the problem. I don't think it's what *he* wants." I spoke so low I wasn't sure if either of them heard, but Zara took a deep breath, and Dot's little hand landed on my shoulder. I shook it off as gently as I could. Now wasn't the time.

"Can we just focus on one infuriating, impossible Variant at a time?" I said much louder, getting the boys' attention too. "I've procrastinated enough. We need to find Alec. Maybe we should split up and—"

"Nope." Kyo's voice was firm. "No splitting up." I narrowed my eyes at him, but he kept talking before I could argue. "No need to. I know where they are."

"Well, why didn't you say something sooner?"

"Because I'm still not convinced this is good idea. And you're the one who demanded tequila, so . . ."

"What? That's not . . ." I took a deep breath, closing my eyes for a second. "Whatever. Kyo, where is he?"

He dropped the mischievous smirk. "He'll be in one of the back rooms—it's where the fighters wait until it's time."

He pointed to the opposite side of the space, where a corridor led off the main area. As I took off in that direction, a firm hand fell on my shoulder.

"I lead the way. Don't let the shots and music fool you. This is a dangerous place, kitten."

I nodded, and he took Dot's hand before heading down the stairs. Jamie appeared next to me, and Zara and Marcus followed behind. But as we made our way around the less-crowded middle level, the music lowered again, and the light on the cage brightened.

Our group stopped dead.

Alec was making his way to the cage. The other three were with him, but my focus was on the idiot in the front. He was wearing nothing but a navy-blue pair of shorts, every tattoo, scar, and ripped muscle on display, his face a hard, emotionless mask.

Jamie cursed. Kyo ran one hand over the top of his head in agitation.

"Shit." I made for the nearest stairs, but both Kyo and Jamie blocked my path, their hands closing over my upper arms.

"Get out of my way!" I was out of time. I needed to get down there immediately.

"Lower your voice," Jamie growled into my ear as I wriggled, trying fruitlessly to escape the grip of not one but two Melior Group agents.

"Eve," Zara said, "it's too late."

"What? Let me go. They haven't started yet. I can still stop him." Panic gripped my chest. Alec was already in the cage, another man stepping in behind him.

"No, you can't." Zara got in my face, blocking my view. "If you'd managed to convince him to pull out, then maybe this could have worked. But now that he's already down there, now that they've seen him . . ."

"Look around you." Kyo's grip on me loosened, his attention split between preventing me from doing something stupid and keeping an eye on Dot. She was hanging back, being way quieter than usual. "Listen to the crowd. If they don't get what they came for, all hell will break loose."

All around, people shouted over each other and pressed closer to the barriers.

"Thirty on the Master of Pain!" a guy with more piercings than I thought could fit on a single face yelled, and a bookie pushed through the crowd to take the bet. Similar exclamations echoed throughout the room. This round of bets was taking much longer than the first round. People were getting restless.

A fight broke out next to Dot. She grabbed a pitcher of beer and dumped it over the two Neanderthals throwing punches, and Kyo finally released me to yank her away from them.

I pushed past Zara and stood right up against the barrier, wrenching my other arm out of Jamie's grip to clutch the steel bar with both hands. They were right. These people were gagging for this fight; I wouldn't put it past them to kill me if I tried to stop it.

Alec had his back to us, his arms loose by his sides, his head slightly tilted to the side. He looked almost bored. In complete contrast, his opponent was a bundle of movement, bouncing up and down on his toes and punching the air. The other fighter was a mountain, bigger even than Ethan, but where Ethan's physique was toned and naturally large, this man was sinewy; he looked as if he had 0 percent body fat.

The bookies were nearly done taking bets, and my heart jumped into my throat. My eyes darted around the room, desperately looking for another solution, but no bright ideas presented themselves.

Then my eyes met calm gray ones.

Busted.

Tyler was gripping the chain-link as he leaned on it. When our eyes met, his widened for a beat, then narrowed, his lips pressing into a tight line. Ethan and Josh stood behind him, their postures screaming tension.

I refused to feel awkward for getting caught. Instead, a surge of defiance straightened my spine, lifted my chin. How dare they keep this from me? And then get upset when I kept something from them? I tightened my grip on the railing and allowed every bit of indignation I had to enter my gaze. Tyler didn't flinch, but he did break eye contact, turning to speak to the other two idiots.

I focused on the cage. Alec still looked bored; his opponent was still posturing, bouncing around the edges of the cage, gesturing and shouting to the crowd. They were lapping it up.

When I turned back to the spot where Tyler had been, it was empty. The next thing I knew, my hand was being removed from the barrier, and a male chest was completely blocking my view.

The reprimand in Tyler's beautiful gray eyes was even more intense up close, and it was tinged with something else—fear or maybe anger. I couldn't be sure. I was too distracted by what he was wearing to try to decipher his facial expression.

Tyler was in jeans and boots and a *leather jacket*. I'd seen him in a T-shirt maybe three times. Usually he was in perfectly tailored pants and collared shirts, his messy hair a constant contrast to his clean-cut look. The messy hair wasn't a bit out of place now.

"Get out of the way. I can't see," I ground out, twisting my wrist out of his grip. He released me, but big gentle hands landed on my shoulders, keeping me grounded to the spot. Ethan.

His eyes still trained on me, Tyler spoke loudly enough to be heard by the rest of our group. "Kyo, take Dot and Zara home."

His tone was pure authority, but it didn't escape my notice that he hadn't explicitly stated it was an order.

"Understood," Kyo replied, and Jamie and Marcus began shuffling Dot and Zara toward the exit. Even Zara didn't argue against Tyler's firm demand, his rigid posture, his deceptively calm eyes.

I was exactly where I wanted to be, but nothing was going right. And my anger and hurt at being lied to was not subsiding.

Just as I opened my mouth, Tyler spoke again. "I have to speak to a man about a Lighthunter," he declared in a quieter tone. He was still watching me with reproach, but he hadn't touched me again since I'd wrenched out of his grip. "You two stay with her. First sign of anything even remotely out of the ordinary, get her out." Without waiting for acknowledgment, he turned and disappeared into the crowd.

They were here to contact the Lighthunter? Had I misread this whole thing completely? I thought Alec was against it. Why would he offer to jump into a cage fight so Tyler could make his enquiries? It was far more likely this was Alec being his asshole self and Tyler was just using the opportunity to do something productive.

"You may not want to watch this." Josh took Tyler's spot in front of me, but he wasn't blocking my view as much. He was giving me a choice. The fight had begun.

I placed my hand on Josh's chest, intending to push him farther out of the way, but what I saw had me bunching the fabric of his Tool T-shirt in my fist.

Alec and the big show-off were throwing punches, and neither was holding back. Alec landed several blows to the other man's face, causing blood to spurt from his mouth, but that left Alec's torso unprotected, and his opponent took advantage of the opening. Large fists slammed into Alec's ribs and stomach.

The psychopathic crowd was loving it, yelling encouragement or taunts so loudly they drowned out the sound of flesh crushing flesh. It was the most violent thing I'd seen in my life, and I'd watched Tyler shoot a man dead right next to me.

Bile rose in my throat, and the back of my eyes began to sting. Every blow that connected with Alec's flesh had me cringing, yet I couldn't look away. If I looked away, something even worse might happen. Ethan's hands tightened on my shoulders, and I spared him a quick glance. He was watching the fight intently too, his body rigid.

A tiny bit of relief washed over me when I looked back to see Alec had the upper hand. Somehow they'd ended up on the ground, a tangle of limbs, but Alec was on top, and he was pummeling the other man mercilessly. It was in that moment I realized Alec was lethal even without his ability. His control was impeccable, his mercy for his opponent nonexistent.

Josh covered my fist with his hand and twisted slightly so he could see better. He was as tense as Ethan and me, even if he didn't show it as much. His face was a mostly calm mask, but his grip on my hand was flexing and relaxing in an unsteady rhythm.

A swell in the cheering had me whipping my head back to the cage. Alec was now the one getting the shit beat out of him. Somehow the beefcake had managed to get the fight back off the ground. He'd pinned Alec against the fencing and was raining down a stream of heavy blows.

Sweat mingled with the blood dripping from the man's nose and forehead. They were both getting tired. Yet neither one's concentration had slipped enough to allow their ability to take over.

"Why does he do this?" I gritted out between clenched teeth, not speaking to anyone in particular or expecting an answer.

Ethan's hands squeezed my shoulders again, and he stepped closer behind me, his heat pressing up at my back.

"To prove he's in control of his ability," Josh answered, his eyes never leaving the horror below. "That *he* controls *it* and not the other way around. To prove he's dangerous even without it. Those are the obvious reasons . . ."

"Sometimes I think he does it because he likes the pain." Ethan's voice was strained, and the lump in my throat became impossible to ignore. He was watching someone who was more than a brother to him get beaten. They both were.

I cursed Alec again for putting us all through this, even as I cringed at more blows landing to his ribs, his head.

"Not the pain." Josh picked up Ethan's comment. "I think he likes the punishment. With his ability, no one can touch him. But here, he can punish himself."

His words rang true. Too true. A deep kind of sadness settled into the gamut of emotions I was feeling.

As if he heard us talking about him, Alec turned into the metal fencing, trying to angle his front away from the onslaught of his opponent's fists, and his eyes met mine. My tears spilled over. I allowed every single awful thing I was feeling to pervade my gaze as I held his as steadily as I could through the blur of tears.

His eyes widened a fraction, and then his opponent was screaming. The massive, obscenely muscled man sprang away from Alec as the light above the cage flashed on. It didn't take a genius to figure out whose ability had triggered it.

Alec's opponent crumpled to the floor, his blood-curdling screams cutting through the music and the sounds of the cheering, gasping, writhing crowd. He curled into a squirming ball, his body contorting grotesquely. I'd seen Alec's ability in action—we'd taken down an entire campus full of people together—but that had been diffused over a wide area and so fast and intense that everyone passed out almost immediately.

This was something else; the full force of Alec's unassisted ability was making a grown man writhe and sob in pain.

As if surprised to hear the screaming, Alec whipped his head around to take in the man on the ground, then whipped back to me. The surprise in his expression was gone—he was pissed off. He sneered at me and pounded the fencing with his palms. I had the distinct feeling it was me he actually wanted to pound.

He turned around and took several deep breaths, visibly calming himself and getting his ability under control. The crowd started to boo, disappointed they'd been robbed of more bloodshed.

The man's screaming subsided into shuddering breaths. Only when it was clear Alec's ability was under control did the bouncers enter the cage. They went to the crying man, and Alec exited unassisted.

NINE

Alec disappeared down the corridor Kyo had pointed out.

"Let's go." Josh dislodged my hand from his T-shirt and pulled me in the same direction.

"What the fuck just happened?" Ethan's big hand stayed pressed to my lower back as we waded through the agitated crowd.

I let them take the lead, just glad it was finally over. "What do you mean?"

"Alec never loses like that," Josh explained as we entered the barely lit corridor. "Sure, he's lost from time to time, but never by using his ability."

"Shit . . ." He'd lost control because of me. He saw me and then his opponent started screaming.

I wasn't so sure I wanted to see him anymore. I'd done what I set out to do—I stopped the fight. Even if it was halfway through. Even if it had resulted in more pain for the poor man in the cage than he would have endured at Alec's bare hands.

But we'd reached the last door on the left, and it was too late to bail. Josh pushed the door open and dragged me inside.

He dropped my hand as soon as we stepped in.

"Alec, stop!" Dana yelled in frustration. "What the hell is wrong with you? Just sit down so I can clean your knuckles, you idiot!"

She was standing by a bench on the right wall, a small dark bottle in one hand and a wad of gauze in the other. Even in jeans and a hoodie she looked hot, her messy blonde hair falling around her shoulders. In the same outfit, I looked like a bum, while she looked like an advertisement for Calvin Klein. *So unfair.*

Alec was pacing the length of the room like a caged tiger, his shoulders bunched, his fists clenched by his sides—as if he were still in that cage, ready to throw a punch. He spotted us by the door and froze, his eyes trained on me. At the same moment, the door opened again, briefly letting the sound of the music and crowd filter in. Tyler walked halfway into the room, placed his hands on his hips, and sighed.

Alec's eyes on me didn't budge. I tried hard not to wither under his stare, but he'd had a lot of time to perfect it. It was a really good stare. I lowered my gaze and leaned into Ethan, who immediately wrapped an arm around my shoulders and held me close. Maybe if Dana hadn't been there, it would've been easier for me to speak up, or do anything other than shrink into my boyfriend.

Tyler took a look around the room. "OK, let's just—"

"Dana," Alec cut him off, his voice strained, "can you give us a minute, please?"

No one said anything for a few moments, and I finally looked up to see what was happening.

Alec was still staring at me. Dana was staring at Alec. Tyler's hands were still on his hips, his gun showing in the waistband of his jeans, and as he looked between the three of us, his serious gray eyes were wary.

"Did that steroid on legs damage your brain or something?" she snapped back, but I had a feeling she was similar to Zara in this respect—the sarcasm was a defense mechanism. "Your wounds need cleaning and dressing. You know your control slips after a fight. Is one of these spoiled brats supposed to whine through it? You need me."

At the less-than-kind evaluation of his family, Alec's gaze finally flew to hers. "Dana. Leave." His voice sounded barely restrained.

She looked between him and me, then dropped the bottle and the gauze on the bench and stalked toward the door.

She stopped right in front of me and stared at me for a beat, her breaths coming fast. "Who the fuck are you?" she half whispered, half growled.

Before anyone could spin another lie in our already complex web, she wrenched the door open and stormed out.

As soon as the door closed behind her, we all relaxed a little. Even in a situation as charged as this one, being alone, just me and my Bond, made everything feel a little easier to handle. Yes, our connection was rife with secrets and stresses, but it was there nonetheless.

Alec dragged himself to the bench. Tyler helped him sit up as Josh opened a few lockers on the opposite wall. Eventually he found a duffel and brought it over to them.

I remained in Ethan's arms, unsure what to do, but then a familiar ache in my chest made itself known. I rubbed at it. How much of his ability had he used? No wonder his opponent was left whimpering on the floor. Alec wasn't completely drained, but he was depleted. His physical wounds would heal faster if he had some Light.

I stepped away from Ethan's comforting warmth and tentatively made my way to Alec. Tyler was trying and failing to open a bottle of iodine with a childproof lid, muttering curses under his breath.

I placed a hand over Tyler's, and he looked up at me through the unruly tuft of hair over his eyes. I smiled and ran my other hand down his arm, giving his elbow a squeeze, asking him silently to move out of the way. He let me take the bottle, swiping at his hair as he stepped aside.

Alec's breathing was getting slower, the fight draining out of his slumped body. His legs were spread wide; his arms hung limply over his thighs. He was watching my every move with a blank expression. The scrutiny was making me a little uncomfortable, but I focused on the task at hand. Sure, I was still pissed at him for putting us all through this, but he was hurting and he was mine. I had to do something. I would tear strips off him later. And then I'd probably patch those wounds up too.

Yeah, our relationship was fucked up. Whatever.

I opened the iodine and, with a steadiness to my hands that surprised me, extracted some swabs from the first aid kit Dana had abandoned. Josh handed me a damp face towel; I hadn't even noticed him move to get it.

I paused, my eyes running over Alec, unsure where to start.

A gash above his eyebrow—the one with the scar in it—had created a trail of blood down the side of his face. His other eye was already puffing up, I didn't want to think about the state of his ribs, and he'd somehow managed to get a cut just above his right knee. But his knuckles were the worst by far, so that's where I started.

I gently cleaned away as much blood as I could, moving on to his other wounds once the knuckles were clean. I focused as hard as I could on my Light flow as I went, drip-feeding him tiny amounts as I touched him on his head, his hands, his legs, hoping he wouldn't notice.

"Can someone get some ice for his eye?" I said without turning, and the door immediately opened and closed. Probably Ethan; he was the closest.

As if my voice had roused him from his trance, Alec spoke. "What are you doing here?"

I paused for only a moment, trying to push aside the anger and frustration his question brought up. "What are *you* doing here?" I parroted, giving him a firm look as I dripped some iodine onto a cotton pad and dabbed at the wounds on his knuckles.

He hissed, and my patience with him ran out.

"Really 'Master of Pain'?" I said, dripping sarcasm. "You take that kind of beating and you can't handle a bit of iodine?"

He frowned, but as I swabbed the rest of his wounds, he didn't react, only wincing slightly for the worst ones.

I dressed his cuts and grazes as best I could. Just as I was finishing up with the one on his knee, Ethan came back with ice wrapped in a tea towel. Alec reached for it, but I snatched it from him.

He could easily do this part himself, but I needed another excuse to keep touching him. The ache in my chest had eased, but it was still there. The tiny amounts of Light I'd transferred were being used up as fast as I could give them, boosting his healing.

I pressed the ice to the swollen eye. With nothing left to do, I casually lowered my hand to his thigh, just above the dressing, and pushed just a little more Light to him, hoping the biting cold and the sting of his injury would distract him.

I was wrong.

"Eve . . ." He said my name on a sigh as he extracted the ice from my grasp, dropping it on the bench.

"You need to ice your eye." I reached for it, but his hand grabbed mine and held on.

"I know what you're doing." His eyes flicked down to my hand on his bare leg. I opened my mouth but hesitated, so he kept speaking. "Just do it properly."

He placed my palm flat against his chest, over his heart, and looked away.

I didn't waste time questioning his sudden openness to having a Light transfer. I just closed my eyes and put all my focus on the energy flowing through me and into him.

With the now steady, strong flow, my palms tingled where they touched his skin. I carefully monitored the ache in my chest, using it as a guide for when to stop. Within minutes the ache was gone, and I pushed just a little extra to him for good measure before dropping my hands and stepping away.

He gave me a disparaging look that told me he knew exactly what I'd done. But he looked better. He was sitting up straighter, his face less pale. His Variant body would heal itself at the accelerated rate that it was capable of now that I'd given it all the Light it needed.

"Let's get out of here." Tyler handed Alec some clothing, and Josh packed the rest of his stuff into the duffel. "I'm going to kill Kyo for bringing you here."

"Disciplinary action for sure," Alec ground out as he pulled the sweatpants on.

"No one 'brought me here.'" I frowned. They were treating me like a child. "I *decided* to come here. Zara and Dot came with me because they knew I would go regardless. Kyo, very intelligently, made the same decision. You should be thanking them for having my back. Would you rather I showed up in this dump on my own?"

"That's beside the point." Alec's voice was muffled behind the T-shirt he was pulling over his head—black, of course. "You should never have known this was even happening."

Tyler crossed his arms, putting on his in-charge voice. "Eve, this might seem like a shady bar, but it's so much more. There are some seriously dangerous people here."

"What a load of shit." I kept my voice level, refusing to look immature by raising it.

"Eve, baby—"

"No!" I cut across Ethan. Even Josh was looking at me disapprovingly. "That's bullshit. You're all ganging up on me for coming here instead of focusing on the actual issue." I gestured to "the issue," who was now pulling on his shoes. "This whole thing is bullshit. You went on about how I'm part of your family. That our Bond is special and unbreakable. And then you *all* lie to me and come here without me. What the fuck?"

I was supposed to be their Vital—the thing that brought us all together as a Bond. Yet they'd lied to me and left me out. *They left me out.*

I'd spent my entire life feeling as if I belonged nowhere, had no family, was alone in the world, especially after my mother died. Then I'd found out I had four people whom I would always be connected to, no matter what. And they deliberately left me out? It cut me to my core.

Naturally Josh was the first to realize my anger was masking pain. He stepped over to me, remorse and worry in his beautiful green eyes, and reached out as if to hug me.

I took a step away. If I let him comfort me, I would break down crying, and I wasn't done ripping them all a new one yet.

Giving myself something to do seemed like a much better idea. I marched over to Tyler and took his left hand. My other hand went to his neck, and I pushed Light into him with a determination I hadn't felt since the night of the invasion. He looked surprised at the new way I was touching him, his hand coming to rest over mine on his neck.

Soon the surprise was replaced with suspicion as he felt the force of the Light flowing into him. His hand wrapped around my wrist, but before he could yank it away, I broke the contact myself and took a step back.

"Ask him," I demanded.

"Eve . . ." He sighed. "It's not that simple. My ability isn't destructive like the others, but it can be a real burden. You have no idea how many secrets I keep. Because they're not mine. I believe in truth above all else, but I also have to respect other people's privacy. Sometimes you need to let people tell you things in their own time."

"And sometimes they need a push. I'm his Vital. It's *my* business. Ask."

"I don't know . . ." He looked behind me, searching for assistance from the other three guys.

"You're the one who told me we should be more open with each other. That we need to trust each other. That I should come to you if I ever want to know something. Well, I'm coming to you now. Alec's actions tonight have caused massive tension between all of us. I know me showing up as your Vital has changed a lot, but you need to accept it's changed things between *you* all as well. You're not just cousins and friends and brothers anymore. You're more. *Ask.*"

"I think you should ask." Ethan came to stand behind me. He didn't touch me, but I could feel his warmth at my back.

"Me too." Josh stayed where he was but added his support.

Alec cursed under his breath. "Fine. Whatever. Just ask me, man." He sighed, sounding resigned.

We all turned to face him. He was leaning back against the bench, his arms gripping it on either side of his hips. He stared intently at the ground, refusing to look at any of us.

Tyler sighed. "Alec, why did you come here tonight? Why did you fight?"

For a beat no one spoke or moved. Tyler's eyes lost focus as his ability gave him the answers that were left unspoken. Once his eyes focused on Alec again, they filled with despair.

Instead of filling us all in on the answer, he marched over to his oldest friend and gave him a hug. Alec returned it, and the two men held each other tight for a long time.

"Please, just talk to me." Tyler finally pulled away, his voice pleading.

"I can't. It's not just up to me." Alec looked straight at me, and Tyler sighed again.

"This is about Studygate?" Josh sounded surprised. "What the fuck happened, you guys?"

"Not entirely," Tyler answered.

"I came here for the same reason I always come here," Alec said, his voice hard. "I needed to prove to myself I have control. Of my ability, of . . . I don't know, my own life? Ever since she came back into it, it's like every ounce of control I'd built up over a lifetime just crumbles in her presence. Regardless of the fact that I'm not getting any extra Light from her. It's fucking terrifying. I needed to prove to myself I could still do it. That I'm not a danger to everyone around me . . ."

"Are you fucking kidding me?" Everyone turned to me. It was good to get an answer, but it wasn't complete. They'd hinted this had something to do with what had happened between us in the study, but I was artfully ignoring that. I knew, realistically, how selfish that was—to focus on Alec's shit while ignoring my own. But it was much easier to give in to the anger. Let it distract me.

"You came here for some manufactured sense of control? To prove some ridiculous point to yourself? Do you have any idea what you put us all through? These three are worried out of their minds for you!" I was too, but again, I wasn't ready to admit it. He had come here for a beating anyway, right? "Tyler used Melior Group resources so he could be here to watch you get your ass beaten. Ethan and Josh felt every blow as if it were landing on their flesh. Because they *care*. They love you, you complete fucking moron."

His face became redder as I continued my tirade, a thick vein appearing in the middle of his forehead, his fists clenching and unclenching, straining the bandages over his knuckles.

He stepped right into my space and opened and closed his mouth several times, as if about to say something. But instead he settled on just growling in frustration while making a choking motion with his hands. Then he turned around and stalked out.

Tyler shook his head wearily. "Let's just go."

We followed Alec up a steep set of stairs, through a back entrance off the dingy corridor, and past several rows of parked cars.

He stopped by a yellow Dodge Challenger. At least he was waiting for us.

"Give me the keys," he demanded. "I'll take the bike back. I can't be in the same car as her right now."

"You know what?" I moved forward, ready to get in his face again, but Tyler stepped into my path.

"Enough!" The finality in his voice made us both pause. "You're both acting like children, and I've had it. Alec, you're in no state to take the bike. Get in the fucking car. Eve can come with me."

Alec didn't wait another second, wrenching the passenger door open and folding his tall frame into the seat.

Josh closed the trunk, having swapped the duffel for a helmet, which he handed to me. A little surprised, I looked at Tyler. He already had his on, zipping his leather jacket up as he swung his leg over a motorcycle.

"Uh . . ." I'd never been on the back of a bike.

"You'll be safe with Gabe." Josh gave me a small smile, then took the helmet back and lowered it over my head. He secured it and gave me a little kiss on the nose before lowering the visor and getting into the driver's seat of the car.

Ethan helped me into a leather jacket. I was swimming in it, but it wasn't down to my knees, so it was probably Josh's and not Ethan's. He rolled the sleeves up, lifted the visor, gave me another kiss on the nose, and jumped in the back of the car. Josh pulled out of the spot immediately.

I pulled the visor back down. I didn't want Tyler to see the awkward look on my face. I may not have been on a bike before, but I knew we were about to be pressed up against each other for at least an hour. I had no idea how he felt about that. I wasn't entirely sure how I felt about it either.

I shuffled over and stopped just out of his reach. He finished putting on his gloves and looked up.

"It's OK. I got you." His voice was clear and confident even from behind the helmet. I couldn't see his eyes, but somehow I knew they were looking at me with warmth and encouragement. Despite the fact that I'd been a major pain in his ass.

I closed the distance and swung my leg over the bike, settling behind him as best I could without touching him. My toes brushed the ground on either side.

Tyler reached back, grabbed my right ankle, and positioned my foot on a little bar. I lifted the other foot into the same position. Then he started the engine, which came to life with a loud, angry roar.

Tentatively, I placed my hands on his waist. There was nothing else to hold on to. Not that I looked too hard.

He grabbed my wrists with his gloved hands and tugged until my arms wrapped around his chest and my front was flush with his back.

"Hold on tight." He had to speak up over the roar of the engine. "If something's wrong or you need me to pull over, tap my shoulder, OK?"

I gave him a thumbs-up; forming words was beyond me in that moment. With training and tutoring and all the Light transfers, I probably spent more time with Tyler than any of the others, but he wasn't the one I was closest to.

We'd hugged a few times, mostly in life-or-death situations, but touching him like this made me relive that first day at Bradford Hills, when I was trying not to get a crush on him and failing miserably. I tried not to pine for him, but with my arms feeling the taut muscles under his jacket, my chest and belly feeling his heat pressed into me . . .

We took off, and my heart hammered in my chest from fear as well as from the close proximity to Tyler, but after a while, I relaxed and started to enjoy the ride. We passed the Challenger on the freeway after only ten or fifteen minutes, but we whizzed by so fast I couldn't see inside.

I admired the twinkling lights of the city, then the darkness as we drove deeper into the country, the headlights illuminating trees and a short stretch of black road ahead. With every turn, every bend in the road, every little correction he had to make, Tyler's core muscles clenched and relaxed. Tight against him—my front to his back, my legs against his, my hips pressed into his ass—I was acutely aware of his every movement, of every inch of contact between us, and I reveled in it.

I may have been spending more time with Tyler than any of them, but I also craved him more. Ethan and Josh were giving in to their physical pull as much as they could without it becoming dangerous. With Tyler, I wasn't sure he even felt a pull.

I definitely felt it though.

The Light was pushing me to deepen the Bond with all of them. It was all I could think about at times. Every time I shared a heated kiss with Ethan or Josh, I remembered how Alec had made me feel that night on the couch, how his hands had touched me exactly how I'd wanted them to. Then I'd immediately start wondering what Tyler's hands would feel like on parts of my body I knew he'd never touch, what his lips would feel like pressed to mine.

I craved Tyler in a way I didn't crave the others—in the one way I couldn't have him.

The vibrations of the engine only added to my heightened state, driving me a bit crazy. All the drama of the night melted away. At least that was one good thing—the ride back, the fresh air, and the distraction of Tyler's body were enough to calm my rage toward Alec.

Too soon we were pulling through the gates of Bradford Hills Institute. Tyler checked us in with the guards at the gate, reminding them about their confidentiality responsibilities, and then we were at the back of my res hall, and he was shutting the engine off.

He straightened, leaning away from the handlebars, and my body reacted to his instinctively. I arched my back and rolled my hips forward, seeking more contact in the one place all my blood seemed to be flowing to—between my legs.

He paused, and because my arms were still wrapped around him, I felt him release a deep breath. He removed his gloves and placed his warm hands over mine. "Your hands are freezing."

Hearing him speak brought me out of my lust haze enough to feel embarrassed at how I'd basically ground myself on him. I'd practically sexually harassed him. He was handling it like a champ though, keeping his cool and not calling me out on it.

I pulled my hands out of his and got off the bike, immediately missing his warmth. My legs were shaky, and my numb fingers struggled to unclasp the helmet.

He stayed on the bike but reached out to pull me closer, then undid the helmet for me. I handed it to him and tried to gulp in the fresh cool air without making it obvious I was trying to calm myself.

"Thanks . . ." My voice was croaky, so I cleared my throat. "Thanks for the ride."

I turned to leave.

"Eve . . ." He sounded as if he was about to say something serious, something that might crush me, but I wasn't ready to hear it. His persistent and careful boundaries hurt enough. I couldn't stand to hear him *say* he didn't want me in that way, articulate it in no uncertain terms.

"Oh, right! You can't hold the helmet and ride the bike." I latched on to the first thing I saw. "Silly me."

I took the helmet back and forced myself to walk and not run up the stairs to my building. As I waited for the elevator, I heard the engine of the bike start up.

TEN

It was nearly midnight by the time I unlocked all the deadbolts on my door and stepped inside, but Zara and Dot were waiting for me. We dragged mattresses, blankets, and pillows into the living area, and I told them everything, completely giving in to all the emotions I'd been holding back and breaking down in tears several times. They listened, soothed, and plied me with junk food until we all fell asleep with the TV on.

When my alarm went off at eight the next morning, I nearly decided to skip my session with Tyler for more sleep. But regardless of how unbearable my pining for him was becoming, I couldn't pass up an opportunity to see him.

I managed to get ready without waking my still-sleeping friends and let myself out silently. I wished I had time to walk to the Starbucks across campus for coffee, but I was cutting it close and didn't want to be late.

The thick gray clouds threatening rain matched my somber mood perfectly. I was glad I'd thrown my oversized cardigan on over my jeans and T-shirt. It was the same warm one I'd worn on my first day at Bradford

Hills—when I met Tyler and fell hopelessly in lust with him.

"Eve!" Ethan's loud voice pulled me up short, and I turned to see him and Josh jogging to catch up with me.

"Hey." I sounded flat and disinterested even to my own ears, but it had more to do with my sleep deprivation and not wanting to be late than the fact that I was still a bit pissed at them.

Neither one of them made a move to touch me in any way, and I wasn't in the mood for chitchat, so we just walked in silence.

Ethan ran his hands through his hair and sighed heavily. "I'm really sorry about last night, Eve. We shouldn't have lied to you."

Josh hastened to add, "I'm sorry too. Really sorry. We're still figuring this all out, and sometimes it's hard to know where the line between protecting you and excluding you is. We fucked up."

I sighed and stopped walking, turning to face them. "You're forgiven. Just don't exclude me anymore, OK?" The last part was delivered on a near whisper as I looked down at our shoes—my black flats, Ethan's sneakers, Josh's loafers.

Ethan rushed forward and wrapped me up in a hug that nearly lifted my feet off the ground. "Thank god! I barely got any sleep. I wanted to come over to your place so bad, but Josh made me leave you alone."

I hugged him back as I flashed Josh a grateful look. I needed to unload to my friends and have some time away from the guys to process—Josh knew that, as usual. He smiled and nodded.

We kept walking. I increased our pace, once again wary of being late.

"Where you off to this early anyway?" Josh asked. "We were coming to see if you wanted to get coffee while we groveled for your forgiveness."

I cocked my head at him, confused. "My session with Tyler." Had I gotten the days wrong?

They exchanged a worried glance before Ethan asked, "He didn't cancel?"

"No. Why would he?" I faltered. Had my behavior last night put him off more than I realized? Was he so repelled by me that he didn't even want to tutor me anymore?

"Today is his mom's birthday," Josh explained. "He usually takes the day off . . ."

"Oh." Tyler was grieving. That just made me want to go to him more. Maybe it was selfish, but I wanted to see him, see if there was anything I could do to help. After all, I knew exactly how he was feeling. We all did.

"Well, he hasn't told me not to come, so I might just check if he's up for it anyway." We'd already reached the front of the admin building.

"I think that's a good idea." Ethan nodded. "Maybe he could use the distraction."

Josh sighed. "I think you're right. Can't be worse than how he usually deals with it."

They both nudged me in the direction of the front doors, not giving me a chance to interrogate them about how Tyler usually dealt with this difficult day.

Riding in the elevator up to Tyler's office, I wasn't sure what to expect. After my mother died, I hated the look of pity in people's eyes. Their over-the-top reactions made me think about it all over again. I just wanted them to treat me normally so I could get through one hour without feeling like bursting into tears.

As I slowly approached his door, fidgeting with my cardigan sleeves, I took a deep breath and did my best to put a neutral expression on my face. I refused to look at Tyler with pity. I'd let him take the lead. If he wanted to tell me about his mother, I would listen. If he wanted to just have a normal session, I would ask a million questions and stick to the plan.

I rapped on the door and pushed it open. I never waited for him to invite me in anymore. But maybe I should have.

He was leaning back in his chair, and perched on the desk facing him was some woman. Dressed in a tight skirt and a soft blue sweater, her blonde hair in a neat, understated bun, she was leaning into him with her hand on his arm, speaking softly.

They both looked in my direction, and I saw it was Stacey from admissions. I resisted the urge to cross the room and rip her arm out of its socket. Tyler wasn't my boyfriend, I reminded myself; it was just the Bond making me react possessively, and I'd only a second ago decided I would do whatever he needed. The neutral look remained plastered to my face as I took my emotion out on the door handle, gripping it tight.

"Oh, Eve, right?" Stacey stood up. "Gabe is actually not feeling well today, so he's going to cancel all his appointments, sweetie. I'm sorry you came up here before I had a chance to let you know."

She placed a hand on his shoulder. It took all my self-control not to stare daggers at the exact spot where her hand rested.

Before I had a chance to answer, Tyler stood up, dislodging Stacey's hand. "Actually, I might keep this appointment." He lowered his voice, but I could still hear him perfectly well. "Might be good to have a distraction, you know? Focus on work for a bit."

"Of course." She had concern painted all over her face. Pity too. "You just let me know if you need anything. *Anything.*"

That last "anything" had an edge of suggestion to it. How transparent could a grown woman be?

"Right. Yes. Thank you." Tyler gave her a tight smile and turned his attention to me. "Come in, Eve. We have a lot to cover today."

Stacey finally went to the door and, with a last pitying smile, left the room.

Tyler and I stared at each other as her soft footsteps retreated down the carpet. When we heard the ding of the elevator, he slumped back against the side of his desk, his shoulders sagging. "I thought she would never leave."

I chuckled nervously, putting my bag down by the door before closing it. "I thought I was interrupting."

"Oh, you were," he said slowly, his eyes downcast. "And I'm so glad you did. The last thing I need today is . . ." He trailed off, staring into space.

It was so unlike him to have incomplete thoughts that my concern kicked up a notch. "I was so worried about Alec last night."

He kept staring, unfocused, at a spot low on the wall behind me. "He puts me through hell every time he fights. It's even worse for Kid and Josh. There's no stopping him, so I just try to manage the fallout as best I can—try to keep everyone . . . I don't even know. Safe? That's why I tried to keep you away last night. Not just because The Hole is dangerous. I wanted to protect you from seeing that, seeing how it affects us all. And then I see Dot, and I'm reminded of Charlie and what he must be going through, and I feel like we're not doing enough to find him. Like *I'm* not doing enough . . . and then my mom's birthday comes around, and I just feel like a twelve-year-old kid again, missing her, and I don't know how I can do it all anymore."

I twisted the edge of my cardigan between my hands. Tyler carried *so much* on his shoulders. How could I even begin to help him with the weight of that burden?

Should I ask about his mother? Should I make a start on our study session? I'd decided to let him take the lead, but he was just sitting there, looking broken.

I decided the best thing would be to ask what he wanted. It's what he would do. Be clear and direct.

I cleared my throat. "Tyler . . ."

As soon as his name was off my lips, spoken softer than I'd intended, he raised his head and looked at me.

The emotion in his gaze made me completely forget what I'd been trying to ask. His beautiful gray eyes, usually so bright with intelligence and curiosity, looked glassy and bloodshot, and his hair was even messier than usual, as if he'd been running his hands through it.

He held the intense stare for a few moments, then dropped his head again with a sigh. He needed something from me, but I wasn't sure what it was, and my attempt to ask him had failed miserably.

Without thinking about it too much, I raised my hand and ran it gently through his hair, pushing the mess off his forehead. He leaned into my touch, and I did it again, this time softly scraping my nails over his scalp. On my third pass, I rested my other arm gently on his shoulder, letting my fingers gently scratch the nape of his neck.

He raised his hands and tentatively placed them high on my hips, over my jeans. He wanted more of whatever it was I was giving him, and I was happy to oblige. I stepped farther into him, positioning myself between his legs but still not leaning into him fully. I didn't want him to get the wrong idea after the way I'd pressed myself into him on the bike the night before.

But as soon as I stepped into his space, he pulled me in the rest of the way and buried his head against my neck. And then his shoulders started to bob up and down, and his breathing became uneven. He was *crying*. After a split second of frozen shock, I wrapped my arms around him, one cradling his head and the other curving around his shoulders. He banded both arms around my middle and held me tightly.

He didn't sob or make any dramatic sounds. He just cried softly as I held him, my heart breaking.

A lump formed in my throat, and tears stung my own eyes. I was doing my best to be strong for him, but seeing him so upset was incredibly hard. The wetness in my eyes reminded me to keep my Light in check. It tended to go haywire when I got emotional, and I didn't want it to distract Tyler. He'd always been there for me to expel excess Light into when it overwhelmed me.

This moment needed to be about what *I* could do for *him*.

I checked my mental barriers; my control had slipped, and excess Light was coursing through our contact. I took a deep breath and concentrated on keeping it in check while I gently moved my hand away from the skin on Tyler's neck.

His head snapped up. "Don't," he whispered softly, his hands once again landing on my hips.

"I'm so sorry. I've got it under control now. You don't have to do that for me today."

"No, that's not what I meant. Don't stop." He grabbed my hand and placed it on his cheek. "It feels good."

"Oh. OK." If he wanted whatever the Light made him feel, then I would give it to him.

I held his face on both sides and let my instincts take over, let his needs speak directly to the Light, let the Light flow. It trickled out of my hands as I wiped the tears off his cheeks with my thumbs, and his eyes widened slightly before drooping closed. A smile tugged at the corners of his lips, and he leaned forward with a small sigh until our foreheads were touching.

We stood like that for a long time, letting our supernatural connection tether us closer, healing unspoken wounds.

After a while Tyler started to speak. As if opening ourselves to our Vital Bond had opened some emotional block, he began telling me about his mother. He told me she was a single parent, and he never knew his father. She was a ballroom dancer and used to drag him to the classes she taught in the evenings.

As he told me how close she was to my mother, I got a lump in my throat. His pain directly mirrored mine. I felt every affectionate smile on his face, every chuckle at a silly memory, every wistful look as if they were my own.

We slowly moved to a more comfortable position on the floor, me leaning back against his desk, his head in my lap.

"And she loved ice cream. Used to make it from scratch. It was the creamiest, most delicious ice cream you would've ever tasted. And whenever it was her birthday or my birthday, there would be ice cream. It didn't matter that my birthday's in the middle of winter." He chuckled, his shoulders bumping against the side of my thigh. "She would make it anyway, and we would bundle up under a million blankets and eat it."

His ice cream story gave me an idea. "Keep talking, I'm listening," I murmured as I pulled my phone out of my pocket.

I absentmindedly ran my fingers through his hair again as I typed out a quick text to Josh.

Can you guys come to Tyler's office please? Bring ice cream.

I hit send and then hesitated, not sure I wanted to send the next bit. Reminding myself this was about Tyler, I typed it out quickly.

And bring the "Master of Pain."

Josh's reply came quickly.

Great idea! Done and done. :)

I smiled.

And get the good stuff. Ben and Jerry's or something. None of that cheap shit.

Yes, ma'am.

I put the phone away and focused on Tyler once more.

It couldn't have been more than ten minutes later that we heard footsteps in the hallway and the door handle turned.

Tyler sucked in a sharp breath and shot up from his horizontal position. He was propped up on his elbows, one knee bent and ready to push himself up farther, when he realized it was Josh walking through the door, with Ethan behind him and Alec bringing up the rear.

Josh paused but didn't allow any surprise to enter his expression. "Chill, man. It's just us."

Tyler relaxed, although he didn't return his head to my lap. Instead he shifted into a sitting position next to me, our backs against the desk. I immediately missed the warmth of his head on my legs and bent my knees up to ease the empty feeling.

The guys joined us on the floor, and Alec extracted three tubs of ice cream from a little plastic bag. It wasn't Ben and Jerry's, but it was amazing.

"It's from a small local producer," Ethan explained, getting that spark in his eye he had whenever he talked about food. "There's only one grocer in the area that stocks it. Luckily it was on Alec's way here."

He smiled at his cousin, a genuine smile that made his dimples appear. Surprisingly Alec smiled back. It was the most relaxed I'd seen him since Studygate, and it reminded me of honey-voiced Alec. A pang of longing slowly blossomed inside me and settled somewhere deep inside my chest.

What had caused such an improvement in his mood since last night? I studied his face as he'd been studying me lately, trying to puzzle it out, but all I could see was the physical damage from the fight. The cut over his eyebrow still had a dressing on it, but the eye was less puffy, and he wasn't moving as if he had a broken rib anymore.

Our talk of dead mothers was abandoned in favor of lighter topics. Josh played some music on his phone, and we chatted and joked, the guys teasing each other. Even Alec joined in, giving me a rare glimpse into their group dynamic. It was nice to see them like that, to see how people who weren't related by blood could still be a family. It was even nicer to be included in it—another stark contrast to the previous night.

I hoped things would keep moving in this direction. That we could have more of this and less of the tension between me and Tyler, less of the hostility between me and Alec, less of the barely restrained physical pull between me and Ethan and Josh. Less of the drama and angst of the night before.

We polished off the ice cream, passing the three tubs around our little circle as we talked. Then we picked ourselves up off the floor.

Stacey had canceled the rest of Tyler's commitments for the day, and Ethan, Josh, and I agreed we would ditch the rest of our classes. Even Alec made a few hushed phone calls before we piled into the elevator and headed off campus. The fat gray clouds hadn't dissipated, but it wasn't raining either, so we walked past the heavy security and headed into town on foot.

As we strolled the tree-lined streets of Bradford Hills, Tyler fell into step next to me, the other three having become engaged in a heated discussion around football, guaranteeing I'd tune out immediately. He grabbed my hand and gave it a firm squeeze before quickly releasing it.

"Thank you, Eve," he said softly into my ear.

I'd actually managed to make a difference. Even if it was only our supernatural connection that had done it, I walked with a lightness to my steps, knowing that something in me had helped to heal something in him.

"Don't mention it." I smiled, injecting every bit of my affection for him into my expression. I hoped he could see how happy I was to do something for him when he'd already done so much for me.

ELEVEN

Things settled down over the next week, and we all fell back into our routines. On the morning of my next session with Ty, I woke from a dreamless, deep sleep to the sound of my backup alarm.

I knew he wouldn't mind me being a little late, but I still swore under my breath as I threw back the covers and jumped out of bed.

The time for showering had long passed, so I just brushed my teeth, splashed some water on my face, and pulled my hair up into a messy bun. Rushing back into my room, I realized I had another problem. Between classes, the drama of the past week, training (of the Variant *and* the self-defense type), and taking care of basic human needs like food and bathing, I'd severely neglected doing my laundry.

I was pretty casual in what I wore, perfectly happy to get around in jeans, leggings, and loose cardigans, but even I wasn't so blasé about my appearance as to spend the day in public in a stained pair of sweatpants and one of Ethan's white T-shirts that I'd stolen. But that was all I could find that wasn't in my overflowing basket in the corner.

"Zara!" I yelled, reaching into the back of my closet and praying for a miracle.

"What?" she replied, sounding just as hurried.

"Can I borrow some clothes? Literally everything I own is dirty."

"Eew!" I heard her unlocking the several locks on our door. "Help yourself to anything in my room, you slob. I gotta run." The door slammed behind her just as I pulled an item of clothing I'd completely forgotten I owned out of my wardrobe—a white linen shirt. It buttoned up the front but was soft and flowy, not at all constrictive. Slipping it over my head, I ran into Zara's room. I only had five minutes to get out the door.

Zara and I were similar in size, but her hips were a little narrower than mine, so I ignored the jeans and grabbed the first skirt I found, figuring if I wore it a little higher on my waist, it should fit. I pulled the black plaid number on as I hopped awkwardly back to my own room. It fit pretty well but was a little shorter than I was used to. The only pair of socks I could find were a knee-high white sports pair. I shoved them down so they pooled around my ankles before quickly pulling on my Converse.

I didn't have time to check myself in the mirror, but surely I couldn't go wrong with black and white. Hopefully I wouldn't be too cold with my legs so exposed.

I grabbed my bag and my oversized cardigan, shoved an apple into my mouth, and rushed out the door, racing through campus.

I made it to the admin building in record time, dumping the chewed apple core in the trash as I approached the stairs. A large group of black-clad Melior Group agents were standing together off to the side, and I cursed mentally when I saw Alec with them, seemingly giving instructions. He had his back turned to me, one hand resting on his hip near his gun. Not that he needed a gun—I'd seen him incapacitate dozens of people with a single focused look. Hell, I'd helped him do it.

I slowed my pace and made my steps as light as possible, keeping an eye on his broad back. As if he had a sixth sense for people avoiding him, he turned just as I reached the bottom of the stairs and looked at me over his shoulder. The expression on my face must have been shifty, but his attention was drawn down, his eyes flicking over my body before he muttered something to the agents and walked over.

Before I had a chance to declare I was late and run off, he leveled me with an incomprehensible look, crossing his arms. "Is that what you're wearing for your session with Gabe?"

I blinked at him slowly, unsure I'd heard him correctly. A sarcastic comment, a grumble about my presence, an exclamation declaring I was the most irritating person in the world—any of those would have made sense. Alec caring about what I was wearing? It just didn't compute.

I went into worry mode. "Oh shit! Is there a stain or something?" I twisted awkwardly on the spot to try to look at the back of my outfit. "I woke up so late, and I didn't get a chance to check myself in the mirror, and then . . ."

My eyes narrowed in suspicion. He was smirking, mischief dancing in his bright blue eyes. His face had almost lost the constant underlying intensity and broodiness. Almost, but not quite. He was amused, but there was a cruel tilt to his smirk.

He was making fun of me. He broke his important work conversation, came over here, and was making me late just to make fun of me.

"You are such a fucking asshole," I muttered as I spun on my heel and stomped up the stairs.

"Have a great lesson, precious," he called after me with mirth in his deep voice.

I gave him the finger over my shoulder. As the glass doors slid closed behind me, I could have sworn I heard a chorus of manly voices laughing.

In the elevator up to Tyler's office, I huffed, annoyed, but then took a few deep breaths, trying not to let Alec get to me. My day had started off badly, and he'd made it worse, but I was trying to wipe the slate clean and go into my lesson with a fresh attitude.

As I entered Tyler's office, however, my day got weirder.

The door was ajar and I let myself in. "Hi."

He was sitting behind his desk, his face buried in a pile of paperwork as his pen scribbled furiously across the page.

"Hey." He glanced up, returning my greeting before dropping his head back down. "Let me just . . ."

The pen stilled, and he raised his eyes once more, slowly. His gaze flitted up and down my body very quickly, as if he were worried he'd go blind if he looked in my direction too long.

Eventually he cleared his throat and placed the pen down with unusual stiffness. His fingers raked through his hair, pushing that persistent messy bit off his face, as he glanced at me *again* before looking away.

"Have a seat." His voice sounded strained. "We should get started. We're behind."

As I took my notebook out of my bag and made my way over to his desk, my brow creased. Why was everyone acting so strange? "No, we're not. We're way ahead."

"Right. Yes. Ahead." He punctuated every word with a glance at me.

"Are you OK?" I was getting worried. Did this have something to do with the events on the night of Alec's fight? We'd never talked about the way I'd rubbed myself on him on the back of the bike. I was still mortified every time I thought about it and was living in fear of him bringing it up.

He took a deep breath, closing his eyes as he exhaled, then looked at me directly.

"Yes," he said with a reassuring smile. But it didn't reach his eyes, and I could still see tightness in his shoulders. "Let's begin."

I thought about pressing the issue, but he launched into the history of Variant suppression in Eastern Europe during the eighties, and I dropped it, focusing on our work.

The rest of the hour lacked the light atmosphere and casual back and forth of our usual conversations. He remained seated behind his desk, and considering that every other time so far he'd come around to sit with me, that was odd in itself.

By the end of the session, though, he was almost acting normally, telling me which journals were good if I wanted to do extra reading. "There's another one, but I can't remember . . . I think it was on one of the printouts . . ."

He started rummaging through the books and papers on his desk, but I knew what he was looking for.

"Oh, it's under this . . ." We reached for the same book at the same time, and our hands accidentally touched. I froze, my words dying in my throat. To my utter astonishment, he stopped moving too.

For a beat we just sat there, the tips of our fingers touching. Then his hand moved, brushing the backs of his fingers against mine. My lips parted, my breathing becoming shallow. I dared not look up for fear of breaking the spell.

With slow, cautious movements, I turned my hand to rest palm up on the desk. He responded by covering it with his, the tips of his fingers at my wrist. As he dragged his hand lightly over mine, our fingers caressing each other's palms, I slowly lifted my gaze.

His other hand was flat against the desk, fingers splayed, and his downcast eyes looked almost hooded. He was staring at my chest, which, I realized, was heaving with how hard I was breathing.

Sudden, loud laughter in the corridor snapped us almost violently out of the moment. I startled, flinching, and he pulled his hand back quickly. Our eyes met for the briefest of seconds; then he looked away and cleared his throat.

Both of us rushed through goodbyes as I scrambled to pack up, and I walked out of his office thoroughly confused and a little crestfallen. Despite the perplexing moment of intimacy, I saw him heave a sigh of relief as I closed the door behind me. I'd thought we'd taken a step forward last week, that he was finally letting his carefully built barriers down a little.

As I walked through the lobby on my way out, I saw Alec coming my way. With considerable effort I squared my shoulders, pressed my lips together, and avoided looking at him.

He laughed, drawing the attention of the women at reception, and then mumbled at me as he walked past, "Went well, then?"

I kept walking, determined to ignore him, but as I stepped into the sunshine, I wondered if maybe Tyler had told Alec about our bike ride and Alec was using it to make my life miserable. They were both acting strange, and clearly I was missing something.

Ethan and Josh confirmed my suspicion when they came up to me at the bottom of the stairs. They slowed their walk, and both of their eyebrows shot up as they looked me up and down. Ethan grinned, while Josh puffed his cheeks and blew the air out slowly.

Either I'd been hallucinating the clothes on my body and had actually been nude all morning, or there was some tear in the space-time continuum and they were seeing something I wasn't. Either way, I'd had enough. My morning was ruined and I wanted answers.

I crossed my arms and jutted out one hip. "OK. What the hell is going on? Alec was a dick to me this morning, which isn't that weird, but he went out of his way to do it, and then Tyler was acting strange through our whole session. Now you two are giving me weird looks. Start talking."

They exchanged a glance.

"It probably has something to do with the fact that you're walking around dressed like Gabe's wet dream, honeybunch." Ethan sounded as if he was explaining things, but his statement only made me scrunch my face up in confusion.

Josh snorted. "Eloquently put, Kid."

"Thanks, bro!" Ethan slapped him on the shoulder and beamed at me. I just frowned and turned back to Josh.

"Tyler has a . . ." His eyes darted around uncomfortably as if looking for the right words. "A thing . . . for . . ."

"Eloquently put, Joshy!" Ethan mocked.

"He has a private schoolgirl fantasy," he whispered, pressing his lips together and shoving his hands into the pockets of his perfectly pressed pants.

"What?" The conversation had taken a turn I definitely hadn't expected.

"Like, sexually," Josh elaborated, looking a little worried.

I rolled my eyes at him. "Yes. Thank you, captain obvious. What the hell does that have to do with me?"

"Seriously?" Ethan couldn't seem to stop smiling. "You're basically wearing a school uniform."

"The knee-high socks." Josh pointed at my feet.

"The pleated skirt." Ethan lowered his voice, lightly caressing the fabric at the hem of the skirt in question.

"The white shirt." Considering we were in public, I was a little surprised when Josh stepped forward and gently tugged at the collar of my shirt.

"The sexy messy hair you have going on, and . . ." Ethan tucked a loose strand behind my ear. They were no longer smiling, the situation having apparently lost its humor. Stupidly, I was fixating on Ethan's use of the word *sexy*.

I got there in the end though. "I look like a disheveled private schoolgirl!" I said a little too loudly, and they both chuckled. "Shit!"

I wasn't sure how to feel. I didn't want Tyler to think I'd intentionally done this to provoke him. Or did I? Of course I was attracted to him, but I also respected him, and he'd very clearly set this particular boundary from day one.

Before I could continue to unpack the situation, I heard the man in question coming our way, his voice carrying through the building's front door. We were standing at the bottom of the stairs and off to the side, not immediately visible but close enough to make out his words.

"... longest hour of my life." He groaned as he emerged from the building, Alec by his side. Ethan and Josh both turned at the sound of his voice, and Josh took a breath. Without even thinking about it, I shot my hand out and covered his mouth. Then I did the same to Ethan for good measure. I spent entirely too much time behind the eight ball in my own Bond. If they were going to talk about something pertinent in public, who were we to stop them? Ethan and Josh both gave me disapproving looks, but they stayed quiet.

"And you knew she was coming to see me dressed like *that*. You are such a fucking asshole." I smirked as Tyler echoed my words to Alec.

"What was I supposed to do, man?" Alec somehow managed to sound defensive and chastised at the same time. "Tell her to go home and change? Yeah, that would have gone over real well. Especially coming from *me*."

"You know I'm doing this for you, right?" Tyler was beginning to sound less amused. "I don't know how much—"

His mouth clamped shut. They'd seen us. We must have looked ridiculous, standing there, my hands over Ethan and Josh's mouths. Tyler's eyebrows shot up, his hand frozen in mid-gesture in front of him, while Alec threw his head back and laughed.

My eyes widened. I'd just been busted by my hot older tutor doing something naughty while inadvertently dressed like a private schoolgirl. The irony was not lost on me.

I dropped my hands, turned on my heel, and walked away as fast as I could.

I was mortified. About all of it—my unfortunate outfit, the new bit of knowledge about Tyler, the blatant eavesdropping on their conversation. *What was I thinking?* Of course he was going to spot us! And now Tyler surely thought my maturity matched my outfit—high school level. I couldn't fathom what Alec thought, but he was a mystery most of the time anyway.

The first words I'd heard Tyler say kept replaying over and over in my mind: *longest hour of my life*. Our session that morning had been awkward for me too, but I wouldn't say it was the "longest hour of my life." He hated it more than I realized. Not enduring my stupid outfit in his face for an hour. *Me*. It was our Bond he hated. Maybe even resented.

His power was passive; he'd never expected or wanted a Vital. It was a burden to him. That's why he'd put such clear boundaries in place. The few moments that made me think he might feel the same way as I did were simply Light-driven, instinctual reactions to our Bond. I'd probably completely ruined this fantasy for him.

I really wanted to go home and change, put on the stained sweatpants and questionable-smelling T-shirt, but we were already late for biology, and I didn't want to miss any classes. So I did my best to pull the skirt down as far as it would go and shove more of my hair into my bun in an attempt to look less . . . provocative.

The boys were following me, and I could hear them talking quietly behind me, probably *about* me. I forced myself to put one foot in front of the other and gripped the strap of my bag tighter. Ethan fell into step next to me. I didn't look at him, but I felt his fingertips gently drag down my arm from my elbow to my wrist—a warning he was about to take my hand.

I did a quick mental check and saw that, in my emotional state, I'd let more Light in than I wanted to. I took a deep breath and clamped down on the flow of Light, scrunching it up into a tight little ball deep inside me. Then I met Ethan halfway. His big, warm hand swallowed mine, giving me a little squeeze, and I instantly felt better. Josh was walking a pace or two behind us, allowing us to look like the couple the whole campus thought we were while still staying close enough to let me know he was there.

As we approached the science building, Ethan tugged me gently toward the side of the building as Josh overtook us. I wrenched my hand out of Ethan's grasp and planted my feet, facing both of them.

"No." I injected as much determination into my voice as I could. They were trying to pull that tag-team shit again—that thing where they crowd my personal space and fry my brain so I'll tell them what I'm thinking even when I'm not sure I want to. I refused. All I wanted to do was focus on science for a while. "We are going to class. I don't want to talk about it right now."

I gave them each a pointed look before turning around and walking to class. Thankfully they behaved, following me into the lecture hall and taking seats on either side of me. We made it just a few moments before class started, and Dot joined us, a few minutes late herself. We exchanged quick hellos before the lecture began.

I stared at the front of the room, oblivious to the information, my notebook remaining blank in front of me. After about ten minutes of this, Josh's hand landed on my leg. He gave me a little squeeze, his fingers digging into my skin below the hem of the skirt, and then he flipped his hand, his palm up in invitation. I placed my hand in his. It snapped me out of my distraction, and after a few minutes I took my hand back and started paying attention.

The rest of the day passed without incident. My classes went well, and no one commented on my outfit. I had lunch with Zara and Dot, but I stayed quiet for most of it, lost in my own thoughts.

When I got back to my res hall at the end of the day, I put on the stained sweats and dragged all my dirty laundry down to the laundry room in the basement. My third load was halfway through when Ethan and Josh came in.

I looked up from the assignment I'd been working on and groaned.

Ethan chuckled. "Well, hello to you too, cutie." He dropped a kiss to the top of my head. I stayed seated, not making it easy for him.

"Hey, pumpkin," I finally replied. I wasn't actually mad at them. "Hey, Josh."

Josh tapped me under my chin, and I raised my gaze to his face. The pure affection in his green eyes made me relax a little. He kissed me softly on the cheek before going to lean against a dryer across from me. Ethan sat on top of the one next to him, and I briefly worried for the structural integrity of the machine; his hulking frame looked as if it could crush it.

They weren't crowding me, as I'd worried they would earlier in the day, cajoling confessions out of me with their searching eyes and probing hands.

"Look, Eve," Josh started, "we don't want to force you into talking about anything. We just want to clear shit up. In case you may have gotten the wrong idea."

"OK." I folded my hands on the table, resting them on the pile of forgotten textbooks and notepads. "Clear away."

"When we told you about Gabe's . . ."

"Proclivities," I finished for him, raising an eyebrow.

"Yes. Thank you. When we told you about that, we didn't consider that it might make him out to seem more . . ."

"Like a perv," Ethan supplied helpfully.

Josh threw him an annoyed glance. "Like he's crossed some boundaries when he actually hasn't."

"What the hell are you talking about?" I was really struggling to keep up with conversations today.

"We just don't want you to think he's actually crossed that line with a high school student before, or even with someone who's underage. He used to watch a lot of anime, and it's just a harmless fantasy he's shared with us because . . . well, we're guys and we talk about that shit. Anyway, Ethan and I gave you an incomplete picture of the situation, and we figured it was up to us to make sure it was cleared up. Because, you know he would never, *ever* . . ." Josh was beginning to ramble, and it was adorable. His perfectly put-together preppy outfit was in total contrast to the slightly frantic look in his eyes.

"Stop." I looked between the two of them—serious, if a little sheepish—and laughed. "It didn't even cross my mind. I think I know Tyler fairly well by now, and I can't imagine him abusing his position of power to do something so . . ."

"Pervy?" Ethan once again supplied helpfully.

"Pervy," I confirmed, giving him an affectionate smile and hoping we could drop the conversation and forget this whole day had happened.

Naturally, Josh was not going to let me off the hook so easily. "Then what's had you so preoccupied all day? What's going on?"

. . . longest hour of my life. Tyler's words ran through my mind again, and I slumped in my seat.

I didn't know how to talk about this with them. They both had feelings for me—feelings that were returned and getting stronger by the day. I loved Ethan's infectious smile, his boundless energy, his gentle touch despite being bigger in stature than anyone I'd ever met. I loved Josh's unpretentious intelligence, his calm nature, his ever-vigilant eyes.

How was I supposed to tell them it wasn't enough? I had two amazing guys, and I spent the day pining for a third. I sounded selfish and petulant even to myself. I was attracted to Tyler, I wanted him badly, and he didn't want me back. But I couldn't say that out loud.

"I'm just embarrassed, that's all." It wasn't a lie. I *was* embarrassed. I just wasn't specifying *what* I was embarrassed about.

"Understandable." Josh nodded. "But you shouldn't be. It's not a big deal."

"Agreed!" I spat out a little too enthusiastically, and they both chuckled. "So can we just stop talking about it and move on? Please."

"Sure," Josh agreed readily.

Ethan opened his arms wide in invitation. I didn't hesitate to leave my seat and step into them, my thighs flush with the dryer he was still sitting on as I relaxed into his chest. After a few moments Josh stepped up behind me to rub soothing circles into my shoulders. With my hands still resting on Ethan's knees, I leaned back into Josh, and his arms encircled my front. I sighed contentedly.

It felt so good to be surrounded by them, Josh pressed to my back, Ethan inching forward to press into my front, his hands snaking into my hair, Josh's breathing becoming shallower, Ethan's eyes looking at my lips as he swallowed . . .

As Ethan leaned in for a kiss, movement in the corner of my eye made me stiffen. We all turned to see various bits of my dirty clothing floating around the room.

"Shit." Josh stepped away and visibly composed himself, returning all the floating items to their spots.

Ethan groaned in frustration, and flames flicked into existence all up and down his muscular arms. Luckily his hands were still in my impervious-to-his-ability hair and not touching something flammable.

I stepped out of his reach and wrapped my arms around myself, bringing my Light back under control as Ethan extinguished his flames. My emotional day had resulted in lack of control, and I was frustrated that they were the ones who had to deal with it. I was also *sexually* frustrated; once again we had to stop things before they'd really started.

Even so, it wasn't the best time or place for all that anyway. While the basement laundry room wasn't exactly public, anyone could walk in at any moment. Plus, I had to finish my laundry. That was of paramount importance.

Josh shifted the bulge in his pants as he turned away, and Ethan jumped down off the dryer.

We all took a few deep breaths at opposite ends of the room, then Ethan folded all my newly clean clothes while Josh helped me with my assignment. I didn't really need the help, but it was good to have a discussion partner and get another perspective on the problem.

After helping me carry all my washing back upstairs, they left with chaste kisses on my cheeks.

TWELVE

The next day, I found a way to use the whole embarrassing situation to my advantage.

Walking out of my last class, I slung my bag over my shoulder and made a beeline for my res hall. I was supposed to be heading to the boys' house for more training, but I needed to speak to Dot privately, and there hadn't been a chance for us to do that in weeks. Zara had messaged me telling me she'd be back late but hadn't specified when.

I texted Dot to come over ASAP without actually telling her what I wanted to discuss. Hopefully the message was firm enough despite the vagueness. I also texted the guys, telling them I needed some alone time and was skipping the afternoon's sessions. I hoped they would leave it at that, but of course that was naive.

"Eve!" Ethan's distinctive voice pulled me up short just around the corner from my building. I mouthed *fuck* before schooling my features into a neutral expression and turning around. He jogged a little to catch up to me, dressed in his standard jeans and white T-shirt. I tugged my jacket tighter around my body to ward off the chilly wind and wondered for the hundredth time how he wasn't cold.

"Hey, snuggleface." I gave him a big smile, which he returned, showing off his dimples.

"Hey, cuddlebum." He rested his hands on my hips and leaned in. "What's going on? You never miss an opportunity to play around with our abilities. I mean, to train." He chuckled lightly. My fascination with Variant abilities had not even remotely waned since I'd learned I was a Vital. If anything, it had intensified.

"I know. I just . . ." I tucked my face into his chest, giving myself some time to think of something. The previous day's events provided the perfect excuse. "I'm just not ready to see Tyler yet," I mumbled.

He sighed and gave me a squeeze, pulling back so I had to look him in the eyes. "I thought we cleared all that up yesterday. You have nothing to worry about."

"I know, I know. But it's easier said than done. I'm still embarrassed, and I just need a day. OK?"

He looked skeptical. "I get it, but I haven't seen you all day."

"I'll come over tomorrow, I promise. Dot's on her way over, so I'd better get going."

"Oh, cool. We can just hang with you. I'll text Josh." His boyish face looked ridiculously eager.

"No!" I blurted out too quickly, then panicked. Thinking quick, I pushed up onto my toes and pressed my lips to his, sparing a moment to make sure my Light was in control. He responded immediately, as he always did, tenderly kissing me back.

Eventually we pulled apart with reluctance. My plan may have backfired;

my brain was as fuzzy after that kiss as I was hoping to make his.

"Are you trying to distract me with your womanly wiles?" He wiggled his eyebrows suggestively.

I laughed. "Would you be opposed to that?"

"No . . ."

With a conscious effort, I stepped out of his arms, giving myself some space to breathe and think. "I just need some girl time with Dot, OK? I'm not trying to avoid you, big guy. I swear."

Over his shoulder I spotted Josh coming our way, impeccably dressed as always; his checked shirt looked as if he'd only just put it on, not as if he'd been sitting in classes all day, and not a blond hair of his slicked-back style was out of place. I knew I had to get going before he joined us. I couldn't hide anything from Josh.

"I don't want to keep Dot waiting, OK? I gotta run. Can you update Josh?"

Ethan nodded, and I gave him another peck on the lips, waving to Josh as I rushed toward my building. His brow creased as I turned to leave, but I didn't give him a chance to stop me.

Dot was waiting outside my room. Her face in her phone, she was leaning next to the door dressed in jeans and a plain sweater, her hair pulled up, her face clear of makeup. My heart broke to see her like that.

She'd been less and less herself. Her moods had been a little better since I'd figured out how to transfer Light to her, but the transfers always made her feel guilty, and she only let me do it whenever she started losing the ability to call out to animals remotely.

Watching her turn into a shell of the vibrant, enthusiastic woman I'd first met—it only solidified my determination to do what I was about to do.

My footsteps echoing down the hall caught her attention.

"Finally." She rolled her eyes. "What's with the vague text?"

"Nothing. I just wanted some girl time." She watched me suspiciously as I unlocked the million locks.

"Is Zara joining us?" She dumped her bag on the couch and rifled through the stash of snacks we had in the little makeshift kitchen.

"Um, no. She has a thing," I said over my shoulder as I checked the window. Then I checked the bedrooms too, just to be sure. It wasn't that I didn't trust Zara, but the fewer people knew about my plan, the more likely I was to succeed, especially considering Tyler's ability. I wouldn't even be telling Dot if I could avoid it, but I needed her help.

As I shut the door of what used to be Beth's room, Dot gave me a funny look while stuffing chips into her mouth. I could tell she was about to ask me what the hell I was doing. I shook my head at her and bugged my eyes out, which made her look even more confused.

"So"—I cleared my throat—"something kind of embarrassing happened yesterday."

At this she perked up. That girl lived for gossip. I slipped my necklace off and placed it gently on the couch. I wouldn't put it past Alec to have placed a listening device in there along with the tracker and distress beacon. Sure, I was being paranoid, but I had no idea who on campus had which ability—which student or Melior Group guard might have super hearing and could grind this thing to a halt before it even started.

"OK . . ." Dot stopped eating and fully focused on me.

"Yeah, so I was on my way to my session with Tyler and . . ." I double-checked that the locks on the door were secure. "Actually, while we talk, can you help me with . . . um . . . my hair? In the bathroom?"

I led the way into the tiny bathroom and closed the door behind us. Immediately I turned the shower on and stood as close to it as I could without getting soaked, gesturing to Dot to come stand next to me.

She hesitated for a moment, looking as if she was questioning my sanity, then finally joined me.

"I have a plan," I rushed out. I knew we couldn't have much time if someone was listening.

"Eve, what the fuck . . ." Her voice was much louder than mine, bouncing off the bathroom tiles.

I slammed my hand over her mouth, putting my finger to my lips. Her eyes bugged out but she stayed silent.

"Just listen, OK?" She nodded and I removed my hand. "I couldn't stop thinking about the Lighthunter and how there's no way to authenticate that she can do what she says, but there *is* a way. *I'm* the way. She doesn't know me. She's never met me. No one even knows my real name, and how would they find out? Plus, if there's one thing my mother taught me to do well, it's disappear."

I paused, waiting for her reaction, but Dot just stared at me for a few moments, dumbfounded. "What exactly are you saying?"

"I'm going to run. And the guys can't know about it." I cringed even as I said it. I knew exactly how hard this would be to pull off, and I knew how pissed they would be when I did it. But it would all be worth it. For Charlie.

"Eve, no. I can't ask you to do that." She shook her head, but I didn't miss the spark of hope in her eyes. "It's too dangerous."

"You're not asking." I took her by the elbows, leaning my face close to hers. "I'm offering. No, I'm not just offering. I'm telling you I'm doing this. For Charlie. I've felt so useless and helpless the past few months, and finally here's an opportunity to actually do something about it. I'm not going to miss it."

"I get it, but why can't we ask for help? I would be livid if Charlie pulled something like this. Your Bond is fucking scary, and they're not gonna like it. Why can't some of them go with you while the others stay behind to test the

Lighthunter?"

"They have rare abilities, they're Lucian Zacarias's nephews, they're too high profile. It would be way too easy to track their passports, find them using facial recognition. I can't have them with me, and they'd never let me go alone."

"What about Alec? I'm sure he has secret identities, considering what he does."

"Probably. But again, that would mean using Melior Group resources, which would leave a paper trail. No one knows me, Dot. If they knew I was Evelyn Maynard and heard some of the stories about us as kids, they might have connected the dots and guessed I was Alec's Vital. But no one even knows I *am* a Vital. There is nothing to connect me to them in any way."

"What if something goes wrong? What if they catch you? There has to be another way." She had three questions for every answer I gave, but she was looking at me as though she hoped beyond hope I would keep answering them.

"It's a risk I'm willing to take." I didn't want to think too hard about the ominous "they"—about the possibility of ending up in the same position we were trying so hard to get Charlie out of. "Having a good plan and thinking through the contingencies will help us minimize it."

"But Tyler might not even be able to get in touch with this so-called Lighthunter."

"But if he does, I want to be prepared. The second we hear that he's made contact, I want to be ready to go."

"I still think we should tell them. They can help—"

"Dot," I cut her off, "you and I both know they will never let me do this. They won't even let me out of their sight from the mansion to the campus. And the only way to be sure is if I go alone."

She watched me for a moment, chewing on her bottom lip. "What does that mean? What would you need to be ready to go?"

I smiled, finally allowing a little excitement to take over. She hadn't said it outright, but Dot was in.

"I'll need ID, and I can't trust some hack to do it for me. I'll need some equipment so I can make a passport and maybe a driver's license. And I'll need a disguise—just something to get me out of Bradford Hills without being recognized."

"A passport? Where would you go?"

"I can't tell you. All it would take would be for Tyler to ask, and . . ."

"He'd know," she finished for me. "Right."

"I'll make you a list, you let me know if you can get the stuff, and we can take it from there. We'd better get out of the bathroom now. If someone actually is listening in, they'll think we're getting it on in here."

I chuckled, and Dot let out a big laugh. "That explains the paranoid behavior."

I turned the shower off and followed her into the living room. We spent the next few hours working on our biology homework and expertly avoiding any mention of what we'd discussed in the bathroom. She clearly had a bunch of burning questions—I could practically read them in her eyes—but she controlled herself like a pro. Dot loved gossip, but this was about saving her brother's life. There was no way she would jeopardize that.

On her way out, she gave me a big hug, holding me longer than usual, and whispered into my ear, "Thank you. I don't deserve you."

We pulled apart and shared a meaningful look before she walked away, her head held a little higher, her steps a little lighter.

Dot was halfway down the corridor when the elevator dinged and Zara stepped out. She appeared to be deep in thought, staring at the ground, so she didn't see Dot until the smaller girl was wrapping her up in a hug.

I laughed, both delighted to see Dot happy and amused by the surprised look on Zara's face.

"I'm heading off, but I'm glad I bumped into you, Zee." Dot gave her a kiss on the cheek and rushed to catch the elevator before the doors closed.

"See ya!" Zara yelled after her and rolled her eyes, tucking a silky strand of red hair behind her ear. A reluctant smile pulled at her lips.

"How was your night?" I asked as she let herself in, removing her leather jacket and sitting down on the couch to get her boots off.

"Yeah, OK." She struggled with the left one. They were the pull-on kind—no zips.

I stepped forward to yank on the heel. "Who'd you catch up with?"

We both strained until the boot slid off, and I stumbled to catch my balance.

"No one you know." Zara held her other leg out, and we repeated the process until she was boot-free.

"What'd you do? Where'd you go?" I started to tidy up the main living area. Neither one of us had really had time to clean. The place was a mess.

Zara narrowed her eyes. "What's with the interrogation?"

I paused halfway through wiping down the little dining table by the door. I was deflecting, trying to keep focus on Zara in order to avoid talking about what Dot and I had discussed, and it was getting obvious. I hadn't even realized I was doing it. I felt like shit not telling Zara, excluding her from something so important.

"Sorry." I hoped my smile didn't look too guilty. "Just making conversation. I didn't mean to pry."

I finished wiping down the table, then braced myself as I moved on to the little bar fridge. Something had gone off in there several days ago, and I was about to find out what it was.

"That's OK. Oh . . . ugh!" Zara and I both gagged at the putrid smell. I had to lean back and cover my nose with my elbow as I extracted every single item, not willing to get close enough to identify the culprit.

Zara put some music on. My cleaning frenzy must have infected her—either that or she felt guilty I was the only one doing it—and she put on some gloves and started scrubbing the bathroom.

We spent the next hour cleaning, chatting about easy, pointless things. By the time I went to bed, I was sure she didn't suspect anything, but the spot just under my ribs was no less twisted at the thought of deceiving her.

THIRTEEN

Dot's black hair was gliding through the straightener when "Side to Side" by Ariana Grande began to play through the speaker in the corner.

It was Dot's nineteenth birthday, and we were in the spare room of Lucian's apartment on the Upper East Side. I hadn't been back there since the night of the gala, when I was too drunk and then too hung over to really appreciate it.

The beautiful apartment was modern and sleek in every way the mansion in Bradford Hills was old-world and classic. Every room had stunning views of Manhattan. While we put on makeup and did our hair, Dot and I watched the city lights start to twinkle as the sun went down.

I paused, holding the straightener over Dot's head as I grooved along to the beat. "I like this song."

I'd been listening to a lot of rock, discovering bands I'd never heard of thanks to Josh and his obsession. With all the new playlists he'd been making for me, I hardly ever heard the radio, let alone a new pop song, anymore.

"Me too! It's so dirty." Dot grinned at me in the mirror.

"Dirty?" I frowned as I pulled her shoulders back against the chair, trying to finish doing her hair.

"It's pretty much about being fucked so hard you can't walk straight." She chuckled. "What did you think it was about?"

I laughed, throwing my head back. "I don't know. I've never really paid attention to the lyrics. I just like the beat."

"I hope tonight ends with me walking side to side," she declared. "It's been way too long since I had *good* sex."

"You and me both. Except it's more like *never* for me. All the sex I've had has been mediocre at best." I shook my head as I finished smoothing out the last section of her perfectly straight hair, then set the hot straightener down on the vanity, somehow finding a clear space in among all the makeup, hair products, jewelry, and for some reason, a bra.

"Well it's lucky you have four seriously hot guys in your Bond who won't be able to resist hitting that pretty soon." Dot jumped out of her seat, smacked me on the ass, and rushed over to the little speaker.

I snorted. "Whatever. I think it could be pretty good with Josh and Ethan, anyway." I didn't want to get into the whole "half my Bond finds me repugnant" thing.

"At the same time?" She wiggled her perfect brows suggestively and restarted the song.

"That would certainly leave me walking side to side," I answered, intentionally vague, as she cranked the volume up.

She bounced over to me as the lyrics began, doing the silliest, least sexy dance I'd ever seen. "Dance with me!"

I rolled my eyes at her, but her excited energy was infectious, especially when seeing a genuine smile on her face felt so great. For the next three minutes, we bounced around the room with the kind of energy I got when I had an overflow of Light.

Once the song ended, more upbeat "going out" music blasted through the speaker. We left it on loud as we finished getting ready.

When Dot had declared she wanted to have a night on the town for her birthday, we were all a little surprised. But she'd explained we'd all been working like crazy and worried out of our minds for Charlie, and it was time to put a pause on it all.

"I just want one night to pretend like everything is normal, go out, have too much to drink, and just . . . forget for a little while."

No one could begrudge her that, and within two days, she and Ethan had organized it and invited more people than I'd ever met.

Dot was in all white, a dress that combined patent leather and velvet and somehow managed to look high fashion and edgy, especially when paired with her white thigh-high boots.

In contrast, I was in all black. Dot had talked me into a pair of very tight black pants—which, admittedly, did make my ass look pretty good—and a shimmery top that left way too little to the imagination. My distress beacon necklace was tucked snugly into my cleavage, out of sight except for the silver chain. Because it was her birthday and she kept gushing about how hot I looked, I let her complete the look by straightening my hair and putting it in a very high ponytail.

Before we headed to the front door, I put my coat on. I was a bit self-conscious about the outfit and wasn't ready for everyone to see it in the bright hall lights; hopefully I'd be more comfortable in the dim lighting of a club. Dot complained that with her birthday being in December, it was always too cold to go anywhere without a coat, which ruined her outfit—even though the coat she had on was faux polar bear fur that matched what she was wearing perfectly.

As Dot and I, along with my four Variants, squeezed into the elevator, she sighed. "I wish Zara was coming."

"Me too." I gave her a sad smile.

Zara was reluctant about any event involving a large group of Variants together in one place, but she'd reluctantly agreed to come celebrate Dot's birthday. Then, the day before, she'd come down with a stomach bug. Dot and I were both suspicious; the timing was just a little too convenient. But hearing her vomiting in the bathroom as I packed my overnight bag had convinced me she wasn't faking it.

"You think she'll be OK?" Dot asked. "Maybe we should've just canceled it."

"Stop looking for excuses to cancel this!" Ethan gave her a nudge with his shoulder—or rather the side of his arm, because his shoulder was level with the top of her head. "It was your idea, and Zara will be fine."

"It's just a stomach bug, and she said a friend was coming over to check on her," I reassured her.

"Who?" Dot frowned. "Everyone we know is coming tonight."

I shrugged. Once again, Zara had been vague about who she was spending her time with, and I wasn't going to pry. I was keeping things from her too. "I think it might be the mystery man or woman she's been seeing."

"Do I need to run a background check on this person?" Tyler held the door open, frowning, and we all filed out.

I gave him a warning look. "Can we rein in the stalking for one night?"

He laughed and held his hands up in surrender, but Alec brushed past and said simply, "No."

I chose not to engage. It was Dot's birthday.

We decided to walk to the club. It was a clear night, and while the crisp air hinted at snow, it was likely to stay clear. The six of us bundled more tightly into our coats as we started the four-block walk.

Ethan and Josh took the lead, joking and laughing, their broad backs covered in thick wool. Dot and I walked arm in arm behind them, much more quietly. I had a feeling she needed some time alone with her thoughts, and I was more than happy to simply walk with her. Alec and Tyler stayed behind us, speaking softly and, I'm sure, keeping an eye on everything.

When we were about halfway there, something occurred to me. "Wait a minute. How are we going to get into a club? Isn't the legal drinking age here twenty-one? I could have made a fake ID if you guys had given me notice."

In response, everyone laughed. Ethan turned around without missing a step, walking backward as he spoke. "Uncle Lucian owns the club." He flashed me his dimples, then turned back around and kept walking.

Of course he did. Why wouldn't he own an exclusive club in New York?

"That's a useful skill to have," Alec piped up.

I flashed him a confused look over my shoulder before I realized I'd casually announced I could falsify identification documents. "Oh, that. Yeah. My mother taught me when I turned twelve, I think, or eleven. Around then. She wanted me to know how to do it in case she . . ." *died*. But I really didn't want to go there. The mood of the night was heavy enough, with Charlie's absence constantly hanging over us. "Umm . . . In case I needed to."

I felt a squeeze on my arm. My eyes met Dot's, and we shared a meaningful look. We were both missing people we loved, but tonight was about having a little fun. About allowing ourselves to feel good for one night.

As we rounded the corner into a side street, I got my first glimpse of an exclusive New York nightclub. A line of people at least fifty deep, cordoned off behind a long stretch of velvet rope, led to the front doors. We walked past them, none of my companions even missing a step, and stopped in front of the entrance. The sleek doors were painted black, like the rest of the building, and were at least ten feet tall, with chunky round handles in their centers. Above them, red neon spelled out the words *Black Cherry*.

In front of the doors stood two large men, the bouncers, dressed in matching suits. "You'll have to go to the back of the line." One of them leaned forward and pointed, his tone not aggressive, simply matter-of-fact.

The two girls at the front of that very line, their hair pulled back tight, their makeup slightly overdone, smugly looked us up and down. I gave them a sickly sweet smile and turned my attention back to my friends.

Tyler, phone in hand as he texted, held up his other hand to the bouncer in a "wait just a sec" gesture, not even looking at the man.

He finished his quick text, returned his phone to his pocket, and just stood there casually as the other guys chatted. The bouncer looked to his companion, neither of them sure what to do. Before either could say anything, however, the doors behind them opened, and a tall thin man in a gray suit emerged. The music's booming bass released into the night for a brief moment before the doors closed again.

The man smiled wide as he hopped down the stairs, and the two bouncers went back to ignoring us.

"Tyler!" He moved in for a firm handshake, then repeated the same greeting with the other three guys.

"He's the manager," Dot stage-whispered to me. "We could have just told the bouncers we were on the list, but that would have meant going through an ID check. This way, we go straight in."

I nodded and chuckled to myself. I guess there really is no need for such pesky things as proof-of-age when your family is loaded and owns the club.

He greeted Dot with a kiss on each cheek and a jovial "happy birthday." He greeted me last but just as warmly.

As he led us past the bouncers and straight through the big doors, I caught the looks of the two girls at the front, their faces much less smug now. I couldn't help myself; I gave them another wide smile before heading inside.

The inside of the club was draped in black, the walls covered in expensive-looking intricate wallpaper, the bars the same slick black finish as the doors, the seating a rich velvet. It was spread over a few interconnecting levels, with several bars and a large central dance floor.

The manager said a few quiet words to Tyler and then disappeared up a side staircase. Dot took the lead, taking me by the hand and walking to a VIP area in a back corner, which had its own bar with bench seating running the length of the wall and small tables scattered throughout. A large sign above the seating read, "Happy Birthday, Dot" in curving script.

At least twenty people were already there, a few of whom I recognized from the Institute. Dot made her way around, saying hi to everyone. The guys led me to a corner near the bar, all taking their coats off and handing them to the pretty blonde bartender. I started to unbutton my coat, but just as I reached the top, Josh stepped behind me.

"Let me help you with that." The music wasn't quite so loud in the VIP area, but he still had to lean in close to be heard, and it sent a little shiver down my spine. He grabbed my coat by the collar and dragged it down my arms. With the heat in the club, I was glad to be rid of it, my hesitation at the outfit momentarily forgotten.

I turned slightly, thanking Josh with a smile. He swallowed hard, returned my smile, then promptly handed my coat off to the bar girls. When I turned back to the front, Tyler and Alec were both staring at me, their gazes taking in the tight pants, the cleavage, the sliver of skin between the hem of my shimmery top and the waistband of the pants. They exchanged a charged look and, as one, turned to the bar. Alec barked something at the poor bar girl, and she immediately poured two shots of some clear liquid. As soon as they were full, the two men threw them back, smacking the little glasses back down.

Tyler lifted his hand, calling the bartender back, but my view of them was suddenly blocked by a very wide chest in a white button-down, open at the top. I looked up into Ethan's face and returned his naughty smile.

"You look smokin'." He planted his warm hands on my waist and pulled me in.

"Thanks, puddin', you look pretty hot yourself." I lifted my hands to his shoulders and gave him my best flirty look.

Making sure my Light flow was in check, I lifted onto my toes and softly pressed my lips to Ethan's. He smiled gently against my mouth and pulled me closer. The kiss didn't last long, but it was enough to give me butterflies. Endorphins released; mission accomplished. I was a little wary about the night, but feeling Ethan's strong body pressed to mine, I allowed myself to let go and embrace the party.

"Let's get you a drink." Ethan kissed me once more on the mouth before leading me to the bar.

Tyler and Alec were still in the same spot, now facing us, their elbows leaning on the bar behind them and their gazes trained on where Ethan's hand met my exposed lower back.

Dot appeared out of nowhere. "What're we having?" she asked, a hint of the lightness that had disappeared along with Charlie back in her voice.

"Whatever the birthday girl desires!" I answered, injecting some pep into my own voice. Anything to keep that easy look in her eyes.

"Cocktails it is then!"

I watched, horrified at the amount of alcohol being poured into the small martini glass, but Dot clapped her hands excitedly. If me drinking copious amounts of alcohol would make her feel better, then I was prepared to be carried home.

Surprisingly, it didn't taste like turpentine, as I'd expected. You could definitely taste the alcohol, but it was fruity and not too sweet. I raised my eyebrows in surprise and gave her a thumbs-up as I took another sip.

"Careful." I hadn't noticed Alec move to stand next to me. "It might taste like peach tea, but there is a lot of alcohol in that."

I rolled my eyes. "Yes. Thank you. I did watch her make it."

He frowned, disapproving, and I felt that familiar Alec-fueled irritation sneaking in to ruin my good vibes. "Look, can we just agree to stay on opposite sides of the room? Then maybe we can both have a good night. Yes? Great!"

I didn't wait for a response before turning back to Dot and Ethan, who had a drink of his own now.

More people began to arrive, slowly filling the VIP area, and Dot was pulled away to accept birthday wishes and gifts. I sipped my cocktail and chatted to a few people I knew from my classes, but either Ethan or Josh was always nearby, if not right next to me. We were all doing our best to have a good night for Dot, but their less-than-subtle hovering was sending a clear message: they were still on alert for any potential threats. It didn't escape my notice that Josh was only drinking soda, and the others were nursing their drinks slowly.

By the time Dot managed to find her way back to us, I was on my third delicious cocktail. As much as I hated to admit it though, Alec was right. They were potent, and I was beginning to feel a little happy.

"I'm so over talking to these posers and pretending I like them while they pretend they care about how I'm doing. You know, with 'the whole Charlie thing.'" Dot made air quotes around 'the whole Charlie thing,' putting on a fake voice as she rolled her eyes. She was being sardonic, but I could see the angry downturn to her lips.

"Let's get you walking side to side!" I burst out at the top of my lungs, gaining a few weird looks and a laugh from Dot and Ethan. "Let's dance and see if we can find someone to . . . !"

A wide, knowing smile reappeared on Dot's face, and I slammed the rest of my cocktail back, smacked the empty glass on the nearest table, grabbed Dot by the wrist, and marched out toward the mass of writhing bodies.

Ethan stuck to our side like glue, his intimidating size keeping sleazy guys far away. At first he crossed his arms over his chest and just stood there, glaring at things as we danced, channeling his cousin a little too well. But after Dot and I poked him repeatedly until he cracked a smile, he gave in and started to dance. Surprisingly, he was pretty good at it. A few of Dot's other friends joined us too.

Every few minutes my eyes were drawn to the VIP area. Every single time, Josh, Tyler, or Alec was looking in our direction. Sometimes more than one of them would be casually leaning on the railing, sipping a drink. They were taking turns, swapping out every so often so it wouldn't be so obvious. At one point all three of them stood there, looking impossibly gorgeous in their collared shirts and their unique eyes and their perfect faces. I waved at them, and they all waved back at the same time in the exact same way, reminding me once again how close they were despite not being related by blood.

Tyler and Alec seemed to be hanging back more. I wasn't sure if it was a conscious effort on their part or simply because people gave Alec a wide berth wherever he went and Tyler refused to leave him alone. Probably a combination of both. They were deep in conversation every time I spotted them—not the light, laughing kind you usually have in a club, but the heads bent and eyebrows furrowed serious kind.

Someone delivered another round of drinks to the dance floor, and I managed to down most of mine without spilling too much as the music changed to a more sultry rhythm, the beat deeper and slower.

A flash of white to my right caught my attention: Dot was dancing with Kyo. I smiled and nudged Ethan, pointing them out.

Several Melior Group operatives were present—some on security detail for specific Vitals, others for added security—but Alec's team were all off duty. Marcus and Jamie were nearby talking to a curvy blonde, but they were both watching Dot and Kyo as intently as I was.

The two of them were completely engrossed in each other, moving to the beat, their bodies inching closer and closer until they wrapped their arms around each other and started kissing! Ethan and I whooped, and Marcus and Jamie hollered from the other side. Kyo grinned against Dot's lips, and Dot just flipped me off, not taking her focus off Kyo for a second.

I got back to dancing but couldn't wipe the smile off my face.

Ethan stepped up behind me, placing one hand flat against my stomach and pressing his body against my back. We started to move together, our bodies swaying. I was tipsy but still had the presence of mind to make sure my Light was locked down tight. I covered his hand with mine and reached my other hand up behind his neck, bringing his head closer.

His free hand brushed my jaw gently, nudging it to the side, away from his face, and then he placed a feather-soft kiss on my neck. I dropped my hand and let it hang loose at my side as I bent my knees lower, arched my back a little more.

With my head turned, I realized we had an audience. All three of my other guys were at the barrier staring at us, their expressions indecipherable.

Ethan dragged his lips up the side of my neck, and I gasped, my lips parting as I kept my eyes trained on the others. Alec's hands on the barrier tightened, the muscles in his forearms popping, and a stormy expression crossed his features. He turned abruptly and stalked off. Tyler whispered something to Josh, took one more look at us, and went after him. Josh leaned his elbows on the barrier, settling in, and flashed me a secret smile.

A guy with bright blue hair and a full tattoo sleeve came up to him, and they started to talk. I looked away so we wouldn't get caught making eyes at each other while I dirty-danced with my "boyfriend."

We let the music hypnotize us, ignoring everything else. Ethan's hands trailed up my sides, his fingers tracing the curve under my breasts. Blessedly the music was loud enough to cover my groan. The several cocktails swimming through my bloodstream, the sultry beats of the music reverberating through my body, and Ethan's confident, smooth moves were just about unravelling any sense of propriety I had.

I turned to face him and pressed my body flush with his, wrapping my arms around his neck. He pushed one knee between my legs and pressed his lips to mine. We kissed and we danced, not an inch of space between us, and I couldn't help imagining what this would be like without any clothing in the way.

Deciding it was probably not a good idea to have sex in the middle of the dance floor, I reluctantly leaned away to give myself some breathing room. We shared a heated look and then put a bit more distance between us.

I looked around, hoping for a distraction. When I glanced toward the VIP area, the guy with the blue hair was still there.

Josh was keeping an eye on us while also maintaining a conversation with the stranger, but there was something off about their body language. I cocked my head, distracted. Behind me, Ethan froze, and I turned to look at him, the question in my eyes. He cringed slightly.

"Who is that?" I asked, raising my voice over the music.

"Uh . . . Just an old . . . um . . ."

An uneasy feeling settled into the pit of my stomach. I turned back to

Josh, and he looked as awkward as Ethan sounded. To the casual observer he would have seemed fine—just having a chat. But I could see the tension in his shoulders, the way his usually careful, attentive eyes darted around the room. The guy with the blue hair was leaning into Josh as he spoke, gently touching his arm from time to time. He seemed interested . . .

My eyes widened, and I stepped out of Ethan's arms. He shoved one hand into his pocket, the other rubbing the back of his head as he eyed me warily. I crossed my arms and gave him a stern look.

He sighed, defeated, and leaned down to speak into my ear. "That's Ben. Josh's ex."

What? My mind wasn't sure what to do with that information. Was Josh gay? Was our Bond forcing him into a relationship he otherwise wouldn't have even considered? I didn't want that. I didn't want him to push down a vital part of who he was because of the stupid Light. Because of *me.*

I looked back at my beautiful, kind, observant Joshy, and my heart sank.

Was I about to lose another one of my Bonded Variants before I even had him? Was I reading them *all* completely wrong?

FOURTEEN

"Is he gay?" My voice was high and uneven.

Ethan chuckled and gave me an odd look. "Ben? Yeah, he's gay."

"I meant Josh and you know it."

"No. He's bi. Eve, you know how hot we are for you. He's mad about you."

Now that he mentioned it, I knew our attraction was mutual. I'd felt it on many occasions. Tyler and Alec fried my brain, I was so unsure of where they stood when it came to a romantic relationship, but Ethan and Josh had never given me a reason to wonder. They'd been into me, and all in, from day one. It was only alcohol-fueled insecurity making me question it. And yet . . .

I nodded and gave Ethan a reassuring smile before looking back at Josh. Ben was leaning right into him, saying something into his ear, his tattooed hand on Josh's shoulder. On *my* secret boyfriend's shoulder!

My eyes narrowed, and Josh saw me looking. He shook his head a little, warning me off. But it was too late; I needed to get to him.

"Shit!" Ethan yelled, taking off after me, but his big frame couldn't navigate the crowd as easily, so I managed to get to the VIP area before he had a chance to divert my attention.

As much as I wanted to, walking up and removing Ben's tattoo sleeve with a cheese grater would probably draw too much attention, so instead I headed to the bar, ordering another cocktail for myself and a soda for Josh. Ethan caught up to me just as the bargirl served me the drinks.

"God, you're fast," he said, sounding a little impressed. I gave him a devious smile as I grabbed the drinks and ducked past him, narrowly skirting past Tyler and Alec, who were walking in the opposite direction. Both of them shot me confused glances.

When I reached the railing where Josh was still speaking with Ben, I pasted a friendly smile on my face, then shoved the arm holding the soda between the two men. "Hey, Josh! I got you another drink. Who's this?"

They both stared at me as if I were a crazy person, and then Josh took the drink. "Uh, thanks, Eve. This is Ben. He's . . ."

Ethan came barreling through the crowd again. "Would you stop doing that?" he admonished me. Then he turned to Ben, his signature wide smile on his face and his hand out to shake. "Hey, man, how you been?"

"Good, good. You?" He shook Ethan's hand while giving all of us a confused look, finally settling on me. "And who's this?"

I inched closer to Josh, my arm pressing against his.

"This is Eve." Ethan pulled me away from Josh and wrapped his arms around me. "My *girlfriend*." He put a bit of emphasis on the word, trying to remind me that the rest of the world thought we were exclusive. I couldn't seem to find it in me to care, the Light-driven instinct pushing me to remove any perceived threat to my Bond. In this case, the perceived threat was a tall guy with blue hair, lots of tattoos, and sharp cheekbones.

"Nice to meet you, Eve." Ben smiled politely. "How long have you guys been together?"

Alec and Tyler chose that moment to join us.

"Oh, hey, the whole gang's here!" Ben smiled wide and greeted them both in turn, although he didn't shake Alec's hand.

They engaged him in conversation, diverting his attention from me and, thankfully, from Josh. After five minutes of this torture, Dot showed up. Ignoring Ben, she declared she needed me to come with her, extracted me from Ethan's iron grip, and pulled me toward the dark corridor leading to the bathrooms. I threw Josh a pointed look over my shoulder.

We rounded the corner and she released me. "So, I'm guessing you know that's Josh's ex?"

"Yep." I crossed my arms and tapped my foot, fighting the urge to run back there.

"You OK?"

"I don't know. What are we doing here?"

"I figured you guys needed to talk before the situation imploded."

"Yeah, probably. But that would require us to be in the same place."

"No shit. Don't get bitchy with me. He'll follow."

I flashed her an apologetic look. It was her birthday, and here she was dealing with *my* drama. She smiled back before looking over my shoulder and walking back out to the club.

Josh took her place in front of me, but I couldn't look at him, opting to focus on his very expensive shoes instead. They were deep red suede, and he'd combined them with black pants and a midnight-blue shirt, the dark hues accentuating his light features.

"Eve?" Josh sounded as unsure as I felt. He sighed and moved a little closer. "Please say something. Is it . . . Do you have a problem with the fact that I'm . . ."

"No!" My head whipped up, and my hands went to his shoulders. His green eyes were mesmerizing, dark in the dim lighting of the club. I'd never seen so much insecurity in them. "That's not it, Josh."

He nodded, still looking unsure, and covered my wrists with his hands, dragging them down to his chest.

"I mean, when Ethan first told me Ben was your ex, I thought you might be gay, and I was horrified the Bond was *making* you have feelings for me, but that's it. I don't care what label society puts on you. As long as this"—I gestured between us awkwardly, his hand still closed around my wrist—"is genuine and you don't have to be someone you're not in order to be Bonded to me."

"That's not what's happening here. I was attracted to you from the start, before I even realized what you were. Remember? In my room that night, the first time we kissed. How could I have known? That was pure chemistry."

I smiled and gravitated farther toward him. "I know. Ethan covered that too."

Josh rolled his eyes. "Ethan's been covering a lot of things I'd like to cover tonight." His eyes trailed unashamedly down my body, and I smiled, feeling better already. "So, if Ethan explained these things, what's going on? What was with the weirdness back there?"

I cringed.

"Eve." His voice had that slight scolding tone to it; he wasn't going to let this go. He released one of my wrists and ghosted his fingers down my jaw, tilting my chin up.

"Fine." I caved. "I was jealous." I put on the most stoic look I could muster, trying to hide my embarrassment "I know that part of it was Light-driven, this force that gets all agitated whenever it feels threatened. But I would be lying if I said it was all Light. I don't like seeing another person all over you."

He smiled, not mocking or indulgent, just open and loving. "I can understand that. I broke up with Ben last year. It wasn't working. Tonight he was hitting on me. He hopes we might be able to get back together, but I'm not even remotely interested. OK?"

I nodded and swallowed around the lump in my throat. The possessive jealousy, the worry, the happiness at hearing how he felt about me were all a little overwhelming. The four cocktails probably weren't helping either. I took a shaky breath, struggling to pull myself back together so we could go back to the party.

As if he knew what I was feeling, he flicked his eyes over my shoulder, in the direction of the music and flashing lights, then pulled me into himself, wrapping his arms around my waist and pressing a searing, determined kiss to my lips. He'd told me how he felt; now he was showing me, and it was exactly what I needed. The feelings Ethan had stirred on the dance floor slammed back into me with a vengeance, and I moaned into his mouth as his tongue found mine.

A booming laugh made my eyes fly open.

"So this is why you were so disinterested before, J. You're into girls now?" Ben walked into the corridor, some vaguely familiar blonde girl by his side. "Your best friend's girl, apparently." His eyebrows rose in surprise as Josh and I took a small step away from each other.

This was bad for our cover story. Really bad. But I had no idea what to say or do. Something in me demanded I stick close to Josh though, and since my brain had checked out, I went with my instincts. I wrapped an arm around his waist, pressing my side to his.

"This isn't what it looks like." Josh's voice was calm, even a little bored, his arm draping casually over my shoulders. It was a complete contrast to the tension in his muscles, which pressed up against me like stone.

"Really?" The blonde girl's smile was ecstatic as she tossed her perfectly styled hair. "Because it looks like *Eve* here is cheating on Kid. With you."

I recognized her. The reason I'd had trouble placing her at first was because I'd never seen her smile. The only time I'd seen her she was crying, sitting between Zara and Beth on the couch in my res hall.

"Anna?" Fantastic. Another ex to deal with. Wasn't one enough for the night?

"Oh, good. You remember me." She sneered, her face taking on a slightly manic quality. "You took my spot at Bradford, my friends, and my boyfriend, bitch. I want you to know it's *me* who took him away from *you* this time. Kind of poetic, don't you think?"

I frowned; she was clearly unhinged.

"Ooookay then." Ben rocked back on his heels, looking between the three of us. "Nice to see you, Anna. Nice to meet you, Eve. Josh, call me if you get over your boobs stage. I'm out. Bye." He turned and casually walked out of the corridor.

"Oh, this is gold!" Anna laughed heartily, waving goodbye as she sauntered away.

Josh cursed under his breath and ripped his phone out of his pocket, shooting off a quick text to Ethan. "Let's go. Time for damage control."

I followed him back out into the writhing, loud, craziness of the club, where we pushed past drunk people to get to Tyler at the bar. Josh leaned over and spoke quickly, pointing at me. Tyler's face fell and he nodded, his mouth forming a tight line.

Without looking at me, Josh took off again, leaving me with Tyler.

"This is all my fault." I groaned and leaned back against the bar, defeated.

"No, it's not. Something like this was bound to happen eventually. Much as I'd like to, it's impossible to control everything." He gave me a lopsided smile, and amused by his own dig at himself, I returned it.

"We can't control everything, but I should have at least been able to control myself."

Tyler shrugged. "The Light is a powerful force. It influences our emotions more than we realize, pushing us to act in ways that are truer to what we're actually feeling rather than ways that are . . . socially acceptable."

I was pretty certain he was referring to the fact that many Vitals ended up in romantic relationships with two or three people at once—their Variant Bond members. But why was Tyler bringing up polyamory in the Variant population now? Was he trying to distract me? The topic had been on our list of Variant studies subjects to cover for some time, but we always seemed to skip it.

Before I could dwell on it further, I was distracted by Alec. He was at the opposite end of the bar, ordering.

"You have got to be fucking kidding me," I ground out, my nails digging into my palms.

Tyler stood up straight, on the alert. "What?"

"Oh, nothing," I answered in my best sarcastic voice. "Just yet another ex for me to have an overwhelming and confusing reaction to."

My eyes glued to Dana as she stepped up behind Alec. She was in a black dress that revealed just the right amount of skin, somehow sophisticated and scandalous at the same time, and her dead-straight blonde hair accentuated the strong lines of her cheekbones. Alec hadn't noticed her yet. She leisurely looked him up and down in a predatory way, her eyes lingering on his ass. Then she wrapped her annoyingly sexy body around his from behind, whispering something in his ear.

His shoulders tensed when her hands first made contact, but he threw his head back and laughed at whatever she said.

Tyler cursed, his hand closing around my forearm, as if I might take off at any second to gouge someone's eyes out. I couldn't blame him.

Alec's eyes found mine, staring at me down the length of the bar. The crooked, mischievous smile slowly dropped from his face.

I turned away. I couldn't look anymore. My relationship with Alec was the most confusing of all. He had been there for me during some of the toughest moments of my life, in a way that was hard to put into words. Yet he'd been so antagonistic—avoidant and downright hurtful at the same time. I was drawn to him, yet he made me want to throw things. *At him.*

I didn't *want* to be attracted to someone openly hostile toward me.

Regardless, watching Dana's hands crawl all over him made my gut clench. Flashes of what I'd seen in the limo on the night of the gala kept popping into my mind, unbidden and disturbingly detailed. I knew what her bare ass looked like, and I really didn't want to. The thought that he could end up in that situation with her again tonight . . .

I faced Tyler, zeroing in on one particular button of his shirt as I tried to calm my breathing. One of my hands was resting on the bar, my fingers clenching and unclenching in time to my grinding teeth. Tyler's grip had loosened, and he was now rubbing my arm soothingly.

"Try to breathe, Eve." He lowered his voice. "Your Light is flowing like crazy."

"Shit!" I slammed my fist down onto the bar, drawing a few looks. I was fighting the urge to march over to Alec and cause another scene, to drag Dana off him by the hair. My control had completely slipped.

"Just breathe, Eve," Tyler soothed, taking a relaxed sip of his drink.

Once no one was looking in our direction anymore, he nudged me and led the way to a back corner of the VIP area. It was next to another smaller bar that was closed for the evening, and the lack of lighting provided some semblance of privacy.

I leaned on the abandoned bar as Tyler once again reminded me to breathe. Trying to get my Light flow back under control was, at least, a good distraction from what was happening at the main bar. I focused on my breathing, on the loud music, on the thumping base reverberating through my feet, and within a few minutes I had it contained again.

"Good." Tyler smiled encouragingly, and I smiled back.

Now that one potential catastrophe had been averted, the other one refused to be ignored. I tried, I really did, but I couldn't help myself. I turned to look.

They were gone.

My heart sank, a hint of panic sending adrenaline through my system. While I was having my Light overflow crisis, they'd left to . . . Ugh! I couldn't think about it. I turned to Tyler, hoping he could do something to distract me so I wouldn't go looking for him, but just then, Alec approached us through the crowd.

Relief flooded through me. He was here. He wasn't with her. But I didn't know how to express the clusterfuck of emotions that had slammed through me in the space of half an hour, so I switched to my default Alec setting—sarcastic and baiting.

"That was quick. I didn't take you for a one-minute man." I propped one hand on my hip and smirked at him in what I hoped was as cruel and detached a way as he so often smirked at me. "Or did you decide not to have slutty car sex tonight?"

His eyes briefly widened. "You're one to talk, precious. I'm not the one who's made out with two separate people in one night, in a very public place."

He crossed his arms over his chest and cocked an eyebrow, the scar becoming more prominent. He was in all black, as usual—black jeans and a black shirt that pulled tightly over the taut muscles in his arms.

"It's not the same and you know it," I spat.

"Guys." Tyler tried to get between us. "Don't start. We've got enough fires to put out for one—"

"Oh, don't I know it!" Alec cut across him. "I just turned down a sure thing for . . ." He waved his arms up and down in my general direction. "I don't even know what!"

Tyler sighed, rubbing the bridge of his nose. "I guess we're doing this, then," he muttered.

"Wait. Did you reject Dana?"

"Yes, OK?" He stepped closer, but I stood my ground, squaring my shoulders and looking up to meet his stormy eyes. I'd never seen the blue in them look so dark. "Yes. You want to know what happened? She came on to me, in no uncertain terms. I mean, we could have been . . . like, right now. But no. I said no to the only woman I've ever met who makes me feel normal. Because of *you*."

He ground the last bit out between gritted teeth, punctuating his statement with a stab at my chest. He left the finger there, leaning in as he continued. "I looked down the bar and saw you, with that broken yet somehow furious look on your face, and all I wanted to do was come over and wipe it off. Is that what you want to hear, Evelyn? That I watch you so closely I feel like I can read your mind? You want to know how I haven't gotten laid since Studygate because I can't *fucking* stop thinking about it? You want to know that if it wasn't for the fact that you gush Light out of every pore every time one of us touches you, I would be slamming you up against a wall and bruising your lips with mine? There, now you know!"

He finally dropped his hand and took a small step back. I hadn't shrunk away from him during his tirade. I'd frozen, my eyes wide with shock, but I'd kept my gaze steady on his and my feet planted.

The tone in his voice and the tension coursing through his body were palpable. He was furious. But in a fucked-up, intense, uniquely Alec way, he'd told me he wanted me.

I blame what I did next on the haze of desire that coursed through my veins at hearing his words. They were violent and slightly disturbing—he'd spoken about slamming and bruising—but they made me think of the way we'd all but battled each other on the couch in Tyler's study that night. Something had to be fucking wrong with me, but I wanted more of that. It made me feel alive.

I blinked, breaking the stare we were in, and my lips parted to release a shuddering breath. "If that's all you're worried about, I have a solution," I rushed out, barely considering what I was saying.

Ethan had run his hands all over me on the dance floor, and Josh's kiss had been exactly what I'd needed in that moment, but they'd both left me needing more. The Light was straining to strengthen my connection to each of them by any means necessary, and my body was providing the means, reacting to each touch, each look, each hint at deeper intimacy with a longing so fierce I had no idea how much of it was my own desire and how much could be attributed to our supernatural Bond.

Now, here was Alec, telling me in his own messed-up way that he desired me too. That it was only the Light transference that was holding him back. For the first time since we'd met, we seemed to want the same thing, and for once I had a solution.

I glanced at Tyler, then reached out to grasp his hand in mine. "Accidental transfer is not an issue for at least a few hours after I've expelled excess Light to Tyler. It would be perfectly safe for us to . . ." I trailed off, partly because in my rush to explain how we could get it on, I hadn't properly considered how to phrase it, and partly because Alec's eyebrows shot up in surprise.

"You can't just . . ." Tyler stared at our joined hands, his brows creased. "I'm not . . . how can you . . ." He looked up at me, his mouth forming a tight line, his eyes turning hard. He wrenched his hand out of mine, making me tip to the side and grab on to the bar for balance.

"You know what? Screw you both." He gave each of us a stern look and then stormed away, shoving Alec with his shoulder as he passed.

I turned to Alec, completely confused. "What the hell just happened?"

He looked as deflated as I felt, his shoulders drooping as he watched Tyler disappear into the crowd. But unlike me, he didn't look confused.

"Fuck." The curse was not an outburst of emotion. It sounded resigned and defeated. Instead of answering my question, he went back to the bar and ordered a drink, giving me his back.

I'd been dismissed and rejected, and I still had no idea why. I needed to get out of this club and away from all these people and all this noise. My best bet was probably to try to find Ethan or Josh, so I headed toward the main club area. Just as I reached the velvet rope, Alec appeared, halting me with one hand around my wrist.

I tried to twist out of his grip, but he rooted me to the spot with an intense look.

"Where are you going?" he demanded as his grip loosened.

"Anywhere but here."

"Ethan and Josh took off a while ago, trying to fix the clusterfuck you three created tonight. They're meeting us at the apartment. And Tyler is going to need some time to get over the fact that his Vital just made him feel used. So we're stuck with each other, precious. I'm the only protector you have left tonight, and I'm your only way home."

"Used?" That was the only thing he'd said I could fixate on. Just the suggestion I'd made Tyler feel bad was giving me an awful tightness in my chest.

"Don't worry. It wasn't just you. I fucked up just as badly. I should never have asked him to keep his distance for my . . . Never mind. The point is, every man has his limit. You trying to use him so it would be safe for us to fuck was his limit."

He shoved my coat—which he must have collected at the bar—at me before taking the lead toward the exit. I followed, absentmindedly putting my coat on as my mind processed what he'd said.

As we emerged into the cold night, the full realization of what I'd done hit me.

"Fuck!" I pulled up short on the sidewalk, shoving my hands into my hair and ruining the perfectly sleek style.

Alec turned to look at me, his expression annoyed.

"Oh, I am such an *asshole*!" I whined. Alec wasn't my first choice of confidant, but he was the only one there.

"Don't worry about it. I'm an even bigger one. Let's go before we freeze." He nudged me forward with a firm hand on my lower back.

I crossed my arms, partly to ward off the cold and partly to stop myself from crying.

Tyler had been there for me from the beginning. Before he even knew I was his Vital, he'd been willing to help me with excess Light flow. He'd taught me about the Variant world, guided me through an incredibly confusing part of my life, and been a solid, constant presence I could always rely on. And I'd taken him for granted.

I didn't even think about how he would feel when I reached for him to expel Light so I could fulfil a physical urge. Of course he felt used.

Despite my best efforts, as we stepped into the warm, brightly lit lobby, my tears spilled over. I turned my head away from Alec and tried to surreptitiously wipe the wetness from my cheeks, but I couldn't stop my shoulders from shaking a little.

As the doors of the elevator closed, shutting us away from the prying eyes of the doorman, Alec surprised me by wrapping one big arm around my shoulders. He pulled me into himself and sighed heavily. The unexpected gesture of comfort made me cry even harder, and I leaned into him.

"It's going to be OK, Evie. He'll get over it. This is mostly my fault anyway."

I had no idea what he meant by that, but before I had a chance to ask, the elevator doors were opening and he was stepping away from me.

As he unlocked the front door of their apartment, another thought struck me.

"Fuck!" I yelled into the quiet hallway.

"God, you have a mouth on you tonight." Alec looked back with a mixture of amusement and worry. "What now?"

"Dot!" If it wasn't bad enough that I'd made Tyler feel like crap, I'd completely forgotten about Dot. "We just left her there. We have to go back! I am a terrible person."

I made to march back toward the elevator, but Alec grabbed a fistful of the back of my coat.

"Dot came home half an hour ago with Kyo. They left around the time you were propositioning me at the bar." He nudged me into the apartment as he spoke, punctuating the last sentence by closing and locking the door. "She's in her room, but I wouldn't go checking on her. I don't know what you might walk in on."

With that, he stalked off down the dark hallway and disappeared into his room.

I trudged to another of the rooms, my irritation with Alec returning. He'd been nice in the elevator—sweet even—and then he had to go and ruin it by making baiting comments about me propositioning him.

I was pissed off at him, but I went to bed more pissed off at myself than anyone else.

FIFTEEN

The next morning I was equally looking forward to and dreading seeing Tyler.

They'd come in about an hour after us, and I'd lain there in my giant bed and expensive sheets, straining to hear what they were saying in the hall. All I could make out was the low bass of Ethan's voice, the whispered responses from Tyler.

Then the door handle rattled. I'd locked it, and after a heavy pause, two sets of footsteps moved away. I couldn't stand to have Ethan and Josh hold me, comfort me, make me feel better when I knew Tyler was down the hall on his own, feeling like shit. Because I'd *made* him feel like shit. I rolled away from the door and stared at the beautiful city view, my silent tears soaking the pillowcase.

I'd hardly slept all night.

The large windows were letting in the morning sun as I slowly walked into the living space, wringing my hands. Everyone was already up.

Ethan and Josh were in the kitchen making breakfast. Dot was curled up in an armchair by the windows, a mug of coffee in her hands, looking out over the city. Tyler had his head in his phone, eating a bowl of cereal at the dining table. Alec was nowhere to be seen. The only noise came from the kitchen and a news program playing softly on the TV.

Ethan spotted me first.

"Morning, babe," he said in a much more muted tone than what I was used to. He came over, dropped a kiss on my head, grabbed a frying pan from a drawer near me, and got back to what he was doing.

I kept my eyes trained on the dining table. Tyler froze, his spoon halfway to his mouth, his thumb midscroll. For a beat he just stared at nothing, and then he lowered the spoon and the phone and took a few deep breaths, still refusing to look at me.

Indecision rooted me to the spot, my heart hammering in my chest. I had no idea how to fix this, how to make him understand I hadn't meant to hurt him.

Josh must have been watching me as intently as I'd been watching Tyler, because he stepped up behind me and placed a firm hand on my shoulder. "Don't overthink it," he whispered before kissing me softly on the cheek and giving me a gentle push toward the dining table.

I took a deep breath and cleared my throat. "Ty . . ."

He shot out of the chair. "I have to go," he declared in a flat voice, stuffing his phone into his pocket and walking toward the front door.

I panicked. I couldn't let him run out again. I jumped into his path, hands held wide as if I were wrangling velociraptors, and yelled, "Stop!"

Amazingly, it worked. He huffed and put his hands on his hips but still wouldn't meet my eyes. "Move, Evelyn," he demanded in a quiet, cold voice.

"No," I replied in a much shakier one. "We need to talk. Can we go into the other room, please?"

"I have nothing to say," he told the lamp behind me, every muscle in his body tense. Despite his original statement, however, he had quite a bit to say. "I shouldn't have waited this long to tell you I want you in the exact same way the others do. That's on me. But even if I didn't, even if *you* don't feel attracted to *me* like that . . . I'm not going to be your supernatural contraceptive. I am not OK with that."

My jaw dropped. I knew I'd hurt and insulted him, but I hadn't expected him to tell me he was attracted to me. As fast as joy raced through me, it was snuffed out by anxiety. Just because he was attracted didn't mean he wanted to act on it—not after I'd wounded him as much as I had. I *needed* him to forgive me, for things to be OK between us again; my skin crawled with the knowledge I'd hurt one of my Bond members.

"Fine, then just listen." I dropped my arms to my sides tentatively. He still seemed ready to bolt at any moment.

He rolled his eyes. As controlled as he usually was, Tyler could be a little juvenile when he was hurt. But I really had no right to judge his reaction. "I don't want to hear—"

"I'm sorry!" I cut over him loudly.

He crossed his arms, his brow pulling down stubbornly. He still wasn't looking at me. His body language said he didn't believe me, but considering his ability, he had to know I was telling the truth. I guess emotional pain can be a powerful distraction.

"Ty, just use your ability. *Please*. Tell me if I'm lying."

His eyes started to dart left to right, his mind calculating.

I kept speaking, hoping I'd appealed to his rational side. "I'm sorry about the way I treated you last night, Tyler. Am I telling the truth?"

With a huff, he nodded, a quiet "yes" falling from his lips.

It was working! "I'm sorry I hurt you. Am I telling the truth?"

"Yes." A tiny bit louder.

"Knowing I made you feel used or unappreciated has made me feel completely gutted. Am I telling the truth?"

"Yes." But his eyes were still locked on a spot on the ground behind me.

"Tyler, I appreciate so much all you do for me. The lessons, the Light transfers, your protecting me, *everything*. I would be lost without you. Am I telling the truth?"

"Yes." A slightly defeated tone this time, and he dropped his arms to his sides. I was getting through to him, but it wasn't enough.

I didn't want to go back to the way things were.

Tyler had built his defenses up so high I had a better chance of cracking Alec again. But he needed to know I wanted intimacy with him as much as I did with the others. I needed to bring this issue we'd been skirting around for months into the forefront. I tried not to think about everyone around us listening as I steeled myself for my next move.

"I care about you. Am I telling the truth?"

"Yes."

"I enjoy your company. Am I telling the truth?"

"Yes."

"I think you're an amazing, intelligent, caring man. Am I telling the truth?"

"Yes."

"I'm . . ." I faltered, incredibly nervous, but I had to get it all out. "I'm attracted to you. Am I telling the truth?"

Finally his head whipped up, and he looked at me, his gray eyes intense. "Yes."

"I like you, Tyler, and not because of all the things that have forced us together. I like you for *you*. Am I telling the truth?"

"Yes." A tiny twitch of his lips pulled them into a near smile.

"I want *you*. Am I—"

"Yes," he cut across me before I could finish my question, taking two long strides forward. With determination, he cupped my face in his hands and pressed his lips to mine.

Finally, *finally*, Tyler kissed me! I'd wanted this since the day we realized we were connected, and now, at last, it was happening. He was knocking down that barrier between us. I didn't even care that three other people were in the room watching us make out; I was so fucking happy to finally touch him how I really wanted to, to have him touch me.

I clasped my arms around his middle, leaving not even an inch of space between us. He deepened the kiss, leaving one hand cradling my cheek and pressing the other to the curve of my spine, making me arch my back. His tongue darted out, and I didn't even hesitate, opening my mouth and embracing every level of deeper connection to him. He was an amazing kisser, his lips soft but firm on my mouth, his tongue finding a steady rhythm against mine.

For minutes, or maybe hours, Tyler kissed me as though he was in the desert and I was a waterfall. It was intoxicating. My Light flowed freely in and out of me; I didn't have to worry about containing it with Tyler.

I was giving in to my desire in a way I couldn't with the others, and it was consuming my mind and my body, making me completely forget where we were. I lifted my right leg slightly, wanting to wrap my body completely around his. The hand that had been holding my face flew down to grip the back of my thigh firmly. I moaned into his mouth and started thinking about where the nearest flat surface was. I wanted more; I needed to feel him on top of me. Maybe the floor would be fine. Marble tiles were totally comfortable.

But thinking about the floor made me remember where we were. Tyler must have realized the same thing, because we reluctantly broke apart.

I found myself staring directly into Tyler's eyes, the gray almost swirling. I'd seen the amber in Ethan's and the green in Josh's just as alive plenty of times, but during the many instances Tyler had willingly taken my excess Light, I'd never been close enough to see it in him so clearly.

I was mesmerized, and he looked away first, his eyes darting around the room. He removed his hand from my thigh and took a measured step back, and I followed his lead. The chair by the window was empty. Dot had slipped out to give me some privacy with my Bond.

Ethan and Josh were standing shoulder to shoulder, staring at us with varying degrees of shock and excitement playing over their expressions. I started to feel a little awkward. I wasn't ashamed of my attraction to Tyler, but I was worried about how this decidedly more physical development between us would make them feel.

By equal measure, I was also a little . . . excited. To know they'd been watching us sent a jolt of confusing arousal through me. I decided to examine it later, but before I could say anything, a fire erupted in the kitchen.

It wasn't Ethan losing control of his ability; the bacon grease in the forgotten frying pan had ignited. Before I even had a chance to react, Josh made a small hand gesture, turning the knob controlling the burner to the off position. Ethan, glancing back almost absently, made a lazy swipe of his arm, and the fire went out.

A big smile crossed my face. Tyler stepped up behind me, wrapping his arms loosely around my front. I looked up to see him beaming at Ethan. Both of us had realized something the other two hadn't caught on to yet. Their focus was on Tyler's arms, so casually draped around me.

"Kid," Tyler said, his voice excited. "Do you realize what you just did?"

Josh realized it before Ethan. He gasped and turned to face him, his finger pointing to Ethan and then to the stove. "Dude! You put the fire out."

Ethan's confused eyes flicked between us and Josh. Slowly, the crease between his eyebrows smoothed out, and his face broke into a big smile. "I put the fire out . . . I put the fire *out*!" he repeated, much louder, and laughed excitedly before jumping and punching the air.

Ethan's excitement was infectious, and I found myself laughing with him, folding forward a little at the hips. But that resulted in my ass bumping back against Tyler, and the evidence of his arousal pressed into me for the briefest of moments before he took a step back, clearing his throat.

"This is great, Kid." Tyler moved next to me. "We should practice—"

"Oh, I don't think so!" Josh cut across him. "You don't get to deflect from talking about that little show you two just put on."

"Can't we deflect for just a little longer?" I shot him a pleading look. I didn't want to overanalyze it.

"No," Josh and Ethan answered together, standing side by side again, presenting a united front. My shoulders slumped and I huffed.

"They're right, Eve," Tyler said, the ever-present voice of reason. "If Anna has anything to do about it, everyone will be gossiping about what she saw. We need to get on the same page, and we need to get ahead of it."

He walked over to the dining table, sat down in the chair he'd abandoned earlier, and looked at us all expectantly. The three of us joined him, me dragging my feet, trying to delay this as long as I could.

I really wanted to bask in the fuzzy feeling that had settled around my shoulders now that I'd deepened my Bond with Tyler. Kissing him had been like a daydream come true. I didn't want to ruin that warmth in my belly by talking about complicated things.

But my mind could never resist the opportunity to gain more knowledge, so I sat next to Tyler.

Ethan placed a plate full of waffles with berries and ice cream in front of me, and Tyler scooted his chair closer to mine, resting his arm on the back of it. He swiped my hair to the side and placed his gentle fingers on the nape of my neck. I smiled into my waffles, biting my bottom lip.

A simple touch was giving me butterflies. I shoved a huge bite of waffles into my mouth to cover up my embarrassing reaction. When Josh set a latte—made on a very expensive espresso machine they had in the kitchen—next to my plate, I finally looked up.

They were all watching me. Josh and Ethan were sipping on their own coffees across from us, and Tyler was just smiling, his eyes trained on my mouth.

I swallowed my food, and in the interest of not getting sidetracked by wondering what he was thinking while he looked at my mouth like that, I started the conversation I'd so wanted to avoid.

"What made you change your mind?" I asked, drawing Tyler's focus away from my mouth to my eyes.

He frowned. "What do you mean?"

"I told you how I felt about you because I couldn't stand the thought of you thinking I didn't care. I knew you didn't want me like that, but I needed you to understand that you matter to me more than you know. But what made you change *your* mind?"

"You thought I didn't want you like that . . ." A sad look crossed his face.

"Have you given her any reason not to, Gabe?" Josh's words were gentle, but they cut right to the crux of the matter.

"No, I suppose I haven't." Tyler sighed and half faced me in his chair, the hand at my neck beginning to stroke me softly. "Eve, I've always wanted you like that."

I frowned and took another bite of the amazing waffles. I didn't know how to respond; his behavior had told me otherwise for months.

"From the first day you walked into my office, I was attracted to you. But you were a student, and even with Bradford's lax attitude in regard to some staff dating students, it felt like I would be crossing a line of propriety to even consider it. Then we learned you were Bonded to Ethan and Josh, and I knew I needed to put your safety and theirs above all else."

His fingers kept up the gentle massage at my neck, and I kept eating my waffles, my eyes on my plate. I couldn't make myself look at him.

"When I realized we were Bonded too, I could have cried from happiness, but I knew immediately how much more danger we were in—how powerful you really are. I resolved to keep our connection restrained so you could have time to learn to control your Light, so these two could learn to control their dangerous abilities."

He gestured to Ethan and Josh. Ethan was leaning on his elbows, listening as intently as I was, and Josh was reclined in his chair, casually sipping his coffee, as if he'd heard this all before.

"The night of the gala"—at his mention of that night, my eyes whipped over to Tyler—"my resolve broke. You'd gotten closer to Ethan and Josh, and even me, in every other way, but that day, the physical connection stepped up a notch, and then you came down those stairs in that dress, and I just wanted to rip it off you."

I swallowed, the sweet taste of my breakfast still on my tongue, but I'd already forgotten how good it was. At his words, all I could think about was tasting his mouth again.

"I made the decision that night to pursue you romantically as enthusiastically as the others, and I'd deal with the consequences of the increased levels of Light. But then Alec . . ."

I cringed, looked away. The memory of what had happened between us that night still made me sick to my stomach. "And then I ran away, and then

Bradford Hills was invaded, and everything turned to shit," I deadpanned.

He chuckled, nudging my chin with his free hand until I was looking at him again. "Yeah, things got more complicated. And once the truth about Alec was revealed . . ." He sighed. "He asked me to keep my distance. He begged me to keep things platonic between us until he could deal with some of his shit. That night after you ran away, you slept in the arms of Ethan and Josh while Alec pleaded with me for time. Maybe it was the wrong thing to do, but I agreed."

I stared at him, eyebrows raised in growing disbelief. "Maybe? *Maybe* that was the wrong thing?"

Un-*fucking*-believable. Hours after promising to be honest with me, he had vowed to keep a massive secret. With Alec of all people.

"Oh shit," Josh whispered, sounding genuinely worried.

"Dude, even I know that was a bad move." Ethan shook his head. I looked between him and Josh, my eyes narrowed. It was a small relief to see they both looked just as shocked as I was.

"Tyler, you promised me no more secrets, and then you went and made another one." Just as quickly as the anger had risen, it dissipated, leaving me feeling deflated and hurt.

"Eve, I'm sorry." He took my hands in his and looked into my eyes, his gaze brimming with sincerity. "It wasn't my secret to tell. You don't know all that Alec's been through. You weren't around all those years to see how much he struggled with his ability, with losing you, with losing our parents. I was afraid I would lose *him*."

I pulled away from Tyler and stood, teeth clenched. My hands tightened into fists at my sides. "So you couldn't stand to lose him, but you could stand to never have me?" I ground out, tears blurring my vision.

"No!" Tyler stood too, his face determined. "Every second I stayed away from you, every moment I kept myself back, was torture, and I never intended to keep this distance forever. But I didn't do it just for him."

"Then *why?*" I hugged myself with one arm, wiping the tears away with quick, frustrated movements. I didn't want to be crying, weak.

To his credit, Tyler kept explaining, *pleading*. Alec would have stormed out in a huff ages ago.

"It was the right thing to do for all of us."

I wasn't the only one who huffed at that. Ethan and Josh added their protests to mine, and we all started speaking over each other.

The sound of the front door slamming broke the cacophony, and we all turned to look at Alec. He came to a stop halfway between the door and the dining table, taking the scene in.

"So you told her?" he asked in a calm, clear voice, removing his coat and dropping it over the back of the couch. There was no anger or resentment; he said it as if he'd expected as much.

"Yes. I kissed her too. I can't do this anymore, man." As he spoke, Tyler moved to stand next to me, wrapping an arm over my shoulders.

And I forgave him. I still didn't fully understand why he'd done it, but he'd apologized immediately, hadn't run away from a difficult situation, and now had my back, standing by his decision to be honest and to be with me. His actions spoke louder than his words, and I couldn't stay mad at him.

To my utter astonishment, Alec didn't rage and yell, storm out and push us all away. He nodded and took a deep breath. "I should never have asked you to do it in the first place."

He looked down and placed his hands on his hips, looking all kinds of awkward and apologetic.

But he hadn't actually said he was sorry.

"So that's it? You're not even going to apologize?" I crossed my arms and leaned into Tyler.

"I was getting there." His ice-blue eyes snapped up, his ire rising to meet mine, as it always did.

A loud, deep groan brought all our attention over to Ethan, who was looking up at the ceiling. "Can we not get into another screaming match, please? I feel like we have bigger fish to fry."

I was a little taken aback that Ethan, the goofball, was the one talking sense. The others must have agreed, because we all sat down again, Alec joining us at the head of the table.

"So how did things go with Anna?" Tyler asked, his hand returning to the nape of my neck.

But before the guys could fill us in, Alec interrupted. "Wait, I just . . ." He looked between me and Tyler uncertainly, his knee bouncing under the table. "I need to apologize to both of you. I am sorry . . ."

"We both made a bad call. Let's just move on." Tyler reached out, and they gave each other a quick hand squeeze while I stared in astonishment. That was it? *Men.*

I could only give Alec a little nod. I couldn't find it in me to speak the words. I wasn't sure if I meant them yet.

"Eve." Alec directed the next part just at me. "I know this doesn't excuse it, but I want to at least explain it. It's not easy for me to talk about this, but I do want you to understand."

When I didn't say anything, he took it as a sign to keep speaking. "Please just know it wasn't personal. I wasn't being malicious or deliberately trying to keep your Bondmates from you to hurt you. I just . . . you don't know how . . . I *hate* my ability," he finally spit out.

I leaned forward. Alec was showing vulnerability, being honest and real for once. I didn't want to blink and miss it.

"What do you mean?" It was the best I could manage to encourage him.

"They call me the 'Master of Pain' like it's something I lord over people—like I enjoy it. But I hate hurting people, and there is nothing I can do to switch it off. Having you . . . being with you, in your Bond, it makes my ability stronger. Eve, your Light is so fucking bright it's blinding."

I stared at him, at the intensity in his eyes. The way he looked at me, with so many conflicting emotions in his face, reminded me of the night in Tyler's study.

Even if it makes me an even bigger monster than I already am? His words rang through my mind, and they finally made sense.

Being with me, letting my Bond deepen with all four of them, would have meant amplifying Alec's ability—the thing about himself he despised the most. He was so stoic most of the time, so solid in his frame and posture, hard in his voice and actions. But underneath all that, he was suffering—had been for a long time.

I stared at him, not sure what to say, how to express that I understood but it still didn't excuse the lying.

"You could have just told me." My voice was low, sad. "Both of you."

"I should have." He nodded. "I didn't know how."

"And it wasn't my story to tell," Tyler piped in. "I'm sorry I deceived you, Eve. I am. But I've watched Alec struggle with this since we were kids. I've watched it bring him to the brink of destruction. It was too heavy for me to just blurt out to you. He needed to do it when he was ready."

"He was never going to be ready." Had they planned to just hold off sex with me for life for the sake of Alec's messed-up attitude? I got the sense the three of them had been letting him get away with a lot over the years. I wasn't about to fall into the same pattern.

"No, I wasn't," Alec agreed, "but it's out now, and I'm glad, because at least now I'm not hurting you both anymore. Regardless of my ability, I'm constantly hurting people." The last part was spoken more to himself as he sat back, dragging his hands down his face.

"If I'm being completely honest, that's not the only reason I held off getting physical with you, Eve." I turned back to Tyler, frowning. "I wasn't ready either."

"What?" Ethan said. He and Josh had been very quiet, letting Tyler and Alec put everything on the table, but they both looked confused at this.

I threw my hands up. "Do guys talk about anything?"

Tyler chuckled, catching my hand and pressing a kiss to my palm. "I never even thought I'd have a Vital. The . . . sharing thing is much more accepted in Variant society, regardless of whether you're in a Bond or not. But I kind of always figured I'd find that one person, and that would be it. I never expected I'd have to share you—and that's OK," he rushed to add. "It really is. I just needed some time to get used to the idea."

At the mention of "sharing," everyone went silent. I glanced around the table to see they were all looking at me, as if waiting for my lead. Josh had a smirk on his face. Fucker.

Yes, there were worries and insecurities about how we would make this work—how we would balance all the emotional scars, needs, and strong personalities without being at each other's throats all the time. But there were other thoughts too—dirtier, more difficult to verbalize thoughts.

I averted my gaze and squirmed in my chair.

"Are you guys done making out?" Dot chose the absolute perfect moment to interrupt. I loved her a little more for it, even as I wondered if she'd been eavesdropping; her timing was a little *too* good. "Because we really should talk about the 'Eve getting caught kissing Josh' debacle." She stopped next to Alec's chair and gave us all a withering look. "I love gossip, but you guys are doing a shitty job of keeping all this"—she gestured around the table with one hand—"a secret."

"Yes, we need to talk about that. Any news?" Tyler slipped back into his leader role seamlessly.

"Oh yeah!" Dot held her phone up as evidence. "All the news. You're trending, and it's not even ten a.m."

"Trending?" Alec asked, even as Josh groaned and Ethan started softly banging his head on the table.

"Hashtag ScandalAtTheClub, hashtag VariantSlut."

"Oh, Lord Kelvin." I dropped my head into my hands.

"What happened with Anna?" Tyler's voice still sounded even; I held on to that to keep myself from descending into full-blown panic. "Did you catch up to her?"

"We couldn't find her," Josh answered. "She left pretty fast, and we decided calling her would only add fuel to the fire, so we left it. Obviously that was a mistake."

"No," Tyler assured him, "it wasn't. Urging her to keep it a secret would only have given her more to gossip about. This way we can have some control over what we say about it."

"What do we do?" I turned my pleading eyes to my friend—the gossip expert.

Her lips widened into a crafty smile, and she tossed her messy black hair. It was still unbrushed from whatever she'd been doing with Kyo the previous night, adding to the slightly unhinged vibe she had going.

"We confuse the fuck out of them," she declared, as if it were obvious.

SIXTEEN

As I zipped up my boots and gathered my stuff for the first day of classes since Dot's birthday, I tried my best to remain calm. I'd woken up before my alarm, and worst-case scenarios had been running through my head all morning.

What if Dot's plan didn't work? What if no one believed us?

I hated being the center of attention. I'd spent my whole life learning how to disappear, and I much preferred the company of dead scientists. But what really had me taking deep breaths to calm my nerves was the thought of my Vital status coming out and putting us all in danger.

I could've really used some of Zara's no-bullshit straight talking—she would have told me to calm the fuck down with an eye-roll—but she'd left for an early class.

She'd asked me what happened as soon as I'd come home after Dot's birthday. Her stomach bug seemed to have completely passed, and she'd held her phone up to show me the gossip all of the vulture Variants of Bradford

Hills were eating up.

I told her the whole awful story, including the bits no one else knew about—how I'd been terrible to Tyler and come on to Alec. I told her about the kiss with Tyler too, barely concealing the grin on my face.

She agreed Dot's plan was probably the best course of action but did try to present another option.

"Have you thought about just coming clean?" She asked as we sat on the couch, sipping hot chocolate—it made us both think of Beth, in a good way. "I mean, maybe it's not worth the effort anymore. And you might be more protected if it comes out you're a Vital. They'd probably give you a Melior Group personal bodyguard."

She'd rolled her eyes, and we'd both chuckled, but she wasn't far from the truth. Most Vitals were under some kind of protection, especially at Bradford Hills. The Institute was probably the safest place for a Variant or Vital to be. But after talking about it for a bit, I'd dismissed the idea. The longer we kept this on the down low, the better. Especially considering how tenuous my connection still was to all my Bond members. We weren't steady enough to present a united front yet.

I put on my thick coat and took one final deep breath before opening the door. Josh was standing on the other side, his fist poised to knock.

He was in a peacoat, his dirty-blond hair parted on one side and styled meticulously, a Burberry scarf around his neck. He gave me a brilliant smile, flashing his perfectly straight teeth, and held up his other hand. "Hey. As your boyfriend, I figured it was my duty to bring you coffee."

"You bring me coffee all the time." I chuckled, taking the cup and inspecting it. "And the boyfriend thing is not new."

I was focused on the double helixes covering my new reusable cup. When I looked back up at him, he was smiling from ear to ear.

"What?" I smiled back, uncertain.

"I just like hearing you call me your boyfriend." He shrugged, taking a sip from his own reusable cup. His had the Rolling Stones mouth on a black background.

I pulled the door closed behind me and gave him a kiss. The taste of coffee on both our lips mingled with the warm, clean smell that always clung to Josh, and I sighed. "You know you're much more than that," I whispered against his lips, eliciting another smile.

Outside, I was glad for my coat and boots. The snow hadn't arrived yet, but the chill in the air announced it was just around the corner. As we walked toward the science buildings, some of the nervousness returned.

"What's going through that head of yours?" Josh leaned in as people started looking in our direction, not being at all subtle about the fact they were talking about us. It reminded me of the day my blood test results came out and every Variant on campus wanted a piece of me. All the attention made my skin crawl.

Unfortunately, Dot's plan hinged on us gaining that attention.

"I'm not entirely sure how to go about this," I admitted. "I don't like having everyone watch my every move."

"How about we just start with this?" He intertwined his fingers with mine, giving me another brilliant smile.

I squeezed his hand, double-checking that my Light flow was under control. If that slipped, the whole plan would crumble.

"It feels so good not to have to stop myself from doing that anymore." He kept his voice low, his words just for me. To anyone looking, we were simply whispering sweet nothings to each other, our hands locked and our sides pressed together, our steps synchronized as we walked.

"Guess this means Ethan's single again," a girl said to her friend, throwing me a smug look.

"It was only a matter of time," her friend responded, and they moved off, not waiting for a response. Not that I was going to dignify them with one. But my hand did tighten around Josh's, my baser instincts driving me to defend what was mine.

"Deep breath," Josh whispered. "We know the truth."

I nodded and did as he said, letting the cool air in my lungs push the mean comments out of my mind.

"I'll see you at lunch." He leaned in and kissed me. It was a chaste kiss in comparison to some of the others we'd shared, but it was still intimate, and it was in front of all the people walking past us into the building.

We separated, but before he had a chance to walk away, Dot marched up to us in black thigh-high boots and her polar bear coat, with a confidence I hadn't seen in her for a long time. She stopped right in front of me, a devious smile on her face.

"Hello, lover," she said at a volume that wasn't trying to be heard or hidden. Then she draped her arms over my shoulders and pressed her lips to mine in an over-the-top kiss.

I chuckled against her lips, and the kiss ended as abruptly as it had begun. She pulled me into a hug, and I returned it, but I wasn't expecting her to rub her whole body up against mine in a deliberately sexual move. If people hadn't been paying attention earlier, they certainly were now.

"What are you doing?" I whispered into her ear. "I don't recall this part of the plan."

"The plan was to confuse them," she whispered back, finally pulling away, "act so erratically that no one has any idea who you're dating or screwing or what the hell is happening."

"She's a little too good at this." Josh sighed, lowering his own voice. "But when you factor in the fact that you've been giving her your Light, I might actually be getting jealous."

He narrowed his eyes at us, but a smile was playing on his lips. He dropped one last kiss on my forehead and headed off, hunching his shoulders against the cold.

Dot looped her arm through mine, and we headed inside to our classes. People who'd been stealing looks before were outright staring now. A few even had cameras out.

I did my best to ignore it and focus on my classes, but I was on my own until lunch, and all the eyes on me made me feel vulnerable. At lunchtime, I speed-walked to the cafeteria.

Zara and I reached the entrance at the same time.

"How's it going so far?" she asked, not bothering with petty things like greetings and pleasantries.

"It's been half a day, and it already feels like torture," I deadpanned, removing my coat as she did the same. We picked a table and sat.

"Well, it's already working, if that makes you feel any better. Some of the rumors I've heard are ridiculous." She smirked, leaning forward so we could keep our voices down.

"Excellent." I rolled my eyes. It was what we intended, but I hated that there was an element we couldn't control.

Dot and Josh joined us soon after, and we were about halfway through our meals when Ethan made his entrance. No doubt it was by Dot's design that he arrived late, his big frame ensuring all eyes were on him as he came through the doors.

He paused, removing his bomber jacket as he scanned the crowd. He found our table and smirked, the dimple appearing for only a moment, but he moved off toward the food instead of joining us.

The chatter in the room lessened, everyone watching Ethan's every move as he piled his tray high with food, then marched straight over to us, his big shoulders pulled back, his eyes dancing. I could tell he was fighting laughter; he found the gossip as amusing as I found it frustrating and awkward.

He lowered his tray, deposited his bag and jacket in a chair, and faced Josh. Josh remained in his seat, one arm resting on the back of my chair, the picture of relaxed.

There was a moment's pause.

The two of them looked at each other.

The room held its breath.

"Hey, bro!" Ethan finally released his brilliant smile.

"What's up?" Josh reached his hand out, and they did some weird horizontal high five before fist-bumping.

I figured if we were going to do this, we may as well do it right. I stood up and wrapped my arms around Ethan's neck. He had to bend to meet me halfway, but we shared a brief kiss hello.

The room descended into confused murmurs. Some people went back to their food and conversations now that the drama they'd been expecting hadn't happened. Others started whispering.

I reveled in Ethan's warmth, the strength of his gentle arms around me, and used it to ground myself.

He stole my seat and pulled me into his lap, and we spent the rest of the hour talking about anything other than the plan we were, so far, flawlessly putting into action.

Two weeks later, Dot's plan was working like a charm. The attention had died down after some furious speculation about who I was actually dating. When no dramatic fights or breakups happened, everyone got bored and moved on to other things. I was no longer trending.

No one had even speculated that I might be a Vital; Dot throwing her attention into the ring had put a stop to that. Everyone knew Charlie was her Vital, and no one wanted to be reminded of the fact he was missing.

Even Zara had joined in the fun, walking through campus with me with our arms around each other. She probably only did it because she enjoyed glaring death at anyone who dared to look at us, but I was grateful anyway.

But there was one unexpected side effect of having the whole campus think I was dating multiple people.

The bitchy comments from girls when they realized Ethan wasn't actually back on the market and people calling me a slut were not a surprise. But the extra advances I received, just the sheer volume of attention, were a bit unsettling. I'd been asked out and propositioned more in two weeks than I had in my whole life before. Both guys and girls were coming up to me, some of them subtler in their flirting than others.

I would have thought that with most Vitals having multiple partners, the Variants of Bradford Hills wouldn't be quite so affected by the idea of someone dating more than one person. But I was wrong. So wrong.

As I headed to my next session with Tyler, yet another guy zeroed in on me, stepping into my path and waving. "Hey, girlie!"

I scowled at him. We were both bundled up in warm clothing, but I could see his face clearly. The last conversation I'd had with Franklyn was at Ethan's party, when he'd come on to me in the grossest way possible on the dance floor.

He kept pace with me as I sped past him. "No bodyguards today?"

The guys had been sticking closer to me than usual with all the extra attention; it hadn't gone unnoticed.

I didn't spare him a glance. The admin building was in view. "No, but I have snipers watching my move at every moment."

Franklyn faltered for a beat, his eyes scanning the bare treetops as if he actually expected to see a gun pointed at him. "Haha! Good one."

We reached the square housing the admin building. There were more people there, and I felt a little safer.

"So, I'm not really into guys, but I'd be up for a three-way with you and the short one with black hair. Her brother's dead, right?"

His words were so insensitive, so rude and presumptuous, that I actually did stop. I stared at him, slack-jawed, wondering how he didn't know Dot's name when they'd been in the same classes for years, how he could talk so casually about Charlie's disappearance, how he thought it was OK to say shit like that to a woman.

He took my pause as a sign to move in, and before my stunned mind could process what was happening, he was lowering his face as if to kiss me.

The invasion of my personal space snapped me out of my shock. A jolt of fear tinged with anger shot through my limbs, and I stepped back, shoving him with my hands flat against his chest. Adrenaline was coursing through me, my fight, flight, or freeze instincts settling on *fight*. My nostrils flared, and I bared my teeth as I prepared to shove him again, to tell him exactly where he could shove his callous comments.

But before I had a chance, his face scrunched up in pain, and he flinched away from me.

"Every time I see you near her, I'll zap you," a deep, angry voice said from behind me. "I won't even pause to find out if you're behaving yourself, understand?"

Franklyn looked as if he was considering fighting back, but then he just turned away and stalked off, rubbing a spot on his chest.

I turned around to see Rick scowling at Franklyn's retreating form. Electricity was still dancing between his fingers, but he snuffed it out as his gaze focused on me.

"Thanks." I didn't really know what else to say. Every time I saw him, the image of his electric ability slamming into Beth assaulted my mind.

He looked like shit. I hadn't spoken to him since he'd come up to me and Zara on the first day of classes, but I still saw him occasionally around campus. He kept to himself these days, seeming to focus more on his studies instead of goofing around with all the loud, athletic guys who hung around Ethan. He looked older too, more tired.

I knew Ethan still hung out with him occasionally, trying to be a good friend. He'd asked me if I was OK with it, and I'd told him he should follow his conscience; I just didn't want to hear about it or see it. I respected that he had a big heart and couldn't help seeing the good in everyone.

We were all still reeling from Beth's death, but as I stood in the square in front of Rick, feeling the cold wind whip my hair around, I realized it couldn't be easy to live with the knowledge you'd killed another person either.

"Anytime," he responded, then hesitated. He looked over my shoulder, then spoke again, his words coming a little quicker, his voice low. "I don't know exactly what you guys are playing at, but be careful, OK?"

"What?" I narrowed my eyes, leaned in a little closer. The hairs on the back of my neck were standing up, and it wasn't because of the cold.

"Just be careful. Watch your back. Don't be precious about your . . . friends being overprotective. You may have confused all these *children* with the show you've put on, but there are other people paying closer attention." He flicked his eyes over my shoulder again and backed away. "I have to go," he rushed out, turning to leave.

"Wait!" I grabbed his arm, and he flinched, hissing as if I'd hurt him, but he pulled a neutral mask over his features quickly. "I don't believe you meant to . . . I believe it was an accident." I'd meant to question him further, demand what he was being so cryptic about, but this had been in the back of my mind too long. Zara may have drawn strength from her anger, but I couldn't hold on to mine. Beth wouldn't have wanted me to.

He nodded once, the barest of smiles pulling at the corners of his mouth. Then he turned and rushed off.

The thud of boots on concrete made me turn back toward the admin building. Kyo and Marcus were jogging up to me.

"You OK?" Kyo demanded as Marcus kept his focus on Rick's retreating back, his hand on the gun at his waist.

"I'm fine." They both looked skeptical. "I'm fine, I swear. Stand down."

The pair relaxed visibly and chuckled at me.

"Only Alec can order us to stand down, kitten." Marcus crossed his arms over his chest.

"Technically, so can Tyler. And I don't know how Alec would feel about either of you calling me 'kitten.'" I raised my eyebrows at them. Alec was still keeping his distance from me, but he was pretty intense about my safety.

Marcus looked genuinely worried, even checking that Alec wasn't standing behind him, but Kyo just laughed.

I waved at them as I rushed off for my session with Tyler.

For the first time in weeks, I found Tyler alone in his office. No Melior Group operatives asking for direction, no Bradford Hills staff wanting updates, no Stacey being "helpful."

I dropped my bag by the door and removed my coat while he finished up a phone call.

"Perfect. Thanks, man. I really appreciate this." He sounded more casual than he usually did on official calls. He was standing by the window, one hand in his pocket, the sleeves of his slate-gray shirt rolled up, as always. "I'll wait for your call. Bye."

He hung up, dropped the phone on his desk, and turned to face me with a brilliant smile. I hadn't seen him smile like that since the day after Dot's birthday, when we finally kissed.

He'd been so busy and stressed, jumping straight back into work. But he was much more affectionate. The look he was giving me held all the warmth and caring it used to when our relationship was closer to friendship, but now it also held a little heat. He wasn't shy about letting his eyes trail down my body, checking out what was visible of my curves under the layers of warm winter clothing.

He also didn't hesitate to meet me halfway when I walked toward him.

I wrapped my arms around his neck, but he surprised me by gripping tightly around my middle and lifting me into a spin on the spot. I let out a startled whoop, and we both paused, our eyes flying to the door to double-check it was closed.

Then his lips were on mine, and I didn't care about anything anymore. His hands roamed up and down my back as we kissed, and I lost myself in the feel of him. I didn't care who might have heard me; I forgot about Rick and his cryptic warnings, Franklyn and his disturbing comments.

There was only Tyler.

I let my hands explore his back, feeling the tight muscles I'd noticed within minutes of first meeting him. I traced downward all the way to his ass. He had such a tight ass, and I'd recently learned I quite enjoyed groping it. Not that he minded. He mirrored my movements, dropping both hands to my ass and giving me a firm squeeze as he ground his very prominent erection into my front.

With a grunt he pulled away, resting his hands on my hips and raising a warning brow.

"Hey, you started it." I was unapologetic, punctuating my statement with another grope of his butt.

He was starting things whenever he could—we both were, as if we were making up for lost time. He constantly stole kisses in his office, pulling me into private corners of the mansion to get a brief hot moment alone. I reveled in being able to touch him, in being able to drop every guard and reservation with him.

"What's got you so excited? Not that I'm complaining." I finally released my hold on his ass, lifting my arms back to his shoulders. His messy brown hair had fallen over his forehead again, and I pushed it back, running my fingers through the soft locks. I was doing that every chance I got.

"I just heard from my guy at The Hole. He's made contact with the Lighthunter." He grinned, releasing me to return to his desk.

My heart jumped into my throat; I made myself swallow around the lump and respond in an even voice.

"Oh? That's great. When can you meet?" I had to be very careful about what I said. I'd just transferred a massive amount of Light to him; his ability would be hypersensitive.

"Hopefully next week. He's going to get back to me. I really have a good feeling about this." He turned back to me with some papers in his hands and sat in one of the chairs, gesturing to the other.

I took a seat, pulling my books out of my bag. "Well, I know I wouldn't bet against one of your feelings."

"Just have to wait and see what happens. Let's focus on what we need to get through for today."

Relieved he'd changed the subject, I forced my mind to focus on the textbooks and the academic discussion.

I waited until I was out of the building before texting Dot. We needed to get things in motion.

SEVENTEEN

The plan was simple. The biggest chance of it getting derailed was before I even made it out of Bradford Hills: I had to make it past the Melior Group guards posted at Dot's house.

I'd been doing more sleepovers at her place over the past few weeks instead of hanging out at the Zacarias mansion. We explained it as wanting more "girls only" time and invited Zara as much as we could, even though we hadn't told her what we were planning.

That night it was dumb luck that Zara had something else to do. Dot and I did the same things we always did—we ordered a pizza and watched a movie while Dot did my nails. But we were so quiet, knowing what was to come, that her mom asked us several times if everything was OK.

Eventually we headed upstairs and went through our usual bedtime routine. Then we shut ourselves in Dot's room and waited for the house to fall silent. Her mom's footsteps came past Dot's room a little after eleven.

"Are you sure about this?" Dot whispered. She'd been asking me some variation of that question ever since I'd clued her in on my plan, even as she procured everything I needed to make a fake passport and helped me pack my go bag.

"Yes." There wasn't an ounce of doubt in my voice. "For Charlie." That always shut her up.

Quietly, we got ready. Dot inserted bright pink and purple hair extensions into my hair as I applied heavy black makeup and fake nose and eyebrow piercings. It couldn't have been more different from my casual look.

I put on some of Dot's ripped-up, crazy clothes, slipped on my sneakers, and grabbed my duffel. It was small enough to not draw too much attention but big enough for the essentials.

"OK." Dot looked around the room, swallowing hard and taking another nervous breath.

I slipped the tracker necklace off. Holding it in the palm of my hand, I felt a pang of guilt. They would be so worried. And mad. Alec was going to lose his shit. And Ethan . . . I'd promised Ethan I would never leave him again, and here I was doing exactly that. I was a shit girlfriend.

I reminded myself I was doing this for Charlie. And Dot. My guys would understand once it was all over.

I pulled the note I'd written from my pocket and handed it, along with the tracker necklace, to Dot, and she hid them in a desk drawer.

I'd agonized over the note for a good hour, staring at the blank page with no idea what I could possibly write to make this easier for them. When I finally realized nothing I could say would alleviate their worry and anger, I decided to keep it simple.

I'm sorry.

Come find me.

I miss you already.

"Say it back to me," I whispered under the light of the one lamp we'd left on.

"I give the note and the necklace to Gabe. He's the only one who can't stop me or slow me down with his ability. I don't wait for him to read it or ask questions. I just tell him to use the Lighthunter, and I hightail it out of there. I camp in the woods for a night, and I keep this on me." She held up a disposable cell phone. I was the only one with the number.

I nodded. We'd gone over the plan a million times, but it made us both feel better to repeat it. With everything ready, there was only one thing left to do. Dot and I stepped closer and held hands. I closed my eyes and let the Light flow out of me while making sure none was allowed in to replace it. I'd been practicing this too—expelling all my Light to see how long I could go without it leaking back in and becoming unbearable.

It was difficult to test, as the guys constantly wanted to train and Tyler asked for boosts almost daily as he tried to puzzle out who was behind the kidnappings.

I'd managed to somehow get a stretch of nearly three days without transferring; that seemed to be close to my limit. By the end of the third day, I was feeling the itchiness at my wrists and ankles, the increased levels of energy, the pull toward my guys to release it.

"Twenty-four hours." I nodded, dropping Dot's hands.

"Twenty-four hours," she whispered back. "I'll come back after one day, and if the Lighthunter is bogus, you tell me where you are, and we come get you."

We stared at each other, then we hugged, holding tight.

"Thank you so much for doing this," she whispered, her voice shaky.

"Hey." I pulled back, my own throat getting tight. "None of that. We need to stay focused. And you can stop thanking me."

Because you're my family. I left that unsaid. I wasn't ready to verbalize it, but that's how I thought of them. It felt good to be so close to people, to feel so safe with them, that I could give them the same label my mother had—*family*. But on some level, it also felt like a betrayal of her.

But I couldn't afford to get into that now, to get emotional. My full focus needed to be on getting past the Melior Group guards posted outside and keeping my Light in check.

I put on a dark coat with a hood, and we quietly made our way downstairs and into the garage. The plan was to hide me in the trunk of Dot's hatchback and have her drive out, telling the guard she was popping out for snacks. The guards were there for general security, but anyone Tyler posted on duty near me was briefed to make me a top priority. If the guard thought I was still in the house, he wouldn't try to accompany Dot. I hoped.

In the garage, we left the light off and walked straight to the car. As Dot opened the driver's side and I reached for the trunk, the side door leading outside opened, and a light flicked on, illuminating the space in a harsh fluorescent light.

Dot's mom, Olivia, stood at the door, one hand clutching the handle, the other holding a half-smoked cigarette between elegant fingers.

"Mom?" Dot sounded outraged more than surprised. "When did you start smoking?"

"I . . . well, I quit a long time ago. But lately, with all the stress, I just . . ." The guilty look on her face melted away as she zeroed in on the bag slung over my shoulder, my new look. She straightened and crossed her arms, keeping the lit tip of the cigarette away from her fluffy white robe. "What are you two up to?"

"Uh . . ." Dot's eyes flew between me and her mom's. If their relationship was anything like mine had been with my mother, Dot wouldn't be able to lie to her. There was no point anyway. Even if we managed to convince her we were just going for snacks, she would insist on the guard coming with us.

"It's for Charlie!" I blurted out. Trying to convince her of some half-baked, last-minute lie would never work. Olivia was too smart and already suspicious. The only chance we had was to appeal to her own worry. Her own grief. Her own need to do whatever possible to find her son. "This could help us find Charlie. But we don't have a lot of time. Please . . ."

I wasn't sure how to finish. Her eyes narrowed, looking between me and Dot but eventually settling on me. "Explain."

"There's no time." The plane ticket was booked, and I had a narrow window to take a convoluted enough path so I disappeared before going to the airport. "I need to get to the train station without the nice men in black knowing. Then, hopefully, in a day or two, we'll know where Charlie is."

It was the best I could do, giving her as much info as I could without jeopardizing the plan.

"Evelyn." She sighed, flicking her cigarette. "I can't let you head out without a guard. It's too dangerous, sweetie."

She wasn't convinced. I was touched that she cared enough about me to want to keep me safe. It was so motherly . . . But once again I couldn't let myself think about mothers and family. I had a mission.

"I miss him, Mom." Dot's voice was low, but it broke on the last word.

She was standing by her car, her fingers clasped around her keys. Every bit of worry, grief, frustration, fear, and longing that Dot had felt since her brother and Vital had been taken was written all over her face. It was in her upturned eyebrows, her hunched shoulders, her glassy eyes. Every painful emotion she'd dealt with in private, or even tried to push down, came out.

"I can't do this anymore." Fat tears started rolling down her face, her breathing becoming labored. "I need him. I need to know . . . Charlie deserves this. We have to try."

Olivia's own expression was full of pain as she watched her daughter break down for her son. "Shit," she cursed under her breath. Then she took one last long drag of her cigarette and threw it to the ground, putting it out with her fluffy white slippers.

"Dorothy, go back inside." Her tone brooked no arguments. "Evelyn, get into the back seat of my Escalade. The windows are tinted."

Dot made a sound that was something between a sob and a surprised laugh, watching with wide eyes as her mother disappeared inside and came back a few seconds later with the car keys and her purse.

"Get in," she ordered, jumping into the driver's side and starting the engine, "before I change my mind." Dot and I exchanged one more meaningful glance, and I climbed into the back seat.

Olivia pulled out of the garage as soon as I closed the door. I covered myself with a blanket and crouched in the footwell for good measure.

At the gate, there was a quick exchange. Olivia said she was out of cigarettes and moved off without incident. The guard didn't even look in the back seat, hardly even giving her an answer past a polite "yes, ma'am." It was so easy. I hoped I hadn't just cost a man his job, but I couldn't afford to worry about that either.

"Where am I going?" Olivia asked uncertainly.

"The train station," I replied, making sure *my* voice sounded nothing but confident. "But park around the corner, on Baker Street." There weren't any cameras there to record which car I'd arrived in, and my altered appearance should be enough to keep me anonymous from the cameras in the station. Dot and I had cased the joint on one of our coffee dates.

She nodded and kept driving. It took only ten minutes to get there, and Olivia spent most of the time nervously adjusting her grip on the steering wheel and muttering to herself. "Must be out of my mind . . . so stupid . . . I should turn this car around . . . supposed to be the adult . . ."

But the car continued to move at a steady, sure pace toward the station, so I kept quiet.

When we came to a stop, her muttering stopped too. She remained facing forward, her breathing labored. "Maybe this isn't such a good—"

"It's for Charlie," I cut her off. "Mrs. Vanderford, Olivia, I need to do this for him. For Dot. For *me*. For all of us."

She finally turned to look at me, her eyes watering. She searched my face for a long time and then, as her tears spilled, gave me a tiny nod and turned back to the front.

I didn't wait for her to change her mind; Dot would make sure she didn't crack. I got out of the car and walked away without looking back, keeping my pace steady, my head turned down under the hood.

My train pulled in just as I made it onto the platform, and I chose a seat near the back. Other than one other guy in a safety vest—probably a shift worker—I was the only one to board. The train moved off, and the shift worker almost immediately fell asleep, his head propped up against the window.

I leaned back in my seat but kept my hood up and my face down. I spent the hour-long ride into the city fortifying my control of my Light and mentally going over the next steps, keeping a careful eye on the handful of people who boarded the train as we got closer to my destination.

But I couldn't help my mind wandering a little, remembering the last time I'd taken this trip. The two experiences couldn't have been more different.

When I'd tried to run away all those months ago, I'd been overly emotional, paranoid, and irrational, constantly looking over my shoulder and completely ignoring the amounts of Light pouring into me. I hadn't even had a go bag ready. I hadn't created a new identity in months!

This time, I was nothing if not prepared. I'd created a passport and other IDs, with the name Gracie-Lou Freebush on the perfect forgeries. I'd altered my appearance. The cash I'd been slowly withdrawing from my account and storing in the pages of my physics textbook was now tucked into my purse. I'd remembered every lesson my mother had taught me.

And I'd thought of every possible outcome. Some of them were more daunting than others, like the scenario in which black-clad men jumped out of the shadows with one of those black devices, identified me as a Vital, and made me disappear for real. But I'd never get through this if I allowed fear to enter my mind. I had to be brave.

I could do this.

I got off the train a few stops before Grand Central. It was easy to get lost in the jostling New York crowd and make my way outside, where I hailed a cab.

I spent the next hour taking several cabs and walking around between them in various directions. I changed my coat twice and put my hair up and down, altering my appearance when I could.

The last cab deposited me at World Trade Center station with just enough time to get onto the train heading to JFK.

Another uneventful train ride later, I was at the airport, making my way past more armed guards to get in line for passport control. My work was impeccable, and the man checking my ID hardly even looked at me.

Waiting in the departure lounge, another pang of doubt stabbed my gut. The guys would be pissed—and worried. And what if I was caught, abducted, killed? Maybe we should have included them in the plan. But they would never have agreed to it!

No, it was better this way. I shut my worries down and, after a tense hour, boarded the plane with the other tourists, businessmen, and families with screaming children. Before I had a chance to doubt myself again, we were taking off as the sun began to rise over New York.

New York to Melbourne is one of the longest routes in the world. I had to do two layovers, and one of my connecting flights was delayed, but thirty-five hours of travel time later, I arrived—tired, disheveled, and smelly. All I wanted was to collapse into a bed and sleep until my guys found me, but I couldn't let my guard down just yet.

I still had to get somewhere safe—somewhere without police and CCTV. But for that, I needed help.

After brushing my teeth and changing my top in the airport bathroom, I stuffed my jacket into the duffel bag—both to change my appearance again and because it was a hot day. I made it past customs and passport control without incident and took another paid-in-cash taxi to my old stomping ground of Fitzroy.

It was midmorning as I slowly rounded the corner. The café was two doors down, a post office and a milk bar separating us. I wanted to take it all in before making my move.

Greville's Café was our regular hangout when I lived in Melbourne. It took up two shop fronts in the middle of a small strip of stores located in a mostly residential area, a few blocks from my old school and within walking distance of both where I'd lived and Harvey's house. People drove out of their way for the best fair-trade, organic coffee in the city, as well as the homemade jam doughnuts.

At least a dozen alfresco tables were situated out front, boxed in by low planters with succulents. Several oversized umbrellas provided necessary shade—a respite from the harsh Australian sun.

Harvey was sure to come here at least once, although I worried he'd already been today and wasn't planning to come back. I had no idea what his schedule was. He'd finished high school the year before and would have started his graphic design course by now. It was all he could talk about when we were together.

I really didn't want to go to his house and risk his sister or parents answering the door. I couldn't hang out inside all day either—too many people I knew frequented the place. But loitering on the corner of a residential street all day would be way too suspicious.

I chewed my bottom lip, fidgeting with the strap of my duffel. The strong sun beat down on my back, making me sweat, and when my stomach growled, I decided to take the risk and go in.

The morning rush had ended, and I didn't recognize any of the few seated patrons. I ordered a cheese toastie, a friand, and a latte. The food came out before the coffee, but when the barista placed the little glass full of happiness down in front of me, I abandoned the sandwich and immediately took a slow sip. I moaned loudly, my eyes closed, as the exquisite, smooth, creamy flavor hit my tongue.

When I opened my eyes, the hipster barista was looking at me with raised eyebrows, fighting a smile.

I cleared my throat. "I really needed that—rough morning. It's really good."

"No worries." He chuckled, moving back to the coffee machine to make more liquid pleasure.

I stayed at my table for nearly two hours, ordering another coffee and taking my time with the food while pretending to read a magazine. But as the lunch rush started, I got worried about looking suspicious; I'd already drawn the barista's attention.

I paid with cash and got up to leave. Halfway across the room, the little bell above the door tinkled as two girls my age walked in, chatting. My heart flew into my throat. They'd gone to my school when I lived here and had hung out with us sometimes at Harvey's house. I cast my eyes down and hunched my shoulders, hoping my heavy makeup and crazy hair were enough of a disguise.

One of them glanced in my direction as we passed each other, but by some miracle, she didn't seem to recognize me.

I walked to the park across the street, on the opposite corner, and hid behind the slide, my heart hammering against my ribcage until they came out and strolled away. I stayed in the park to keep watching the café, praying to the universe Harvey would show up.

It was two thirty, the café buzzing with moms grabbing an afternoon caffeine hit before school pickup, when I spotted him. He was with two other guys I didn't know. *Uni friends?* I smiled to myself.

I wondered from time to time what might have become of Harvey and me had I not screwed up and started us on a course that changed my entire life. But I'd realized, ultimately, there was no avoiding that course. I was made for those four incredible, loving, frustrating men. I was their Vital, and we were always going to find each other, one way or another.

What I'd had with Harvey was superficial by comparison. I was sad about how it had ended—he would have been confused and scared when I just disappeared like that—but I harbored no unresolved feelings for my old boyfriend, just a strange kind of nostalgia and a hope that he was happy. Seeing him laughing and joking with friends made me feel better about it all.

I crossed the street again and stood around the corner, watching. When they came out of the café, takeaway cups in hand, I started to worry they would leave together and I'd have to go to his house. But his two friends took off in the opposite direction, and Harvey headed toward me.

I pulled back and leaned against the rough brick, my palms a little sweaty and not just from the oppressive heat. What if he was really mad and refused to speak to me? What if Variant Valor had somehow got to him, and *he* kidnapped me? What if he didn't remember me?

My paranoid thoughts were interrupted by their subject walking around the corner. He was in a Deadpool T-shirt, his backpack slung over one shoulder. He looked taller.

He was tapping away at his phone and didn't even notice me standing there.

"Harvey," I called out.

He pulled up, turning distractedly, his attention still half on his phone. He lifted his eyes to mine, a mildly curious expression on his face, before dropping them down to his screen again. Then he froze, his fingers tightening around his takeaway cup, his eyes flying back to mine.

Shock and disbelief were heavy in his raised eyebrows, his parted lips. "Holy shit." The words came out on a breath.

Suddenly unsure what to do, I gave him an awkward smile and a pathetic little wave.

"Holy shit, Eve!" That time he practically yelled the words, throwing his almost full coffee to the ground as he lunged forward.

"No need to waste perfectly good coffee . . . *oof*." He knocked the breath out of me as he enveloped me in his arms, giving Josh a run for his money when it came to lung-crushing hugs. He was definitely taller. We used to be about the same height, but now he had almost a head on me. His voice sounded deeper too. The boy who had been so many firsts for me had turned into a man.

I returned his hug, feeling comfort and nostalgia in his arms but not a scrap of the angst-ridden pining I used to feel. I'd found something much deeper with my Bond than Harvey and I could ever have had.

"Can't breathe," I managed to get out with the last bit of air in my lungs.

He released me only to grasp my shoulders and stare into my eyes. "My god. It's really you!" His volume was still high.

"Shh!" I glanced around.

His eyebrows pulled together in suspicion. "Eve . . ." He dropped his arms by his sides but kept staring at me as though he couldn't quite believe what he was seeing.

"I know this is a lot—me showing up like this."

"I . . . there are just so many questions. I don't even know which one to ask first."

"Do you hate me?" It wasn't exactly the question I'd planned to ask, but it had been playing on my mind since the night my mother forced us to pack up and leave. Of course he would have worried, but how long had that lasted? How long before he'd turned to anger, looked for someone to blame? If he still held a grudge, my chances of getting his help were significantly lower. Harvey could be almost as stubborn as Alec. Almost.

"Hate you? No." He chuckled, shoving his phone into his pocket. "Eve, I knew you would never leave like that for no reason. I could never hate you . . ." He looked a little awkward, and it struck me in that moment that we'd never actually broken up. It would be the logical conclusion after not seeing each other for over a year and a half, but technically . . .

I breathed a sigh of relief, choosing to focus on my current situation. The afternoon was slipping away and taking the light with it. I needed to get on the road soon.

"Harvey, I'm sorry for so many things, and I wish I had all the time in the world to explain them to you, but . . ."

"But you're in trouble." Tension returned to his posture.

"Kind of, I guess." I wasn't technically, but I could be. "I need your help."

"What do you need?" I knew he burned for answers, but he put that aside and was willing to do what I needed. He reminded me of Ethan in that moment; my big guy was the most selfless, caring person I knew.

I pushed the longing down, making sure to shut my Light flow down with it. "I need to borrow your car, and I need the keys to the Carboor house, just for a few days, and then everything will be OK." I didn't sound convinced, but I really hoped what I was saying was true.

"Who are you running from, Eve?" He stepped closer, lowering his voice. "Is it the same people as before? Is that why you left? Maybe I can help. Maybe we could call my uncle Steve. He knows some guys in the federal police . . ."

"No!" My voice rose. "Harvey, no police." I fixed him with a firm look, poised to just run away from him again if I had to.

"OK, OK. No police. Just please tell me what's going on?"

"I can't." I sighed. "There just isn't time. I need to get going before it gets too dark to navigate the dirt roads. Please, Harvey!"

I injected as much desperation into my look as I could. He watched me for a beat, then sighed and rolled his eyes, and I knew I had him.

"Come on then." He headed toward his green Range Rover. "Don't suppose there's time to get another coffee."

"I wish." I looked longingly back toward the source of the best coffee I'd ever tasted.

EIGHTEEN

Harvey drove in silence, and it almost started to feel awkward, but his house was really close, and we were pulling up in no time. I took in the big eucalyptus tree in the front yard, the red mailbox, the curving path to the front door. It looked exactly the same as when I used to come over after school, and another pang of longing shot through me for something that almost was but never really could have been.

Harvey wasn't getting out of the car. "It's getting late, Eve. It could be dark by the time you get out there. Maybe you should just stay the night. Mum and Dad won't mind, and Mia will be ecstatic to see you—"

"Harvey," I cut him off, "you can't tell them I'm here." The fewer people knew I was in the country, the safer. Plus, while Harvey had talked about his family's holiday property often, I'd never been and would be relying on GPS to get me there. I needed to get going.

It had been over forty hours since I'd left. Dot would have told my guys about it by now. If the Lighthunter was legit, they were probably already on a plane on their way here. I needed to be somewhere isolated, and I needed to stay put until they found me. It was safer for me—away from creepy little Vital-identifying machines—and it was safer for the general public; I wasn't sure how well I could control the amount of Light that would come gushing out when we reunited.

"Will you explain things after . . . whatever this is? When you bring my car back. You *will* bring my car back, right?" He flashed me a smile, but it didn't reach his eyes.

"I'll do my best to explain it all." I owed him that much.

Harvey nodded, got out of the car, and walked up the curved path. I shifted over to the driver's side and fastened the belt, ready to head off.

He came back after ten minutes, just as I was beginning to panic he'd blabbed to Mia. But he emerged on his own, carrying a bag and a cooler. He dropped both in the back before coming around to the window, playing with a set of keys.

"I packed some extra supplies for you."

"Thank you, Harvey. For all of it."

"Just be safe." He handed the keys to me.

Not knowing what else to say, I nodded and started the engine. He stepped away from the car as I moved off. I could see him for a while in the rearview mirror, watching me drive away.

Once I was past the rush-hour traffic of the city and on country roads, the rolling hills in shades of muted green and brown soothed my nerves. No cars followed me out of the city, and Harvey's GPS guided me toward my destination.

The sun had set by the time I had to navigate the dirt roads on the approach to Harvey's vacation home, so I put the high beams on and took it slow, looking out for wombats and kangaroos. I finally arrived around nine, unloaded the car, took a quick shower, and collapsed into the first bed I found, not willing to walk even the few extra steps to the master.

It had been over forty-eight hours since I'd slept in an actual bed, and I was beyond tired. I fell asleep as soon as my head hit the pillow.

When I woke up to the sound of kookaburras outside the window, my arms and legs were itchy. I'd done my best to keep the Light at bay, but there wasn't much I could do while I slept.

I groaned, getting out of bed. After another long shower, I removed my brightly colored extensions and got dressed in shorts and a tank top; even though it was only ten, it was already sweltering hot. Scratching at my arms, I rifled through the supplies Harvey had packed. The extra bag had spare blankets, flashlights, a first aid kit—the kind of things I'd need if the car broke down. The cooler had food.

Thank the Milky Way. Food was the one thing I hadn't thought about. If my ex-boyfriend hadn't raided what looked like half his fridge, I would've had to drive into town, and I couldn't risk being seen or having the guys find me there.

Ten minutes later, I was sitting on the porch with a plate of scrambled eggs and bacon, a mug of instant coffee (it would have to do) next to me. I took my time eating, watching the birds fly from tree to tree and breathing in the warm air. The beautiful view helped me focus as I tried for the millionth time that morning to bring my Light flow under control.

But the itchiness had already spread to my shoulders and hips, and it wouldn't be long before it reached my torso. I had no doubt that within twenty-four hours, I would be glowing like a Christmas tree.

Sighing, I took another sip of coffee, turned on the phone only Dot had the number to, and dialed. It had barely started ringing before she answered.

"Are you OK?!" my crazy friend shouted down the line, startling a flock of birds that had settled into the branches of a nearby tree. I cringed, pulling the phone away from my ear. Then I chuckled.

"Yes, Dot. I'm fine. Everything went to plan. Are you OK?"

"Oh, thank fuck." She sighed. "Yes, just . . . just wait, Mom . . ." I could hear Olivia in the background. "I'm talking to her . . . She's fine . . . You can't talk to her because *I'm* talking to her . . . Mom!"

I laughed, listening patiently to scuffling sounds on the other end of the phone, followed by a door slamming.

"That woman has been driving me mad. I had to take her camping with me so she wouldn't blab. You owe me for that one."

"I am eternally in your debt."

"You put your life at risk to help me find my brother—we can call it even."

"Haha! Deal!"

"So how you holding up?"

"I'm fine. No issues getting here, but my Light levels are starting to get uncomfortable. What happened after I left?"

"Well, I didn't sleep all night. Partly because I was worried sick about you and partly because Mom was worried sick about you. She regretted her decision, like, immediately. She walked through the door and started freaking out, and the only way I could keep her from running off to Uncle Lucian was to answer her million questions. Thank god Dad is away or this whole plan would've imploded the second he saw her."

"So rough night, then?"

"Yeah, you could say that. The next day I somehow managed to convince her to come camping with me. So we drove to campus, and I made her stay in the car while I waited for Gabe. He showed up with Alec."

I cringed. "Shit."

"Yeah. Shit. So I pretty much threw the scrunched up piece of paper at him and sprinted to the car, and Mom and I sped out of there. But, man, was he pissed."

"Who?"

"Who do you think? Gabe just stood there frowning at the note, but Alec . . . the words coming out of his mouth made even me blush. I could hear him loud and clear despite the fact that we were already driving away."

"So are they on the way? Did it work?" I needed to know if it had all been for nothing. I'd never received the call from Dot—the one we'd planned on if the Lighthunter was bogus and I had to tell them where I was—but I needed to hear it.

"Well, after another sleepless night in the woods, once again courtesy of my mother—I mean, I had a bear guarding us from all the dangerous animals, but apparently that made her uncomfortable. I swear . . ."

"Dot!" I laughed, the itchiness creeping up my collarbones momentarily forgotten.

"Anyway, I called them in the morning, and they were already in the air. I spoke to Josh. Gabe was busy ordering people around, and the other two were pissed and refused to speak to me."

"Ethan was pissed?" I knew he'd be hurt and worried, but I'd never seen my big guy lose his temper.

"Yeah. Punched a hole in the wall, apparently."

"Shit."

"Yeah, you're in *so* much trouble."

I groaned. "How did they know where to go, Dot?"

"The Lighthunter." She sounded excited. "Josh said they drove to The Hole immediately and demanded to know where to find her from Gabe's contact. The guy needed a little persuading, but he spilled eventually." I didn't want to know what kind of "persuading" they'd done, but I could guess. "Then they went straight to wherever that was, and within an hour they were in the air. So how's your ex?"

I spluttered, dribbling coffee all over myself as I laughed and coughed at the same time. "What?!"

"Well, Josh said they were heading to Australia. I figured you hit the Aussie up for some help. Is he still hot?"

"Yes. I mean, no! I mean, yes, I did ask Harvey for some help, and when it comes to his level of hotness, I don't know. I don't look at him like that anymore. I have three new boyfriends, remember?"

"Four boyfriends," she replied without missing a beat, and I rolled my eyes. "Alec has issues, but he's into you. Trust me. And bitch, please! You cannot tell me that you reunited with a guy you've seen naked and didn't appraise whether he got hotter or notter."

"Notter?" I chuckled.

"I'm coining a new term. Just roll with it."

"You know what? This conversation has turned pointless. I need to go burn some of this Light off."

"Fine. Be like that. Just don't get eaten by a kangaroo out there."

"Aren't you supposed to be an animal expert? You know kangaroos don't eat humans, right?"

"Oh, hey, my mom is calling me. Gotta go!"

"Whatever." I was barely containing my laughter.

Before I could actually hang up though, Dot spoke again, her tone much more serious. "Thank you for doing this, Eve. I love you."

"I love you too, Dot."

"Good luck with your boyfriends."

"All three of them? Thanks!"

"Fou—" I hung up before she could get the word out.

I propped my feet on the railing and sipped my coffee, smiling to myself. Now that I knew my guys were on their way, I felt much more relaxed, despite the itchiness.

It had worked. The Lighthunter was real, and we might actually have a chance at finding Charlie.

After a punishing, hour-long run, I jumped into the shower to wash away the dust of the dirt trail. As I headed into the bedroom, wrapped in a towel, my hair piled on top of my head in a messy bun, I heard the distinct sound of a car engine.

That can't possibly be them yet. Fear spiked, making my stomach clench, my spine straighten.

I peeked out the window at the dark truck approaching, leaving clouds of dry dust in its wake. It was too late to make a run for it. I had no way of getting away, and they were already pulling up next to Harvey's Range Rover.

I pulled the towel tighter around myself and swallowed around the ball of fear that had lodged in my throat, making it hard to breathe, talk, or scream.

And then all four car doors opened at once, and I breathed a sigh of relief.

The mental walls I'd so diligently constructed were instantly dust, pulverized by the mere sight of my Variants within touching distance. The itching was all over my body, but now it wasn't just itching. My skin felt as if it were humming, practically vibrating with the amount of Light straining at my seams.

To my dismay, a soft glow illuminated my skin, making me look like a nightlight. It was the first time since the invasion my Light overflow had gotten this bad. The glow faded and then intensified again, appearing and disappearing as though it weren't sure if it wanted to be there yet. But I couldn't waste any more time.

I rushed onto the porch as they all piled out of the car. I was down the few stairs and halfway to them before I realized Tyler and Alec both had their guns out.

My steps faltered. "It's OK. We're safe here . . ."

They ignored me. Everyone was moving forward, but none of them were looking directly at me except Ethan. He was the only one heading straight for me, and he was the only one unarmed.

"Stop!" Tyler's commanding voice halted them all. "No one fucking touch her until I do. I can practically smell the amount of Light coursing through her body. Alec, Josh. Perimeter. Kid, watch her."

I huffed and rolled my eyes. "This really isn't nec . . ."

But the three of them had already moved off. Only Ethan stayed, his gaze never having wavered from mine.

A fifth person had also exited the car, but I barely registered what they even looked like. My focus was on my big guy.

His shoulders were hunched, his huge chest heaving, his fists clenching and unclenching. He looked as if he was a split second away from ignoring Tyler's command and launching himself at me. I knew because I felt the same way. The Light inside me was throwing its full weight against the inside of my skin, reaching with outstretched hands to get to one of my Variants.

But it was his face that kept me glued to the spot. His eyes were blazing, and considering his ability, that was scary in itself. He somehow looked both furious and scared at the same time.

I really just wanted to hold him, but I tried speaking to him instead, my voice soft. "Hey, marshmallow."

Apparently now was not a good time for our nickname game. His lips pressed together, and he looked away, staring at the gravel by his feet.

My heart cracked in two, and I couldn't wait any longer to go to him, to try to wipe that devastating look off his face. But before I could take a step, Alec's serious voice sounded behind me. "Clear."

"Clear" came Josh's reply, followed by his footsteps pounding down the stairs.

"Clear." Tyler finished off the routine, but it was *his* voice, the voice of my logical leader, that sounded uneven, insecure. I turned to face him, completely shocked for the second time in fifteen minutes. He was striding toward me, tucking his gun into the back of his pants.

Alec and Josh were halfway between me and the house, Alec's hand on Josh's shoulder, as if to hold him back. But Tyler was demanding my full attention. He took me in his arms, one hand banding around the middle of my back, the other splayed flat against the bare skin above the towel. My hands instinctively flew to his neck.

We both grunted at the force of the Light that gushed out of me and slammed into him as soon as we made contact. And then he kissed me—one searing kiss, filled with all the intensity of the moment. Too soon he pulled away, but he didn't let go. If anything, his grip on me tightened, his fingers pressing into my skin.

"Don't hold back." He panted into my mouth, his lips nearly on mine again. "Let me have it all. I want it all."

I had a feeling he wasn't just talking about the Light, but I didn't have a chance to think about it; my body was already reacting to his words. Lifting onto my toes, I pressed my lips to his and pushed my tongue into his mouth.

He responded, kissing me with a passion I hadn't felt in his kisses before but had sensed all along, underneath his careful control.

He broke the kiss again but only to pick me up and hold me against his chest as he turned and walked purposefully toward the house. I wanted to lift my legs and wrap them around his waist, but I remembered just in time I was in nothing but a towel, and my ass was already an inch away from being exposed to the Australian countryside, as well as our other companions. So I left my legs hanging, bending them at the knees to avoid kicking Tyler in the shins as he went up the steps.

I lifted my head just as Tyler carried me into the house.

Josh's eyes were glued to the spot where Tyler and I were touching, and the envy in his narrowed eyes was warring with another emotion, one that had his lips almost twitching into a smile.

Alec was watching my face, his hand still on Josh's shoulder, and his expression could not be mistaken for anything other than longing. The intensity in his ice-blue eyes as they met mine surprised me and confused me so much that I had to look away.

I only caught a glimpse of Ethan before Tyler carried me deeper into the house. He was still standing in the same spot, still not looking at me.

I ached for them. Each of them. I wanted to comfort Ethan, reassure him I was OK. I wanted to make Josh's smile break through, prove I wanted him as much as any of them. I even wanted to wipe that look of longing off Alec's face, show him he could have what he longed for if only he would drop his stubbornness, reach out, and take it.

I wanted to be touching them all. But I was touching Tyler, and that was nothing to complain about.

He carried me into the bedroom. His hands were everywhere—fast, frenzied—as if he didn't know where he wanted to touch me first. He was more out of control than I'd ever seen him, his breathing ragged, his blue shirt crumpled.

I pushed his messy hair back, threading my fingers through his soft locks as he came in for another kiss. I got completely swept up in the taste of him, the smell of his cologne mingling with a hint of sweat, the feel of his perfect body against mine, his greedy hands grabbing my arms, my back, my waist, my ass.

We ended up on the bed, Tyler half on top of me. One of his legs pushed between mine, and I could feel his arousal pressing into my side. I moaned into his mouth. After all those months of being sure he didn't want me in the way that I wanted him, feeling the evidence of his desire was the ultimate turn-on.

I hiked my leg over his hip and drew him even closer, wedging my hands between us to access his shirt buttons. I had half of them undone before he broke the kiss, his breathing uneven. His gray eyes were bright, almost silver, and swirling.

"Why"—his voice was low and strained—"are you wearing a towel?"

He was holding himself above me with one arm, but his other hand was gripping my hip, his fingers flexing and relaxing on my bare flesh. The towel had come completely untucked, and the whole right side of my body was exposed.

"I wanted to be naked when you all got here." I meant it to come out more lighthearted than my breathy voice and swollen lips made it sound. Tyler's eyes narrowed, and he groaned, dropping his forehead to mine.

"Kidding." I chuckled. "I was in the shower and . . ." I didn't bother to finish, focusing instead on what my hands were doing. I undid the top button on his black pants and dragged the zipper down, sliding my hand inside his underwear.

The silky-smooth skin was warm in my hand as I wrapped my fingers around him and started to stroke. His eyes closed, and his hips started to move in rhythm with my hand.

He trailed his fingers up my side, over my shoulder, and down my front. He paused at my breast long enough to give it one firm squeeze that made my back arch off the bed just a little. Then he moved lower.

I dropped my leg off his hip to give him better access. His fingers reached the spot where I wanted them most, spreading the moisture with slow, deliberate movements that made me falter in my strokes, and then, as he started to push his finger in . . .

"Gabe!" the hard, almost growl-like quality in Alec's voice was punctuated by loud thumps on the bedroom door.

"Fuck," Tyler whispered against my lips. He pushed his finger in the rest of the way in one swift move, swallowing my exclamation of surprise with one last searing kiss. Then he pulled away, extracted my hand from his underwear, and left me panting and naked on the bed.

He fixed his pants and ran a hand through his hair as he opened the door a crack, murmuring something too quietly for me to hear.

Alec's voice wasn't quiet at all. "You have two minutes."

Tyler shut the door and turned, his hands going to the buttons on his shirt, but he paused when he noticed I hadn't moved.

"Much as I love this view," he growled, pausing to bite his lip and rake his eyes all over my nakedness, "you need to get dressed. The others are getting impatient."

I took a deep breath, relishing the way his eyes followed my chest's rise and fall. Then I got up and pulled on some shorts and another clean tank top.

He moved to open the door. "It's probably better that we stopped."

"What?" I halted, his words bringing back every insecurity I'd ever had about his feelings for me. Did he regret taking our relationship to this new physical level? Was I a disappointment? "I thought we were past this shit." I somehow managed to get the words out on a firm, annoyed tone, my arms crossing over my chest.

"Oh, Eve, no . . ." He abandoned the half-open door and faced me fully. "I'm not saying I wanted to stop."

"OK . . ." What was he saying, then?

I had a feeling this was related to what we'd briefly talked about the morning after Dot's birthday: Alec's conflicted feelings, Tyler's getting used to sharing me, both of them needing time. Maybe I just needed to be more patient? But I kept my mouth shut, waiting to hear what he had to say.

"It's just . . . the physical stuff is a little complicated. You know how intense and steady the Light transfer is when you're touching us, especially in that way."

"Yeah." I propped my hands on my hips. "Stop being obtuse. It's not your style. Spit it out, Ty."

He smiled and wrapped his arms loosely around my waist. I returned the embrace, resting my hands on his shoulders and doing my damnedest not to let his proximity distract me.

"When you give to one of us—when you share your affection and your Light—the others are naturally drawn to you. When the"—he paused, searching for the right words—"pleasure is received by you, it's a little easier to resist the urge. But when it's *given*, it's almost impossible. It's like my ability has a mind of its own, instincts of its own, and it demands I claim you—get my share of the Light and the attention that comes with."

My mind went to the night of the invasion, when Alec had refused to let me touch him in the way he'd touched me, refused to let me give him the kind of pleasure he'd given me. He wasn't just denying me the closeness I craved; he was making sure the others wouldn't have extra temptation to cross the same line. I wasn't sure if he was being thoughtful or selfish. Once again my feelings toward Alec were ambiguous.

"So you're all refusing to let me pleasure you because you know the others will be tempted too?" I arched a brow, skeptical.

Tyler chuckled but nodded. "That, yes, but also . . . Eve, I'm trying to be mindful of you. Of what you are and aren't ready for. It's—"

"That's my decision to make. Not yours." Who did he think he was to decide when I was ready to have sex?

"I'm not trying to control you!" Tyler wasn't quick to anger, but he wasn't one to back down when he believed in something. "I'm just trying to give you the space to make that decision yourself—to not have it made for you by the pull of the Light. Eve, there's four of us. Once you cross that line with one, the other three won't be able to resist much longer. You won't be able to either. Are you sure you're ready for that?"

My immediate gut reaction was "Yes! Sweet baby Einstein, yes!" But I didn't speak. My instincts were screaming at me to jump him, tear his clothes off, and deal with the consequences later. But my pesky logical brain was throwing up all kinds of doubts. Like how it could be dangerous if my Light control slipped. Or how I wasn't entirely sure Alec wanted it. Or how I wasn't sure I wanted it with *him* after the way he'd treated me. I wanted the physical—the way he made me feel was undeniable—but did I want all the emotional baggage that came with the physical pleasure?

"We're just trying to give you time." Tyler smiled reassuringly before giving me a kiss on the forehead. "At least some of us are," he mumbled under his breath, and it made me smile.

It also made me realize I had yet to have a proper reunion with the rest of my Bond.

I followed Tyler out of the bedroom only to find Alec stalking across the living room toward us.

"Well, at least you're dressed this time," he grumbled, crossing his arms. "I can't get Kid to move or speak or anything. He's starting to freak me out. Fix it, precious."

I ignored his pompous attitude, already brushing past him on the way to my big guy.

NINETEEN

Ethan was still in the same spot in front of the car, his shoulders tense, his gaze fixed on the ground.

I marched right up to him, my heart aching, but he wouldn't meet my eyes. I'd expected him to be upset with me—he'd been the most hurt when I'd attempted to run away the first time—but I hadn't expected this.

"Ethan? Talk to me," I pleaded, petrified I'd pushed him too far—that yet another one of my Bond connections was about to fracture—but I knew he needed more than words.

I burrowed up against him, pressing my face into his chest and tucking my arms under his to wrap them around his waist. The back of his shirt was damp with sweat, and I could feel the tension in every rigid muscle. But it was the million-miles-per-hour hammering of his strong heart under my cheek that took my breath away.

He was scared.

My eyes started to sting, an unbearable ache growing in my chest that had nothing to do with the Light.

"I'm sorry," I murmured into his white T-shirt.

I pulled away only long enough to lift onto my toes and move my arms upward. He still wasn't looking at me, but his body was responding to mine, his head dipping so I could reach his neck.

I took it as a positive sign and forged on, doing what felt natural. I lifted one leg, winding it around his hip, and then held on tight to his shoulders as I lifted the other too, wrapping myself around him completely.

His hands remained by his sides, so I ended up clinging to him like a monkey. I didn't care how ridiculous I looked or that my arms were already starting to ache from the effort. I'd hang there all day if that's what it took to wipe that heart-wrenching look off his face.

"I'm sorry," I murmured again into his neck and pressed a soft kiss to the same spot. His breathing shallowed, his big chest jostling me with every inhale.

My thighs were already in a jellylike state from what Tyler had done between them. My legs started to tremble, and I slipped just a fraction, nearly losing my grip. I caught myself, but Ethan moved in the same instant.

The sensation of me slipping away from him once again, even a tiny bit, was enough to break whatever spell he was under. He took a sharp breath as his arms finally flew around me. One went to my ass, holding me up, and the other banded around my back.

His head dipped, and he took a long inhale before mirroring my action and lightly kissing my neck. His lips lingered as I spoke again.

"I'm so sorry I put you through this again, baby. I wasn't running away from *you*. I was only trying to help save Charlie. I would never run away from you again, ever."

He sighed, his breath against my neck sending goosebumps over my entire body despite the stifling heat—and despite the fact that every inch of me was flush against someone who was known to spontaneously combust from time to time.

He pressed his lips once more to the same spot, darting his tongue out just a little before trailing his lips up the side of my neck, across my jaw, and over to my mouth. He kissed me, pouring all his frustration and fear into it. I kissed him back with all I had, pushing my tongue into his mouth, crushing my breasts against him, grabbing a handful of his hair.

He needed me to show him I wanted him as much as he wanted me, but I did it because it felt right.

Someone cleared their throat.

"I hate to break this up"—Josh's quiet, steady voice made us pull away from each other—"but we have company."

Ethan's eyes finally met mine, and I was more than relieved to see a smile pulling at his mouth. I pressed one more quick kiss to his full lips, and he lowered me to the ground.

I kept my hands on his shoulders. "Are we OK?"

"Not by a long shot." His usually booming voice was pitched low and ragged. "But I'm glad you're safe."

Before I could say anything else, he grabbed me firmly by the hips and turned me to face Josh.

Josh's green eyes were practically shining in the bright Australian sun, and his gaze was making up for the way Ethan's had avoided me.

He didn't come to me as Tyler had. I didn't go to him as I'd known Ethan needed me to. No, with Josh, I was always on an equal footing. We leaned into each other at the same time, and he pulled me into one of his bone-crushing hugs.

I dropped my forehead to his shoulder. Ethan let me go, even encouraged me to go to Josh; he knew that's what we both needed. But he stayed close because that's what *he* needed. I could still feel his heat behind me, one of his hands on my hip.

Josh pulled back, threaded one hand into the hair at the base of my head, and kissed me. I returned the kiss with all the intensity he was throwing into it.

He grunted and stepped forward farther. My back connected with Ethan's chest as the evidence of Josh's arousal pressed into my front. Solid as always, Ethan didn't lose his footing; he only lifted his other hand to grab my hip, his fingers seeking out the exposed skin above my shorts.

Knowing Josh was hard and ready to go made me want to drag him into the house to finish what Tyler had started—maybe grab Tyler on the way too. My desire, my need for them, was dizzying. I didn't even think before I arched my back, rubbing my ass against Ethan. The hardness I felt there as he met my grinding motion with one of his own proved he was just as ready.

I was trying to decide whose shirt to remove first when Josh broke the kiss. I gave him a questioning look, both of us breathing hard, and he licked his lips and glanced over my shoulder, having one of his silent conversations with Ethan. Ethan took a deep breath and squeezed my hips one last time. Then his searing heat at my back disappeared.

It helped sober me up. Tyler was right; I was having trouble controlling my sexual impulses, and I couldn't entirely be sure if it was my own desire—the estrogen, dopamine, and oxytocin my brain was releasing—or the Light that was driving it.

I also remembered the extra person. My eyes widened, and I backed away from Josh while still keeping my hands on his shoulders, not quite ready to let go. I was a little surprised to see Tyler standing close on my left, his hands on his hips, his body blocking us from the striking woman behind him.

He gave me a smile and a little nod, and I turned back to Josh.

He had that knowing look in his eyes. Of course Josh would have been aware Tyler had come over to give us some semblance of privacy while the three of us pawed at each other like animals with no impulse control.

I kept my eyes locked on Josh's, reveling in the connection we shared, but his smile slowly dropped from his lips, his eyebrows knitting together as he searched my face. "When are you going to stop running?"

His words hit me with the weight of an eighteen-wheeler. The question cut to the core of who I was as a person.

I'd spent my life running, spurred on by my mother, her eyes always looking over her shoulder. But I'd run from her too, hiding things about myself I knew she would disapprove of—like Harvey. I'd grown so much since meeting my guys, but I was still running from some things. Like the fucked-up situation with Alec and what that meant for the rest of us.

Josh watched me intently as half-formed thoughts and conclusions ran through my mind. But after a moment he simply kissed me on the forehead and stepped out of our embrace. Now was not the time for that conversation.

He turned to face Tyler and cleared his throat. "Eve, this is Nina. Nina, this is our Vital, Eve."

Tyler stepped out of the way so I could face the woman, the Lighthunter, properly. She was tall and had an athletic build—the toned muscles in her arms and midsection making her every movement seem effortless—and her complexion was a rich umber. The black hair on her head was buzzed very short, but her graceful movements and the delicate lines of her face and hands made it impossible to mistake her for a man. She was wearing a red crop top and tan pants with rips all over them.

She looked right at me with almost black eyes and smiled wide. "So this is your Light? Hello." She spoke with a heavy French accent. "Nice to meet you."

"Nice to meet you too." I stepped away from my guys, extending my hand in greeting. If I could blush, I would have. She'd seen every kiss, heard every moan, as I reunited with my Bond. "Sorry about . . . uh . . ."

"Not to worry." She shook my hand. "I am well acquainted with the dynamics of Bonds."

"Right. Because you're a Lighthunter?"

She nodded with a small smile.

"Nina has more than proven she's the real deal," Tyler said, placing a hand at my lower back and making me sigh with pleasure. Even though I no longer felt as if the Light were about to burst out of my skin, tearing me apart in the process, something still felt off; there was still an *almost* pulling sensation in my chest.

"You scared your Bond half to death. I don't know what they would have done to me had I refused to locate you." Her words were ominous, but she looked very amused. Then her smile faltered as something behind me drew her eyes. "Why do you not reunite with all your Bondmates?"

"What?" I'd never heard the term *Bondmates*, but it was obvious she was talking about my Variants. Specifically the one Variant I had yet to properly deal with.

"Your Light clearly flows through him, but it is dim. The connection is strained." Her gaze wandered to the spot on my chest right where I could feel that dull ache. I raised my hand to rub at it, not particularly wanting to discuss with a total stranger the clusterfuck that was my relationship with Alec.

She stepped forward and gently pulled my hand away, immediately replacing it with hers. My eyes widened, and my mouth opened to say something, but all that came out was a small gasp of surprise.

"So much tension . . ."

For some reason, I felt compelled to explain it to her. "Yeah, Alec and I, we—"

"Not just that one thread," she interrupted. "All your threads are tense.

Your Bond is unsteady."

"What? No . . ." I knew where I stood with the others. I knew where I wanted our relationships to go.

"Yes." She chuckled and dropped her hand. "You are all connected. You are *as* one. But you are *not* one. If there is tension with one Mate, there is tension with the whole Bond."

"Oh . . ." The complicated situation between Alec and I was making things more difficult with the others too. They felt they had to take sides at times, and hadn't I just had a conversation with Tyler about why they were holding off on physical intimacy?

"Why does he not come to her?" Nina asked Tyler.

"He doesn't feel it would be received well. And he doesn't think he deserves it. It's complicated . . ."

"Oh, for Galileo's sake." I rolled my eyes and marched over to where Alec sat on the steps. If we could just hug it out and mute this annoying ache in my chest, maybe we could all get on with the important stuff—finding Charlie.

I stopped in front of him, determined, tiny puffs of dust settling around my feet. He had his head in his hands, his fingers digging into his scalp, his elbows resting on his knees. It reminded me a lot of the first time I'd seen him. He'd been sitting exactly like that in the corner of my hospital room after he'd saved my life.

Suddenly, I found myself wanting more than a means-to-an-end hug. I wanted him to look at me with those ice-blue eyes and speak to me with the honey in his voice.

I wanted the man who'd been kind and made me believe I wasn't alone in the world. Not the one who had been cruel to me, ignored me, and pushed me away. I was finding it increasingly difficult to reconcile the two.

"Alec," I said uncertainly.

He looked up, his eyes searching mine, his expression somehow simultaneously vulnerable and angry. "I know that I . . . I'm sorry . . . I just . . . fuck!"

He leaned back and looked up, rubbing his thigh with one hand. His other was tightening and relaxing rhythmically around something in his fist.

Usually he bailed well before this level of emotion was allowed to surface.

He reached out as if to touch me but pulled his hand back. I shuffled my feet, unsure.

Then I huffed—at him, at me, at this whole situation. My gaze zeroed in on his clenched fist and the delicate sliver string peeking out from between his fingers.

I reached out and covered his fist with my hand, and his nervous movements stilled. Using both hands, I uncurled his fingers to reveal my necklace—the tracking device. I took it and slipped it over my head.

His striking eyes followed my movements. I gripped the little silver rod pendant with one hand and placed the other back in his still upturned one. His calloused fingers closed around mine immediately.

I gave him a nod, hoping it conveyed what I couldn't seem to find words for.

Part of me wanted to apologize for running away, for putting him through that again. The words had come easily with Ethan, but with Alec they just didn't sit right. I couldn't make myself say sorry to him when he hadn't said sorry to me for so many things.

He gave me a little nod in return, the tension in his shoulders relaxing slightly. Folding both his big hands around mine, he opened his mouth to say something, then closed it again, his eyes flying from side to side.

I waited patiently, my heart beating a little faster. This was the most sincerity I'd seen in his face for a long time, the most vulnerability.

He looked back into my eyes.

"Evie." His voice was like honey, and I nearly melted. "I am so sorry . . ."

Whatever he was about to apologize for, it was interrupted by Tyler rushing up to us, his gun by his side. "We have company."

Alec stood and pulled his own weapon immediately, his face going hard again, all the rigidity returning to his posture. They moved together and nudged me behind them, shielding me from the oncoming threat.

I craned my neck and spotted an unfamiliar car coming up the driveway. This must have been the most action that driveway had seen in months.

A tiny jolt of fear spiked in my chest. I stepped closer to the two broad backs in front of me, resting a hand on each. I needed something to hold on to.

Tyler reached around to hold me closer to his hip. Alec leaned back into my touch but kept both hands firmly on his weapon. Ethan and Josh moved cautiously to stand off to the side and in front of us. Nina simply got back into the car; it was most likely bulletproof if it had come from Melior Group.

The silver Holden Commodore slid to a stop in the gravel, the driver having slammed the brakes a little too hard.

When Harvey got out and raked his confused glance over the scene, I breathed an audible sigh of relief. The sound drew his attention, and he spotted my face between Alec and Tyler's shoulders. Then his eyes took in the weapons in their hands.

"Hey!" He marched toward us. "Get away from her!" His voice carried, the squawk of nearby galahs punctuating it further.

He had no idea these guys were my Bond; he knew only that I was on the run from someone dangerous, and here were a bunch of armed men literally holding on to me.

My guys had no way of knowing Harvey wasn't a threat either. This could turn ugly real fast.

"Wait, wait," I rushed out, tapping both Alec and Tyler on the shoulder.

"It's OK, he's—"

"Stay back." Tyler's command was calm but firm.

"I said get the fuck away from her!" Harvey was undeterred by the fact that both Tyler and Alec were raising their weapons, but it was Josh who reacted first.

He moved both hands in a shoving motion, and Harvey was thrown off his feet, sliding on his back almost all the way back to his car.

My eyes widened; Josh looked furious. I'd never seen him like that. He was always the calm one.

My attention shifted to Ethan and the angry ball of blue fire in his hand.

Harvey slowly got to his feet.

Tyler and Alec's guns were both pointed at him.

To say their show of force to protect me from a *human boy* was overkill would be a massive understatement. But I was fast learning their protective instincts knew no bounds. Just like my own toward them.

I wrenched myself out of Tyler's grip and planted myself between my ex-boyfriend, who had managed to regain his feet, and my four Bondmates, as the Lighthunter had called them.

Tyler and Alec immediately dropped their guns but kept their eyes on Harvey.

"Stop!" I held my hands up to either side, as if I were separating misbehaving children. "He is not going to hurt me. This is his house. He helped me. He kept me *safe*."

Logic worked with Tyler; his posture relaxed visibly, and he even tucked his gun away. Alec kept scowling at everything, but that was nothing new. I turned to check that Ethan had extinguished that angry flame, and breathed a sigh of relief when no fire was in sight. My big guy was doing a good impression of his older cousin, scowling with his arms crossed.

That's when Harvey made another mistake. He came up behind me and placed a hand on my shoulder, speaking in a low, suspicious voice. "Eve, what the hell is—"

His words were cut off by Josh using his ability again, only this time it wasn't directed at Harvey. I found myself flying through the air backward, the wind knocked out of me. The sensation was like when you miss a step walking down stairs, and your stomach ends up in your throat while your whole life flashes before your eyes.

But unlike Harvey, I didn't land on my ass. In a split second my back hit something, and strong arms encircled my waist protectively. Josh had used his ability to pull me to himself. I was equally annoyed at his overreaction and proud that his telekinetic control was improving.

"Josh, it's OK. He's not a threat. This is—"

"Harvey," he finished for me, his green eyes meeting mine over my shoulder. "Yeah, I know."

I narrowed my eyes.

"His first reaction when he got here was to protect you. He ran *at* two loaded guns to get to you. I knew he wasn't a threat. I figured he must be the ex."

I gaped at him. "Joshua," I scolded, extracting myself from his arms and turning to face him with my hands on my hips. "Not cool!"

He had the decency to look sheepish, rubbing the back of his neck and looking down at his feet. His dirty-blond hair was a mess, and he was in one of his band T-shirts and shorts. His neat chinos-and-shirt combo was nowhere to be seen.

"Sorry," Josh mumbled to the ground.

"This is your ex?" Ethan came to stand by me, another ball of fire appearing in his hand, his signature cocky grin pulling at his lips. "This should be fun."

"Ethan!" I was just about at my limit of testosterone for the day.

The fire was yellow, meaning it was harmless and would fizzle to nothing if he threw it, but Harvey didn't know that. To his credit he stood his ground—a human facing the crazy Variants down despite the growing fear in his eyes. This was why I'd fallen for Harvey; he really stood up for what he believed in. He was brave.

"If the one who pulled you away with his ability, which is totally cheating, by the way"—Harvey was scowling, his fists clenched by his sides—"is your boyfriend, then who's this fuckwit?"

"What the fuck did you just call me?" The fire in Ethan's hand started to turn blue.

"Enough!" I yelled. "Unless you want to whip 'em out and measure 'em, it's time to behave like adults."

All three of them looked as if they actually considered it for a moment, sizing each other up, but finally Ethan extinguished the fire, Josh stuffed his hands into his pockets, and Harvey rolled his neck while taking a deep breath.

"That's better." I looked over my shoulder, wondering why Tyler hadn't stepped in sooner. He and Alec were standing shoulder to shoulder, both wearing matching amused expressions. He was too proud to act as juvenile as Ethan and Josh had, but he was enjoying the way they were staking their claim.

I shook my head.

"Guys, this is Harvey." I chose not to put a label on him. He was definitely no longer my boyfriend, but he was much more than just a friend. "Harvey, this is Josh."

"Her boyfriend," Josh added as he waved, but at least his tone was friendlier.

"And this is Ethan."

"Her boyfriend." Ethan dropped one big arm over my shoulders, his grin widening at the confusion on Harvey's face.

Tyler walked over to us and took my hand. He extended his other to

Harvey. "I'm Tyler, her boyfriend." I rolled my eyes, but laughter was starting to bubble up in my chest from the ridiculousness of it all. "Sorry about the rocky start."

"Um . . . OK." Harvey shook Tyler's hand, then looked at me with raised eyebrows. "How many boyfriends do you have?"

We all turned to Alec, who was now leaning on the railing, his arms crossed and his cool blue eyes narrowed.

"Uh, it's complicated," I answered. "And that's Alec. You should probably just . . . stay away from him."

"Yeah, you definitely want to steer clear of Alec," Tyler reinforced my warning.

But we'd spoken of the devil, so he appeared. Alec walked right up to Harvey, a smile tugging at his lips. There was nothing friendly about it. He extended his hand. "Hi, I'm Alec."

Harvey's manners won, and he returned the greeting, reaching his hand out.

As soon as their hands clasped, Harvey yelped in pain and yanked his back to his chest, rubbing at the palm.

The creepy smile was still on Alec's face. "That's just a little taste of my ability."

I rounded on him. "Alec, what the fuck?"

His fake smile fell away. "So this is why you flew halfway across the world? To see your ex?"

"Man, you know she came here to help find Charlie." Tyler sounded as frustrated as I was angry. "Calm down."

"I'm not a fucking moron," I seethed. "I'm not going to put my life in danger to have a chat with an old friend. I came here for Charlie. I went to Harvey for help. He was gracious enough to provide it."

"How convenient. Isn't four enough? You looking to add another to your collection?"

I flinched but didn't hesitate in my response. "I don't have four. I have three."

He watched me for a long moment, neither one of us willing to back down, look away.

"You have four," he said with such certainty I almost wavered and reached out for him. Almost.

"You've got a funny way of showing it."

"What?" It was his turn to look confused.

"Dana," I ground out between clenched teeth. I'd tried to pretend I wasn't jealous. I'd tried to tell myself Alec and I weren't together, so he was free to do whatever he wanted. But I was his Vital. He was in my Bond. He was *mine*.

"Dana?" Bit by bit, the confusion in his furrowed brow turned to anger. "Dana?! I haven't fucking touched Dana in . . . since the fucking gala. I told you that the morning after Dot's birthday. I fucking want *you*."

"Oh, I'm sorry, am I supposed to read your mind? How the fuck am I supposed to know . . ."

"Stop fighting!" Ethan's voice was so loud and sudden I actually startled. "Just stop. I'm so sick of this. I can't take it anymore. Please . . ."

His voice lost its booming quality, his shoulders sagging. He looked so tired. Had he slept? Had any of them? They all looked disheveled and haggard, hair messy, expensive shirts rumpled.

"I have never seen so much tension in a Bond." Nina had exited the car and was standing next to Harvey, who looked somewhere between confused and uncomfortable. "She has more than enough Light to sustain all four abilities."

"Light? Abilities?" Harvey's eyes widened. "Eve, what is going on?"

Harvey deserved answers. Though he wasn't a part of my life anymore, at one point he'd been my whole world. His kindness had meant everything at a time when I'd felt so isolated. Then I'd just disappeared. And now I'd just shown up out of nowhere, bringing all my drama and baggage into his life. I was surprised he wasn't being more forceful about getting the truth.

"A lot has changed since we saw each other last, Harvey." I smiled sadly, nostalgic for how simple my life had been back then, when all I had to worry about was keeping my boyfriend a secret from my mother—and occasionally about what we were running from. Simpler times . . .

"Yeah, I'm starting to get that." He smiled back.

"Put the kettle on?" I nodded toward the house. "I'll tell you all about it over a cuppa."

He nodded and walked into the house, running his hands through his brown hair and releasing a deep breath.

"Eve," Tyler said tentatively, "we don't really have time to—"

"Yes, we do," I interrupted with a smile. I wasn't going to run off on Harvey again. There were very few people I'd ever gotten close enough with to care about. I needed to stop hurting them. Might as well start here, in the scorching heat of a dusty Australian sun.

TWENTY

My cup of tea with Harvey turned into lunch. The seven of us crowded around the little round table, and the guys let me do most of the talking. Nina observed every interaction, every little touch between us, as if she were trying to put together a jigsaw.

Harvey wasn't stupid; the talk of Light and all the guys' abilities led him to the conclusion I was a Vital. But he had a million questions. I answered them all, despite the other men's disapproving looks and even attempts to stop me. I trusted Harvey, and other than the Melior Group stuff I wasn't supposed to know, I wanted him to have the truth.

I did, however, make the gravity of the situation clear. "You understand you can't repeat any of this to anyone, right? You can't tell Mia or your parents you even saw me. People's lives are at stake. *My* life could be at stake."

Harvey frowned but nodded. "This have something to do with the Vital abductions I've been seeing all over the news?"

Tyler's voice was patient but firm. "Yes. It's very complicated, and we can't tell you much more—for your own safety as much as anyone else's."

The guys, realizing they couldn't stop me from telling him as much as I could, ended up just imploring Harvey to stay quiet. Tyler used logic and his naturally authoritative demeanor; Josh had seen how much he genuinely cared for me, so he appealed to those feelings; Ethan poured his big heart out, telling him how much I meant to them, how much it would hurt to lose me. He made me get all emotional, but he still wasn't meeting my eyes most of the time. Alec just glared, his threat evident in his posture and facial expression.

After lunch, we drove for hours, past the city and to a private airstrip. At least that explained how they'd gotten to me so fast. Leaving as soon as you want and refueling in the air certainly saves time.

I gave Harvey a brief hug on the tarmac, hyperaware of the four sets of eyes watching us intently.

"Keep in touch this time?" he joked, but his smile didn't quite reach his eyes.

"I'll text you when we land. Thank you so much, Harvey."

He nodded, and I turned away, walking to my guys and onto the plane.

In a much shorter time than it had taken me to cover the same distance, we were back home.

Everyone filed through the entryway and into the massive foyer of the Zacarias mansion. Extravagant Christmas decorations had appeared in the few days I'd been away. Next to the curving staircase stood a massive tree, resplendent in red and gold decoration, and poinsettias had replaced the usual vase of fresh flowers on the side table. Even the banister was decked out in garlands.

Nina smiled as she stepped inside, lowering her bag onto the pile of coats and luggage by the door. "You must be Dorothy."

Dot looked more nervous than I'd ever seen her. She was standing between her parents, Lucian hanging back by the stairs. "You can call me

Dot." She cleared her throat uncertainly.

"Hi, I'm Olivia." Dot's mom waved. "And I have to be honest here, I don't really understand how this works, and I'm not entirely convinced it's a good idea."

"I understand your concerns, madame. My name is Nina, and I would be happy to explain to you as much as I can how my connection to the Light works, but I have a feeling everyone in the room would prefer if I tried to track your son first?"

"Yes, please!" Dot's eyes were wet, and my own throat tightened. We'd been waiting for this so long; the anticipation, the hope that we could be so close to finding Charlie, was palpable.

Josh circled his arms around my front. Ethan had been very quiet the whole way back, and while he wasn't rejecting me when I hugged him or leaned on him, he wasn't initiating any affection. He was still pissed at me.

"Come." Nina gestured to Dot. "Let me get a proper feel for you."

Nina took Dot's hands in hers and closed her eyes. After only a moment, she opened them again and sighed, giving a sad, tight smile. "I'm sorry—"

"No!" Dot wrenched her hands back as her mom started to cry. Dot's dad, Henry, folded his wife into his arms, his own eyes tired and misty.

"No, you misunderstand," Nina rushed out, her French accent becoming more pronounced. "I am not saying he has, how you say, passed away. Only that I cannot track him as—"

"I knew it!" Alec burst out. "This was a waste of fucking time. She's a fraud. Now she'll ask for money."

Everyone started speaking over each other, and Nina looked more than a little frustrated.

"Let her speak!" I yelled, and miraculously, everyone quieted down. Alec huffed and crossed his arms over his chest. The frown on Lucian's face was just as skeptical, but at least he was controlling himself.

"I cannot track him *now*," Nina continued, "but I will be able to once the foreign Light is out of Dot's system."

"What do you mean?" Dot asked, wiping tears away.

"I mean that you have too much of someone else's Light coursing through you." She looked pointedly in my direction. "The connection is not strained toward your Vital because your ability is sustained. Once Eve's Light is cleared, I will be able to track your brother."

"Shit." Guilt gripped my lungs, making it hard to breathe. It was my fault we couldn't get to Charlie right away. I'd only been trying to help Dot, make her feel better, but I'd ruined everything.

"You could not have known." Nina smiled at me, then frowned. "You have been very generous with your friend. There is more of your Light in Dot than in some of your Variants."

Her dark eyes traveled to Alec. She had very expressive eyes.

"OK, how does this work?" Henry stepped forward, demanding answers, daring to hope.

"I will be more than happy to answer any questions you have, but I do need a shower. We may have flown in a private jet, but twenty-two hours on a plane is still twenty-two hours on a plane."

"Of course!" Tyler stepped in. "I'll show you to the guest room."

He took off up the stairs, carrying Nina's bag. The other guys dispersed too, in search of showers and fresh clothes.

Dot came up and enveloped me in a big hug. "I'm so glad you're OK," she whispered into my neck, "but you smell like shit." She pulled back, making a face.

"I'm sorry about the Light." I looked down, not finding any humor in the situation. "If I'd known . . . and now we have to wait longer."

"Stop." Olivia pulled me into another hug. "You have nothing to apologize for, Evelyn. I'm glad you're OK. Thank you for doing this. You have no idea how much I appreciate it."

She was starting to cry again. She gave me another squeeze and moved off after Lucian and Henry, muttering about making tea.

Olivia may have let me off the hook, but I was still nervous about what Dot had to say.

"Don't even worry about it." She waved me off, moving to sit on the stairs. I breathed a sigh of relief and sat next to her.

"So, you took the private jet, huh?" She nudged me with her shoulder. "I've never been in it. What's it like?"

"It was actually really cool." I couldn't help grinning. Extravagant things didn't usually faze me, but the jet was amazing. "I loved not having to deal with customs or passport control or waiting for ages to board, and it has a bed!"

"A bed, eh?" She gave me a knowing look, but I rolled my eyes.

"As if. We had company. Plus, Alec won't touch me, Tyler had to work most of the time, and Ethan's still pissed at me. I took a nap with Josh though."

"Yeah, Ethan was pretty upset."

"I know. I feel really bad. I'm constantly hurting someone or letting someone down. I've just never had this many people in my life, you know? I'm still learning how to not only think about myself."

"Speaking of pissed . . ." Dot cringed, and I groaned.

"What now?"

"Zara. I talked to her, explained the situation. I think she gets it, but she feels like we lied to her."

"We kinda did." I sighed.

"I know, but this was about Charlie, and I'd do it again a hundred times over if it meant getting him back. I just think you should talk to her."

"I will. I'll go home . . . soon." I yawned, leaning my head on Dot's shoulder.

My phone vibrated. It was Harvey, replying to the text I'd sent him when we landed. It felt good to have him back in my life, to have some connection to my past. I smiled as Dot read over my shoulder.

"So, how'd the guys do with meeting the ex?"

I groaned. "About as well as could be expected."

"Oh, so he's dead? Then who's texting you?"

I laughed. "OK, slightly better than expected. They gave him a hard time, and it started a fight with Alec. But I made them all be nice."

Dot chuckled, jostling me on her shoulder.

I lifted my head to glare at her. "It's not funny. He could've been hurt. You should've seen them all when they realized his last name is Blackburn."

"Wait! You gave yourself his last name? Oh, this is gold!"

"I created this identity before we got together, OK? I had a crush. How was I supposed to know I'd be stuck with it indefinitely?"

"Maybe not indefinitely. You could start using your real name once it's safe. Have you figured out why your mom ran in the first place?"

"No. It's on my long list of mysteries to solve." I sighed and stared at the beautiful, glowing tree.

"OK, Veronica Mars." Dot chuckled and followed my gaze, leaning her head on my shoulder.

I'd been meaning to raise it with Lucian, but it was proving more difficult than I'd anticipated, partly because he worked more than even Tyler and partly because I had no idea how to broach the subject. I'd spoken to the guys about it at length, but they knew about as much as I did—jack shit.

Part of me was afraid to find the answer, but what terrified me even more was a lack of any insight at all.

Would I live the rest of my life not knowing why my mother had taken me away from our home?

Josh, Ethan, and Dot had already headed off to shower, but I needed another minute for my breathing to recover. It had been a leg-heavy session in the gym, and I was skeptical the noodles currently attached to my hips could make it up the next two flights of stairs. It didn't matter that it was three days before Christmas; Kane refused to give us a break.

"Your enemies will not take a break to bake gingerbread cookies while plotting your downfall" was his reasoning, delivered with a scowl. He had a point.

I pushed the sweaty strands of hair off my forehead and hobbled toward the front of the house. At the bottom of the curving main staircase, I paused, resting one hand on the banister.

"Come on, Eve," I whispered to myself. "You can do this. It's just stairs. You climb them all the time."

But my legs refused, so I lowered my forehead to rest on the back of my hand and took a little standing nap.

Voices from Tyler's office drew my attention, and I turned my head, resting my cheek on my hand instead of my forehead.

The door was ajar, and Tyler's voice came through clearly.

" . . . don't understand. It's been confirmed and verified as well as we could have hoped for. What are we waiting for?"

"It's not that simple. I may be the director, but I still have a board I have to answer to, Gabe." Lucian sounded just as frustrated. "And it would seem we don't have the full support of the board."

There was a pause, and I found myself straightening up, leaning toward the door in order to hear better. Then I realized what I was doing and shook my head.

If it was important, Tyler would tell me. They knew what they were doing when it came to Melior Group operations.

"So this has become political, then." Tyler sounded resigned, if a little angry.

I abandoned the stairs and headed back toward the kitchen.

"It always was," Lucian replied. "We need to tread carefully, be smart about . . ."

The voices faded as I continued to the back of the house.

I looked at the pool longingly. It would have been great to jump in and cool off, let the water support my aching muscles for a while. But it was covered up for the winter and way too cold anyway.

It wasn't too cold for a steam though. There were multiple studies expounding the benefits of a steam room post-workout for recovery, heart health, respiratory health, and skin, just to name a few.

I grabbed one of Ethan's hoodies off the back of the couch before rushing across the yard to the pool house. The smell of snow was in the air, and the cold was biting. As a freezing gust of wind cut through Ethan's big hoodie as if it were a scrap of lace, I envied Zara.

She was spending the holidays with her family in California. She'd sent me a photo of herself at the beach just that morning, and I'd sent one back of the heavy gray clouds that had been hanging over Bradford Hills for the past three days.

She'd left a few days after my return from Australia. I'd done my best to explain to her why we'd kept it from her, but understandably she still felt left out. I'd spent as much time with her as possible before she left, but there was still a distance, a coldness in her eyes when she said goodbye.

Hopefully the warm Californian weather would thaw her out.

Inside the pool house, I headed straight to the large bathroom at the back, taking my shoes off at the door and moaning when the heated tiles made contact with my frozen toes.

"Hello?" a heavily accented female voice called out, and I looked up. The steam room was already occupied, the heavy moisture behind the glass making it difficult to see inside.

"Oh, hey, Nina. It's Eve. Sorry, I'll come back."

I turned to leave, but she called out again. "No need, darling. There is plenty of room."

"Oh, OK." I hesitated. I'd been planning to steam naked, but I eyed the pile of thin Turkish towels on the bench next to the sink. I guess that would work too.

I undressed and wrapped the pale purple cloth around myself before stepping into the steam room and closing the glass door.

The hot, humid air enveloped my body, relaxing me almost immediately. I took a deep breath and rolled my shoulders, releasing the tense posture I'd held since the frigid air first hit me outside.

Nina sat in the middle of the bench, leaning against the wall, completely relaxed and completely naked. Her lithe body, her long legs, and all the private bits were just . . . there. The humidity glistened against her smooth skin.

Once again I hesitated. She cracked one eye open. "Are you going to sit? The steam can make you dizzy."

"Oh, yeah." I averted my eyes and quickly sat to her left, leaning back against the warm tiles. I tightened the towel around my chest, then paused. I was being ridiculous.

She was an adult, I was an adult. There was nothing sexual or inappropriate about sitting in a steam room together.

Making a conscious decision not to be ashamed of my natural human state, I let the towel fall at my sides, reveling in the warm moisture caressing every inch of my skin, the heat soothing my aching muscles.

"How are you finding your stay here?" I asked. I hadn't had too many opportunities to speak with the Lighthunter one-on-one. After everyone had showered and slept off the massive trip, Nina had sat down with Dot and her parents, with Tyler and Lucian present, and answered all their questions.

I wasn't there for that conversation—I was busy having my own big conversation with Zara—but Dot had filled me in later.

It would take a few weeks at least for my Light to drain out of Dot enough for her ability to strain toward her Bonded Vital, Charlie. They would continue to check in regularly, but in the meantime we had to wait. Alec had insisted that Nina stay at the Zacarias mansion, with thinly veiled threats to inflict pain if she put any more of his family in danger. As if it were her fault I ran away. Lucian smoothed it over with an invitation to *host* her for the duration of the wait and a promise to pay her generously for leading them to Charlie.

She'd refused any kind of payment until she could prove herself to even the staunchest of skeptics—namely Alec and Dot's dad, Henry—but had accepted the offer of a place to stay, as she didn't know many people in the area.

She mostly kept to herself but did join us for meals and the occasional discussion. No one could resist Ethan's food or Josh's subtle ways of pulling you into a fascinating chat.

"It is very comfortable. The Zacarias family has a lovely home," she answered.

"I'm sorry if Alec has been difficult. He's just . . . I don't even know. He treats me with the same level of hostility, if it makes you feel any better."

She chuckled. "Alec does not bother me." She waved a lazy hand in the humid air. "He is only motivated by his strong protective instincts toward you. It is plain to see."

"Not to me," I mumbled.

"You know, I can see the ties in a Bond almost as physical things at times."

"Really?" I turned to her. She and the things she could do fascinated me, and there wasn't a single book on the topic I could read. "How does that work?"

She shrugged. "It does not matter how. I just can. Just like I can't tell you how I track a Variant or Vital through the others in their Bond. Just like you can't describe the color green or any other color."

"What do you mean? Green is the color of leaves, grass, the combination of blue and yellow—"

"Yes," she cut me off, "you can point to things that are green, but you cannot describe the color itself. We both know what a Variant is, what a Vital is, the DNA behind it. There are theories behind what exactly the Light is, but no one can really explain it. I can't really explain how I do what I do. I just do it. It is like breathing."

I thought about what she was saying. The stuff about colors was blowing my mind a little. How *do* you describe green without pointing to something green? My default was always to understand things, to learn them, unpack them. But some things just . . . are.

"What does it look like? The Bonds?" I decided to focus on what information she *could* give me—her own experience of it.

"When the Bond members are in close proximity, sometimes it's like a wisp of smoke from one to the other, moving and shifting like it has a mind of its own. Usually, though, it is just a feeling. A sense of something that is difficult to articulate. I just know that two people are connected."

"Kind of like Tyler just knows when someone is lying?"

"Yes, very similar."

We fell silent for a few moments. The heat had completely relaxed my muscles, and I was taking long, deep breaths.

"I have never seen so much tension in a Bond as I have in yours, Eve."

Her tone had become more serious, and I stayed silent, waiting for her to elaborate. "With Tyler, Josh, and Ethan there is a lot of positive energy, even if it is restrained, not fully actualized. But with Alec, so much uncertainty, so much resistance. Yet it is the most established of all."

I frowned, running my hands down my slick thighs. "What do you mean? How is that possible?"

"The connection to Alec was made many years ago. Before the Light had begun to course through you even. The Bond was made but not actualized."

The glass door opened, letting some of the steam out and a gust of fresh air in. Dot waltzed in completely nude and plonked herself down on Nina's other side.

"Yeah, even an idiot could see that the Bond is strained because of Alec." She inserted herself into our conversation seamlessly, leaning back and taking a deep breath. "No offense. I've just known him for a long time."

"None taken." Nina's voice held a bit of humor. "But it is not only because of Alec."

"Do tell." Dot angled her body toward us, giving Nina her full attention.

"Yes, Alec is . . . ambiguous. He is already irrevocably connected to you, but he is fighting it."

"He hates his ability, and I only amplify it. Therefore, he hates *me*." I couldn't keep the bitterness from my voice.

"Dramatic much?" Dot added helpfully as Nina chuckled.

"He definitely does not hate you. But that does explain the tension. The others are holding back too for this reason? To help him have distance?"

"Yeah, pretty much," I grumbled.

"But you do not wish to wait any longer." That was not posed as a question.

"Yeah, my girl has a major case of blue ovaries." I was beginning to think Dot had only joined us to make my life difficult.

"I do not understand this phrase 'blue ovaries.'" Nina looked between us, confused.

"What my friend is so helpfully trying to say is that, yes, I would very much like to . . . take the next step." I'd pretty much just admitted I wanted to fuck four guys. "The attraction is getting difficult to hold back. My feelings toward Alec are complicated—he hurt me a lot recently—but I'm even attracted to him . . . physically."

"Naturally. He is in your Bond. There is nothing to be ashamed of, Eve. But the longer you drag this out, the more tension there will be, the more intensely the Light will pull you together. If you let nature take its course, follow your instincts, trust your body, the Light will settle. Alec is afraid of his ability, you are all cautious about the damage Ethan and Josh could do, but you fail to realize that once it is settled—once the tethers of the Bond are sealed—the Light will not be quite so intense. It will be easier for you to control, easier for them to manage. The amount that transfers will not be excessive, because the Light will not be straining you to deepen the Bond."

"So you're saying once I sleep with them, the Light will be *less* intense, not more?"

"Exactly. Lean into it, and everything will fall into place. Dot can tell you. Her Bond is established and settled. You only receive the exact amount of Light you need at any moment, unless your Vital consciously pushes more at you, correct?"

"Yeah, but he's my brother. I didn't have to sleep with him to seal the Bond." She shuddered. "Plus, it wasn't something we had to build—it was always there. It was a normal part of our sibling relationship growing up."

"I think I know what you're saying." I sighed. We were all so concerned about keeping our distance—keeping the Light at bay so we could learn to control it, so Alec could get his shit together emotionally—that we weren't allowing the Bond to deepen and settle naturally. "I don't know how to even raise this topic with them," I grumbled.

"Why must everything be discussed?" Nina stood as she spoke. "You are perfectly capable of making your intentions clear with your actions and your body."

She winked at me and exited the steam room. A minute later we heard the shower start up.

I sighed. "Why does this have to be so fucking hard?"

Dot snorted. "That's kind of necessary for the sex stuff."

I rolled my eyes. She was almost as good as Ethan at making everything into a dirty joke. "I'm serious, Dot. Things are impossible with Alec, but it's not just him. We keep hurting each other. I can understand why they're holding off on the physical stuff for now, but I can't understand why they keep hiding things from me—not including me in the decisions. I'm supposed to be their Vital. We're supposed to be this tighter-than-family unit, but it doesn't feel like it."

"Maybe it's *because* you're their Vital that they do it? All I've seen from them is that they're trying to protect you."

"They can't protect me while keeping me in the loop? That's bullshit." I crossed my arms, then dropped them down to the bench immediately. It was too hot to have any part of my body touching another.

"We didn't keep them in the loop about Australia either," she pointed out.

"I know." I looked down. "I knew they'd be pissed—Ethan's still keeping his distance, even while he watches me like I might evaporate if he blinks. I just didn't realize how hurt they'd be. I was on my own for so long. I guess I'm still learning how much my actions impact them too. I just . . . How do we stop doing this to each other?"

"Look, those boys have been tight for a long time. I mean, I'm their cousin, and we moved back here not long after their parents died, but even Charlie and I aren't a part of their little inner circle. They've spent so much time together, sometimes they communicate without speaking. You may be their Vital, but having you be a part of that is going to change that dynamic. And you're still learning what it means to have a family. Those kind of changes take time."

"So what do I do? I can't wait for them to slowly realize I'm part of their little group now, and I don't want to feel like an invader in my own Bond."

"Just be patient." She shrugged. "Try to make your feelings on the matter clear, but try not to get too frustrated when they fail from time to time."

I leaned back, watching the white steam obscuring the top of the steam room as I thought about that. It was actually really good, mature advice. And then she had to go and add to it.

"Or if you want, I can get Squiggles to spy on them." She smiled wide.

"No!" I stood up slowly and wrapped the thin towel around myself. "No more spying." Before I closed the door, I added, "But thanks for the advice."

She just smiled and closed her eyes, settling in for a bit longer.

As I showered and dressed, I thought about all I'd discussed with Nina and Dot. Relationships were complicated enough with just two people trying to navigate life together. I had to deal with *four* guys who all had their own issues and insecurities, a supernatural force that tied us all together, and dangerous, powerful people who were after Vitals like me for an unknown, probably horrific reason.

It was probably easier to deal with the sex stuff first.

TWENTY ONE

As Zara and I strolled in the direction of the town center, I fingered the cool metal pendant hanging around my neck. Zara was right—we needed to get out for a bit—but one of the guys was most likely monitoring the tracker at that very moment. I kept expecting my phone to blow up with calls and messages demanding to know why I'd left the safety of campus.

It was early January, a few days before classes were due to resume, and both of us were in boots and coats, mine big and black, Zara's fitted and almost the same color as her bright red hair.

"I'm not sure about this, Zara. Ethan is still pissed at me. I'm just going to text them so they know I'm off campus."

"Nooo," she whined. "Come on, Eve. You know one of them will come down here, and it's supposed to be just you and me. And do you know the things I had to do to get Derek to agree to this?" She grinned, hinting that she actually rather enjoyed those things.

Derek was the Melior Group guard currently manning the east gate at Bradford Hills Institute. On our way out the gate, Zara had planted a kiss on Derek's lips. "I really appreciate this, babe."

He'd winked at her as he let us pass. "You have one hour max. I don't want to lose my job."

I'd gaped at her. The mystery of who she'd been seeing in secret had been solved, but as we continued into town, she'd persisted in acting totally unaffected by it all, even under my onslaught of questions.

Normally students had to sign in and out at the gates. All Vitals had a personal security detail, but I wasn't a Vital as far as anyone knew, so all the agents were under instructions to report my absence to Tyler. This was really only a safety precaution in case someone forced me to leave under duress; I never left campus without one of my guys or someone under Tyler's orders.

At least, not until today.

"I don't know." I chewed on my bottom lip, feeling as if I was doing something behind my guys' backs. "What if something bad happens?"

Zara rolled her eyes. "We are literally in the most heavily guarded place on the East Coast right now. Even if shit goes down, there are Melior Group badasses everywhere."

As if to illustrate her point, two black-clad, armed women passed us, heading in the opposite direction. Bradford Hills was crawling with them.

We fell into a companionable silence, walking side by side. As we rounded a corner onto Main Street, Zara turned to me.

"OK. We need a better distraction. Want to get some ice cream?"

"I don't know. It's freezing." I pulled my scarf a little tighter around my neck, tucking the pendant into the front of my shirt. If I couldn't see it, maybe

I would stop worrying.

"Who cares? Do you want ice cream or not?"

I smiled, glad she seemed to be getting over the fact that Dot and I had lied to her. "Let's do it."

With a satisfied nod, she pulled me along. "There's a little gelato place at the other end of Main."

"Thanks for talking me into this." I kept my eyes on the street ahead as we passed boutique shops, little cafés, cozy restaurants, and lovely old buildings, with giant oaks lining the street the whole way, their branches bare. "I hardly know the town, and I've been living here almost a year. It's really nice. And I wouldn't mind trying some of these restaurants."

Zara remained silent. I looked over to see a deep frown on her face, her eyes fixed on the sidewalk.

"Red? You OK?"

"Huh?" Her head snapped up. "Sorry. I was in my own world."

I smiled warmly. "That's OK. I was just saying thanks for talking me into this. It's nice. I wish Beth was here."

"Me too," she whispered sadly as we slowed to a stop in front of the gelato shop. It was a little separated from the rest of the Main Street buildings, its front door on a diagonal, almost hidden from the main road.

"Oh no. I think it's closed." The shop's Closed sign hung unmistakably on the door. I glanced around for another café, but there were no other establishments at this end of Main, the street curving up a hill and disappearing into the trees.

"Is it?" Zara stiffened next to me, the arm looped through mine going rigid. "You sure?"

She dragged me right up to the door.

"Pretty sure." I chuckled. "I know you want ice cream, but the sign is pretty clear."

"Yeah . . ." She looked behind me, scanning the street with nervous eyes.

I frowned. She was acting strange.

"Let's just walk back up the street. We can get coffee and cake instead." I tried to tug her away, but her grip on my arm was like steel. "Zara, what the hell—"

An unassuming gray van suddenly pulled into the driveway leading to the back of the building, cutting my words short. It stopped right next to us, blocking the footpath and the view of the rest of Main Street.

I hardly had time to register the prickles on the back of my neck before the door slid open and two masked men stepped out.

They moved fast. Two sets of rough hands closed, vicelike, around my upper arms. As they wrenched me away from my friend, she released her hold. I didn't even have time to try to run, yell at Zara to run, do *anything*.

They dragged me backward toward the van, and one of them shoved a face mask over my nose and mouth—the kind you would see in a hospital operating room. Something sweet smelling with a sharp alcoholic tinge filled my lungs, probably some form of ether.

All the training I'd done had been for nothing. The endless hours of torture in the gym with Kane, the runs with Ethan, the sparring—I still had no idea what I was doing.

As the ether did its job, stealing my consciousness away at an alarming rate, my mind registered only two things.

The first was the chemical formula of ether: $C_4H_{10}O$. Completely useless in this situation.

The second was the cold, hard look in Zara's eyes as she willingly climbed into the van after us.

The last thing I heard before blacking out was the thud of the van door slamming shut as the betrayal slammed through my heart.

My eyes slowly opened, the sense that something wasn't right pushing through the haze in my brain.

I groaned and rolled onto my back, screwing my eyes shut again. The ground was cold—concrete—and I could hear rain, a rhythmic metallic sound in the background. If it weren't for the fact that I was freezing and on the hard ground, the noise would have been soothing. I lifted my right hand to rub my temple, and my left came with it.

They were bound at the wrists with a zip tie.

A jolt of adrenaline shot through me, fear finally catching up to the murkiness in my head, but I tried to shove it down. I had to remain calm. I had to assess the situation.

I was in what looked like a basement. The concrete floor matched dank, dirty concrete walls, and timber beams ran across the low ceiling. It was dark, but thin windows situated high on one wall were still letting in some faint light, so it couldn't have been more than a few hours since I was taken. Zara and I had headed out around midafternoon.

Zara!

The detached look in her eyes as she closed the van door flashed through my memory.

Confusion, worry, betrayal, and fear churned inside me, all battling for dominance. But I couldn't give in to the overwhelming feelings. I needed to stay focused.

Moving my legs, I realized my ankles were bound too. I tried to push myself up, but halfway there my stomach did a flip, and I collapsed onto my elbows, vomiting—a side effect of the large dose of ether they must have given me to knock me out so fast. I puked until there was nothing left, fighting my body to stop dry retching.

Once my breathing calmed a little, I managed to scoot into a sitting position, away from my own vomit, and look around for something, *anything*, to tell me where I was or what was happening.

There didn't seem to be anyone around, but the basement looked large, the area farthest away from the windows cast in shadow. Stacks of crates sat at intervals along the length of one wall, and multiple shelves held neatly arranged gardening implements and tools. A wall was at my back, and stacks of crates towered over me on either side. Metal bars stretched between the two stacks and, I realized as my eyes adjusted, all the way around, completely enclosing me.

A cage.

Panic began to set in. I lifted my bound hands to swipe away the tears pricking at my eyes while my brain grasped for control by providing relevant statistics. Kidnapping statistics for US adults are elusive, as the *crime* of kidnapping is not recorded separately to all missing persons cases. When it comes to minors, 86 percent of perpetrators in non-family kidnappings are male, while the victims are predominantly female. Nearly half of all victims are sexually assaulted.

I was fairly certain my particular situation had more to do with my being a Vital than with someone wanting to rape me, but the idea only added to the terror clawing at me from the inside out.

My wrists were beginning to hurt from the tight restraints, but they were also itchy. I cursed under my breath; I'd completely dropped my control of the Light flow, distracted by dread and nausea.

I leaned my head against the cold metal bars and closed my eyes, consciously taking deep, slow breaths. Without any of the guys here to transfer to, the Light could get overwhelming very quickly.

My eyes flew open. *The guys!* I had a way out! It was on a chain around my neck. My bound hands flew to my chest, where the feeling of the little metal bar had become so familiar I forgot it was there most of the time.

I couldn't find it.

How could they have known to take it off me? I hadn't told Zara about the little distress beacon.

Forcing myself to take another calming breath, I pulled my scarf away, running my fingers over my throat more carefully. The chain was there! The pendant had just gotten twisted so it hung down my back.

I tugged on the chain, pulling the little metal bar to the front, and didn't waste any time, yanking the two pieces apart with shaking fingers.

I knew four alarms on four cell phones had instantly gone off, but for me it was a little anticlimactic. I was still bound and caged, sitting on the cold concrete with no idea where I was or how long I'd been there.

My shoulders slumped. I stuffed the silver bit into the pocket of my jacket, then did my best to pull the jacket closer around myself. The adrenaline was beginning to wear off, and the cold seeping into my bones was taking its place. All I could do now was wait and hope they got to me before . . . I didn't let myself entertain the myriad horrible possibilities, focusing instead on bringing my Light flow under control.

But my mind wouldn't stop trying to puzzle things out. The men who had grabbed me were trained, efficient, and identically dressed in black, with masks that brought back gruesome memories of the invasion. Judging by what I knew about Melior Group's suspicions, and about how the Vitals had been taken, I was pretty certain I was firmly in the clutches of Variant Valor.

And Zara had told them my secret.

My gut twisted. I pushed the thought out of my mind and counted my breaths instead.

After at least an hour, I managed to get into a meditative state and bring my Light flow under control. But it slipped away again violently the moment a painful tugging sensation stabbed through my chest. I gasped, my hands flying to the spot to try to rub the ache away.

One of the guys was in trouble. I hadn't felt the pull this bad since that first night when Ethan had blown up a car and I'd run to him in the middle of the night.

Panic squeezed my lungs as the Light poured into me, desperate to be released into whoever had me feeling as if I might die if I didn't get to him *now*. Would I have to sit here, feeling the pain in my chest get worse and worse as one of them lay dying? A sob of hopeless frustration choked me, my body folding in on itself; the pain and the pull were becoming unbearable.

Just as I was about to curl into a fetal position, a loud metallic clang shattered the basement's quiet.

A light flipped on, illuminating the area in front of my cage as boots thudded down the stairs.

I sat up straighter, on alert, but the tears continued to slide down my cheeks, the pain in my chest refusing to be ignored.

As the group came into view, I released a strangled sound—something between a sob and a wail.

Two men were hauling a limp Josh across the concrete. They each had a firm grip on one of his arms, his feet dragging across the ground, his head hanging. His chinos were covered in dirt from the calf down, and his white shirt was torn at the right shoulder and crumpled.

Blood was everywhere. A thick, gluggy drop of it fell from someplace on his face I couldn't see and, as his feet dragged through it, left a macabre streak on the dirty concrete floor.

Behind them walked Zara and another woman, whose pantsuit and neat hairdo seemed out of place in the dank basement. The woman was looking down at her phone as she walked, her heels clicking.

The two men dragged Josh over to my cage, one of them reaching for the lock. I awkwardly shuffled over to the bars, everything in me screaming to get to Josh.

"I wouldn't put him in there. She's his Vital." Zara's detached voice made them pause, and they both looked over to the older lady. There was something vaguely familiar about her, but all my attention was on Josh.

She looked up, sparing me a disinterested glance. "Put him in another cage. We can't have a fully charged telekinetic disrupting the schedule." Her voice was quiet, her words articulate, and I once again got a pang of familiarity before she turned and focused again on her phone.

My kidnappers dragged Josh away from me, and the ache in my chest got impossibly worse, making me sob. They opened the door to another cage, on the other side of the crates to my left and at a right angle, and dumped him inside, his body crumpling lifelessly to the concrete.

They locked the door and walked back the way they'd come, the fancy lady leading the way.

"Right, now I'd like a full report. How the hell did he find us? Are you idiots sure you weren't followed?"

"Yes, ma'am," one of them answered. "We followed protocol to the letter and . . ." His voice trailed off as their footsteps got fainter.

I switched my attention to Zara. She was just standing there, looking at Josh's prone form. I couldn't make myself look at him again. Not yet. I needed to talk sense into Zara. There was no point in pleading with the black-clad men or their boss, but Zara was my friend. Or so I thought.

"Zara." My voice was strained and gravelly. More tears fell down my face.

She just kept staring at Josh, her expression disturbingly flat.

"Zara!" I managed to yell, and she turned her blank eyes to me slowly. A sick, hollow feeling settled in my stomach. She was *not* OK, and I'd been so wrapped up in my own shit, in supporting Dot through losing Charlie, that I hadn't paid attention to what was going on with my other friend. I'd always seen Zara as such a strong person; it never occurred to me that she could be the one struggling the most.

"What are you doing, Red?" My voice broke again, but I hoped the use of my nickname for her would spark some emotion. "Why?"

All she did was blink slowly, her arms slack. I began to worry she was having some kind of mental break.

Another sickening stab of tugging pain made me double over, struggling to breathe. When I looked back up, she'd moved closer to my cage. Her expression was still indifferent, but she'd tilted her head to the side and seemed to be focusing on me better.

"Zara?"

Before I could formulate another way to get through to her, she spoke. "We're doing important work. We are. We need Vitals to fix it. And you're a Vital. I told them. I helped them get a Vital. A powerful one. We need more powerful ones. The others keep failing. Dying. It will all be worth it in the end. She'll understand once it's over. Once we fix it."

She looked away as she spoke, gazing at some imagined sight in the middle distance. Her right hand began to twitch next to her leg, little flicks of the wrist that didn't look deliberate.

"Fix what? What are you trying to fix, Zara?"

Her hand stilled. "The genes. The Light can switch them on. I think Josh is going to die."

She wasn't making any sense, and the rapid change of topic had me crying harder. I'd lost another friend. She was standing right in front of me, but Zara was gone. And if the excruciating pain in my chest was anything to go by, I was about to lose one of my Variants too.

"I think you're right. Josh is dying." I fought hard not to break down completely, my breaths becoming more and more erratic, my tears soaking the scarf at my neck. "Help me save him, Zara. Just let me touch him. He doesn't have to die. Please, we can—"

"No," she cut me off. "He doesn't matter. Only you matter."

She turned on her heel and left. I crumpled to the ground, watching my last hope of saving Josh walk away, indifferent.

With my face on the cold hard ground, my tears staining the gray concrete black, I finally looked through the two sets of bars at a dying Josh. He was on his front, his head angled toward me. The half of his face that wasn't squished into the ground was red with blood.

He didn't even look as if he was breathing, but the awful pain in my chest told me he was still alive. As long as the pain was there, there was something for the Light to be drawn to. I was dreading the pain disappearing.

I pushed my hands between the bars, reaching in his direction; it was pointless—our cages were feet away from each other—but I couldn't help trying. The tight zip ties around my wrists dug in, angrily chafing my skin, but that wasn't what demanded my attention as I moved my arms in front of me.

I was glowing. There was so much Light pushing inside of me in anticipation of releasing into Josh that I had gone nuclear again.

TWENTY TWO

At the sight of my glowing skin, I cracked. The pain, the worry, the despair, and the hopelessness churned together into something closer to frustrated anger. I growled, screwing my eyes shut and bunching my hands into fists, my nails digging into my palms hard enough to leave marks. Then I opened my fingers, stretching them wide.

My eyes flew open at the warm, tingly sensation that spread through my hands, as if I were holding them under a giant faucet, the running water firm but pleasant. But it wasn't water flowing over my hands. It was Light. And it wasn't flowing over me. It was flowing *out* of me.

I watched, mesmerized, as the Light shot across the distance between the two cages and slammed into Josh.

I didn't dare move a muscle or think a thought. I had no idea how the Light could transfer without contact, but I wasn't about to question it.

Not when it was saving Josh's life. I knew I'd done it that day on the train platform—my Light had leaked out to Ethan and Josh even though I hadn't been touching them—but I hadn't done it since, and we still had no idea how it worked.

The glow on my skin slowly faded, the pain in my chest abating until it no longer felt as if I were being torn in two. Eventually the Light pouring out of me stopped.

Josh's eyes flew open, and he took a deep, shuddering breath. Trying to push himself up, he coughed, spluttering blood everywhere, then groaned and rolled over onto his back.

"Josh!" I did my best not to shout. I didn't want the guards to come back.

He looked over at the sound of my voice, his eyes widening as they landed on mine. He tried to get up again but winced, clutching his side.

I winced too. "Don't move. Just take it easy, OK?"

"Are you OK?" His voice sounded strained. I'd been drugged, kidnapped, and betrayed, and I'd nearly had to witness him die. I was definitely *not* OK.

He watched me in that way only he could, then nodded. Our gazes stayed locked across the space of the dirty concrete floor, both of our heads on the ground, both of us reaching for the other through the metal bars.

"We need to get out of here," he ground out after a few minutes, pushing himself to a sitting position.

I sat up too, my restraints cutting painfully into my skin. "How?" I was really hoping if he had a plan, it was better than the one that had gotten him all bloody and caged. "And where are the others?"

"I was the closest when the alarm went off. Hopefully they're not too far behind." He looked around the basement, paying special attention to his cage. Pulling himself to his knees, he studied the cage door intently. I heard the metallic *click* of the lock turning, and the door swung outward.

The tug in my chest increased a little. My glowing Light transfer had managed to get him off death's doorstep, but he was nowhere near fully healed and shouldn't have been using his ability at all. I kept my mouth shut though. He was doing it to save our lives, and there was nothing I could say to convince him not to.

He rushed over to my cage. As soon as he was within reach, my bound hands went to his, and I immediately started pushing Light into him.

He paused and sharply inhaled as his eyes closed for a moment, but he didn't indulge in the sensation for long. He unlocked my cage the same way he'd done his. In an instant, he'd pulled me to my feet and wrapped me in one of his crushing hugs, my bound hands squished awkwardly between us.

The hug didn't last long either. Someone could come in at any moment.

"I need something to cut you free," he whispered into my hair before moving off. I only nodded. I didn't want him away from me, but short of hopping around with my feet bound and probably face-planting onto the concrete floor, there wasn't much I could do to follow him. So I just stood there in the open door of my cage, my heart hammering in my chest, listening intently for the sound of boots on rickety stairs.

Josh returned quickly, a pair of giant bolt cutters in his hands. "It was all I could find." He shrugged before bending down and cutting the zip tie around my ankles. He made quick work of my wrists too, and I rubbed them, wincing at the raw skin.

Josh grabbed me with one hand and held on to the bolt cutters with the other, taking the lead toward the far end of the basement—the area cast in shadow. We couldn't risk going through the same door the kidnappers had taken. There had to be another way out.

Unfortunately, we hadn't made it more than a few steps before the dreaded metallic sound of the door opening rang through the cold space.

"... why we have to knock her out again. She's tied up already," one of the kidnappers whined.

"Man, shut the fuck up and pass me the tank." His gruffer-voiced companion didn't sound as if he was in a good mood.

They were on the stairs, about to come around the corner—too close for us to make a run for it, and we had nowhere to hide. I started to panic; we didn't have time to jump back into the cages and pretend we were still tied up and knocked out.

Josh reached the obvious conclusion before I did. We had to fight.

He pushed me behind him, raised the bolt cutters over his head, and waited. I prayed that neither one of them had their guns drawn as I stuck my hands under Josh's shirt and pushed as much Light into him as possible.

But as the two men came into view, three quick, loud bangs—the sound of muted gunfire—came from somewhere above us, followed by shouting voices. The two men turned their heads, their hands going to their weapons.

Josh didn't hesitate, bringing the heavy metal tool down over the first man's head. His target crumpled to the ground, the tank I recognized from my kidnapping clanging to the ground next to him. But it was the other man who howled in pain, doubling over and clutching his head.

Had I not seen countless other people doubled over in pain just like that, I would have wondered if my mind was playing tricks on me. But I knew exactly what was causing it.

"Alec," I breathed, a tentative kind of relief flooding through me. We were still in danger, we had no idea how many people we had to fight through to get out of this situation alive, but at least the reinforcements had arrived.

Josh dropped the bolt cutters, and with a flick of his wrist, a heavy wooden crate tumbled off a nearby shelf onto the second man's head. He joined his companion on the ground, unconscious.

I crouched next to the pile of passed-out kidnappers and extracted the first man's gun from its place on his hip. Josh picked up the other weapon and reached over for mine, but instead of taking the gun away from me, he flicked the safety off and fixed me with a steady look.

"Hold it with both hands, point, squeeze the trigger, and be ready for the recoil."

I gave him a shaky nod, swallowing around the lump in my throat. He nodded sharply and turned back around, positioning himself at the corner and pointing his gun up the stairs. I stayed behind him, the heavy gun trembling in my raised hands, my brain helpfully reminding me I had no idea what I was doing.

A *bang*, like a door slamming against a wall, came from the top of the stairs. I jumped, nearly firing the gun I had no business handling. The loud noise was followed by the sound of several feet on timber.

Josh lowered his gun and slumped against the wall, but I couldn't make myself do the same. Logically I knew by his reaction that whoever was coming toward us wasn't a threat, but the horror of the situation was catching up to me, and something at the edges of my being was starting to crumble. The gun provided an illusion of safety I wasn't ready to part from.

Tyler came into view first, his gun raised as he moved forward purposefully. He was wearing a thick black vest, which was probably bulletproof, and the pale yellow shirt underneath jarred with the gritty situation we were in. The color was too cheery; his signature rolled-up sleeves, too casual. He cast his eyes over me and Josh but kept moving past us, still on alert.

Alec followed, wearing the same vest, but his combat boots, black pants, and long-sleeved top fit right in. Despite his pain ability, he too was armed, his stance almost identical to Tyler's. With his ice-blue eyes, he scanned me, then Josh, just as Tyler had, but he didn't move off immediately. He lowered his gun, extending his left hand toward me, palm out.

"Eve." His voice was level, his face blank. My eyes were darting between his face and the gun I was pointing directly at his chest. Or almost directly—my hands were shaking so badly I couldn't even aim properly.

A split second later, Ethan came around the corner. He wasn't armed, but one raised hand held a deadly ball of blue fire. His eyes went straight to me, and all the emotions he must have been holding back cracked through and poured into his expression. All the fear and worry and anger were right there in his amber eyes.

"Evie." Alec drew my attention back to him.

Fat tears began rolling down my filthy cheeks. I took my finger off the trigger, my shoulders slumping as I finally let my arms go slack.

Alec grabbed the gun by the barrel, removing it from my tenuous grip in one swift movement.

"Watch them," he said to Ethan over his shoulder, passing him the gun. Then he raised his own weapon and went after Tyler.

Ethan secured the gun in the back of his pants before stepping forward and enfolding my terrified shaking body in his big warm one. He tucked me into his side, standing between me and Josh and keeping a vigilant eye on our surroundings. I clutched at his bulletproof vest but couldn't find anywhere to grip the rigid material, so I settled for nestling my arms between us and turning my face into his shoulder.

I could feel Ethan trembling, tiny little shivers coursing through his body as he gripped me as if I might disappear into thin air at any moment. As confident as he'd looked coming around the corner, he was clearly just as freaked out as I was.

After only a few moments, Tyler's firm voice yelled, "Clear." A beat later Alec answered him with a "Clear" of his own, from the opposite end of the basement.

I lifted my head. Tyler was stalking back toward us, holstering his weapon at his hip. His gray eyes, usually so calm, were staring right at me, filled with fear. As he got within a few feet, I instinctively reached for him, and he took hold of my outstretched wrist and tugged me out of Ethan's grasp. I winced from the friction on the spot where the zip ties had cut in, but he didn't see it. He'd already pulled me into a hug.

He wrapped his arms around my shoulders, one hand at the back of my head, holding me firm to his chest. I focused on the feeling of being held by one of my Variants, on the way his fingers were flexing against my scalp.

Ethan turned to Josh and gave him a hug too before pulling away and letting Alec take his place. Alec grabbed the back of Josh's neck and pressed their foreheads together, his back and shoulders rigid. As he straightened, he said something I couldn't hear. Josh nodded weakly, raising his hand up to squeeze Alec's shoulder before they both took a step back.

"We've got company," Alec ground out, his eyes on the little windows near the ceiling.

"What about our guys?" Tyler released me to reload his gun.

Alec turned back around. "On the way. Probably another five."

"This basement is a death trap, we can't let them corner us down here." Tyler didn't wait for a response, taking the lead up the rickety stairs.

"Wait." My voice was shaky. So were my knees. "What are we doing? What do I do?"

But Ethan was already helping Josh up the stairs, and Alec was firmly nudging my back with one hand. I started climbing, my heart simultaneously climbing into my throat. At least the extra adrenaline was helping energy return to my limbs.

"Just stick close to me." Alec spoke low. "I'll keep you safe, Evie."

I had no other choice but to let them take the lead. Alec overtook me at the top of the stairs, placing his body between mine and the rest of the house.

Then things started happening fast.

Shouting and banging—the sound of glass breaking.

Alec pulled me through the door and darted down a hallway, stopping near a bathroom. When Tyler appeared next to me and grabbed my hand, I barely managed to stop myself from calling out. Josh and Ethan crowded next to us in the bathroom doorway.

"I need a little more Light, baby," Tyler whispered close to my ear, his eyes glued on the hallway, his gun raised.

Immediately, I pushed as much Light into him as I could. He dropped my hand within seconds and took off again, gesturing to Alec. I didn't understand what the hand movements meant, but Alec must have, because we followed Tyler in the opposite direction to where we'd been heading. Ethan supported a limping Josh, and we moved as a unit though the house.

Eventually I forced myself to look up from the back of Alec's bulletproof vest. We were at a front door, waning afternoon light streaming in through the side panel.

"Bulk of force coming in through the back. This is our best chance, but they're not stupid—they have a few out front as well," Tyler filled us in.

Before anyone could respond, deafening gunfire made me jump again, and this time I couldn't hold in the panicked scream that came tearing out of my throat.

It was Tyler who'd started firing. Armed men were coming down the hallway toward us. They took cover in the rooms off the hallway but soon returned fire.

Alec spun around, firing over my shoulder with one hand and pushing me behind him with the other.

To my right, a large cabinet tumbled to the floor with a tremendous *crash*, blocking the path of more assailants who were coming at us from an elaborately decorated sitting room. It wouldn't stop them, but it would slow them down.

Unfortunately, the use of his ability would slow Josh down too. The sudden pain in my chest made me cry out, the Light desperate to get to him. He wavered, but Ethan caught him, at the same time throwing an angry blue ball of fire that engulfed the cabinet in flames.

Bright light streamed into the foyer from the now open front door, and Alec pulled me through, once again keeping me behind him.

But as soon as we were outside, the gunshots started up again. Three more assailants came toward us, big black vans blocking the street behind them.

We had danger behind us and danger in front of us, and Josh was fading fast.

I didn't hesitate. I made everything else fall away—time itself seemed to stand still—as I put all my focus on Alec. My fingers tightened around his hand, and I pushed Light to him almost violently, raising my other hand to the back of his neck—the only other bit of exposed skin I could see.

I grit my teeth and growled. I was weak too. Bringing Josh back from the brink had drained me, and I couldn't get that level of power again so soon, but I pulled Light into me as hard as I could, and I shoved it all into Alec.

Within seconds, everyone was on the ground, moaning in pain, gripping their heads and stomachs. It wasn't instantaneous, as when we'd done it that first time at Bradford Hills, but eventually they all lost consciousness.

At first, my own wheezing breath was the only sound I registered. Then traffic, a loud car alarm nearby. As the wail of sirens announced we were about to have more company, my other senses joined the party too. I let go of Alec and stepped back.

We were at the top of the stairs leading into a large, elegant home.

At that moment, something clicked into place—the reason why the woman from the basement had looked so familiar. She was Senator Christine Anderson—the same woman who had delivered the rousing speech the night of the gala and was all over the TV lately. How deeply connected was she to Variant Valor? And how the fuck did Zara know her?

This had to be the senator's house. Similar homes lined both sides of the street, and tall concrete-and-glass buildings cut into the skyline a little farther away. Were we in Manhattan? Surely they couldn't have been so brazen as to keep people locked in the basement of a home in the city? And come to think of it, where was the senator? Where was Zara? Had they been involved in the gunfight inside? Had my friend shot at me? Tried to kill me?

My eyes scanned the quiet street, the bodies on the ground. When they landed on Josh, I remembered the pain in my chest.

Rubbing at the ache, I took the few steps to reach him, my hands going straight to the sides of his neck. I let the Light do its thing as best I could. I was running on empty; anything coming into me was going straight back out to him.

"Time to go," Tyler announced, reloading his gun. "Ethan, are you hurt? Help Josh to the car?"

"Yeah, I got him." Ethan's voice was shaky.

"Alec, go." Tyler turned to Alec, who was still facing the unconscious assailants. "I'll try to clean this mess up."

"What?" I croaked, whipping my head around to look at him. "You're not coming with—holy shit!"

Tyler's chest was drenched with blood. Crimson covered the entire right shoulder and right side of his shirt, the original color of the fabric not even discernible.

I was torn. Josh needed me—he was leaning heavily against Ethan, his eyes closed as he enjoyed the sensation of the Light transfer. But I ached to go to Tyler too, check where the blood was coming from, how badly he was hurt.

He must have read the torment in my face, because he came to me, pulling the collar of his shirt down. "A bullet grazed my neck. I barely felt it. I'm OK." He kissed me on the forehead, one hand in my hair, before looking me level in the eyes. "Evelyn, I'm OK. It's already stopped bleeding. Josh needs you. You need to get him home. Alec!"

But Alec was already moving. He wrapped one of my hands around Josh's, took the other, and hurried down the stairs. As we headed up the street, I looked over my shoulder to see Tyler standing by the door, watching us.

"Wait!" I tugged on Alec's hand, but he kept a firm grip, a steady pace. "Alec, we can't leave him there alone. What if they wake up? What if more come?"

He stopped, then turned me by the shoulders to fully face where we'd come from.

"Melior Group has arrived," he said evenly. "See Kyo?" He pointed to a group of three heavily armed men moving toward Tyler. More followed behind them. "Tyler is fine." He turned me back toward himself, his hands on my shoulders. "We have to go, precious. Josh needs you more than any of us right now."

I nodded. Tyler was OK—I'd seen it with my own eyes—and the panic was beginning to settle. My head didn't feel so light; my ears weren't ringing quite so much. I'd made it out. Now I had to make sure Josh did too.

TWENTY THREE

Alec resumed his lead, and I tried to focus on his wide back, his shoulders tense under the black fabric. Some people had come out of their homes to see what all the noise was about; a crowd had gathered on the street, and phones were out. I tried to take in their faces, anything to distract me from how loose Josh's grip was on my hand, how much my chest still ached even though I was transferring as much Light as our contact would allow.

As we rounded a corner, coming to a stop next to Tyler's black Escalade, it began to snow.

I had to let Josh's hand go for the few seconds it took the guys to get him into the car, and those few seconds just about tore my chest open. He lost consciousness as I doubled over in pain, the ache and urgency unbearable.

As soon as Ethan had lifted Josh's legs inside, I shoved past him and found contact at the exposed part of Josh's neck where his shirt was torn. He was slumped in the middle of the back seat, his head lolling to one side, his blood-streaked hair falling over his eyes.

The boys tried to get me to move so they could strap Josh in, but I ignored them. "Just go!"

I didn't even know where I wanted them to take us; I just needed to be on the move.

The door behind me slammed shut, and a moment later Alec was behind the wheel with Ethan in the seat next to him. He started the car and pulled away with a jolt. They'd both taken the time to strip down to T-shirts, and Ethan was cranking the heat up.

Josh needed me and my Light more than anything, but keeping him warm would help. He could use every advantage we could give him.

Sitting on my knees, I had one hand on his neck and the other clutching his limp hand on the seat. It wasn't enough. The Light was practically humming with how quickly it was flowing between us, but it was still straining against my skin. Josh needed more.

Making sure to keep contact with the backs of my hands as I went, I undid what was left of his shirt and pushed it off his shoulders. Then I pressed my forehead to his as I shrugged off my jacket and sweater, pulling my top over my head in one swift move.

After lifting myself over his lap, I removed my bra for good measure. I vaguely registered protests from the front seat about seatbelts and nudity before pressing my front flush with Josh's.

Slowly, as the car warmed up, my breathing evened out, and Josh's became stronger. We all settled into silence. Thoughts fell away, and I was lulled by the motion of the vehicle. I can't be sure how long we drove, but it must have been at least an hour or two, because my hips were aching from staying in that position for so long.

The sudden absence of the engine's rumble made me open my eyes and lift my head from Josh's shoulder. He roused at the same time, placing his hands flat against my back.

Our eyes met, all we'd been through passing between us unspoken, but the stare wasn't uncomfortable. I could look into those green eyes all day and never get weirded out or bored.

"Let's get you both inside." Ethan was the first to get out of the car, Alec following close behind.

As their doors slammed shut, Josh pressed his forehead to mine and whispered a heartfelt thanks, his hands moving to my hips and giving them a gentle squeeze.

The light pressure made me shift, my hips rolling forward, and he froze. I suddenly became very aware of how naked I was from the waist up. As if to emphasize the point, my breath hitched, and my breasts pushed farther against his chest.

I felt him grow hard under me. And then the car door opened. Alec draped a jacket over my shoulders and stepped back.

"Are you sure we shouldn't take him to a hospital?" Ethan sounded hesitant. I finally lifted my head. We were in the Zacarias mansion's underground garage.

"There's nothing better for him right now than her," Alec answered decidedly. "We'll get him checked out in the morning."

I pushed my hands into the sleeves of the jacket. The view Josh got of my breasts as I pulled back to do so was unavoidable, as was the jolt of desire that shot down my spine at the hungry look in his eyes.

I scrambled out of the car, holding the jacket closed with one hand and trying to balance on my almost numb legs with the other. Alec steadied me while Ethan helped Josh out of the car, and we all headed inside.

Much as I dreaded climbing the two flights of stairs to Josh's bedroom, that's where I suggested we go. He had regained consciousness, but he was still severely depleted, and I itched to get that skin contact back. The pull was still there; the healing was not done.

"I really need a shower first," Josh said.

Despite all our protests, he insisted he felt disgusting. There was a smear of something on his cheek that was such an odd color it couldn't be identified, and his grimy hair looked more brown than blond.

"OK," I conceded, "but then straight to bed. You still need more Light." I chewed on my bottom lip, uncertain. But now that he mentioned it, I really needed a shower too.

"I know." He smiled weakly, and then Ethan practically carried him up the stairs.

I watched them go and took a deep breath, preparing myself for what felt like a climb up Mount Everest. I lifted one foot but couldn't seem to find the energy to follow through, so I ended up twisting awkwardly and lowering myself onto the step.

I leaned my head on the banister. *I may have to ask Ethan to carry me up too.*

Then I noticed Alec standing in the foyer. He looked almost as worn out as Josh, but the ache in my chest was still pulling me up to the third floor, not to the impossible man standing in front of me, so he hadn't overused his ability. He was just emotionally and physically spent.

"You OK?" The words were out of my mouth before I could really think about them. It just seemed like the right thing to say.

His shoulders sagged, and he dragged his feet as he came and sat down next to me, resting his elbows on his knees.

"I'm fine, Evie." His voice was low and tired, but it had honey in it, and it was making my heart ache. "Not that it matters right now. But you're safe, so I'm fine. It's Josh who needs you."

"I know . . ." I was replying to what he'd said about Josh, but it felt loaded all the same. "I bet you're burning to say I told you so." I wasn't sure why I was giving him an opportunity to be an ass. I guess it just felt like our default, a bit of familiarity after so much turmoil and fear. To his credit, he didn't rise to my bait.

"I take no pleasure from any part of this situation, believe me." He looked at me with those icy eyes of his and raised his eyebrows, nothing but sincerity in his voice. "I know I don't deserve it"—he averted his gaze before continuing—"I know I've made a lot of mistakes, but can I please just hold you? Just for a moment?"

He looked so vulnerable, his eyes darting about the room, his hands clenching and unclenching. I leaned into him and rested my head on his shoulder. He released a massive breath and, in one swift move, picked me up and settled me on his lap, crushing me to his chest and burying his face in my filthy hair.

My arms were squished between us, but I managed to extract one to curl around his neck. I hadn't realized how much I'd been craving his embrace. The distance between us had begun to feel insurmountable, but I needed him. I needed him as much as I needed the others. We were incomplete without Alec. I just hoped he realized how much he needed me too.

"I keep losing you," he mumbled into my neck, his voice shaky. "I can't keep losing you, Evie. It's killing me."

"So do something about it." I had so little energy. I knew he was trying to tell me he needed me, that he regretted how things had turned out between us, but I couldn't muster much of a response. It was just too much. My brain was mush.

"I will," he whispered. Then he lifted his head and touched his hand to my cheek, nudging softly until I was looking up at him. "I will," he said with steel in his voice. "I'm going to fix this."

I stared back, at the sincerity in his face, the intensity. I knew how fucking stubborn he was; when he decided something, there was no changing his mind.

But I also knew how much he'd hurt me.

"I need a shower." I wasn't ready to accept his declaration. I wasn't in the right place, mentally or physically, to entertain the idea of trusting Alec with my heart.

He pressed his lips together, and I braced for another screaming match. But he surprised me yet again.

He stood, holding me close to his chest, and started to climb the stairs.

"I can walk." Even my words came out sounding weak.

"I know" was his quiet reply.

I didn't have the energy to struggle, so I let him carry me up the two flights of stairs, through his bedroom, and into his en suite. He set me down on the counter and turned on the hot water in the shower, then disappeared into his room. He returned a few seconds later with a bundle of clothing.

"Do you need help?" He wasn't coming on to me or looking at me with hunger in his eyes, even though the jacket was unbuttoned and my breasts were on display. He didn't look uncomfortable either. He was simply asking what I needed.

"No, I'm OK." I got off the counter. The hot water was filling the bathroom with steam, and the pure white water particles were reminding me how dirty I was. A clump of something disgusting was matted into my hair, and my mouth still tasted like vomit.

Alec nodded and left me alone, closing the door softly.

Slowly but efficiently, I managed to get myself scrubbed, my hair clean, and my teeth brushed. I was painfully aware that it was Alec's bathroom, his shower, his toothbrush I was using, and it was hard to relax under the hot spray sluicing over my aching shoulders. On top of that, the ache in my chest, pulling me to Josh, was impossible to ignore.

I dried off and put on the boxer shorts and soft black T-shirt Alec had left out for me. They smelled like him, and I had no idea how I felt about that.

The room beyond the bathroom was dark. Alec was already in bed. The brightness from the bathroom behind me cast one harsh column of light across his gray sheets. He was under the covers, his face in darkness. I couldn't see what he was looking at, couldn't guess at what he was thinking or feeling. I never could.

I switched the bathroom light off and remained in the threshold. I should go, run to Ethan or Josh—to someone emotionally safer. But then I realized I was doing what Alec always did: standing in a doorway and getting ready to run.

So I chose not to.

I did what I really wanted to do. I sought out what I craved—the comfort he'd provided that night in the hospital what felt like a lifetime ago.

I walked over and sat on the bed, my back to him. He was silent and unmoving behind me. But he wasn't throwing me out, and he wasn't leaving.

I lay down on my side, my back still to him, and screwed my eyes shut, pulling my knees up, hoping beyond hope . . .

After an excruciatingly long second, the sheets rustled, the mattress shifted. My mind convinced me he was getting up, leaving. According to psychological theory, assuming the conditions are the same, the best predictor of future behavior is past behavior.

But he didn't leave. He scooted closer and curved his body around mine. His strong arm wrapped around my front, and he held me tight, his face in my damp hair.

I didn't know what had gotten into him, but I was in no state to question it. Because my honey-voiced stranger was holding me together, and it felt so fucking good.

But that's what he was—a stranger. This side of Alec was much less familiar than the hard, cruel asshole he'd been showing me since I came to Bradford Hills. On some level I knew that wasn't really him. I couldn't describe the reasons why—it likely had more than a little to do with the supernatural tether of Light between us—but I felt as if this was the real him. *This* was how it was meant to be between us.

With his arm holding me tight, just as it had on the two worst nights of my life—when I'd lost my mother and my friend—I mourned for the relationship we could have had, *should* have had.

Pile that on top of everything else I'd been through in the past twenty-four hours, and the emotional breakdown was inevitable.

Tears stung my eyes. Heat spread up my chest, and my breathing became shallower and louder in the dark room. As the tears soaked Alec's pillow, he shifted, lifting himself up a little on his elbow. His strong presence enveloped me like a blanket of steel—comforting, protective, and suffocating all at once.

"It's OK, Evie," he crooned into my ear. "You're OK. I've got you. *We've* got you. You'll never be alone again."

In a moment of indulgence, I let all the emotion come. His declaration had probably been more in relation to my physical safety, but it had hit on one of my biggest fears—being alone in the world. And here was the man who'd pushed me away more than anyone in my life, telling me I wouldn't be. I sobbed into the pillow as Alec stroked my hair and held me, whispering things I could no longer hear.

After a while, the tears subsided, and I nudged him so he would back away a little. He responded immediately, and I rolled onto my back, wiping the tears and snot away with a wad of tissues he handed me.

"I have to go to Josh," I said in a raspy, strained whisper, rubbing my chest. "He needs me. I need him."

I needed all of them. I needed Alec to keep doing exactly what he was doing—it was soothing my soul in a way that was too scary to examine—but Josh needed me more. No, he wasn't going to die, but the ache in my chest wasn't abating. I couldn't keep ignoring it for my own selfish reasons.

Alec nodded and gave me a reassuring smile as I sat up, swinging my legs over the edge of the bed. I braced myself, fighting the fatigue in my muscles in preparation for standing, but Josh beat me to it.

He appeared in the doorway, the light from the hall casting his face in shadow but making his dirty-blond hair look like a halo. He walked over, and I pressed my hand to his bare stomach, finding skin contact as soon as possible. The ache in my chest disappeared immediately, and we both sighed in relief.

I wrapped my arms around his waist, pressing my cheek to his belly, letting the Light flow freely.

After a moment, he pulled back, and I tilted my head to look at him. He gave me a weak smile, rubbing my cheek with his thumb. Dark bags sagged under his eyes, and a cut on his chin looked as if it would probably bruise. His shoulders were slumped, but nothing but warmth emanated from his eyes.

He looked over my shoulder, but the gaze didn't linger, didn't go into a silent conversation with Alec. He just took in the scene, then got into the bed, shuffling me into the middle of the mattress.

We faced each other, my head resting on his arm, our limbs instinctually entwining. Josh's eyes closed. His mouth parted slightly, and he fell asleep almost instantly.

I was ready for oblivion too. Exhaustion was pulling my eyes closed, making me feel as if I were sinking into Alec's soft sheets and Josh's fresh, warm smell. But the sound of movement from the door caught my attention. I lifted my head—it felt like an anvil—and saw Ethan dropping a bundle of bedding on Alec's couch.

Alec sighed. "What is this?" he whispered. "A fucking slumber party?"

Ethan walked over to Alec's side of the bed, making me crane my neck to see him. He was shirtless too, his glorious, muscular body on full display. Why did they all have to sleep in nothing but underwear? It was incredibly distracting—not that I was in any state to do anything about it.

"We all need to be close tonight, bro," Ethan whispered back. He leaned over his cousin to kiss me on the lips, then on the forehead. "It's part of being in a Bond. Sometimes we *all* need her. You're just going to have to get used to it."

I tucked my head back into Josh's chest. I didn't want to see Alec's face, his reaction to Ethan's words. I didn't have the energy to deal with it.

The soft rustle of bedding as Ethan set himself up on the couch lulled me toward sleep. But as I started to drift off, Alec shifted, his movements slow and careful so as not to disturb all the sleeping people who'd dared invade his fortress of solitude.

He grabbed the blanket that had pooled around our knees and pulled it up, covering us all. But his hand lingered on my shoulder, his fingers tentatively caressing it over the fabric of the T-shirt. I stayed still.

His fingers trailed up until they found the exposed skin on my neck, but he didn't pull away. There was no Light left over for him; all I had was going to Josh. My skin tingled where Alec touched it but not because of the Light.

He removed his hand and replaced it with a kiss so soft I questioned whether it was really still him in the bed with us, but there was no denying the honey voice, the one I always craved.

"I promise," he declared, finishing some private train of thought on the barest of whispers. Then he settled himself behind me, resting his hand on my hip.

With Josh in front and Alec behind, I finally felt safe, warm, and unconsciousness took me. I would have to wonder about Alec's promise when I woke up.

TWENTY FOUR

I woke up flat on my back, my head turned toward Alec, my left hand resting on Josh's chest. Slivers of morning light peeked past Alec's heavy drapes, but most of the room was still cast in hazy darkness.

The weight of all that had happened was nudging at me, trying to wake me fully, make me think about it and dissect it and figure it all out. But I pushed it aside, covered it with a warm blanket, and made it go back to sleep. I wanted just a little longer to look at Alec's peaceful, sleeping face in the muted light, feel the steady rise and fall of Josh's chest, feel them there with me.

I sighed softly, letting my eyes rake over the little scar in Alec's eyebrow, the very slight kink in his nose, the stubble on his strong jaw. My fingers itched to reach out and touch the rough prickles, but I didn't want to risk waking him.

Josh was already awake though. He turned onto his side, making my hand drop to his hip. When he pressed his palm against my belly, I turned to face him.

His eyes were half-open, and he was watching me as I'd been watching Alec. I covered his hand with mine and inched it up.

I was making sure to keep the difficult, heavy thoughts away, but I couldn't help remembering the previous times I'd woken up from spending the night in the arms of one of my Variants, restoring their Light—the possessive way Ethan had held me that first night, the way Alec and I had crashed into each other in the study.

My skin was sensitive to every touch, my body painfully aware of the two nearly naked men on either side of me, and all the heat was pooling between my legs. My breathing got faster, my lips parted. It drew Josh's attention to my breasts under the black cotton of Alec's T-shirt.

I nudged his hand again, just a fraction, in the direction I wanted it to go. He trailed it up my ribs and cupped my breast through the fabric, gently but with confidence. The slow, deliberate movements he used to knead the soft flesh were driving me mental, but I let him take the lead for a while. He *had* nearly died after all.

His lips parted, his breath grew heavy. His hooded green eyes watched me with *need*. When I felt his rock-hard length press against my hip, my breath hitched.

Josh rocked his hips against me, and knowing he wanted me as much as I wanted him turned me on even more. I squirmed, rubbing my thighs together.

Our subtle movements must have woken Alec.

He shifted, and I froze, but Josh hadn't noticed, his hips still rocking against me in a steady rhythm, his mouth now at my neck, pressing soft, moist kisses to my burning flesh.

My heart was on the edge of a cliff, ready to fall as soon as Alec realized what was happening and put a stop to it.

But instead, I felt Alec's hand nudge the T-shirt aside, wandering up my torso until my other breast was in his hand. Instead of plummeting, my heart soared, and I moaned—a soft breathy sound as much surprise as it was arousal.

Josh paused what he was doing to look. He took in the fact that Alec had joined in, as well as the desperate, needy look on my face, and smiled a sleepy but excited smile right before he kissed me, *hard,* his hand on my breast becoming less gentle, his tongue immediately invading my mouth. But the kiss didn't last long. He pulled back and nudged me so I faced away from him.

Suddenly I was face-to-face with Alec, Josh's hardness now pressing into the curve of my ass. Alec's stare was laced with lust but a hint of uncertainty too. His hand had come away from my aching flesh as I shifted, and he wasn't making another move. So I did.

I leaned forward and kissed him as forcefully as Josh had kissed me. He responded immediately, fighting my mouth for dominance, growling a little as his strong hand went to my ribs. He was rock hard too, his arousal making itself known against my front.

Squished between them like that, not a breath of space between our writhing bodies, hands roaming everywhere—it was intoxicating. Almost too much. Too much skin, too much heat, too much sensation.

Yet it wasn't enough.

As if he'd read my mind, Josh pushed forward, giving me more. His hand thrust its way between me and Alec to the throbbing flesh between my legs. Alec moved away just enough to give him access, and Josh started rubbing me over my borrowed boxers. The friction was exquisite, and I followed his lead.

I reached down and started rubbing Alec's length the way Josh was rubbing me.

Alec growled again, a low sound that reverberated through his chest, through mine, and elicited a moan from Josh behind me. Alec pressed his forehead to mine, watching how I touched him. Encouraged by his enthusiasm, I moved my hand higher, to the waistband of his underwear. I didn't let myself pause, didn't let the memory of what had happened the last time my hand had been in this position stop me. I reached inside, pushing the fabric down, and wrapped my hand around his warm, engorged flesh.

He didn't swat my hand away. He just closed his eyes and reveled in the sensation. And I smiled in triumph.

I started slow, pumping him up and down in deliberate strokes, slowly increasing the pressure, the speed. He began to move with me, his hips bucking slightly in time with my movements.

Josh moved his hand to the waistband of my boxers before pushing his long fingers under the fabric.

"So wet ..." came Josh's strained whisper at my ear. He licked a path from the curve of my neck to my ear and started nibbling. His words sent a shiver down my spine, and I moaned softly, making Alec open his eyes.

I closed the miniscule distance between us and licked his lips. He crushed his mouth to mine, pushing his tongue inside my mouth.

But just as fast as he'd kissed me, he pulled away. His hips stilled.

The atmosphere between us changed.

Something heavy settled in the pit of my stomach. Alec closed his eyes and took a deep breath. My hand slowed, stopped. I didn't want to suffer the pain of having him remove it again, so I did it myself.

Josh stopped what he was doing too, pulling his hand out of my underwear and resting it on my hip.

Alec rolled onto his back and rubbed his closely cropped hair with both hands, sighing loudly before dragging his hands over his face. He pulled his underwear back up and turned to face me again.

"I want this so bad." His eyes may have been icy in color, but they were *burning* with intensity.

I frowned, confused, disbelieving.

"I do," he declared with more steel in his voice. Steel but also honey. He wasn't returning to his cruel, detached self, but he was still pulling away. "I'm just not ready. I always thought you were mine. Just mine. And now I have to share you—and that's OK, it is—I just need some time."

I was still breathing hard, but I pressed my lips together and looked down. I couldn't think. The throbbing between my legs was relentless, my body not yet aware of the rejection. I knew what he was saying, the words made sense, but I just couldn't process them. All I understood was that I wanted him. I wanted him and Josh and Ethan and Tyler. I wanted them closer, more, *completely*. But he was rejecting me again.

He was ruining it *again*.

"Alec . . ." Josh's whisper sounded exasperated.

"I'm sorry. I'll fix everything. I promise," Alec said softly, answering Josh's unfinished question and all my unspoken ones. Then he pressed a kiss to my head and left, his bare feet silent on the plush carpet.

The soft click of the door closing felt almost worse than if he'd slammed it.

I sat up, staring at the closed door in bewilderment. My mind was struggling to process it all. My body was still wired, still *craved*.

Josh sat up too, resting his chin on my shoulder, his hand running up and down my arm soothingly. Ethan got up from the couch and came to sit in the spot Alec had just abandoned. I'd forgotten he was even in the room. He frowned at the closed door, but when he turned his amber eyes to me, they softened.

"How about I go down and make us some pancakes?" he whispered, cupping my cheek, rubbing his thumb over it softly.

He was always so gentle with me. But I didn't want gentle. I wasn't done. My mind was reeling, but my body was still on fire, my skin tingling, every nerve ending on edge.

"No," I whispered back. For some reason, we were all keeping our voices, our moans and sighs, low. The curtains were still drawn, the room deceptively dark despite the light threatening to burst from behind the heavy drapes.

"No?" Ethan frowned, cocking his head.

"No." I licked my lips, and his eyes dropped to my mouth for a split second. He was in nothing but underwear, the bulge under the thin fabric impossible to hide. Even if he hadn't been a participant, he'd been affected by what we'd started in the bed. He'd heard the rustling of the sheets, our whispers, our soft moans. He was setting his desire aside because he thought that's what I wanted. They both were.

But that wasn't what I wanted. I wanted *more* intimacy with them, not less. If Alec didn't want to be a part of that yet, that was his problem.

"Fuck him," I breathed an inch away from Ethan's mouth. Then I wrapped a hand around his neck and crashed my lips to his. His response was instant, the hand at my cheek threading back into my hair as his tongue met mine.

Josh's hand pushed up under my T-shirt to find my breasts again. My nipples were hard and sensitive, and every touch, every caress, felt impossibly heightened, as though beyond what a human brain was normally capable of processing.

I broke my frenzied kiss with Ethan to rip the T-shirt off over my head.

We all fell back to the pillows in a tangle of limbs and bedding and heavy breathing. Two hands—one with long artistic fingers, one with strong athletic ones—dragged the last scrap of clothing off my body. Alec's boxers disappeared into the void beyond the edge of the mattress.

Nothing existed but the bed; nothing was going to interrupt, stop, or ruin what I'd started up again. While Ethan assaulted my mouth with his, his tongue pushing in and out steadily, Josh moved his hand between my legs once again.

This time there was no fabric hindering his movements. He teased me, spreading the wetness around, circling my clit.

"So fucking wet," he whispered again, his hot mouth at my cheek, inches away from mine, from Ethan's.

Ethan broke the kiss and looked at Josh.

"Is she?" he whispered, his eyes dancing, the amber vibrant even in the dim light of the bedroom.

"Oh yeah. Feel it." Josh punctuated his statement by pushing one finger just inside me and then pulling it out again. We both groaned.

Ethan bit his lip, his eyes flicking between my flushed face and Josh's, all our mouths so close that if I were to lean up just a little, I could probably taste them both.

I tilted my face, and Josh's lips met mine, his tongue darting out. Ethan pressed his forehead to the side of mine, watching us kiss. He didn't join in, but he didn't pull away either, his lips inches from ours. He trailed a big, warm hand down the length of my naked body, and his fingers joined Josh's between my legs.

"Fuck," he groaned, his breath washing over our wet lips. Ethan's face was glorious, his eyes half-closed, his mouth hanging open as he panted, running his fingers up and down my folds.

"I want to taste it . . ." he whispered so quietly I wasn't sure he meant to say it out loud. But his face was so close to mine I heard every word, and it filled me with curiosity and desire so strong I finally broke the kiss with Josh.

Whatever Ethan saw in my face made him smile, his lips slowly turning up into a devious smirk. When he licked his lips, in what I'm sure was a deliberate move to make me imagine what his tongue would feel like on *my* lips, I couldn't help smiling back and nodding.

It was all the encouragement he needed. He shimmied down the bed, kissing and licking my body as he went, taking his time with my breast, nipping at the sensitive spot on my ribs. All the while, Josh kept kissing my neck, his hips rocking against me from behind.

As Ethan's face came level with my hips, Josh moved his hand out of the way. He grabbed my ass firmly and bit down on my neck, making me gasp. Then he moved his fingers back between my legs, only from behind, giving Ethan full access to the front.

Ethan grabbed the inside of my thigh and held my leg out of the way, giving himself enough room to press his mouth to my molten core.

As Ethan's lips started kissing, then sucking my most sensitive flesh, Josh pushed two fingers inside. I was completely lost in the sensations of what the two of them were doing to me. The licking and sucking and pushing and stretching . . . It was almost too much. My mind completely shut off, and I became nothing more than what they were making me feel.

They worked in perfect synchronicity, Josh's fingers and Ethan's mouth finding a steady rhythm that had my ecstasy climbing with increasing intensity.

My body started to tremble, soft little shivers spreading from my core down my limbs. When Josh leaned over and took one of my nipples in his mouth, I reached the peak of pleasure and came plummeting down all at once.

I cried out, a guttural, almost surprised sound that broke the relative quiet that had enveloped the room. The intensity of the orgasm made my back arch off the mattress, lifting me onto my elbows.

Once the stars obscuring my vision cleared, things beyond the edge of the bed faded back into reality.

Tyler was standing in a pile of bedding near the fireplace, wearing tight black briefs and a crumpled shirt, half the buttons undone. He was holding his gun loosely by his side and staring at me as I panted through the aftershocks of my orgasm, his mouth slightly open, as if he didn't quite believe what he was seeing.

Josh laughed—a surprised yet unabashed chuckle, as if he couldn't quite hold it in. That made Ethan lift his face from between my legs. He glanced first at us, then over his shoulder.

His big shoulders started to shake too, and I deliberately, slowly closed my legs. I hadn't known Tyler was in the room. With his mussed hair and glassy eyes, he looked half-asleep. I must have woken him with the unrestrained sound that Ethan and Josh had elicited.

"You all right, Gabe?" Josh asked, the laugh still in his voice as he gently kissed my shoulder, keeping his eyes on Tyler.

"Uh, yeah, I'm . . ." Tyler finally looked away, casting his eyes about the room, to the bedding at his feet, as if he was only just realizing where he was. His mind was catching up, but his voice still had that gritty, sleepy quality to it. "I heard a shout, and I . . . uh . . ."

He lifted the weapon in his hand and frowned at it. Obviously, when my orgasmic outburst had startled him from sleep, his training had kicked in, his senses looking for the threat.

"That was just us," Ethan teased. His head was turned away from me, but I was sure his dimples were showing. "Giving our girl the wakeup call she deserves."

He punctuated his answer by biting the top of my thigh and making me yelp.

Their laid-back attitude put *me* at ease. I'd had a moment of hesitation when I realized someone had been present for such an intimate experience. But it wasn't just someone; it was Tyler. He was part of my Bond, and I was no longer unsure where I wanted our relationship to go.

I laughed too, throwing my head back and letting my sweaty, perfectly satiated body flop back into the soft bedding.

"I'll just . . . ah . . . I need a shower," Tyler mumbled, walking out of the room without waiting for a response. I peeked over Josh's body just in time to see Tyler adjust himself before reaching for the door handle. I laughed again. To know he was as affected as we were—that he wanted it too—filled me with joy. Much as he fought for control of the situation with his mind, there was no hiding what his body wanted.

"Fifty bucks says he's rubbing one out in the shower." Ethan crawled up to settle himself on my other side, still chuckling.

"No way am I taking that bet!" Josh fired back, but he was grinning too. "He's *definitely* rubbing one out in the shower. Plus, how would we settle it? Someone would have to go in there to check."

"I volunteer as tribute!" I yelled, and we all descended into laughter once again. I wasn't even self-conscious about how various parts of my body might be jiggling in unsightly ways. I was too busy wiping tears from the corners of my eyes.

Our giggles subsided, and we all just lay there, catching our breath and staring at the ceiling. Ethan's hand rested easily on my bare thigh while Josh traced lazy patterns up and down my upper arm.

I didn't want to get out of bed, didn't want to break this sickeningly happy, naked bubble we were in by opening the curtains—letting the light illuminate all the shit we still had to deal with.

But my stomach had other ideas. It growled loudly, breaking the moment.

"OK." Ethan slapped me on the thigh and sat up. "Pancake time."

Josh pressed a quick kiss to my cheek and jumped out of bed too.

My eyebrows creased, and I shot up. "Wait."

They were already standing, but they paused and looked at me.

"What about . . ." I gestured to the still obvious bulges in both their underwear. I was beyond satisfied—they'd been generous in the way they'd worshipped my body—but neither of them had finished. "I want to, you know, return the favor."

I let my expression fill with lust, raking my eyes over their amazing bodies, taking in the tattoo on Ethan's strong shoulder and the lithe muscles of Josh's abdomen, dragging my eye lower . . . I wanted to make them feel as good as they'd made me feel. It was making me excited all over again.

They exchanged a loaded look before focusing back on me. Ethan growled and rubbed his short black hair with both hands.

Josh exhaled sharply. "You look so fucking hot, lying there in the tangled sheets, naked and inviting." I arched my back, pressing my breasts forward at his words, illustrating his point for him. "There is nothing we want more than to just crawl back to you and let you . . ." He growled too and rubbed his erection with the palm of his hand, as if it was painful not to touch it any longer. "But if we cross that line, if we receive from you in the same way you've received from us . . . I think it's better that we sort out the situation with Alec first. You need to be sure you're ready for this with all of us."

He was talking about what I'd discussed with Tyler, what I'd done my best to research. The Light demanded equality in my connection to my Bondmates. The deeper the connection—the stronger the next level of intimacy—the harder it was to resist evening the score with the others.

Alec wasn't ready; he'd expressed that clearly. I *was* ready; I wanted them all. But I was apprehensive about taking that step with Alec while so much was unresolved between us emotionally.

Once again, they'd thought of the consequences of our physical relationship, managed to push their own lust aside to put my emotional well-being first. What the fuck I had ever done to deserve them was beyond me.

I pulled the sheet up to cover my naked body and nodded, giving them both a genuine smile to show I understood.

They smiled back, then headed for the door.

"I guess we're all rubbing one out in the shower this morning," Ethan mumbled, but we both heard him clearly. I laughed, happy the moment was ending on a light note.

Once they were out of the room, I started looking for my discarded clothing, focusing on the promise of pancakes as I headed for the shower myself.

TWENTY FIVE

As I headed downstairs, dressed once again in borrowed men's clothing, the heaviness of the past twenty-four hours started to settle in. With every step, the weight on my shoulders increased, wiping the smile off my face.

Step. Alec ran away from you. Again.

Step. You were kidnapped . . .

Step. . . . knocked out . . .

Step. . . . nearly killed.

Step. Zara betrayed you—had possibly been plotting to do it since Beth's death.

As I allowed myself to think about what Zara had done for the first time since coming face-to-face with her in that basement, I had to pause. One hand flew to the railing; the other went to my abdomen as I bent over. I felt sick—both as if I might vomit and as if my stomach were hollow.

After a few deep breaths, I straightened and continued to the kitchen. I was trying to convince myself the hollow feeling had more to do with the fact that I hadn't eaten in nearly a day. Maybe food would help.

Alec and Tyler sat side by side at the dining table, laptops in front of them, both absorbed in what they were doing. They had the exact same posture—shoulders slightly hunched, hands moving furiously over keyboards—and they wore matching creases between furrowed brows. Tyler paused what he was doing and reached for a steaming mug of disgusting black coffee. Alec reached for his own only a beat behind him.

They were so similar in their mannerisms I wondered for a second if they weren't related by blood after all.

I padded into the large open-plan room, the thick socks I'd taken from one of Alec's drawers making my movements soundless.

"Morning, Eve." Tyler greeted me without lifting his eyes from his screen.

"Morning, Evie." Alec did the same thing.

I guess I hadn't been as stealthy as I thought. I cleared my throat before mumbling my own "morning" and shuffling into the kitchen.

At the fridge, I frowned. Alec had called me Evie, and he hadn't sounded pissed off or hostile *at all*. In fact, his voice had that honey quality I craved like an idiot. It was so contradictory to his behavior earlier that it was confusing the shit out of me.

Again, I put all my focus on food instead, pulling a bunch of stuff from the fridge for scrambled eggs. I'd cracked a dozen eggs into a big bowl when Ethan came into the kitchen.

"Morning!" He grinned widely.

The two at the table grunted in acknowledgment. Ethan planted a kiss on my cheek, replaced the fork in my hand with a fancy whisk, and started chopping vegetables, chattering about the omelet we were apparently making.

Josh joined us not long after, giving me a kiss and making coffee. Since I'd started staying over, a shiny new espresso machine had appeared in the butler's pantry. I was never without a good latte anymore.

No one spoke about the heavy shit for the next half hour. We expertly ignored the shaky camera-phone footage of ourselves playing on the muted TV as we ate the omelet and sipped our coffees.

As I finished my latte and dropped my dishes into the sink, Tyler cleared his throat, closing his laptop.

"Eve, in light of the events of last night, I'd like you to consider moving permanently into our place." His voice was even as always, his hands clasped on top of his laptop. But the slight tightness around his eyes gave him away. He was worried about my response.

Ethan's head snapped up, looking from Tyler to me as a huge grin spread over his face.

Josh nodded. "I was going to suggest the same thing."

I leaned back against the sink, gripping the edge of the bench on either side of me. I was trying so hard to ignore all the things threatening to tear us apart; I hadn't expected that to be the first thing he raised. I hadn't even thought about it.

"None of you have even asked me out properly, yet you're asking me to move in?" I joked, trying to buy myself time.

Instead of taking up my teasing tone as he usually did, Ethan fixed me with one of his rare serious looks.

"I think we both know I was never pretending, baby. I'm yours through and through," he declared without a hint of doubt, his big shoulders rolling back.

I couldn't help looking over to Josh as an unfamiliar emotion threatened to choke me, the smile falling from my face.

Josh smiled at me with his knowing look, answering my unasked question, "Me too. Goes without saying."

I looked back to Tyler, and he beckoned me to come away from the sink and rejoin them. When I did, he wrapped his warm fingers around mine. "If words of commitment are what you need, then, yes, I'm in too. Mind, body, and soul. I just want you to be safe, and since Zara . . . I don't like the idea of you staying in the res hall alone."

I didn't like the idea of being alone either. I never wanted to feel alone again.

"You know about Zara?" I asked.

"We saw her at Christine Anderson's house when we arrived." Alec broke my flimsy bubble of pretending he wasn't in the room. "She wasn't tied up or locked in a basement, so we figured she had something to do with your abduction. According to reports from my team, she and the senator are the only ones who got away—with the help of Zara's parents. We're trying to track them down."

"Shit." I pulled my hand out of Tyler's and wiped it across my eyes. Talking about Zara was making it all come back. Betrayal was the worst kind of . . .

"And just so it's clear"—the hard edge in Alec's voice had me lifting my head to look at him—"I want you here just as much as the others. Don't let me stop you from moving in here. I said I would fix things, and I meant it."

"Oh, was that you fixing things this morning?" The snipe was reflexive, born out of the need to protect myself emotionally from Alec's behavior.

"What happened this morning?" Tyler frowned, looking between us. He didn't like not knowing things.

"Dude," Ethan said, "you slept through a lot."

"Evie . . ." Alec's voice was soft, his eyes pleading. Something clenched deep in my gut, but I wasn't ready to let him off the hook.

"You basically pulled the same shit you did that night in Tyler's study.

You know how much that hurt me." I crossed my arms and stared him down, challenging him to disagree.

With a deep sigh, Tyler dropped his head into his hands, running his fingers into his messy hair and leaving them there. "We can't keep doing this." He spoke to the table. "It's getting dangerous. Everyone else knows now anyway."

The rest of us shared confused looks. He was talking to himself, but he wasn't making a lot of sense.

"Gabe?" Josh leaned forward, but before he could formulate a question, Tyler jumped up out of his seat, coming around the table to stand in front of me.

"Enough is enough," he declared in a louder, confident voice. I stood up a little straighter. His shoulders were back, his face determined as he grabbed my face in his hands and kissed me firmly.

I made a muffled sound of surprise, and then my eyes closed of their own volition, my hands lifting to rest on his hips.

He pulled away just a fraction, his lips not even an inch away from mine.

"Let it flow, baby," he whispered, his warm breath washing over my face.

Then his lips were back on mine with a renewed intensity. One hand threaded into the still damp hair on the back of my head while the other circled around my back, pressing our bodies firmly against each other.

I wrapped my arms around him and completely dropped my mental barriers, letting the Light flow freely. It always came most easily when one of them was kissing me—when all my logic went out the window, chased away by the heady feeling at the base of my spine.

Tyler pushed his tongue into my mouth, and I moaned softly, his hard chest pressing against my breasts. With a new wave of desire, a fresh wave of Light came pouring out, and he moaned in response.

"Uh, guys?" Ethan's voice only just managed to penetrate the fog of lust

Tyler had so expertly got us lost in. With a few more soft kisses to my swollen lips, Tyler pulled away but still held me close.

"My ability is not dangerous." He spoke at a volume the others could hear, but his gray eyes focused on mine. "But it can be hard to live with sometimes. I know so many things I'd rather not know. Sometimes I'll ask an innocent question, and my ability fills in the answer in ways I don't expect. It can be a burden carrying others' secrets."

I frowned, not sure where he was going with this, but didn't interrupt. I ran my thumb across his cheek in what I hoped was a soothing gesture and waited for him to continue.

"So when I know that someone has a secret, something they don't want to talk about, I try my best to respect that. I don't ask them about it because I know they don't want me to know."

"Oh, shit." As usual, Josh was the first to figure out what was going on.

"I've respected your privacy." Tyler looked at me pointedly. "I've tried to be there for you in the hope that you would come to trust me enough to tell me yourself, but you're more stubborn than I anticipated."

His mouth quirked up just a fraction, but my eyes widened as I realized what he was doing.

"Shit! Tyler, no!" I injected as much steel into my voice as I could, my shoulders tensing as I pushed him away. He let me put a little distance between us, but his hands came to rest lightly on my hips.

"Eve, we've come so far, the five of us. We're getting closer and working as a team more every day. But this thing between you and Alec, it's hanging over us like a cloud. Shit's getting really serious, and we just can't afford to have any more surprises. Not ones we can prevent. No more secrets."

"This is none of your business, Tyler." Outrage surged through me, my breathing erratic for all the wrong reasons now. But I couldn't seem to make my hands leave his shoulders. I was scared of this thing coming out—this thing festering between Alec and me. I was scared of what they would think of me, how they would react. But even as my anger rose, I knew it wasn't Tyler's fault for pushing it. I *needed* a push.

"It is though." His eyes were sad, as if part of him wished that weren't true. "I'm yours. Don't you get it? This isn't some human relationship with human rules. I'm a Variant and you're my Vital. Your relationship with each of us doesn't exist in a vacuum, separate from the others. We're your Bond—we're *all* yours, and we're *all* in this together. When something affects you, it affects us all."

He was right. The connection we had was far beyond anything that could be described adequately with words. Each one of them was a part of me, and I hadn't known how incomplete I was until I found them.

Tyler had stopped speaking. He'd forced out of me the means by which he could get the information himself, but he was still giving me a chance to tell it first. He'd nudged me to the ledge, but the final leap was mine to take. I just didn't think I had the words. I wasn't sure I could get them all past the emotions lodged in my throat.

I looked up at his patient gray eyes, took a deep breath, and nodded once, giving him permission to finish what he'd started.

"Alec," he said immediately, not giving me a chance to change my mind, "the night of the invasion, when you and Eve—"

"No!" The sound of a chair scraping on the floor was accompanied by Alec's firm voice. "Tyler, I refuse to speak about this."

Neither one of us was looking at Alec. Tyler was focused on me, and I was returning his gaze, even though every fiber of my being wanted to avoid his eyes.

"When you and Eve were in my study, alone"—Alec started cursing, but Tyler just raised his voice and kept speaking—"what happened between you two?"

"Fuck!" Alec stormed around the table, coming to stand right next to us. I could see him out of the corner of my eye but kept my focus on Tyler.

I watched his face closely, making a conscious effort not to cringe at what I knew must be running through his head. His eyes darted back and forth, and his mouth dropped open slightly. I replayed the main highlights of Studygate in my head as I watched him: Alec holding me and telling me I wasn't alone, the matter-of-fact way he'd said he hated me, the frenzied make-out session on the couch, my incredible orgasm, Alec rejecting me, my outburst and the smashed glass all over the floor.

With a sharp intake of breath, Tyler's focus slammed back into the present moment. I dreaded to see what look would cross his face now. Would he be disgusted with me, disappointed in me, pity me, or some other unfathomable combination of awful things?

But none of that came. Instead, he released me, only to push me behind him and give his full attention to Alec.

"What the fuck is wrong with you?" he seethed, and I braced for Alec's response, sure he would explode and start shouting and throwing things. But he remained silent.

I leaned around Tyler to peek at him. Alec was breathing hard, his head hanging low and his shoulders slumped. Ethan and Josh were both staring at us with wide eyes, out of their seats and looking as if they were poised to move at any moment.

"So many things," Alec finally replied, his voice quiet and a little shaky. "I fucked up, OK? I didn't even realize how badly I fucked up at the time, but I know now. I'm an asshole."

I snorted and rolled my eyes. I'd called him that as I threw the glass paperweight in the general direction of his head. I'd been calling him that in my head and out loud for months.

"What were you thinking, man?" Tyler's shoulders were tense, one arm still holding me back protectively. He was keeping me away from Alec. He was protecting me *from Alec*. His ability had shown him not only the facts of what had happened but the truth about how I felt—about how Alec made me feel most of the time—vulnerable.

"I wasn't." Alec finally looked up, pleading. "You've never been depleted like that. You don't know what it's like to feel like you're fading into nothingness, and then you feel the most incredible thing—it's what sunshine would taste like, what warm summer nights smell like, what it feels like to be wrapped up in a warm blanket, naked. And it's the only thing keeping you tethered to this world. And then you start to get some conscious thought back, and you realize all those things are *her*. It's fucking impossible to resist."

I didn't know what it felt like to be on the other side of Light transfer. I knew what it was like for me, but I'd never asked what it felt like for them.

"That's not an excuse." Tyler echoed my thoughts.

"Can someone please clue us in on what the fuck the three of you are talking about?" Ethan's booming voice could never be ignored, but I knew him well enough to hear the note of insecurity in it. He didn't like feeling left out. His big arms were crossed over his chest where he stood, frowning at us.

Josh had sat back down, but he was watching us intently too. "Yeah, even I'm having trouble keeping up."

Tyler rubbed his temple. "I don't even have words . . ."

"Now you know why I refused to talk about it." I stepped around Tyler and fixed him with a firm look.

Alec sighed and turned to face the table. He still hadn't looked at me, and it was beginning to piss me off. "Look, I'm not proud of it, OK? But that night—"

"No. I'll tell it." It was time to put my big-girl panties on anyway. I was sick of people speaking for me, and I was getting sick of Alec's voice. It sounded like honey—gentle and genuine—which told me he was being honest, but I wasn't ready to forgive him. Not that he'd even asked for forgiveness.

Calling up every scrap of maturity I could muster, I took a deep breath and spoke in as even a voice as I could manage. "You both know what happens when you idiots overuse your abilities and I have to juice you up." I looked between Josh and Ethan, fighting the urge to look down out of embarrassment, to hunch my shoulders, to fidget. "You know how drawn we are to each other. The Light pushes me . . . and the urge to just . . . get closer is . . . So I'm sure it's not a surprise that things got physical between Alec and me. But things went further than they'd gone with any of you at that point, and I'm not even entirely sure how, because I tried to . . . and then . . . Fuck, I'm mumbling!"

No one was saying anything, giving me the time I clearly needed. I took a breath and crossed my arms. It made me feel a little stronger.

"OK, basically Alec got me off, and then—"

"You two had sex?" Ethan's voice was higher pitched than I'd ever heard it. Josh's eyebrows shot up. I could almost see the gears turning in his head.

"There is more than one way to get a woman off, little cousin." Alec chose possibly the worst thing he could say at that moment, and he said it with that cocky grin, the one that turned one corner of his mouth up.

Fucking asshole. I stared at him, my mouth agape, my brain trying to process that *he'd actually said that* while also trying not to think about all the other ways he could get me off. I was decidedly pissed off at him, wanted nothing more than to be away from him, yet I was getting turned on at that mere suggestion of feeling his hands, and other things, on me again. I hated it. But that's what the Light did. That's what it meant to be in a Bond. You were drawn to each other no matter what.

"You did not just crack a joke." Tyler groaned.

"Dude, what is wrong with you?" Josh bugged his eyes out at him.

"I thought we already established that many things are wrong with me. I was trying to lighten the mood." Alec groaned. "It came out before I could think about it. I can't fucking think straight when she's around."

"Enough!" I banged my fist on the table. Like the mature adult I was trying so hard to be, I ignored that he'd just blamed his stupid comment on my presence and got back to the task at hand. "I am speaking. No more interruptions."

I fixed each of them with a serious look, and they all looked appropriately chastised. Even Alec.

"As I was saying, he got me off—and I'm not going to elaborate on the details. Then when I tried to return the favor, he pretty much told me I was worthless and ran out of the room." Josh and Ethan were staring at me with horrified expressions on their faces. "He rejected me twice that night, but none of that hurt as bad as when he told me he *fucking hated me*." I ground the last part out between clenched teeth and felt the sting of tears. Blinking furiously, I finally allowed myself to turn away from them and toward the picture windows, staring at the heavy clouds hanging over the massive yard.

Silence filled the room for a beat.

Then sudden movement drew my eyes back around just in time to see Ethan's fist flying at Alec's head.

TWENTY SIX

We all knew Alec was lethal and could've stopped Ethan's punch from landing, but he just stood there and took it. The muscles in Ethan's arms and back bunched as he delivered the blow. Alec's head snapped to the side, and he stumbled a little, catching himself on the edge of the island.

My hands flew to my mouth in shock. Tyler and Josh sprang into action, getting between the two cousins. Tyler pressed both palms flat against Alec's chest, and Josh used his ability, floating Ethan a couple of inches off the ground to drag him back.

"I'm not gonna hit him back." Alec held his arms out at his sides, and Tyler lowered his hands. "I'm not gonna hit any of you back. If that's what you need to feel better, I'll let you all have a free hit."

"Would you stop being a fucking martyr?" Josh rolled his eyes, releasing

Ethan once it became clear the big guy wasn't struggling either.

"I didn't punch you to make myself feel better." Ethan frowned, his voice hard. "I did it because what you did was low, and there need to be consequences for treating our Vital like shit."

He pointed at me as if to illustrate his point. I lowered my hands from my mouth to my chest. I didn't like the violence, but I could appreciate the sentiment. They were standing up for me—defending my honor. It was positively chivalrous, and I was beyond relieved they weren't upset with me, that they weren't judging me.

"May I speak?" Alec asked in a quiet, serious voice, finally looking directly at me.

I sighed and made a "whatever" gesture, then turned back to face the windows, having trouble holding his intense gaze. His footsteps approached, but then he just stood there, not saying anything.

Frustration built inside me, creasing my brow and making my heart rate speed up. I whipped around, ready to demand what the hell he wanted to say.

"I'm sorry!" he blurted out before I'd even opened my mouth.

I don't know what I'd been expecting, but it certainly wasn't that. He knew how much he'd hurt me. He'd had plenty of opportunities to apologize. I'd all but given up on it.

"You're sorry?" My tone suggested it wasn't good enough. Because it wasn't.

"Yes. I'm sorry. I know I should have said it sooner, but I just didn't know how. I tried so many times, but something would interrupt, or I would realize what I was about to say just wasn't . . . enough. I didn't know how to make sure you understood that I meant it. That I fully recognize how much I fucked up."

His shoulders hunched forward, and his eyes darted between mine, pleading, refusing to release me.

I crossed my arms and let him fill the silence.

"I'm sorry I rejected you. I'm sorry I made you feel worthless." He looked disgusted at the mention of that word. "I'm sorry I blamed you for something that was all on me. I'm sorry I suggested that the fact we saved all those people was somehow a bad thing. *I'm sorry I said I hated you.*"

His voice broke a little at the end, and the lump returned to my own throat. I was already on edge, and here was the strongest, hardest man I'd ever encountered getting emotional. It had nothing to do with the fact that he was finally saying what I'd needed to hear from him since that night. Nothing to do with the fact that I was maybe starting to believe him. At least that's what I was trying to convince myself of.

"That's what I'm most sorry about, Evie." At the sound of my childhood nickname, the tears spilled over, and I had to take a shuddering breath. "Because it's not true. It couldn't be further from the truth. It's *me* that I hate."

Tears tracked down my face, but I was also confused. Why was he saying he hated himself?

"My ability makes people literally recoil from me. It causes so much pain. And I've been living with that since I was twelve. It's who I am, and I know I can't change it, but I *hate* it. Your mere presence makes the one thing I hate about myself amplified exponentially. I blamed you for that when I should know better than anyone that you can't control that. It just is what it is. I took my own fucked-up feelings about myself and projected them onto you."

He took a step closer, his hands in front of him, palms turned up. We were both breathing a little hard, both trying to hold back the tears. He was doing better than I was. His eyes were red and misty, but my tears were already soaking the collar of my hoodie.

"I'm so, *so* sorry."

I was finding it really hard not to believe him. The layers of defensive anger I'd built up were slowly crumbling, torn down by the sincerity in his face and words.

And then he delivered the final blow.

"Because the truth is"—he took a deep breath—"I don't hate you at all, Evelyn. I fucking love you."

I definitely was not expecting *that*. My arms dropped to my sides as my jaw unhinged. The tears were still trickling down my cheeks, but I didn't even know why anymore. I was frozen to the spot, no idea how to react.

I chanced a quick glance in the direction of the table. Tyler was wearing a look very similar to mine—shocked. Ethan looked surprised too, but he was also smiling a little, the dimples only just appearing. Josh had a smug grin on his face, suggesting he wasn't surprised at all. Naturally . . .

Alec didn't bother to check the others' reactions. His focus was all on me.

"I've loved you since the day you were born and we went to the hospital to meet you and my mom insisted I hold you. I love you with that same protective, nurturing feeling I had toward you when we were kids. I love you in that uniquely fucked-up, impossible-to-describe way that all Variants love their Vitals—because I can't help that one. I love you for making Ethan feel like he has a family again. I love you for drawing Josh out of his books and making him rejoin the real world. I love you for making Tyler realize he doesn't have to be the strong one all the time.

"I tried to fight it—*riled* against it. But then I saw how fucking smart you are, and I watched you repeatedly get this close"—he held his thumb and forefinger very close together between our faces—"to finding me several times before I could stop it. I watched you show up and fall into this world like you belong here—because you do. I watched you as you embraced the news that you're not only a Variant but a *Vital*. And I watched you constantly push every damn button I have. I realized you're *strong*. Much stronger than

I ever gave you credit for. And I loved every fucking minute of it, even while I was constantly getting frustrated and pissed off. I loved it because I was finally around you all the time. And I love you."

"Stop saying that." Something warm and fuzzy—but also incredibly confusing—was igniting in my chest.

"I can't." He chuckled darkly and looked up to the ceiling. "It's out now. There's no putting it back in."

"I don't want you to put it back in," I replied as Ethan chuckled. His mind was always in the gutter, but I ignored him. "I just don't understand. I'm . . . what does this mean? What do you *want?*"

That was the main issue—what the hell did he want from me? Did he expect us to just start acting like a couple? Going on dates? Cuddling on the couch?

"I want you to forgive me. And I know it won't be this easy—that's why I haven't tried to make it right yet, because I didn't know what I could possibly do or say to atone—but at least it's all out there now. It's a start."

He stopped speaking and just stared at me, the tattoos running up and down his arms projecting the tough guy exterior that completely contrasted with the vulnerable look on his face.

"It's a start," I conceded in a low voice. Because it was. He had at least admitted he was an asshole and apologized for it.

He breathed a massive sigh of relief and nodded. "OK. I'm just going to . . . go. For a little while."

I frowned at him. He was leaving?

"I'm not running away," he rushed out, holding up his hands as if approaching a wild animal. As though *I* was the one who might bolt at any moment. "I'm just going for a walk, and I'm coming right back. *Not* running away. Just giving you some space. OK?"

He wasn't actually leaving. Not this time. I nodded, and he turned around, finally releasing me from his intense stare, and walked toward the front of the house.

I released a massive breath I hadn't realized I'd been holding. Then I turned to Tyler. If he was determined to break every barrier between us, if he felt entitled to know what was between me and Alec, then I felt no qualms about asking him to use his ability to give me some clarity.

"Was he telling the truth?" I braced myself for a fight—for him tell me he had to toe a line between being truthful and betraying others' privacy. But he didn't. He smiled and leaned on the table, staring after Alec, his posture relaxed.

"Alec can be hard to read sometimes." He kept his eyes trained on the middle distance. "He's so conflicted about himself, his place in the world, his feelings about it all, that often, even when I detect truth in what he's saying, it's laced with doubt. But, Eve"—finally he turned his eyes to me—"I have never heard him sound so sure of anything in my life. I've never sensed more truth coming off him than I did just then."

I let his words sink in for a moment. "Still doesn't excuse the way he treated me."

"No, it doesn't." The way Tyler pressed his lips together, a frown pulling at his eyebrows, told me he'd be having another chat with Alec. "But he *is* sorry and he *does* love you. That much you can be sure of."

I nodded and sighed. I didn't know what to say. In true Alec fashion, he'd dropped a massive bombshell and then promptly made his exit, leaving the rest of us to deal with the fallout. Only this time, I needed the space too.

Ethan used the stretching silence to bring the conversation full circle. "So, will you move in with your four boyfriends?"

He flashed me his dimples, obviously attempting to lift the mood, even though I could tell he was anxiously awaiting my answer.

"Yes." I smiled. "I'll move in with my four stalkers. I mean my four Bonded Variants. Tomato, tomato." I waved a hand, but he whooped and lifted me clean off the ground, mashing his lips to mine and making me remember what we'd been up to earlier in Alec's bed.

As soon as Ethan set me down, Josh enfolded me in one of his bone-crushing hugs. "Thank god," he whispered into my hair. "I was already planning a roster so one of us could stay with you on campus every night. This is much more convenient."

"Oh, well, I'm happy to make your stalking habit easier on you." I chuckled as he released me.

"Come on." Tyler pulled me over to the couch and tucked me into his side. "We need a break from the heavy stuff."

He flicked through channels, making the news disappear until he found some shitty sitcom, and we all settled in.

Alec came back and sat in the empty spot next to me, taking my feet and putting them in his lap. Tyler's hold on me tightened, and he placed a reassuring kiss on the top of my head. I decided to leave my feet in Alec's lap. I wasn't sure how I felt about his declarations, but he could have my feet for a little while. I was willing to give him that much.

Halfway into the third episode, Dot bounded into the room.

"What the fuck is this?" She put her hands on her hips, furious. "You assholes promised to tell me when she woke up, and I show up here to find you . . ." She gestured wildly to our various reclined states on the comfy couches. Ethan was snoring lightly, not in the least disturbed by her dramatic entrance.

"Sorry, Dot." Tyler looked guilty. "We had some things to discuss. She's fine, see?" He held up one of my wrists as proof.

"No, I don't see." She sniffed, turning her nose up. "I need a closer look."

I peeled myself off the couch with a groan and went over to her. "I'm fine, Dot. I promise."

She sprang forward and wrapped her arms around me. I held her for a long time, only pulling away when she did.

"I was so worried it had happened again," she whispered, not looking at me.

"It nearly did." I wasn't going to lie to her. "But my guys got me out."

She nodded, taking a few deep breaths.

Tyler and Alec went back to their computers, declaring break time over, and Dot joined me on the couch. We spent most of the day lazing around, watching movies and eating. Nina joined us not long after Dot, saying she was happy to see me well but not asking any questions.

By late afternoon we had cleaned the fridge out of leftovers, which gave Ethan an excuse to start making dinner from scratch. Tyler and Alec moved to stools at the island bench and opened some beers, chatting with him as he chopped things. I ended up in Josh's lap, reveling in messing up his perfectly styled hair with my fingers.

When Lucian walked into the room, his suit crumpled and his tie hanging loose, shoulders hunched from the weight of his day, the mood in the room changed.

He stepped up to lean heavily on the island, palms flat on the cool stone, as Dot muted the TV.

"What the fuck were you thinking?" His quiet voice carried in the now silent room.

I'd never heard Lucian swear. I stood, moving to the opposite end of the island, my full focus on Lucian and whatever fresh hell he was about to rain down on us. Alec and Tyler's postures were rigid in their seats, almost as if they were at attention.

"Lucian," Tyler started, "we—"

"What the fuck were you idiots thinking?!" the older man cut across him, raising his voice. "That shit is all over the news, the senator hasn't been seen since this morning, and now they're starting to speculate that there's some conspiracy in Melior Group to take her out. Not to mention the fact that you've exposed yourselves. Exposed Evelyn."

He finally raised his head, looking mostly at the two older Variants in his employ but also casting his furious gaze to Ethan and Josh, who had joined me at the other end.

"We couldn't just sit around and do nothing. All we knew was that Evie was in danger. We acted to protect her." Alec kept his voice even.

"By bursting in there and causing a national incident, getting on the fucking news?" He gestured to the muted TV, slapping his hand down on the bench. "You should have told me and waited until we could get a stealth team down there to sort this out *quietly*."

"With all due respect," Tyler replied, "we reported it to you immediately, but we couldn't wait. Every second we wasted could've been a second she didn't have. Not to mention Josh happened to be in the city and got to her first. He has barely any training, and it was a stupid move, but he couldn't have stopped himself any more than we could have. They were both in danger. We couldn't wait."

"You should have," Lucian ground out between gritted teeth.

"As if *you* could have." Frustration leaked into Alec's voice. "If it had been Joyce, if it had been *your* Vital, you really think you could've waited?"

Lucian's eyes went wide. He turned to me as I gasped, my hands tightening on the edge of the bench.

"Your . . ." I couldn't get more than a single word out. The room felt as if it had tilted on its axis, and my grip on the bench was the only thing holding me upright. My mother was a Vital? My mother was *Lucian's Vital?*

"Holy shit." Josh laid a comforting hand on my shoulder, but my eyes were fixed on Lucian. "You didn't know Lucian was Joyce's Variant?"

"What?" I couldn't seem to get my voice above a stunned whisper. "I didn't even know my mother *was* a Vital."

I tore my gaze away from Lucian's to look at the guys. They all had varying degrees of shock and confusion on their faces. They thought I knew, but Lucian knew I didn't. Another realization crawled into my mind, and I looked back at him, holding on to the bench tighter. My knees were weak.

"Are you my father?" My voice sounded steady, but there was a tempest raging inside me, and I hoped I could hear his reply over the noise in my head.

"No!" He held a hand out, pleading. "Your mother and I met when you were already six months old. There's no way . . . I would never have kept that from you."

I released a tense breath, relief flooding through me. If Lucian were my father and had been keeping it from me this whole time, I don't think I could have coped. And the implications of him being Ethan and Alec's uncle . . . that would have made us cousins. The things we'd done were certainly *not* familial.

I scrunched up my nose in disgust, and when I looked up, both Ethan and Alec were wearing matching expressions, no doubt thinking about the things they'd done to my body.

Next to me Josh chuckled, and I rolled my eyes at him. Of course he was amused by it. Shit stirrer.

"How is it possible that my mother was a Vital and I had no idea?"

Lucian had been staring into space, but at my question he looked up, eyebrows raised. "Hmm? Oh, yes, she was . . ." He sighed deeply, running his hands through his salt-and-pepper hair in a move that reminded me of Tyler. "I think it's time you and I had a long talk, Evelyn. There are things I haven't said because I didn't want to hurt you, and there are things I simply didn't know if you knew or not. But in light of recent events . . . it's all coming out now, and it won't be long before your father puts two and two together, if he hasn't already."

"My father?" My back straightened, my hands closing into fists. If there was any topic my mother had avoided more than why we were on the run, it was the issue of my paternity. My heart kicked up a beat. Even as the vulnerable, young side of me that pined for a dad got excited, the grown-up, logical one reminded me there was a reason Lucian hadn't told me yet.

"Yes. I think once I explain who he is, and what I suspect him of, you will understand why your mother and I both kept it a secret. Maybe we should sit—"

"Oh!" Nina's surprised exclamation cut Lucian off, and we all turned to her.

She was sitting up on the couch, the loose gray hoodie covering her bald head askew as she stared at Dot on the chair opposite her. Nina's wide dark eyes had a faraway look to them, and a tense silence settled over the room.

Dot sat up straighter in her armchair, dropping her feet to the ground.

"Dot." Nina tilted her head to the side, a tiny twitch of her lips hinting at a smile. "Come."

Dot practically fell over the coffee table in her rush to sit next to her, launching herself into the spot next to Nina and grabbing her outstretched hand.

We all held our breath, watching them intently. After only a fraction of a second, Nina smiled. "I feel him. I have a location," she declared, and Dot burst into tears.

The room exploded in a flurry of activity. Ethan called up Dot's mom, letting her know the news. Lucian, Tyler, and Alec converged on Nina, firing a million questions and already starting to strategize. I wasn't sure what Josh was doing—probably something no one else had thought to do.

I went to Dot and just held her close in the second highly emotional hug we'd shared that day.

"He's alive," she whispered into my shoulder, and I smiled.

TWENTY SEVEN

The formal sitting room off the foyer had not changed one bit since Josh had given me an amazing dress and I'd kissed him silly. It was still immaculately clean, the two velvet couches positioned perfectly on either side of the coffee table, the drapes hanging precisely, a fire roaring in the fireplace. Even the Christmas decorations had disappeared as fast as they'd arrived, leaving the room looking untouched.

I sat on one of the soft couches, reading the latest edition of *New Scientist* and trying to take my mind off the fact that my father was alive and the man who knew his identity was in the house somewhere.

While the room remained unchanged, so much else hadn't. The day I'd first stepped into it with Josh, giddy about the gift and the kiss, I'd had no idea Alec was part of my Bond, no one knew I was a Vital, Beth and Zara were my closest friends, Charlie was safe and well and getting ready for the same gala we were.

Now . . .

We knew where he was, but we still couldn't get him. The news that Nina could now track him had pushed everyone into action the previous night, but my assumption that we would be commandeering the jet within hours was grossly misguided.

There were preparations to be made, approvals to be gained, strategy to finalize. Dot's parents were almost manic in their attempts to get things moving, but Lucian insisted we do things properly.

"We could get him killed if we march in there unprepared," he'd explained. "We don't know what we're walking into, what we're up against. We don't know how big it is, how many Vitals they're holding, who's behind it. The more information we have, the better our chances of success."

Tyler and Alec agreed; it was important to do recon first. They copped some sarcastic remarks from Lucian, considering how they'd handled saving me from the senator, but they were all determined to do this right.

Which left the rest of us sitting on our asses with nothing to do—and left me dying to ask Lucian who my father was. The man didn't have a spare second to eat, let alone talk to me about shit that happened before I was even old enough to remember. Hopefully things would calm down enough for us to have a proper conversation soon; I wasn't sure how much longer I could wait.

I'd spent the previous night in my usual room, in a giant, ridiculously comfortable bed, but I'd spent it alone. As much as I loved being around my guys, I needed the space. I needed to not worry about who was sleeping where, who might be feeling left out, and if I was being a good enough Vital.

I'd grown up pretty much alone, and I was still getting used to being around so many people all the time.

I was *still* alone by midmorning. Everyone was busy preparing to rescue

Charlie, and Josh and Ethan had headed to Bradford Hills Institute to pack up my stuff. I'd considered going with them but decided in the end to let them do it for me. I wasn't ready to walk into those rooms and look at the empty beds—reminders of the two friends I'd lost as fast as I'd made them.

"Eve?" Lucian's call came from somewhere in the house. I stretched, taking my time getting off the couch.

"*Eve?*" His voice was closer this time, mingling with the sound of his loafers on the foyer's marble floor. This time it held a panicked edge.

I rushed to the door, catching him on his way to the kitchen. "Lucian?" He spun around, eyes wide. "What's wrong?"

"Evelyn." He rushed over and placed both hands on my shoulders. "I'm sorry I don't have time to explain everything properly, but I need you to listen and do exactly as I say."

"OK . . ." I fiddled with the hem of my white sweater.

Alec came bounding down the stairs, phone in hand. He ended a call as he reached the bottom. Tyler was hot on his heels, buttoning up a fresh blue shirt.

"She's on the way. She should beat him here," Alec said.

"Good." Some of the anxiety drained out of Lucian's face, but he kept his eyes trained on me. "This is what I was afraid of when visuals of you transferring Light to Alec were plastered all over national television. Now everyone knows what you are, and some people know *who* you are too. One of those people is on his way here now."

"What? Who?" My voice was high. "Why are you guys so freaked out? You're freaking me out!"

"Uncle, you're scaring her." Alec placed a hand on Lucian's shoulder, and the older man released me.

"Sorry, it's just we have no time . . ." Lucian looked more rattled than I'd ever seen the distinguished man look. I wondered how much he'd slept in the past few days.

"Eve, Lucian's business associate Davis Damari is coming here," Tyler said evenly as Lucian visibly pulled himself together, tucking his shirt into his slacks and smoothing his hair.

"OK . . ." I frowned. Davis had popped up in my reading a few times—in the news and online when I was doing research about Variants—but I didn't remember anything alarming.

"He's made up some flimsy excuse to invite himself over," Lucian explained, a little more collected, "but he's really only coming to see you for himself."

"What? Why?" Why would some super-rich hotshot business guy want anything to do with me?

"Because he knows you're *Evelyn Maynard.* He knows what you're capable of."

"How?" Alarms started going off in my mind. Why did everyone seem to know more about me than I did?

"I wish I'd made time to have this conversation with you sooner. Now it's too late." He sighed. "The most important things for you to know are that he's dangerous and he's trying to find out what we're up to. He also has a mind-reading ability—"

"Which is the only reason why we invited . . ." Alec cut in, then trailed off.

"Who?" I was asking all the *W* questions, trying in vain to piece together the puzzle with whatever snippets of information I could drag out of them. I was so sick of being out of the loop.

The doorbell rang. All three of them looked to the door.

"It's not him," Tyler announced, moving to open it.

Dana was the last person I expected to come through the door. She looked almost as irritated as me. As soon as we saw each other, we both crossed our arms.

She was in black pants and combat boots—standard issue gear for Melior Group operatives—but once she took her thick coat off, the white top underneath looked as if it were painted on, showing off her voluptuous breasts and toned arms.

Tyler took her coat and hung it up. "Thanks for coming, Dana."

"Just following orders," she replied.

Lucian inclined his chin. "We still appreciate it."

"What exactly do you want me to do?" She was having trouble keeping her eyes off Alec. He was standing eerily still, his hands in his pockets, and avoiding everyone's eyes.

"Davis is on his way, so just the standard," Lucian answered. "He's here for"—his eyes flicked to me—"other reasons, but we can't have him picking up that we suspect he's behind the Vital disappearances. It would unravel months of hard work."

"Got it." Dana pulled her phone from her pocket, looking bored. From the way Lucian spoke to her, it sounded as if she did this all the time.

But my brain was still processing the bombshell Lucian had dropped. Davis was behind the Vital disappearances?

"Your mouth is hanging open," Tyler whispered into my ear as his gentle hands rubbed my shoulders. I snapped my mouth shut.

"Maybe we should just hide her?" Alec spoke for the first time since Dana had arrived. "Have Tyler take her out for a few hours and say she's not here."

"He'll just find an excuse to stay until they get back," Lucian answered. "He won't leave until he's seen her with his own eyes. It's better if we get it over with quickly, and then I'll steer the conversation toward business. The sooner we can get him out of here, the better."

"I don't want him anywhere near—"

Whatever Alec had been about to say was cut off by the crunch of tires on gravel.

A rush of panic and adrenaline made me fidget again, my eyes darting about the room. I needed to move—to do something—but Tyler's grip on my shoulders tightened, and he leaned in, his heat at my back soothing.

"Calm down, Eve," he whispered. "You need to be calm and polite, and we'll get you out of here in a few minutes. You can do this."

I breathed deep, focusing on the mindfulness techniques Tyler had taught me months ago. He released my shoulders and stood next to me.

Lucian moved to the door, opening it wide and blocking my view. Pleasantries were exchanged, comments about how cold it was, and then three men entered the Zacarias mansion.

Two of them were clearly security detail—dressed almost identically, with weapons strapped to their hips and beady eyes taking everything in. The third was Davis Damari. I recognized his broad shoulders and dark hair, peppered with gray, from the few images I'd seen online, but he was a little taller than I expected.

Their coats were taken by a maid who appeared out of thin air and disappeared just as quickly while the men continued to chat. Davis greeted Alec with a polite head nod in place of a handshake and then shook Dana's hand.

"What a pleasure to see you again, Dana." He smiled warmly but showed just a hint too much teeth for it to not look menacing.

"Nice to see you again too, sir." She smiled politely, her face pleasant but her posture at attention.

"I can't remember the last time we had a meeting without Dana present, Lucian." Davis turned to him. "I must say, it's a pleasure to have a break from the constant chattering in people's heads. Although if I didn't know any better, I'd think you were keeping her around to keep something from me, old friend."

Those teeth again. To his credit, Lucian just chuckled, not looking even slightly nervous about Davis's pointed teasing. As soon as we'd heard the car pull up, Lucian had drawn himself to his full height, and any hint of the panic he'd shown moments before had been wiped off his handsome face. He was giving nothing away.

"You know my ability blocks yours anyway. Dana has been working closely with me lately on a special project."

The guys had mentioned their uncle's ability when I first met him at the gala. While Dana was a blocker—neutralizing the ability of any Variant in her vicinity—Lucian was a shield. He was impervious to others' abilities but could only protect himself, and it worked best against more passive abilities, like Tyler's truth telling or Davis's mind reading. I wondered what he'd been capable of when he had my mom, his Vital, around.

"Oh?" Davis's eyebrows rose. "Sounds intriguing. I don't suppose you can tell your old friend what you're working on?"

"It's classified." Lucian smiled, an amused glint in his eyes, and stuffed his hands into his pockets casually. He looked so relaxed that even I almost started to believe these were just two old friends teasing each other. But Davis wasn't quite as good at covering his true feelings; his eyes narrowed just a fraction.

"Excuse my rudeness." Davis turned toward me and Tyler. "I have yet to greet your right-hand man." He sauntered over and shook Tyler's hand before fixing his intense gaze on me. "And you must be Evelyn Maynard." He smiled wide, looking at me in the same way I'd seen women look at shoes they loved but couldn't afford—with longing and greed.

I patted myself on the back for not flinching at his use of my full name, the name I'd spent my whole life hiding. Hearing it used so casually by someone who was making my skin crawl felt like a siren going off.

Danger! Evacuate! Take cover!

I breathed through it, taking inspiration from Alec's unflappable uncle, and smiled back. "Yes, pleasure to meet you, sir."

I kept my hands loosely clasped. I didn't think I could suppress a shudder if I had to touch him.

"You have no idea how it warms my heart"—he pressed his hand over the organ in question, his eyebrows turning up in a decent imitation of sincerity—"to see you safe and well."

"Yes." I cleared my throat. "It's been a crazy couple of days."

"Couple of days?" He chuckled. "My dear, I was referring to the past dozen *years*. I am sorry to hear your mother is no longer with us. You look so much like her."

I kept my mouth shut, unnerved. How the hell did he know so much? Once again, I wished the guys had told me more, that I'd had time to interrogate them. I looked away from his intense stare but didn't know what to say.

"I don't mean to upset you. I see now that you don't know who I am. It's not all that surprising that your mother kept it from you, I suppose. She did, after all, keep you from *me*."

I looked back into his face, frowning. He seemed to be insinuating *he* was the reason my mother and I had been on the run all those years. Was he threatening me?

Except that didn't sit right. His words weren't *menacing*; they were *griping*. They were the kind of thing a person would say if they were bickering about custody.

My breath hitched.

The ground fell out from under me.

I had my mother's hair, her eye color, her build, but in front of me stood a man with the same *shape* eyes as me, the same full lips, a more masculine, bigger version of my nose.

All sound disappeared as the implications fell into place. I retreated completely into my own mind, momentarily cut off from my senses, incapable of movement, as I processed the bombshell that had gone off inside me.

I tuned back in in time to see Lucian leading Davis to Tyler's study, turning the conversation to business. Tyler said something about getting them coffee and looked at me with concern.

I looked back at him, letting my eyes go wide, letting the realization crash over my features. He pressed his lips together and shook his head before heading off toward the kitchen.

Alec came to stand in front of me, worry and a question in his eyes.

I had questions of my own. Now that my senses had returned, all I had were questions.

What the fuck? I mouthed.

He pressed a finger to his lips and took my hand in his, leading me up the stairs and past a scowling Dana. She was leaning on the wall next to the door to Tyler's study, arms crossed, eyes fixed on Alec's hand gripping mine.

We made it up only one flight of stairs before I couldn't keep quiet any longer.

"He's . . ." I pulled on Alec's hand. I needed to stop, sit, think. "He's my . . . that man is . . ."

I needed to hear someone say it, but I couldn't form the words myself. The word *father* was too unfamiliar to my lips; they didn't know how to shape the letters.

Alec gave up on dragging me up another flight, instead nudging me a little farther down the hall. "He is your biological father, yes." He kept his voice low, looking both angry and wary at the same time.

"Did you know?" I yanked my hand out of his, my rising anger giving me added strength. Was this another thing they'd kept from me? Would the secrets never end?

"No." His answer was firm and definitive. "Lucian did, but it's not something he shared with us until half an hour ago, when he heard Davis was on his way. We've suspected he may be behind the Vital kidnappings for some time—there's a special task force in Melior Group dedicated to investigating the theory—but we haven't been able to find anything concrete. He's very good at keeping his dealings private. A little *too* good for it to not be suspicious. But that had absolutely nothing to do with you, as far as we knew. Now . . ."

His voice had dropped so low I had to strain to hear him, hanging on every word. I believed him that he hadn't known, but I had so many more questions. I needed answers, and almost as much, I needed *comfort*.

I leaned forward and pressed my forehead to his chest, breathing in the clean male scent of him. He closed the remaining distance, wrapping one strong arm around my back and cupping the back of my head with the other.

"He'll be gone soon," he whispered into my hair, pressing a kiss to the spot, "and then we'll have a nice long chat with my uncle. You will have your answers. I promise."

When Alec set his mind to something—like stopping me from finding him for a year, or resisting the pull of the Bond, or keeping my identity a secret from his family—there was no stopping him. He was like the most solid tree in the forest. It was nice to have that force of will on *my* side for a change.

After a while, we separated, and I slid down the wall to sit on the ground. Alec stayed with me, but when we heard movement downstairs, he went to make sure Davis was leaving.

For a few minutes, the sound of several male voices drifted up to me. I caught my name a few times but didn't have the energy to try to listen in. I couldn't even be bothered to move, try to hide, when I heard footsteps coming up the stairs.

A pair of boots, too small to be a man's, came to a stop next to me. I sighed and leaned my head against the wall, drawing my knees up.

Out of the corner of my eye, I watched Dana turn around, but instead of heading back downstairs, she sat on the top step. We were a few feet apart, facing opposite directions but sitting in line with each other.

"He was never mine, was he?" There was no anger in her voice—just a resigned kind of sadness.

"If it makes you feel any better, he fought it really hard. For a long time," I told the ornate hall table in front of me.

"It doesn't," Dana answered.

"I'm sorry." I was just as surprised as anyone to hear myself directing those words at her. But I really did feel bad about how it had all played out. She'd got caught up in our mess, and it wasn't fair to her. Alec had hurt us both.

"Don't be. You didn't do anything. I see that now. I just wish he'd told me."

But I had done something. I'd let him kiss me; I'd kissed him back when I'd thought he was with her. I wasn't sure she knew that, and I didn't want to rub salt in the wound. "He kept things from me too."

"Fucker."

I turned my head in her direction. She met my gaze and rolled her eyes, a tentative smile pulling at her lips.

I smiled back and shook my head.

At least there was one fewer person I had to watch my back with.

TWENTY EIGHT

Ethan and Josh got back just as Dana was leaving, so I let Alec and Tyler catch them up. I needed some time alone. I spent most of the day shut up in my now-permanent room, staring at the ceiling or out the window.

After a subdued dinner where Lucian didn't join us and the guys kept looking at me warily, I decided I couldn't put it off any longer. The guys all got up to go with me, but I wanted to speak with Lucian alone. Much as I appreciated having Alec's determination on my side, he tended to escalate situations.

The older man was on the balcony off his study on the first floor. A single desk lamp cast the room in an eerie yet cozy glow, throwing shadows over the vast bookshelves. I walked through the classically decorated room to the balcony doors.

Lucian stood at the railing, looking out over the yard. I grabbed a blanket off the leather couch and draped it over my shoulders before stepping out to join him.

It was a perfectly still night, so there was no biting wind. Just the snow falling softly, coating everything in white and silence.

A silence it was time to break.

I stood next to him, both of us looking out over the white powder, and waited. He knew all my questions; there was no need to voice them.

He sighed deeply, his breath misting in the cool air, and held a glass out for me. I took it reflexively; he had a matching one in his other hand, and both held a generous amount of scotch. Something exorbitantly expensive, I was sure.

I brought it to my lips but couldn't discern any fancy undertones in the flavor. It just tasted like alcohol. It burned my throat on the way down and made my lungs burn, but it did make me feel warmer.

"Your mother glowed too," Lucian finally said, "when the Light flow got really intense. I only saw it a handful of times, but it was exactly like what you did."

"They told you about that?" I looked at him out of the corner of my eye.

"I saw it in the footage from the train station."

"I thought Alec took care of that."

"He had Charlie delete it all, but I *am* the director of the top security firm in the world. Give me a little credit."

"Fair point." But if he'd found it, who else had?

"Have you figured out yet that when you glow, it allows you to draw Light from Variants?"

"No. Only that I can transfer *to* them remotely. Although I don't know what it is or how it works. My research is yielding no results." I frowned at the amber liquid and took another sip. Could I really draw Light *out* of others? I couldn't remember doing that, but the few times I'd glowed had been under extremely stressful circumstances. I'd been acting on instinct.

"I only experienced it for myself once and saw her do it a few more times, but she told me about it—what little she knew herself. Evelyn, you need to be very careful with it. When you glow like that, when you tap into such intense power, it allows you to *give* a Variant an ability. Someone who doesn't have one, you can give it to them."

"Whoa . . ." I whispered, my mind racing.

"But it kills the Variant you're drawing Light from."

I whipped my head around to look at him. He didn't meet my gaze, continuing to stare out into the silently falling snow.

"The only way to give a Variant an ability is to draw it from another, but you take every scrap of Light they've ever possessed, and it kills them. Have you ever wondered how Davis got his ability?"

"No," I whispered, dread trickling down my spine.

"You may have seen mentions in the media about his ability manifesting in his early thirties—much later than is common." Lucian took a sip of his own whiskey. "Well, it didn't *manifest*. Your mother *gave* it to him."

The implications of that settled in the silence between us.

The snow continued to fall. Soundless. Steady. I knew the answer was right there in front of me. In the icy flakes, in the amber liquid, in Lucian's unsteady voice.

But I just couldn't wrap my mind around the idea that my mother had killed someone.

"What do you mean?" I sniffled, not entirely sure if it was from the cold or the emotion beginning to choke me. I lifted the glass to my lips once more; my hand was shaking.

"She didn't mean to do it. She knew as little as you did about how it works, why she glowed. But Davis is very manipulative, and she thought she was in love. So she drained another Variant dry, not knowing it would kill him. In the weeks after, she realized she was pregnant, and Davis, drunk on his new power to read people's minds, dumped her."

"How do you know all this? You said you didn't meet my mother until after I was born."

"I didn't. I lived in London for most of my youth, working for my father there. When an opportunity with Melior Group came up in New York, I moved back here, returning to my childhood home"—he gestured to the sprawling yard and the beautiful mansion—"and my sisters. Olivia was living in London with her family too. They came back not long after you and Joyce disappeared.

"I met your mother when I moved back, and realized she was my Vital. You were only a baby, but your father—"

"Don't call him that." My voice had the bite that was missing from the cold. I hadn't thought before I spoke, but the reaction felt right. "I don't have a father."

"Fair enough." Lucian nodded. "He was already out of the picture. He got what he wanted from your mother, and he was off, using his new ability to build his empire. It was only when he decided he wanted more from her that he came back."

"What did he want?"

"He wanted her to do it again. To kill for him again. To take another Variant's ability and help him figure out how she did it. He became radicalized, obsessed, had crazy ideas about how he could make more Variants. He wanted to change humans—give them abilities. It's not scientifically possible. Humans simply don't have the DNA, but he was . . . persistent."

"What did he do?" I was afraid of the answer, but I needed to know. I couldn't shy away from asking all the relevant questions, even if the answers pained me.

"Your mother felt awful about what she'd done. She thought a lot about turning herself in to the police, but she didn't have any family, and that would have left you alone in the world. She just couldn't do it. When Davis came back a few years later, he threatened her with exactly that. He said he would turn her in, make it sound like she was the one who'd orchestrated the whole thing. It would be his word against hers—a prominent businessman with friends in high places versus a single mom, trying to figure things out. She was scared. She knew what he was capable of, and once again she chose to put you first. So she ran."

And there it was—the answer to the question I'd been asking for as long as I could remember. I finally knew what my mother had been running from: my father.

I took a deep breath, trying to calm my racing heart. "Why didn't you come with us?"

If he was really her Variant, how did he ever let her leave? If she was his Vital, how could she stand to be away from him? The mere thought of separating from my guys sent a jolt of pain through my chest.

"It was the single hardest thing I've ever had to do, but it was the best way to keep you both safe. I was already well-known in Variant circles, in the business world. My face was recognizable. I had a large family. I couldn't just disappear. I would have been a liability. But by staying behind, I was able to help. I helped her stay hidden, stay one step ahead of him. I used every Melior Group resource at my disposal. Who do you think taught her how to make fake documents?"

I looked over at him and smiled. She'd taught me, but I'd never really thought about who taught her. "Yeah, she passed that skill on. Thanks, I guess."

"You're welcome." He smiled into his glass before taking another sip. "And I've seen your fakes. They're exceptional—better than some of the forgeries my professional guys can do."

"Thanks." My chest swelled a little. He didn't strike me as a man who gave praise frivolously.

"Evelyn, Davis's dogged pursuit of your mother and her ability is why we suspect he might be behind the Vital kidnappings. I never heard him mention it once since Joyce ran, despite the fact I kept him close, made deals with him, pretended to be friends with him—but I believe he never gave up on his mission to give others abilities. I think he just refined it. The fact that you're like your mom—not only a Vital but one with all the extra power—is why she had to keep you from him. She couldn't risk him using you like he did her. Hurting you."

"So she knew. You guys knew I was a Vital even that young?" Abilities and Light access usually didn't manifest until the teens.

"Alec was twelve when his ability started to manifest. You were only four but already showing signs of access to the Light. You weren't transferring to him or anything like that, but it was clear you had a special connection. You felt particularly safe and comforted with him, and he was crazy protective of you. Playing with a toddler for hours on end doesn't exactly top the list of desirable activities for most preteen boys. We all suspected. When you actually glowed one night during a temper tantrum, it was confirmed. Not long after that, Davis showed up again, making his threats."

"And she ran," I whispered, my breath misting in the cold.

"And she ran," Lucian repeated, his voice low, sad.

We were both silent for a while, staring at the snow still falling steadily. If it kept up this pace, we wouldn't be able to get a car down the driveway in the morning. I tried to digest all I'd learned, but it sat heavy in my stomach, making me feel a little lightheaded. Or maybe that was the whiskey.

I put my empty glass down on a table behind me and pulled the throw blanket tighter around myself. "Why did you keep me in the dark? You must have known who I was when you saw me at the gala. Why didn't you tell me?"

"Alec—"

"Fucking Alec," I cut him off.

"He's trying."

"I know."

We both sighed in the exact same way, mutually frustrated and grudgingly understanding.

"When your mother didn't check in at our designated time, I knew something was wrong. Unless, of course, it was a last-second decision, she usually kept me informed about where you were heading next—sometimes I would help her set it up. Then she would check in once she got there."

He looked at me expectantly, his eyes burning with the need to know why we'd abruptly left Melbourne.

"She found out I had a boyfriend," I explained. "We were on a plane within hours."

"Ah." He nodded. "I assumed you were both . . ." He swallowed audibly. This was clearly difficult for him to talk about, and I felt a pang of guilt for putting him through it. But I shoved it aside. I'd been lied to so much my whole life. I deserved some answers.

He refilled his glass and took a big sip. "I knew your mother was gone. There was no way she would have gone that long without getting in touch. When I saw you at the gala, you can't imagine how happy I was, Evelyn. To know you'd survived whatever it was that happened to her. To know we hadn't failed after all . . . but I was so mad at Alec for keeping it from me. For a long time."

"Still doesn't explain why you didn't tell *me*."

"What was I supposed to do? Walk up to you in a room full of gossiping Variants and say, 'Hey, I know you don't know me, but your mom was my Vital, and I was in love with her, and I know who and what you are—by the way, why are you dating Ethan and not Alec?'"

I rolled my eyes. "You could have come to me after."

"Alec begged me not to. He wasn't ready to face it all, and if I'm being completely honest, neither was I. You didn't know any of it, but you were where you belonged. You were safe and happy, and that's all that your mother and I ever wanted, so I decided to let you enjoy it for a little while. Plus, I had to do all I could to keep Davis from finding out you were alive. That's what I focused on."

I should have been angry—what was it about Zacarias men that made them so determined to keep secrets from me?—but I just couldn't seem to find the energy. He may not have handled it how I would have liked, but maybe he'd handled it how *my mother* would have wanted, and I couldn't fault him for that. Besides, considering all he'd told me, all that had happened recently, we couldn't afford to be at odds.

This was my new family. It was time to move forward.

I opened my mouth to say just that, but he beat me to it.

"I'm sorry, Evelyn." It came out on a whisper, his voice quivering slightly. "I only ever wanted to protect you and your mother."

"I know," I answered quickly. "But no more secrets and lies and *classifieds* and keeping things from me for my own good. I'm not a child anymore. I have a right to make my own informed decisions about my life."

"It's hard for me to think of you as anything other than that little four-year-old who was the light of our . . . of your mother's life, but I agree. No more secrets."

His little slip didn't go unnoticed. I was taken aback by just how much he seemed to care for me—I hadn't even known who he was until a few months ago—but knowing what he was to my mother changed everything. I was a Vital too; I knew what it meant to have Variants.

I couldn't trust myself to speak without crying. Instead, I took a tiny step closer to him and slowly lowered my head to his shoulder. After a beat, he wrapped a tentative arm around me and took another sip of whiskey.

The first day back after Christmas break was about as awful as I expected.

Walking to my last class, a Variant studies lecture, I was one-hundred-percent over it. I'd done my best to ignore the whispers and stares all day—to focus on the feel of Josh's hand in mine, the heaviness of Ethan's arm over my shoulder—but it was hard.

Dot's mood wasn't much better; any Light I'd transferred to her was gone, and she'd lost all ability to talk to animals without touching them. Zara's absence was excruciating when I had to attend classes we'd shared and sit by myself—nothing but her betrayal in the seat next to mine and people's gossip settling over me like a heavy cloak of deceit and pain.

I took my bulky coat off inside the building and headed for the lecture hall, juggling it with my book bag.

"Is it true?" A blonde girl who used to date Ethan blocked my path. I remembered her from when we first started dating; she'd never been shy to let me overhear her talk about how there was nothing special about me.

"Hi, my name is Evelyn. How nice of you to finally introduce yourself." Maybe because I was so acutely aware of Zara's absence, my reaction was pure sarcasm. Although it did feel good to finally use my real name. It was freeing, despite the fact that I was introducing myself to a total bitch.

"Come on, are you really a Vital?" She crossed her arms over her chest. She had some friends with her, but a few other people also stopped to listen. Everyone wanted to know; she was just the first one to actually ask.

"I'm sure you've seen the news." I refused to lower my voice. Let them listen. "Clearly I am."

"And you have *three* Bonded Variants?" She asked skeptically. "That's really rare."

"Yeah, I know." I matched her bitchy tone, laying a little more snark on top. It was all out in the open. I had nothing left to lose by being honest. A Melior Group agent was never far away, and they were all on orders to keep an eye on me. "And I don't have three."

She looked satisfied, turning to her friends. "I told you. No one—"

"I have four," I cut her off.

They all turned to face me.

"Bullshit." One of her friends scowled, but her eyes held a heavy dose of uncertainty.

"Believe whatever you want." I sighed, shifting my bag off my shoulder; it was getting heavy.

"Four Bonded Variants is unheard of," the blonde declared, as if I didn't already know. As if everyone in the hallway didn't already know. "You expect us to believe you have four and that the 'Master of Pain' himself is one of them? Please! You're probably just using this to explain away the fact that you're fucking half the school."

"Not half the school. Just four guys—*my* guys." I leaned forward for that last part. I was done being called a slut. I wasn't technically sleeping with them yet, but she didn't know that.

"I don't believe you. No one goes near Alec . . ." Her eyes widened at something over my shoulder. The crowd shifted, shuffling away while still trying to stay within earshot.

Then I felt Alec's solid presence at my back. I could just imagine the scowl he was wearing. If there was anyone who hated attention more than I did, it was him.

"Is there a problem here?" he asked in his cold, unyielding voice as Kyo, Marcus, and Jamie stepped into my field of vision, looking every part the tough Melior Group team they were.

No one answered. I leaned back a tiny fraction and let my back make contact with his chest. He placed one possessive hand on my hip, and I tilted my head up until I was looking at him upside down.

He was wearing the exact scowl I'd pictured—the one that pulled at the scar in his right eyebrow—and I could see up his nose. I don't know why, but that made me chuckle.

He looked down at me, amusement playing at his lips. Instead of explaining myself, I decided to ignore the whole thing.

"Hey, Alec," I whispered, giving him a genuine smile.

"Hey, Evie," he whispered back and smirked at me. "You good?"

"I am now."

He leaned down and planted one quick kiss to my head.

Everyone left me alone in my last lecture, some people even actively avoiding me. Apparently their fear of Alec now extended to me, and I was OK with that, especially if it provided a small reprieve from all the attention.

TWENTY NINE

At the end of the day I got a ride home—I was still getting used to calling it that—from Kyo and Dot. They were now officially an item. Since they'd first kissed on the dance floor on Dot's birthday, every moment that Kyo wasn't on duty they spent together. They weren't the kind of couple who were sickening in their PDA, but Dot had no filter and told me all about it. In great detail. Including their sex life. And about the time Marcus joined them for a threesome. I always told her she was oversharing, but secretly I paid close attention . . . for future reference.

Judging by the way she'd whispered to Jamie before jumping in the car, her hand on his bicep as she leaned in close, I wouldn't be surprised if she ended up in bed with all three of them by the end of the week.

Alec had taken Josh and Ethan into the city to meet with Melior Group management. That was the only reason it wasn't one of them escorting me safely back to where I belonged. Instead, Marcus and Jamie followed us through the streets of Bradford Hills in an unmarked vehicle.

We'd managed to hold off this dreaded meeting for the past few weeks due to all the intense stuff that had happened, but the board had stepped in, and now even Lucian couldn't stop it from happening.

They'd managed to keep me out of it somehow—Lucian, Alec, and Tyler had probably all pulled some serious strings. I suspected Ethan and Josh had also offered themselves up much more easily than they otherwise would have to keep me away a little longer. But even so, one of the things we'd dreaded—one of the reasons we'd kept our Bond secret—had come to fruition. Both Josh and Ethan had formidable abilities, and now that it was known they had a Vital, Melior Group was recruiting them.

That was the first purpose of the meeting. The relationship between Variants and humans had only gotten more strained. There were constant protests outside Variant organizations and businesses. Groups of humans were ganging up on Variants with more benign abilities. Politicians were making outrageous comments in the press, capitalizing on the fear to gain more voters. And throwing fuel on the fire, Senator Christine Anderson was still missing.

The Variants were saying humans had taken her out because of all the work she was doing to bring Variant interests to the forefront in Washington. The humans were saying she'd been plotting to make them second-class citizens, so good riddance. Things were getting increasingly violent. Melior Group wanted all the help they could get.

The second reason for the meeting was even more serious. When any Variant finds a Vital, they have to register the Bond with the government. If the abilities are as dangerous as Alec's, Ethan's, and Josh's, this is taken particularly seriously. We hadn't technically broken any laws—because we *had* reported it to Melior Group (i.e. Lucian), which is tasked with handling the registrations and managing the risk to the general public—but we'd skirted the line by not keeping the humans in the loop.

Now that it had come out in such a public, spectacular way, they were pissed. We'd made them look bad.

Alec, Josh, and Ethan would be gone most of the evening; they might even stay the night in the city apartment if the meetings went long. Tyler was the only one home, working in his study.

That's where I found myself after changing into comfortable leggings and a soft black sweater—pacing the marble floor in front of the study's half-open door. I could hear Tyler inside speaking on the phone, but I wasn't paying attention.

I was thinking about the day I'd had. How freeing it was to say my real name, to not have to hide anymore, to have Alec at my back.

My talk with Lucian flashed through my mind too. How much more I felt like a part of his family with fewer secrets between us all.

Then I remembered what Nina had told me that day in the sauna. How much stronger we would be as a unit if we let the Bond strengthen naturally—if I followed my instincts instead of my mind and let the Light guide me.

I considered how much easier it was to control the Light—that I didn't really even *need* to control it—when we were relaxed and together and connected in the way I wanted us to be. As I'd been with Josh and Ethan in Alec's bed . . .

Decision made, I marched into Tyler's office and closed the door.

He looked up, the phone still to his ear. He was beautiful. He'd been at Bradford Hills most of the day and was still in his slacks and a patterned teal shirt, the sleeves rolled up, of course. His brown hair was messy as always, but his shoulders weren't as slumped as I'd come to expect these past few months; his face wasn't as drawn.

Locating Charlie and knowing he was still alive had lifted all our spirits.

"OK, just get it to me by morning so I can review. I have to go." He listened for a bit and then hung up.

I sat down on the edge of his desk. "You didn't have to hang up on my account."

"I'd been trying to end that call for five minutes." He chuckled, leaning back in his chair. "How was your first day back?"

"I don't want to talk about that." I waved my hand dismissively.

"OK." He stood, stretching his arms over his head and rolling his neck. My eyes couldn't help wandering down to where his shirt was straining to pull out of the waistband of his pants. "I need a break. Want to watch some TV?"

He made to move past me, but I placed one hand firmly against his hard chest.

"No." I shook my head, my voice betraying my nerves. I wanted this, I was sure of it, but I'd been rejected so many times . . .

"Then what do you want to do?" Tyler's voice lowered, and he stepped closer, resting one hand lightly on my knee.

In answer, my hand wandered over his defined shoulder to the back of his neck, and I leaned up, pressing my lips to his. He kissed me back, trailing both hands up the outside of my legs and resting them on my hips. I pulled him closer, opening my legs so he could step between them, and deepened the kiss. His tongue met mine.

After losing myself in his embrace for a while, I knew it was time. I pulled back, my hands still wrapped around his neck, my fingers playing with the crisp collar of his shirt.

"Ask me what I want to do," I demanded on a whisper, holding his gaze.

He indulged me, his swollen lips twitching in amusement. "What do you want to do, Eve?"

As his ability told him my intentions, I drove my point home by slowly and deliberately dragging one hand down his chest, over his abs, and all the way to between his legs. I stroked him, feeling the hardness through the fabric, as realization entered his face.

His breathing sped up and his hands flexed on my hips. "Are you sure?"

"I'm positive." I leaned forward and placed soft, sensual kisses on his neck, keeping a steady pace with my hand.

He groaned, stepping out of my reach. "This will mean taking it to the next level with all of us. You understand that, right? The Light is a powerful force. We're not animals, we can resist it, but it won't be easy. And you won't *want* to either. Are you positive you're ready for that with Alec?"

"Yes." I wasn't, not entirely. Judging by his disapproving look, his ability had told him as much, so I rushed to explain. "Look, I know Alec and I still have a lot to sort out, but I'm done pretending he's not in my Bond. I'm done allowing distance and insecurity to create more tension. Mentally, I may have some doubts, but in every other way, I'm ready. I want this, Tyler. I want you."

I kept my gaze locked on his, even though I felt incredibly vulnerable. His ability had told him I wasn't sure what to expect from my relationship with Alec, but it would also have told him how sure I was about everything else. I was choosing to follow my instincts—put my faith in the Light. I just hoped Tyler would see that.

I finally dropped my eyes, the potential of another rejection weakening my resolve, but that's what seemed to break him out of his own thoughts

He grabbed my hands and pulled me to my feet, then toward the door.

"You're not even going to talk to me about it?" I tried to tug my hand out of his grasp, frustrated, but he held on.

"I'm not saying no." He smirked over his shoulder as he reached the door. "This door doesn't have a lock."

He yanked the door open and quickened his pace toward the stairs.

I snapped out of my shock as we started to climb up, the frustration and fear of rejection wiped away by Tyler's cheeky grin and the lust in his eyes. Giddy anticipation replaced it, giving me a burst of energy, and I overtook him on the stairs.

Now I was the one pulling him behind me, and we ended up running and laughing all the way to his room.

As soon as his bedroom door was locked, the energy changed again. It turned more serious as we came together, his lips devouring mine as he held me close. It turned more intense as he walked me backward toward his bed.

When the backs of my knees hit the mattress, I broke the kiss, and before I could reach the hem of my sweater, Tyler was yanking it over my head.

I wanted his hands all over me. I wanted his mouth on my skin. Once again, he gave me exactly what I wanted, licking and kissing my neck as he unclasped my bra.

My breathing was heavy, my heart hammering with anticipation. The thought alone that I wouldn't have to stop, wouldn't have to hold myself back, was sending jolts of pleasure straight to my core.

I threw my bra aside and made quick work of Tyler's buttons, shoving the shirt off his shoulders. As he pulled it off, I pressed my lips to his chest. He was warm and smelled like the body wash I'd taken to using since the night of the invasion—when he'd let me use his shower. It smelled so much better mingling with his natural scent.

I kissed my way up the flat planes of his chest to his neck, running my hands up the muscled arms that had caught my attention that very first day.

His breathing was loud in my ear as he pressed himself closer and closer, his hands gripping my hips, my waist, my ass; kneading my breasts; never lingering in one spot for too long. As if he didn't know what he wanted to touch first.

But I knew exactly what I wanted. I ghosted my fingers over his shoulders and trailed them down his back as my mouth found his. Once my hands reached the waistband of his pants, I pushed my tongue into his mouth and, without wondering when I should stop, undid the clasp.

I didn't waste time, shoving both the underwear and the pants down. I touched him in the way I'd wanted to for so long, wrapping my hand around his erection and basking in the way he moaned into my mouth, the way his hips thrust forward, encouraging me.

Just as I was increasing my pace, intoxicated by his every reaction to what I was doing to him, his hand clasped around my wrist, and he pulled away.

"If you keep doing that, this will be over before it starts."

"I thought it had already started," I teased.

"I want to come inside you, not in your hand." He looked me dead in the eye as he said it, reminding me that was exactly where I wanted him. *Inside me.*

Suddenly I couldn't think about anything else.

The Light was *purring* as it flitted over my skin and into him in a slow, steady trickle, unrestrained. My body was flushed and ready.

My mouth, however, was apparently determined to ruin the mood.

"You mean you want to come inside a condom inside me, right? Safety first." My breathy voice betrayed how aroused I was, even if my words weren't exactly seductive.

Tyler's lips pulled up in a brilliant, amused grin. "Yes, that's exactly what I meant."

"Sorry . . ." That wasn't the sexiest thing to say with his dick in my hand.

"Don't be. I would never be so reckless."

I circled my arms around his middle, leaning my forehead on his shoulder.

His hand threaded into my hair and nudged my gaze back to his. He looked at me with so much affection and understanding it took my breath away. Or maybe it was his mouth that took my breath away. The kiss he pressed to my lips was intense yet gentle, but he kept his tongue back. He was being sweet and patient, putting me at ease.

But I didn't want gentle; I was ready for *more*.

I smiled against the kiss and then sucked his bottom lip into my mouth, biting it. He gave me a devious grin that reminded me of bad-boy Tyler—the one I'd briefly glimpsed at The Hole, who wore leather jackets and had women gossiping about how good he was in bed.

He stepped out of the pants and underwear that had pooled around his ankles and picked me up roughly. His hands gripped my ass, and I wrapped my legs around his waist, my hands flying to his neck so I wouldn't fall.

He dropped open-mouthed kisses on my collarbone as he moved, then he dropped me onto his bed. I bounced a little on the mattress, giggling, as giddy and excited as I was turned on and ready.

Tyler stood in front of me, gloriously naked, for only a beat before crawling over me, his knees on either side of my thighs. He placed another searing kiss to my lips, but before I could pull him closer, he was moving down my body.

He kissed a trail down the center of my torso, deliberately bypassing my breasts as his hands dragged a path down my sides.

Once his face and his hands reached the waistband of my leggings, he leaned back and pulled them off along with my underwear. He threw the clothing over his shoulder dramatically as his eyes raked over my completely naked body, from my toes all the way to my face. When our eyes met, he leaned forward, and I lifted up onto my elbows. We couldn't resist coming together anymore. We didn't want to.

He crawled back onto the bed and pressed the length of his body over mine as I pulled him down. We kissed deeply, breathing heavily through our noses, our hands roaming, our bodies starting to move to the rhythm of our mouths. I opened my legs wider and felt his hardness. We both groaned, and Tyler broke the kiss, pressing his forehead to mine as his hips continued to grind against me.

"I want you inside me," I whispered against his lips. I'd never been more sure of anything in my life; his ability would have made that clear to him.

"Fuck." He groaned before getting up and going to his bedside table.

As he ripped open the foil packet and put the condom on, I took in his glorious body.

He was a little bit taller than Josh but just as lean; hard muscle hid beneath his pressed shirts and tailored pants. I let my eyes linger on his tight ass before my attention was drawn to a large tattoo across his upper back. Scrawled in a bold but intricate font were the words "Knowledge Is Power." The simple sentiment was so him, and the fact that he had ink under his clean-cut appearance reminded me of his slightly shady, dangerous past.

Condom in place, he came back to the foot of the bed. I moved backward against the pillows as he crawled over the top of me, his eyes full of need, almost feral.

He was letting his instincts take over. And judging by the narrow-eyed look he was giving me, his instincts were to claim me.

He pushed my legs apart and settled between them, holding himself up on one arm. His lips crushed fiercely to mine—repayment for the way I'd bitten him earlier—and his hand roamed, grabbing and feeling and teasing my skin on its jagged path to the spot between my legs.

Once there, he broke the kiss, his eyes closed, his mouth panting.

His fingers trailed up and down, spreading the wetness and rubbing the most sensitive spots with the perfect pressure. He alternated pushing his fingers inside and rubbing my clit, tormenting me in the most delicious way, giving me a taste of exactly what I wanted, then changing it up.

Just as I was starting to get frustrated with his antics, he shifted and slowly, deliberately pressed his length into me. Inch by glorious inch, Tyler filled me until he was all the way in, and we both groaned at the sensation.

Finally, *finally*, I was breaking down one of the last barriers between me and my Bonded Variants, and everything about it felt so fucking right—his smell, the way his hands caressed my body, his weight on top of me, the feel of him inside me.

For a few moments we just stared at each other, the connection deepening in a way clearly fueled by the Light but also in ways that had nothing to do with our supernatural Bond. Yes, I was his Vital and he was my Variant. But I was also a woman and he was a man, and we'd wanted each other in this most intimate, carnal way for a long time.

A messy brown lock fell over his forehead, and I didn't hesitate to brush it away, threading my fingers into his hair, moving my hand to the back of his head and attacking his lips with mine again. He started to move, and I met every thrust with my own hips.

Tyler seemed to know exactly what I wanted. Just as I imagined his fingers twining into my own hair, there was his hand, pulling gently at the strands. Before I'd even fully formed the thought that I wanted my breasts crushed against his hard chest, he was letting a little more of his weight onto me. As I let the sensations take over my mind, chasing the highest form of pleasure, Tyler adjusted his movements and angled his hips in exactly the perfect way.

His thrusts became harder but shallower, barely even pulling out as he ground himself against me.

I pressed my head back into the pillow, not even caring about the sounds coming out of my mouth as I rode the waves of pleasure.

The orgasm lasted longer than I was used to. As I clawed desperately at Tyler's back, the heady, molten sensation built and built. My stomach muscles clenched as I lifted my legs and wrapped them around his hips, making it possible for him to drive deeper into me, drive me higher. I moaned loudly and my vision went blurry as wave after wave washed over me. My thighs started to tremble, and I put my feet back down onto the mattress.

Before I had a chance to catch my breath, Tyler changed it up again, pushing in and out with more force—longer, faster strokes that drew out my own pleasure—then groaned his release into my neck.

He rolled onto his back beside me, and our hands found each other between our naked, panting bodies.

As my breathing evened, I turned my head to him. "You cheated."

He looked at me and smirked. "Are you complaining?"

"No. I couldn't be more satisfied."

THIRTY

Alec arrived back from his meeting at Melior Group headquarters while Tyler was still inside me—for the second time. He pounded on the door, demanding to be let in. We thought he was just feeling the Light's pull and ignored him until we finished. But it turned out he'd been trying to call us for over an hour.

The Melior Group board had finally approved the large-scale attack they'd been planning for weeks, and we needed to move out immediately. The jet was being fueled.

He pointedly ignored the fact that Tyler opened his door in nothing but underwear, as well as me on the bed, nothing but a crisp white sheet covering my still-flushed body. It was only when Tyler disappeared into the bathroom that Alec looked at me.

So many emotions crossed his face I struggled to unpack them, but the way his hands clenched and unclenched by his sides told me at least some of his urgency actually had been driven by his need to get to me.

"Fuck," he breathed, finally letting the lust hood his eyes. Despite my just having had sex with Tyler twice, my body reacted to the desire in his gaze, and I squirmed on the bed. But he turned on his heel and rushed down the hall.

The next few hours were a flurry of activity, everyone packing, preparing, bustling to the airport. Olivia cried on and off, Dot worried about whether to bring Squiggles, and Tyler and Lucian were constantly on the phone, making last-minute arrangements and giving orders.

We hadn't had time for the guys to update me on their meeting. I hadn't had time to tell them about Tyler and me either, but they knew.

I'd showered and dressed and was packing when they got home, but Josh took one look at me, kissed me passionately, and grinned from ear to ear, anticipation and happiness dancing in his eyes.

"Well, OK then," he said before releasing me. Ethan kissed me just as passionately, lifting my feet off the ground, but the look in his face was a little more confused.

Josh dragged him away so they could get packed, and I saw him whisper something, their heads bent together. Then Ethan's back straightened, and he looked back at me with wide eyes. If Josh hadn't pulled him along, I had a feeling he would have marched back to me, locked the door, and forgotten about the mission entirely.

Since then, they'd both been throwing me knowing looks full of promise that made my heart beat a little faster and my mind wander to lascivious thoughts.

Before I had a chance to process though, we were in the air. Then, hours later, we were landing in Bangkok and making our way to the compound.

Only then did Tyler explain to Josh, Ethan, and me that we weren't technically allowed to come. I was only permitted to be there because I was an active operative's Vital. If something happened to Alec in the field, I needed to be close by to transfer Light to him.

It was stinking hot and humid in Thailand. We were in the wilderness somewhere, well off the beaten tourist track, but Melior Group had managed to find a compound with modern amenities and multiple dwellings to use as a base of operations. Charlie and another eighty or so suspected captive Vitals were in a low building a few miles to the south.

For the past week, teams of Melior Group operatives had been moving into the area—some into this compound, some into resorts and other places nearby—and we now had a small army, as well as all the information we could gather about the target location through observation and bribing locals.

All this I'd overheard in the strategy meeting Josh, Ethan, and I had just been thrown out of.

I hadn't been able to help myself; I'd asked a question to clarify something, and everyone in the room had turned to look at me as if I were insane.

"Let me make this perfectly clear . . ." Tyler lectured us in his stern man-in-charge voice as he promptly escorted us out. "You three are here as civilians, just like Nina, Olivia, Henry, and Dot. You will not be assisting in the strategy, and you will not be going in with the highly trained Melior Group agents. Am I understood?"

We all grumbled a response, and he nodded before turning back to the main house.

"We might as well get some sleep." I sighed and started walking toward the cottage at the back of the property. Hopefully we'd only be there a night or two.

"I'm going to see if I can get back in there." Josh gave me a light kiss on the forehead and followed after Tyler. His need to know everything burned as bright as mine. I smiled after him.

"I need to cool off. I'm gonna jump in the pool first," Ethan said.

Personally, I was enjoying the break from the freezing New York winter, but the heat had Ethan struggling to breathe most of the time, and he always planted himself under the AC in every room.

As I walked through the manicured grounds, my flip-flops slapping on the pavers, I pulled my loose tank top away from my sweaty skin and briefly considered joining him. But I desperately needed to lie down. It was early evening, the sun only just dissipating into twilight, but none of us had slept much in the past twenty-four hours.

Anyone here *not* as a civilian spent most of the day planning and going over maps and reports, making sure they were as prepared as possible. They would be going in at four in the morning—while it was still dark and silent.

Hopefully they'd get some rest before.

The cottage was the designated civilian area. It had four bedrooms and a small open kitchen and living space. Dot's parents had one room, Dot and Nina were sharing the one with single beds, and the guys and I had yet to arrange ourselves between the other two rooms.

I showered and crawled into the bed of the closest free room, wearing nothing but underwear and a tank top. Everyone besides me and the guys had already gone to bed, although I'm sure no one was sleeping. We all wanted to be in that meeting, but Tyler was right; we were too emotionally involved, and we needed to let the professionals do their work. It was Charlie's best chance.

As I lay on my back, enjoying the breeze coming in through the window, I tried to will my body to relax, my mind to stop obsessing over what was to come. But it was pointless. My mind was wired, and my body was humming with need.

As if on cue, the door opened, and the perfect distraction entered.

Ethan was shirtless, his broad muscular chest bathed in moonlight. He dropped his towel and shirt to the floor and took two steps toward the bed before stopping.

"You need to tell me if you want me to sleep in another room." His low voice was strained. His jet-black hair was still wet from the pool, and a droplet landed on his shoulder, glistening in the blue light. "Because I can't lie next to you all night and not . . . do things."

"What do you mean?" I put on my best innocent voice. "What things?"

I dragged my fingertips up the front of my thigh, up my belly, between my breasts and propped my head on my hand so I could see him better.

He groaned, dragging his hands down his handsome face, but when he took them away, he was smiling, the dimples showing. "You're teasing me?"

"Nope." That time the innocence was gone. "I fully intend to follow through."

He closed the distance, and I lifted myself onto my knees to meet him. We crashed into each other with such intensity we nearly lost our balance. Kissing and giggling, we ripped the last few scraps of clothing from each other's bodies.

He ran his big hands all over me, and I did the same to him. As he pushed his tongue into my mouth, I grabbed a handful of his ass. It was cool from where the wet fabric of his swim trunks had clung to him, and the skin warmed under my touch.

With Tyler it had been intense, and more serious, and everything I'd needed it to be. With Ethan it was playful, our movements less restrained. I felt giddy. I was aroused but also just plain happy to be in his arms and touching him how I wanted to.

I spared a moment to make sure my Light control was locked down, but I'd transferred to Tyler just an hour ago to give him an extra edge in the planning, and now that I was giving in to my Light-driven instincts, it was nowhere near as pushy as it usually was. I was doing what it wanted me to do.

Satisfied I wouldn't be complicit in starting a bushfire in the Thai wilderness, I finally let my hands drag around to Ethan's belly, eager to properly explore the hardness pressing into my front.

I broke our kiss to see what I was doing as my hand wrapped around the base of his erection. I paused, letting myself fully take in the size of him before dragging my hand up . . . and up and up.

Ethan was a big guy and *every* part of him was in proportion. I took a deep breath, a tiny bit of worry breaking through my lust. He was bigger than Tyler, bigger than any guy I'd ever slept with. But he was my Variant—meant for me in every way. It would be fine. *Right?*

He must have noticed my hesitation, because he chuckled and pressed his forehead to mine. "You'll be fine, baby. We just need to make sure you're real relaxed."

"Mmhmm." I couldn't seem to manage words, let alone entire sentences.

Effortlessly, Ethan picked me up and dropped me onto my back. But instead of lowering himself on top of me, he sank to his knees and put his mouth right between my legs.

I gasped, not having expected him to go straight for the sweet spot, but he was a man on a mission, and my lucky stars, was he good at that! His tongue, his lips, the occasional scrape of his teeth . . . And then he put two fingers inside me, and I was a goner. The orgasm washed over me quickly and intensely, but I somehow managed to stay silent, remembering there were other people on the other side of the walls.

Ethan kissed his way up my body as I caught my breath, but once again, instead of lowering himself on top of me, he pulled me up by the hands and picked me up. I wrapped my legs around his thick waist, and he sat down on the bed with me in his lap, producing a condom seemingly out of nowhere.

He must have had it with him, but I couldn't care less where it had come from. I was as relaxed and wet as I was going to get. He slid the condom down and held his erection at the base.

"You're in control," he whispered, his deep voice sending a shiver down my spine. A light sheen of sweat covered my skin, and I could feel dampness at the nape of Ethan's neck as I held on to it for balance.

I lifted myself onto my knees and looked him in the eye as I slowly took him in. His eyes fluttered at the sensation, his full lips parting as his breathing deepened. My hips met his, and we both groaned, my eyes finally falling closed.

The feeling of fullness was almost overwhelming, and I gave myself a moment to adjust. Ethan waited patiently; the only sign he was aching to move inside me were his hands on my waist, his fingers pressing almost painfully into my flesh.

When I started to move, slowly, deliberately, he released me and leaned back on his hands. The only part of him that moved were his hips, thrusting up to meet mine as we found a steady rhythm. His abdominal muscles clenched and relaxed with every roll of his hips, and I could feel his thick thighs under me.

My hands on his shoulders, I focused on the feeling building deep inside me once again—almost as deep as Ethan's impressive length could reach.

I rolled my head back, and the wavy ends of my hair tickled my lower back.

We were panting, little moans and groans escaping here and there, but we were doing our best to stay mostly silent.

"That's it, ride my cock." Ethan's words came out on a low growl as his hand found my breast and he massaged it, running his thumb over the nipple.

Those words and that hand pushed me over the edge again. I leaned forward, biting his shoulder so I wouldn't call out. He kept pumping his hips under me, losing the rhythm a bit as his movements became more frenzied.

The hand on my breast moved down to grab my ass, squeezing and guiding me on top of him, and then he stiffened too, his groan of release a little too loud. He leaned forward and brought his other arm around my middle, burying his face in my neck.

Then he leaned back, letting me fall on top of him. Despite the oppressive humidity, I pressed my sweaty cheek to his chest and listened to the pounding of his heart.

I was exactly where I wanted to be, and I dozed off with Ethan running his hands through my hair.

Some time later, as I lay half-asleep in Ethan's arms, I heard the door open and close softly. Someone shuffled about the room, and then the bed dipped behind me.

I caught a hint of expensive aftershave as Josh's long, soft fingers caressed my shoulder. He trailed a line down my arm and over my hip, his touch so soft it almost tickled.

And that's all it took to get me going again.

I'd known it was going to be hard to resist them after I crossed this line with Tyler; I just hadn't expected giving in to be so *easy*. It was effortless the way my body responded to his touch, the way I rolled over so I was facing him, the way our lips came together in the softest of kisses.

Tyler and Ethan had both checked with me, making sure I was ready for what we were about to do, but this was Josh. He didn't need to ask; he knew I wanted this, and he was ready to give it to me.

I hadn't bothered to get dressed after Ethan and I had sex, and Josh was completely naked too. He kissed me slowly—his lips pressing into mine in the most torturous way, preventing our tongues from deepening it just yet—and I let my hands explore his body as he was exploring mine, with soft, slow movements.

As I tugged on his hip, shuffling closer, he finally ran his tongue over mine, pressing his body flush against me. He pulled my knee until my leg was hitched over his hip, then he ran his hand down the outside of my thigh until he had a firm but soft grip on my ass.

I felt his erection between us as we both started to rock gently against each other, our bodies no longer able or willing to keep still.

Josh moved his hand just a little farther over and felt how wet I was. He moaned softly into my mouth. It was getting hard to breathe, but neither one of us was willing to break the kiss, which was becoming frantic as the rest of our bodies reacted.

Without taking his lips from mine, he rolled us over so he was on top of me, and I could feel him—hard, smooth, and right where I wanted him. He rocked his hips, rubbing his length up and down, spreading the moisture between my legs with every movement. The friction was driving me wild, making me almost forget there were other people in the house, that Ethan had been lightly snoring right next to me when Josh got into the bed.

I finally pulled away, nudging his shoulders lightly, and he lifted himself higher to look at me. His perfect face was as flushed as my whole body felt, his usually immaculate hair a mess, his vibrant green eyes hooded.

I *needed* him inside me.

"Condom," I whispered, hating that I was breaking the spell of silence but not willing to risk unsafe sex.

I bit my swollen bottom lip, showing him I didn't want to wait any longer.

He smiled, flashing me his perfectly straight teeth, and moved to do as I'd instructed, but a condom appeared instantly between us. It was already out of its packet, pinched lightly between Ethan's fingers.

We both turned to look at him, doubt bubbling up in my chest. Maybe Ethan didn't want to watch Josh fuck me in the exact bed where we'd just done the same thing. Maybe Josh didn't want an audience. It felt right to me—I had nothing to hide from either of them—but I hadn't stopped to consider how *they* wanted this to play out.

Wordlessly, Josh took the condom and sat up to put it on.

Ethan caressed my cheek with the back of his knuckles. His eyes were hooded with lust, but they also held a hint of uncertainty. "I can leave if . . ."

I looked at Josh as he lowered himself back down and caressed my hair.

"Doesn't bother me." To prove his point, he started to press into me slowly, pulling back out and watching my face.

I looked back at Ethan. "Stay."

I returned his lazy smile, and then my focus was back on Josh.

He pushed all the way into me in one slow, smooth movement. He didn't stop, didn't wait for me to adjust. He was done taking his time.

Josh was sure and quietly confident in all he did, and this was no different. He started moving in and out of me at a pace that completely contrasted with the sensual and languorous way this had started. Hard and intense. He watched me the whole time, his eyes drinking in my expression, the way my lips parted on a moan, the way my eyes struggled to stay open.

His hips hit a particular spot every time he slammed into me, and it was driving me to an orgasm; it was going to wash over me any second.

"I can't . . ." I panted, but he was relentless. "Can't keep quiet."

In answer, Josh turned my head gently toward Ethan. As the orgasm crashed through my body like waves against a cliff, Ethan pressed his mouth to mine, swallowing all the noise I couldn't contain. He pulled away just in time for me to watch Josh finally lose control.

His eyes closed, the most beautiful look of serenity wiping the intensity from his features as he held himself inside me, riding out his own release.

He collapsed next to me as Ethan pressed a soft kiss to my cheek.

Once Josh's breathing evened out, he raised one hand in a fist above me. "Thanks for the assist, bro."

Ethan didn't even skip a beat, and they fist-bumped over my naked, sweaty body. "Anytime, man."

"You're both idiots." I rolled my eyes but wasn't entirely able to contain my giggles.

This felt so right. I couldn't believe I'd waited so long to do it.

THIRTY ONE

I never did fully fall asleep that night. The apprehension about what was due to happen in a few short hours was palpable. I stayed in bed between Josh and Ethan, dozing and letting my mind wander.

Ethan's light snores filled the quiet, mingling with the sound of insects from the open window, but even he didn't stay asleep all night. Josh didn't even try. Every time I looked over at him, his eyes were wide open, even though he was lying perfectly still.

As I was contemplating checking the time, the door opened, and Tyler stepped inside. He paused, taking in our naked bodies sprawled on the bed, not a scrap of clothing or sheets in sight.

"Sweet fucking Christ," he breathed, running his hand through his hair.

"No Christ here," Josh answered as Ethan rolled over, rubbing his eyes, "but there was plenty of fucking."

I sat up. "Is it time?"

Tyler took a deep breath and nodded. "It's time. I thought you'd want to know. Plus, I think Alec could use some juice."

I was already half-dressed by the time he finished speaking. I pulled on some shorts and a tank top, not bothering with underwear. I wouldn't know where to look for it anyway.

Tyler led me through the manicured grounds back to the main house; the bright lights still on made me squint.

There was a flurry of activity, some black-clad men strapping on gear, others testing the communication devices that sat snug in their ears. Alec was strapping a belt with more knives than I could count to his right thigh. His team was nearby, also arming up.

I walked straight up to him, weaving through the busy people.

"Hey." I had to raise my voice to be heard over the hubbub. He straightened and turned to face me, his ice-blue eyes taking in my haphazard appearance—the shorts inside out, my hair an absolute mess.

His expression was unreadable; he was already getting into his "dangerous secret organization badass" frame of mind and wasn't giving much away.

"Ty said you might need . . . um . . ." I didn't know why I was so reluctant to voice that I was there to transfer Light to him. He was my Variant. Everyone in the room already knew that.

"Yeah." He nodded, giving me a little smirk before darting his eyes about the room and frowning. Maybe he was feeling as unsure as I was. This wasn't exactly our usual dynamic.

"Just . . ." He lowered his voice and rubbed the back of his neck, scowled at the ground, then straightened to his full height. He looked pissed off, but I didn't feel as if it was directed at me. "It'll be good to have a bit of an edge but not too much. I haven't had a chance to train with extra Light, and it could be a distraction."

I nodded. He'd spent years training to be a killing machine without what I could provide. Giving him too much could actually be counterproductive.

I held my hand out, offering the Light to him in the least intrusive way I knew. But he surprised me by wrapping his calloused hand around my wrist and tugging me forward.

I found myself chest to chest with him, and instead of focusing on the task at hand, my mind helpfully supplied vivid images of what I'd been doing just hours before.

He must have seen the lust in my face, because he smirked again, narrowing his eyes. "Just a little, Eve."

Then he took a breath before pressing his lips to mine.

I wrapped my arms around his neck, his buzzed hair prickling my fingers, and Alec kissed me in a way that was sweeter than I'd thought him capable of.

I knew this was an important moment for him, for us. He was trusting me to do my job as his Vital. I needed to keep that trust by not getting distracted by the ache between my legs.

And so, even as I delighted in his lips on mine, I focused on the tingly, humming sensation of the Light flowing into him. I replenished what he was missing and gave him a little extra—just enough to make his ability reach a little farther, make the pain a little more intense, let him use it a little longer. Then I cut it off. It was easier than I'd ever thought possible.

He took that as a sign to break the kiss, pulling away while still keeping me in his arms.

I licked my lips, wanting to taste him again, drag him back to the dark room in the cottage and complete the connection to my Bond. "Be careful."

I fixed him with a look that I hoped conveyed my sincerity and stepped out of his arms. He nodded once, and I watched him pull his hard, unfeeling mask back into place. He started barking orders as Kyo handed him a very large gun, and I turned away, going to stand just outside the back door.

I couldn't watch them leave.

Dot was sitting on a log, her elbows on her knees. I leaned on the wall next to her, and we listened to the sounds of heavily armed men and women heading out to bring her brother home.

I reached a hand out, and she took it, squeezing it firmly.

I was pacing the kitchen, arms crossed, listening intently to what Tyler, Lucian, and the other Melior Group operatives were doing a few feet away.

A swell of panic within me kept fighting to break through. It would bubble up to my chest, and I would squash it down with a deep breath. It would gurgle up to my throat, and I would only just hold it back by focusing on moving my feet, step by agonizing step, on the pale green tiles.

It couldn't have been more than an hour since the organized force of Melior Group fighters had taken off for the compound. They'd converged on the low structure, taken out the few guards posted at gates, and breached the building.

And then all communications had gone down.

Anyone associated with or employed by Melior Group was keeping their cool.

Lucian leaned on the dining table, still strewn with maps and tablets from the strategy meeting, his intelligent eyes watching everything, monitoring for any missteps.

Tyler flitted from one place to another, typing furiously at a computer one minute, then issuing commands to groups of people the next.

Ethan was sitting on the kitchen bench, his head in his hands. Josh leaned next to him, watching the whole room, but even he couldn't keep the worry off his handsome face.

Dot had run back to the cottage as soon we'd lost contact with our teams, updating her parents. I couldn't imagine how difficult this must be for them.

"Fuck," Ethan growled and looked up, hugging his big arms around his middle. He looked more like a scared kid lost in the mall than he did like the six-foot-four, 250-pound man he was.

Tyler glanced in our direction, murmured something to the computer tech he was standing next to, and came over. He placed a comforting hand on Ethan's shoulder and tucked me into his side.

"It's OK, Kid." He gave Ethan's shoulder a squeeze, then addressed us all. "Guys, we knew this might happen. The comms all went down that day at Bradford Hills. We're pretty sure it was due to a Variant with an ability related to tech. We expected to come up against it again. We're prepared for this. OK?"

"Lucian?" Olivia's panicked voice came from the back door. She'd arrived just in time to hear Tyler's little speech. Dot stood next to her, holding her hand, and Henry was behind her, his eyes bloodshot and drawn.

Lucian got up and went to stand by his family

"He's right, Olivia." He pulled her into a hug. "We've got this under control."

We spent the next hour on a knife's edge. Olivia would burst into tears sporadically, Dot or Henry rubbing soothing circles on her back.

I continued to pace.

Tyler and Lucian continued to work.

The clock continued to tick with no news, not even a report of movement from the scouts watching the area.

"It's time," Lucian finally declared, his voice firm, and the Melior Group staff sprang into action.

"Time for what?" I asked. Tyler had started strapping weapons to his body near the kitchen, and I went to him. "Time for what, Ty?"

"We're going in," he answered, and Josh stepped forward to help him strap on his Kevlar.

"Going in?" The past hour of waiting had been so tense my mind couldn't seem to process the fact that things were happening.

"Yeah." Tyler checked his gun and holstered it. "This is part of the contingency. We gave the A team time to do their job. They haven't been in contact and haven't returned. It's time for backup. That's us."

I looked around the room. By "us" he meant every Melior Group employee left. They may have been computer geniuses and tactical masterminds, but they were all just as highly trained as anyone else permitted to attend this mission. They were all gearing up.

Within five minutes, another twenty people were ready to move out. Other teams from other locations were calling in their readiness over the speakers.

"All right, there won't be anyone left here with you guys, but you're perfectly safe, OK?" Tyler addressed the three of us, then tipped his head in the direction of Dot's family. "Olivia and Henry both worked for Melior Group at some stage. They've had training. They'll know what to do in an emergency." At last he turned to Josh, the only one of us as seemingly calm as the professionals in the room. "If all else fails, stick to the plan. Get her out."

Josh nodded, and I squashed my annoyance at the fact that there was some last resort plan I was unaware of. Instead I focused on Tyler.

I stepped into his space, and he embraced me without hesitation. Pressing my lips to his, I let the Light flow freely, even giving it a little push. I wanted him to have every advantage he could out there, and unlike Alec, he didn't need to worry about controlling his ability in the field.

We pulled apart, and he placed a kiss on my forehead. "I'll be right back." He smiled, but the anxiety threatening to choke me wasn't pacified.

Most of the others were already out the door, but Lucian stood to the side, waiting for Tyler. Without thinking about it too much, I walked up to him.

"Would it help if you had a little boost too?" I asked. His ability was defensive, and I'd perfected transferring Light to non-Bonded Variants. If this was the only way I could help, I'd drain myself dry so my family could be safe.

"It can't hurt." He smiled tentatively.

I reached out my hand, and he took it gently in his. Closing my eyes in concentration, I pushed a decent amount into him, and he gave me a little squeeze when he'd had enough.

"Thank you, Evelyn." His eyes were a little brighter, his posture a little straighter, and I wondered if he'd had any Light transferred to him at all since my mother had taken me and run off into the night.

Acting on instinct, I gave him a quick hug before scurrying back to Ethan's side.

Then they were gone, and we went back to waiting.

Nina joined us not long after they left, and Dot updated her on the situation in minute detail. I think it made her feel better to have something to do, something to say. Nina listened to it all with patience and understanding.

As the first hints of light started to announce the dawn, I rubbed at my chest, feeling a pang of alarm. Had it been too long? Should we be doing something? Calling someone?

The weight on my chest grew heavier, and I started to wonder if I was experiencing the beginnings of a panic attack. I leaned on the bench with one hand as the pressure increased—except it wasn't exactly pressure. It wasn't caused by the crushing anxiety of waiting to see if they were all OK.

It was *pain*. It was that pain that was becoming more and more familiar to me every time one of my Variants put himself in danger and used too much of his ability. And it was getting worse.

"No!" I cried out as I bent over double. The urge to run, to get to him *now*, felt as intense, though not quite as all-consuming, as it had the night I'd run to save Ethan.

"Eve?" That was the first hint of panic I'd heard in Josh's voice. His hands were all over me, checking for injuries. Ethan was on my other side, doing the same.

"Oh no." Nina shot up from the couch. "She feels the pull. Something is wrong with one of her Variants."

There were only seven people in the room, but it erupted into chaos, most of it centered around me. Some of them were talking over each other, trying to decide what to do; some of them were asking me questions.

I focused on my breathing and on Ethan and Josh's soothing touch. The pain, the pull, was still in my chest, but it had stopped getting worse. Whatever my Variant had been doing, he'd stopped doing it. He was drained, weak, but he wasn't dying. *Yet.*

"I have to go there," I whispered. No one heard me over the cacophony of voices. I straightened, squared my shoulders, and looked around. Slowly, one by one, they returned my stare and grew quiet. "I have to go there. I have to help."

"Evelyn, I can't possibly let you do that." Henry was putting on his parent voice, but he wasn't my parent, and I wasn't a child.

"With all due respect, I'm not asking for your permission. Two of my Variants are in there. One of them could be close to death. I'm going." To my surprise, neither Ethan nor Josh was arguing with me.

"What other choice do we have?" Ethan growled, crossing his arms.

Josh sighed. "Tyler is going to kill me, but I can't live with myself if we do nothing and . . ." His unfinished sentence settled heavily over the room.

Olivia stopped crying and stood from the couch, wiping her tears away angrily. "I'm with Eve. I'm sick of sitting around, losing more of my family as every hour passes."

"Olivia!" Henry turned to her, horrified, but the rest of us were already springing into action.

"Henry, Charlie is in there. My brother is in there. Alec, Tyler . . ." She started ticking names off on her fingers.

"Kyo," Dot added, her face desperate. I wondered if she'd realized yet how hopelessly in love with him she was.

I went to Dot and pulled her into a hug.

"I'm thinking it might be a good idea . . ." I started at the same time she said, "I think you should juice me . . ."

We both nodded, no more words necessary, and I took her hands in mine, doing the most efficient and quick Light transfer I'd ever done. When we pulled apart, she ran for the door.

"I'll do recon as I change," she yelled over her shoulder.

Ethan and Josh had already dressed in the leftover gear, decked out from head to toe in black, looking every part the Melior Group agents they weren't.

The next few things happened so fast they were mostly a blur. I must have got dressed in tactical clothing too, because I was in all black when I pressed my lips to Josh's, slamming Light into him as if our lives depended on it. Ethan adjusted my Kevlar before I turned to him and did the same.

When we made for the door, I stopped short and gaped at the sight of Nina with an automatic rifle hanging off her shoulder, her delicate frame draped in weapons.

She smirked as she took the lead toward the jungle. "What? I know a few things I have not told you about."

Even though Henry tried to talk us out of it the whole way there, eventually he gave up and started giving us all advice and instructions on how to stay alive. "This is madness," he ground out between clenched teeth as we crouched in the underbrush about an hour later, near an unassuming green door.

Dot had used her ability to perfection. An orange-bellied leafbird had informed her no one had gone in or out since the backup team. But a mouse that had scurried inside the building said there were "a lot of men in black unconscious inside."

Unconscious gave me hope. Unconscious wasn't dead.

We crept forward. At a flick of Josh's wrist, the door swung open, and we moved inside.

Immediately, everything became fuzzy, muted somehow. I was having trouble holding on to my gun, which felt foreign in my hands anyway. I lost track of the others. My vision kept fading in and out. I couldn't remember where we were.

"You're early, daughter dear."

A voice drew my eyes up. *When did I sit down?*

"I didn't even have to kill him to get you here." A face with eyes similar to mine, only much darker and more cruel, hovered over me.

As Davis Damari grinned, the world around me dissolved into blackness.

THIRTY TWO

I came to slowly, my limbs heavy.

"... takes time. Everyone is different," a female voice I didn't recognize said.

"I need her to wake up. This won't work unless she sparks up." Davis sounded more than a little impatient.

The ache in my chest had returned along with my consciousness, and that made everything else come crashing back. Reflexively, I tried to lift my hand to rub at the pain and discovered I was tied down.

My eyes flew open.

I was in a padded chair, not unlike a dentist's chair, half-reclined, my wrists bound to the armrests. A large circular piece of opaque glass housed in a thick black frame hung above, pointing directly at my chest. I couldn't even begin to guess its purpose. Monitors stuck to my torso and head fed into thin wires leading somewhere behind me.

"Ah, you're up." Davis moved to my side, his hands in his pockets, his posture the picture of casual calm—as if he were about to ask what I wanted for breakfast. I ignored him, my eyes flying about the room.

It was cavernous, white walls and no windows. Benches and workstations were scattered throughout, as well as beds on wheels. The beds were all empty, but I shuddered to think what they were used for.

"I told you, you just needed to wait." The woman speaking had short black hair and sharp glasses perched on her nose. She was holding hands with a man who looked vaguely familiar.

"Yes, yes." Davis moved over to one of the benches. "And the others are still subdued? Wouldn't want any interruptions."

"Yes." The woman rolled her eyes. "Just get on with it."

"Gina." The man holding her hand spoke over his shoulder, directing his words to someone else. "Do you need more Light?"

A short, stocky woman with curly brown hair stepped out from behind him. "Nah, I'm good." Her gaze was fixed on me, as if she were watching fish in a tank. "I'm only shielding us from the passive abilities. I could do this all day."

The man nodded and closed his eyes again. He was clearly a Vital; the two women, I assumed, were his Variants.

Davis murmured to a few other people gathered around the bench, some of them jotting things down on tablets, others fiddling with screens and knobs. Then he sauntered back over to me.

I knew it was pointless, but I pulled on my restraints all the same, testing them. Every instinct I had was screaming at me to get the hell away from this man—not to mention the horrific pain in my chest urging me to do whatever I could to get to my Variants. It now felt as if more than one of them was drained.

I looked around, trying to spot them, but both my brain and body were sluggish from whatever they'd used to knock me out.

"What did you do to me?" I growled.

"Me?" Davis pressed a hand to his chest, amusement playing in his eyes. "Nothing . . . yet. It was my colleague Sarah who incapacitated you and all the others. A very handy ability to have when armed men come storming onto your property, don't you think? And Gina here made sure young Tyler Gabriel knew nothing about it."

The impressive nature of both abilities sent a chill down my spine. To be able to knock people out but choose to leave others in the vicinity conscious was a scary thing to be up against. The fact that the other woman—Gina—was seemingly able to shield whomever she chose explained why Tyler hadn't seen this coming, why they went in not expecting any of this. He would hate that he hadn't been able to warn his teams.

Once again, I frantically scanned the room for my guys, but all I could see were sterile walls, fluorescent lights, clean steel surfaces. The pull in my chest was tugging me to the left, but I couldn't see around the Vital and his two Variants.

"Move out of the way so she can see her Variants, would you?" Davis waved, and they shuffled to the side.

Behind them, all four of my guys were slumped, unconscious and unarmed, on the ground. Guarding them was another couple, one I recognized from when Ethan had pointed them out at the gala. The man was tall; the woman had Zara's silky red hair. Con and Francine Adams—Zara's parents.

A few feet over, leaning on the wall, was Zara herself. She had her arms crossed over her chest, her head tipped back, and she was watching me with a blank look in her eyes.

Seeing her again would have upset me on any day. Seeing her now, as

I was strapped to a chair and out of my mind with worry that one of my Variants was about to die, just about pushed me over the edge.

I ground my teeth as a half growl, half wail ripped from my chest, and hot tears started trailing paths into my hair.

Crouched down next to her, his elbows on his knees and his arms extended in front of him, head hung low, was Rick. For every bit of apathy in Zara's posture, his held defeat.

It shocked me to see them next to each other. He was responsible for Beth's death. Zara *held him responsible* for our friend's death and had refused to even hear his apology. Yet there they were, side by side, watching me fall apart under the hands of a man who I may have called father had my life turned out differently.

Rick looked up, his red-rimmed hazel eyes meeting mine. His jaw trembled as if he was trying to hold back tears. I looked away, and my eyes landed on the Vital whose name I didn't know—the one with the two powerful Variants currently thwarting our rescue mission. He looked familiar because he was an older version of Rick. He had the same honey-blond hair and hazel eyes. I wondered if Sarah or Gina was Rick's mother.

"Bring me one of them." Davis gestured in the general direction of my Variants. Two of his thugs hauled Tyler up and dragged him across the smooth, clean floor as I tried to control the sobs, uselessly struggling against my restraints again.

They propped him up in a chair identical to mine, directly opposite me, not bothering to fasten the straps.

Davis yanked a tablet out of the hands of one of the people—I was reluctant to call them scientists—near the bench and pressed some buttons. The odd glass circle above Tyler's chair lit up with a dull blue light, the machinery in the room making a soft humming, whirring noise.

Immediately, the ache in my chest began to throb. It felt as if someone had sliced me open, reached a hand into my sternum, and was tugging me by the ribcage toward Tyler. My back arched off the chair, and I screamed.

They were draining him.

Whatever the fuck Davis Damari and his lackeys had been doing in this hellhole, one thing was certain: they'd figured out how to harness the Light, and not just from Vitals. They'd figured out how to drain it from anyone with the Variant gene.

They were killing him.

Gritting my teeth against the pain, I sat up as straight as I could and focused on Tyler's prone form. My skin had begun to glow, reacting to his need, and even though I didn't want to expose my secret to these people, I couldn't just sit there and watch them kill Tyler.

I embraced the energy, the power, coursing through me and directed it all at him. With a rush like a waterfall washing over my skin, the Light released and went where it was needed most.

Immediately, the ache in my chest subsided, and I was able to breathe again.

Davis turned his horrific machine off and, before I could turn my attention to my other Variants, came right up to me, grinning maniacally.

"Perfect!" he yelled. "Even brighter than your mother. Dare I say I'm proud, daughter?"

"You're fucking sick, is what you are." My voice was hoarse, my body strained from being under so much stress, despite the fact that it was humming with Light.

He just chuckled as if I'd made a joke and started untying my restraints. He yanked me out of the seat as his thugs dragged Tyler back to the others, dumping him unceremoniously on the ground.

Rick had moved away from Zara and was standing next to his parents. Sarah still had that look of concentration on her face, his father still transferring Light to her, but Rick was pleading with them.

"Come on, Mom, please!" He raked his hands through his hair, not even trying to hide his tears or wipe them way. "We don't have to do this. Let's just go. You're hurting people. I *killed* someone!"

"She was just a Dime, son." His father frowned at him. "Stop worrying yourself over it."

I suppressed the urge to gouge the man's eyes out for referring to my dead friend in such a dismissive, derogatory way, and my eyes flew to Zara. For the first time since before I was abducted, I saw a glimmer, a tiny hint of the old Zara. Her eyes narrowed, and her lips almost pulled into a scowl. But then she met my gaze, and whatever she'd been thinking disappeared from her features as she watched, unblinking, while Davis shoved me toward my Variants.

I didn't question why he was letting me go to them. I just ran.

A blur of movement was all that preceded Zara's father appearing next to me, and I remembered belatedly that he and his wife both had super speed. He jerked me to a stop, his grip on my upper arm painful. I clawed at his hand and thrashed against him, but he pulled me tight against his chest.

"Probably not a good idea to let her recharge the one with the pain ability," he spat out, the sarcasm rolling off him so similar to what I was used to from Zara.

But Davis wasn't paying him any attention. He held his hand out to Zara. "Come, my dear." She went to him without hesitation. "Now that Evelyn has so graciously helped me configure the machine, we can see about gifting you with an ability."

The smile on Zara's lips was a little too wide, her eyes glassy. I may have seen a hint of my friend for a second there, but the promise of an ability—of being everything she never could be before—had driven her to insanity.

"Which ability would you like?" Davis cooed, helping her onto the chair I'd just been torn apart in. Her mother stepped up behind it, running her hands lovingly through Zara's silky hair, as if she were comforting her on a routine visit to the doctor.

All these people were completely unhinged.

"A powerful one" was her answer, her eyes zeroing in on the unconscious bodies just out of my reach. "That one." She lifted her arm and pointed—right at Ethan.

Davis snapped his fingers at his lackeys, and they moved to obey.

"No, no, no!" I thrashed against my captor again. "Leave him alone! Put him down. I will *fucking destroy you*!" My hoarse voice sounded feral; my legs kicked so violently they were leaving the ground.

No one even remotely reacted to my outburst.

The guards struggled under Ethan's weight, and a third stepped forward to help. They hefted Ethan into the chair Tyler had occupied and stepped away, panting with the effort.

"Are you sure this won't hurt her?" Zara's mother asked.

"Her?" Davis answered as he punched buttons on the tablet again. "No, completely harmless to *her*. Him? Well, this is the new part of the experiment. One we haven't been able to test without a particular kind of Vital to configure the machine." He glanced in my direction, and I deflated.

Whatever it was he'd been doing here, I'd just provided him with the final piece of the puzzle. I'd done my glowing thing, drawing Light and sending it remotely to Tyler. I'd walked in here and offered myself to him on a platter. I may have had an IQ of 153, but I was a fucking idiot.

Lucian had told me how Davis had gained his ability. Now he was about to attempt the same thing with Ethan and Zara.

"It may kill him." Davis shrugged as he confirmed my fears, sounding positively chipper. "Let's find out, shall we?"

He pressed one last button, and the machines started to whir to life, the circular glass above both illuminating.

Something inside me cracked.

There was no time to dissect the implications of what was before me. To puzzle out the quantum mechanics behind this new technology. To analyze the unique abilities of the Variants in the room. To *think* of a solution.

I needed to *do* something.

Wrapped in a bigger man's iron grip, with my Variants knocked out cold, there was no way I could do it with my body. So I put my faith in the most powerful aspect of myself.

I planted my feet on the ground, took a deep breath, and unleashed.

I allowed the Light to take over.

I drew on every bit of Light I could access—every tendril I could find. I pulled the Light that was naturally and plentifully always available, but I also drew it from every other source in the room. I counted twelve—twelve other people with Variant DNA and therefore some amount of Light. I pulled it from all of them.

I glowed brighter than I ever had before, the warm white light bouncing off the white walls and shiny surfaces.

And I pushed it all into them. Every bit of Light I siphoned I sent to the four men who each held a piece of me.

At the same time that Davis's macabre machine came to life and I started transferring Light to my Variants, Rick lost his shit.

His pleading with his parents had failed, and in a moment of pure desperation, he used his ability. Other than the day he'd protected me from

Franklyn, this was the first time I'd seen Rick use his ability since the day it had killed Beth. Only this time it wasn't an accident, and it wasn't random. The electricity came to his hands effortlessly, and he let out a pained yell as he aimed it right at his mother, hitting her square in the chest. Her eyes flew open and then went dull as she crumpled, falling into her Vital's arms.

With most people in the room shielding their eyes from my lightshow, I was the only one who saw Rick take down his own mother, then run to Ethan. With strength I didn't know he possessed, Rick hauled his friend out of the seat, shoving him out of the way and taking the brunt of whatever the machine was doing.

As the intensity of my glow began to fade, Rick collapsed onto the chair, facedown.

People started to get nervous, fidgety, but Davis remained fully focused on finishing his experiment. His shouted orders were now all about keeping everyone away from the range of his machines so the process could be finished.

I stopped pulling Light and transferring it to my guys; they were replenished and overflowing. Now I just had to wait for them to come to.

Con's grip on me loosened. He was the closest Variant to me, and I'd pulled the most Light out of him. He was weakened, so I seized my opportunity.

I braced, remembering some of the ruthless drills Kane had put us through, and leaned forward as far as I could before slamming my head back into his face. It hurt like a bitch, but his grip loosened further. Just as I was about to kick him in the shin though, he was wrenched away.

I turned just in time to see Alec swing his fist, knocking the older man out cold.

I'd never been happier to see his scowling, cruel face. Behind him, Tyler and Josh were getting to their feet, shaking the rest of the daze from their heads.

Alec shoved me almost harshly in their direction, and I heard a low growl as he launched himself at the guards between us and Davis.

Before any of them could take a shot, Josh disarmed them, their weapons twisting into unusable chunks of metal over their heads.

"Could've used one of those, man," Tyler grumbled as he pushed me behind him. Josh closed in on my other side until they were boxing me in.

"There you go," Josh answered, and a handgun came flying toward Tyler. He caught it effortlessly and fired, taking out an assailant who was about to hit Alec from the back.

I bent to see around Tyler, and the first thing I caught sight of was Ethan, still sprawled on the ground near that awful machine. Why wasn't he waking up like the others? He was too close to all the dangerous people, all the flying fists and whatever that machine was doing.

I ducked past Tyler and Josh and ran, sliding on the ground to come to a rest next to Ethan.

"Dammit!" Tyler swore, hot on my heels. Josh was swearing too but not following, so I had a feeling he was dealing with something else.

I ran my hands over Ethan's bulky form, placing my palm flat to his neck, but he didn't need more Light, and he was breathing. He was just taking a little longer to wake up. A tiny bit of relief leaked through the panic as he moaned and started to shift beneath my hands.

The machine next to us had finished what it was doing, and the cold light emitting from the round bit of glass faded until it was dull once more.

"Did it work?" A frantic female voice asked, and I looked up to see Francine brushing hair from Zara's forehead, her fearful eyes darting about the room. The guards were managing to keep Alec at bay—only just. There were so many more of them, and for some reason he was refusing to use his ability, mowing them down with his fists.

Gunfire and shouting could be heard from behind the white walls and closed doors. The rest of the Melior Group forces must have come to when Alec did, but who knows what they had to fight through to get to us.

"Time to go!" Davis shouted. He gathered up some items from the bench, and his other scientists did the same, lifting out of their hidden positions behind benches.

Zara sat up in her chair, seemingly oblivious to the chaos. She held shaking hands out in front of her, her head bent, as she took shuddering breaths. She was turning her hands this way and that, seeing or feeling something the rest of us weren't privy to.

Davis yanked her out of the chair by the wrist and dragged her to a discreet door in the back of the room, her mother and some of his other staff hot on his heels.

As more men in black burst into the room, Davis and his group disappeared through the door, slamming it shut behind them.

THIRTY THREE

For a split second my heart sank, convinced the people streaming into the room were Davis's guards. But then Jamie's red hair caught my attention, and I started recognizing the Melior Group operatives who'd been at the compound. Lucian appeared at my side and started helping Ethan sit up as Kyo and the guys fell in beside Alec.

We gained control of the room within seconds, but it was seconds too late to stop Davis.

Lucian looked as if he'd aged ten years as he checked his nephew for injuries, finally pulling him into a hug as Ethan shook the lethargy from his head. As soon as Ethan's eyes found mine, he pulled away from his uncle and scooped me up, one hand holding me close and the other running over me, looking for any harm.

"You OK?" He asked my hair.

"Are you?" I threw back at him.

Neither of us answered the loaded question. We just pulled apart and got to our feet.

Tyler was barking orders to detain the thugs Alec hadn't killed, and a group of agents were trying to force open the door Davis had disappeared through.

With everyone else occupied, Lucian turned to me. "What is this place? What happened?"

My heart was ripped out of my chest. I was betrayed. We nearly died. I didn't know where to start, so I stuck to the facts. "Some kind of fucked-up lab." Lucian didn't even flinch at my swearing. "You were right. He's been trying to figure out how to switch on the dormant Variant gene in Variants without abilities—epigenetics taken to the criminally insane level. He did it. He nearly killed . . ." I swallowed around the lump in my throat, my gaze going to Ethan's back. He was turned away from us, staring at the machines. "I glowed and . . . I couldn't help it, but . . . I gave him . . . I . . . I . . ."

I was losing my shit, but Lucian put one comforting hand on my shoulder and held my gaze, his expression calm. Instead of asking more questions, he gave me some positives to hold on to. "We found the Vitals. We've been getting them free slowly. They should nearly be all out. When the others started waking up, we moved to clear the rest of the building and—"

"The others?" Tyler came to stand next to me, and I leaned into him. "I thought everyone was knocked out."

"When we breached, almost everyone fell. But I had a little help." Lucian gave me a wink. "The extra Light I had from Eve allowed me to shield myself and the three closest operatives to me. We faked being unconscious, and when everything was quiet, we started taking the guards out and moving through the building slowly. After a while we found Nina too, fully conscious and fighting off *two* of Davis's men. If there was any doubt that Lighthunters are impervious to other abilities, she more than dispelled it. She's in the lower levels, helping to free the Vitals."

While we talked, Ethan moved to Rick's side. He checked the spot on his friend's wrist and his neck for a pulse, and then his big shoulders slumped.

The moment Rick had gone limp in that chair, some part of me knew he wouldn't be getting up again. But seeing it in Ethan's defeated posture, his misting eyes and quivering lip as he turned to look at us, was almost too much to bear.

It could have been him lying dead in that chair. It nearly was.

Tears blurred my vision as I wrapped my arms around my torso and tried to stay strong. I couldn't fall apart.

But Ethan reacted differently. Something changed in him. It took maybe a second—his gaze flying around the room, taking in the implications of it all—but then his eyes narrowed; his lips curled in anger.

Without warning, Ethan started conjuring angry blue fireballs and throwing them at the machine, the computers, the walls. He was destroying the room.

I knew his ability couldn't hurt me, but I backed away, frightened by the intensity of his anger.

A massive *boom* sounded from the door Davis had escaped through, and Tyler turned to shield me from the blast. Apparently the door was somehow reinforced, and Melior Group was using explosives to try to remove it.

"Kid, you're destroying evidence!" Lucian yelled, stepping into Ethan's space, despite the fact that Ethan's ability definitely *could* harm him.

Between him and Alec, they managed to calm Ethan down. At the same time, Josh finished off what the detonators around the door had started. He used his ability to twist the door in on itself, and it finally came open.

"All right, let's move!" Alec yelled, his team already forming up at his side.

I grabbed his forearm with both hands. "No!"

That one word came out so forcefully and loudly that several people turned to look before getting back to what they were doing.

Alec turned to me, and I braced for him to sound angry, annoyed that I was getting in his way, but the look on his face was regretful. "I have to go, baby. It's my job."

I tightened my grip on his arm. "Alec Zacarias, don't you leave my sight right now. Don't any of you leave me."

I turned to look at them all, proud of how steady my voice sounded despite the tears that had once again started falling.

By this stage, two other teams had already gone through the busted door after Davis.

"Get these civilians out of here." Lucian rolled his shoulders back. "That's an order."

He gave Alec one firm look before following the last few agents through the busted door. I could have kissed him, but he moved fast for an older guy.

"All right, team, let's move." Alec gently pried my hands from his forearm and took my hand in his. Kyo and Marcus took the lead, and we all headed through the opposite doorway, Jamie bringing up the rear.

As we made our way through the building, which was much larger underground than it looked from the outside, evidence of the fighting was clear: bullet holes in the wall, macabre splatters of blood, doors hanging off their hinges. But Melior Group was efficient, and all the actual people were gone. We came across only one Melior Group operative helping a teammate with an injured leg. Marcus stepped up to assist them, and before long we were emerging into a wide warehouse-like space.

It was much dirtier and rougher than the pristine white lab and maze of corridors we'd just come through. A few all-terrain vehicles were lined up on one wall; massive shelving stacked with different sized boxes took up the other.

And in the corner closest to us were cages.

I shivered, remembering the last time I'd seen black bars like that, in the basement of a house in Manhattan. There were so many of them, more than I could count as we kept walking, heading for the ramp on the other side of the open space. The morning light streamed in through the wide opening at the ramp's top, beckoning us to freedom.

But before we'd even made it a few steps, a massive *boom* reverberated through the structure, shaking the walls, the very ground we stood on. We all bent our knees, throwing our hands out for balance.

We were still one floor below ground level, and it looked as if the structure above was about to come crashing down. Cracks were appearing in the ceiling.

Another *boom* sounded from farther away. People were screaming, yelling. Jittery shadows cut across the sunlight ahead as people ran about frantically.

"We need to get the fuck out of here." Tyler took the lead, but as he stepped forward, a giant chunk of concrete landed in front of him.

Josh pushed past him and threw his hands into the air, every muscle in his body taut, as if he were physically holding the bricks and mortar up with his hands rather than his ability.

I dropped Alec's hand and pressed my palm flat against Josh's bicep—the biggest bit of exposed skin I could find. The only problem was I wasn't sure I had anything left to give. Yes, the Light constantly coursed through me, but I'd used so much recently, and in such an intense way. I was spent, tired, weak.

My skin took on that ethereal glow once again, but there just wasn't that much Light available for me to pull from. I reached mentally for my Variants, for what energy they had.

Ethan's big warm hand found my free one, and the connection made it so much easier to draw Light from him. Next, Tyler's firm grip closed on my forearm. I took from them and gave to Josh—just in time. The ceiling was completely collapsing. We were the only thing holding it up.

At Alec's command, the other operatives with us started to make their way across the wide expanse, keeping to the edges.

"Can you keep that up and move?" Alec asked, panic tinging his words.

Before Josh could answer, another dozen people streamed through the door from where we'd just come. Some of them were Melior Group agents; others were in nothing but gray pajama-looking outfits, the looks in their eyes pure terror and confusion. Many of them were dirty and sooty, their clothing torn. They stayed close to the wall, unwilling to brave the massive piece of concrete now hovering above our heads.

As Alec spoke to his subordinates—asking how many people were still coming, if everyone was out, what the situation was—the slab of concrete burst into flames.

Some of the fire burned blue, and for a moment I wondered why. That only happens when high levels of oxygen are present or when copper, chloride, or butane are added to the flame. But the blue flames were random and flickering in and out, so neither of those explanations fit. The only other blue flame I knew of was Ethan's . . .

But the time for curiosity was over. A mere second after the concrete caught fire, another explosion, farther away, went off.

"Run!" Alec roared, waving at the group of people by the door. "Go! Now!"

They obeyed, shuffled forward by Kyo and the other operatives, some of them helping the injured as they ran for their lives. The five of us were the only ones left on this side of the room.

"We need to secure it!" I yelled.

Ethan was freaking out but keeping his hand firmly around mine. "Why the fuck is everything on fire?"

"Josh, use the shelving!" Tyler gestured to the steel constructions at the edges of the room.

"I'm barely holding it up, Gabe!" Josh's voice was strained with effort.

"Maybe we should retreat, let it fall," Tyler thought out loud.

"No." Alec appeared in front of me, pressing his palm to my cheek. "We'll be trapped. Take it all if you have to."

The last part was directed at only me, his ice-blue eyes determined.

I pulled—took the extra connection and drew on Alec's Light, slamming it all into Josh.

Josh took his first deep breath. He held the concrete in place with one hand and swung the other out, dragging the tall shelving over, letting the boxes and crates stacked there fall to the ground. He positioned the shelves under the collapsing ceiling and lowered it a bit. It was still on fire, the flames licking fast and angry, spreading to some of the cardboard and timber crates.

The concrete slab must have weighed several tons, not counting the above-ground building on top of it. The shelves, solid as they were, wouldn't last long. They simply weren't made for it. Not to mention that the intense fire was weakening the metal and making the concrete crumble further. There was no amount of math I could do to figure this out; I wasn't an engineer. We just had to hope for the best.

"Now!" Tyler yelled, and we ran.

All five of us sprinted across the warehouse floor as flaming chunks of concrete fell around us. Once we made it to the relative safety of the bottom of the ramp, I chanced a look back, and my heart froze, *seized* in my chest.

Halfway to us was Henry, an unconscious Charlie in his arms, dressed in the same gray pajamas I'd seen on the other prisoners. Keeping pace with them was a Melior Group operative carrying one of his comrades in a fireman's hold. Olivia was limping, lagging behind, but they all hauled ass. Menacing balls of fire fell all around them, making them zigzag.

Without even thinking, I turned, ready to launch myself back into the thick of it. But before I could take a step, strong arms closed around my middle and pulled, knocking the wind out of me.

"God dammit!" Alec yelled. He threw me over his shoulder and carried me the rest of the way up the ramp. I struggled against him, but the way he held me allowed me to watch the others make it to safety, my guys helping them up the ramp as Josh used his ability to swat away the flaming obstacles.

As we emerged into the sunshine and the chaos above ground, Alec set me down.

"Where's Dot?" I immediately demanded, craning my neck to see around him. I had to make sure everyone was OK.

Alec grabbed me by the shoulders and turned me toward several parked black vehicles. Dot was enveloped in Kyo's arms, her head on his shoulder, but she was standing, conscious, unhurt.

As soon as the rest of her family emerged, she broke out of Kyo's arms and ran to them, but I didn't get to witness her finally reunite with her brother and Vital. Alec turned me back to face him. With both hands on my shoulders, he leaned down so his intense eyes were level with mine.

"Is Charlie OK?" I tried to ask, but he spoke over me, his expression somewhere between frustration and fury.

"Have you no regard for your own safety whatsoever?"

"Huh?" I lifted my hands, resting them on his elbows.

"You don't have to be the one to do it all. You don't have to save everyone, Evie. There are other people here just as invested in helping and certainly more qualified and trained. It's not all on you." With one thumb, he wiped a tear I hadn't even realized was streaming down my cheek. "You have us. You're not alone anymore, precious. You're *not alone*."

A sob broke out of my chest, and I leaned into him. He held me tight, as if to enforce his statement, as I absorbed the truth of what he'd said.

For all his fucked-up issues, his antisocial tendencies, the giant chip on his shoulder, his emotional stuntedness, Alec always seemed to know when I needed to hear those words the most.

I relaxed against him, finally letting go, and when he passed me to Ethan, I didn't struggle. I let my big guy scoop me up into his arms and buried my head in his neck. I didn't check on what Alec and Tyler were doing. I didn't demand to know what needed to happen next. I just let Ethan hold me—let Josh run his hand through my hair, removing the hair tie and dislodging some of the knots with his fingers.

People were still rushing about—some working to put out the fire, others tending to the wounded—but Davis's remaining men were all restrained, and the sense of danger had abated.

Sitting in a shady spot with her knees drawn up, her shirt torn and her face dusty, was Nina. She chugged an entire bottle of water in one go and took several heaving breaths. Our eyes met, and I gave her a tired smile, hoping it conveyed my gratitude. She winked at me.

The sound of helicopters drew my gaze up.

"Medevac," Josh murmured just as medics began to move some of the worst injured toward a clearing in the distance. One of the people being rushed to the choppers was clearly Charlie; Dot and his parents were running beside his stretcher. I wanted to rush after them, comfort my friend, find out what was happening, but I reminded myself Charlie was in good hands. Kyo jogged to catch up with them and took Dot's hand right before they disappeared behind some trees. I let myself relax a little more to the steady beat of Ethan's heart.

But soon Josh's fingers in my hair faltered, then stopped completely. He cursed low under his breath. Ethan's whole body stiffened, his arms around me tightening.

I hadn't even realized I'd closed my eyes, but I made myself open them, ready for whatever new catastrophe was befalling us now.

Medics were rushing about frantically near the vehicles. Tyler was pointing at things, yelling at people. Alec just stood there, his hands on his hips, his head hung low, his shoulders heaving.

All their attention was centered around a man on a stretcher.

"Who do you think . . ." Josh's question died when a gap in the crowd revealed a glimpse of distinguished features, dark hair peppered with gray.

The man on the stretcher, the man I'd watched be carried out next to Henry and Charlie, was Lucian Zacarias.

The three of us rushed forward at the same time, fear choking the air out of my lungs.

THIRTY FOUR

The blood on Alec's knuckles had crusted over. There were so many people with serious, life-threatening injuries that a couple of busted hands just weren't important.

I focused on the deep red, the bruising already beginning to show, the streaks of dried blood mingling with dirt and dust all over his arms. Anything to distract myself from the screaming.

Charlie's latest blood-curdling scream came to a whimpering stop, and we all took a small breath of relief.

Alec was sitting in a plastic chair across from me, his head in his hands, his shoulders stiff. Ethan mirrored his older cousin's posture in the seat next to him. I could see the resemblance clearly in the dark shade of Ethan's longer hair and Alec's buzz cut, in the set of their tense shoulders, in the way both of their feet were planted wide, the toes slightly turned out.

Josh sat next to me. I had a feeling if he wasn't scared to crush the bones, he would have been gripping my hand as hard as I was gripping his.

Davis had managed to get away with Zara, her mom, Rick's dad, and a small group of the mad scientists.

In the ensuing battle, forty-eight people had died, and several hundred were wounded. There were bullet wounds, broken bones, blunt force trauma, and a myriad other injuries. But the worst were the burns.

They were still trying to figure out what exactly had caused the fire. It had spread fast to many parts of the building, and several people had serious burns. Charlie was one of them.

The medics had managed to stabilize Lucian at the scene, but his injuries were horrific. He'd been shot multiple times in the chest and left arm as he joined the teams trying to stop Davis from getting away. Then, as the last few people were evacuating the building, a wall had collapsed, knocking him unconscious and pulverizing his hips.

He was still in surgery, doctors battling to save his life, while Charlie screamed through his first change of dressings.

"This is my fault," Ethan growled, rocking back and forth, pulling on his hair.

"No, it isn't." I didn't even hesitate to refute him. He'd started blaming himself once we'd realized how badly some of the victims had been burned. By the time we'd arrived at the hospital in Singapore where the worst cases had been airlifted, nothing could convince him his ability hadn't caused the fires.

His anguish had Alec sitting up straighter. "We don't know what happened yet. But, Kid"—he put a firm hand on Ethan's big shoulder—"no one would blame you even if your ability did start it. We were all there because of that fucker in the first place. Aim your anger at him, not at yourself."

The sound of approaching footsteps preceded Tyler's arrival. He came to a stop near the waiting area and propped his hands on his hips.

"Hey." He sighed. We were all tired, dirty, and aching. Tyler's hair was all kinds of crazy, but he was dressed in black, just like the rest of us, so the filth wasn't as visible. "How's Charlie doing?"

We all winced. The doctors had rushed him to surgery as soon as we'd arrived, doing their best to repair the damage to the right side of his body. He'd been resting until a few moments ago.

"They're changing his dressings now. What's going on out there?" Josh asked.

"Chaos, but we're doing our best to contain it. The press has already gotten wind of things. We told everyone to keep it quiet, but a lot of Vitals were being held, and they're reuniting with their families. It's impossible to keep that many people quiet. Also, we found the senator."

"Christine Anderson?" My eyes snapped to his, my back straightening. That woman had been at least partially responsible for my kidnapping, for Josh nearly dying, and she was definitely involved in all this. But she hadn't been seen or heard from since that day.

"Yeah. In one of the cells. And she's not shy about talking. She's a little delusional about her political prospects after all this, but it seems she was working with Davis early on—until he decided she was a liability and locked her up."

"But she's talking?" It was the first time in hours I'd seen a hint of a smile on Josh's face. The hope in his eyes gave *me* hope.

"She won't shut up." Tyler smiled. "She confirmed Variant Valor orchestrated the invasion at Bradford Hills Institute, manipulating the Human Empowerment Network to cause a distraction so they could kidnap Vitals. How they've been transporting them and where to. She's also saying some interesting things about how Variant Valor began—how deeply Damari is involved. There's a long way to go to corroborate her stories but—"

Another gut-wrenching scream, barely recognizable as human, came from Charlie's room. Tyler reached for the gun at his hip, but we all just flinched.

I squeezed Josh's hand again, gritting my teeth. Alec dropped his head back into his hands, and Ethan growled—a sound between pain and frustration.

Josh held his other hand out to Tyler, gesturing for him to lower the gun. "It's the pain from changing the dressings."

"Fuck," Tyler breathed, threading a hand through his hair. "Can't they give him some painkillers or something?"

"They've given him as much as they can," I explained. "This is one of the most painful things a person can experience. The dressings are often put on wet and pulled off dry to tear away dead tissue. There's only so much morphine can do."

My brain was in that weird state where it started firing related yet unhelpful facts and statistics in moments of high stress. Apparently, I was now comfortable enough with my Bond to spew this information out loud instead of just going over it in my mind, despite them all watching me with horrified expressions. "Burns are categorized by thickness. Charlie's burns are bad but *not* full thickness, which means the nerve endings weren't destroyed completely, which means he can still feel it all. Yeah. It fucking hurts."

Alec growled, throwing his hands in front of him as if he could physically throw off the discomfort he was in, and leaned heavily back in his chair. He started rubbing his thighs, then sat up again. His eyebrows were threaded together, the scar in the right one puckering.

Out of all of us, Alec had the most experience with pain, yet he seemed to be struggling the most with listening to Charlie go through it. But he wasn't leaving.

"Has anyone called in a healer?" Tyler asked in the next break between screams.

"Uncle Henry did," Ethan said to his shoes. "But they're coming from Egypt, and it's going to be a while. They can't just not change Charlie's dressings."

Healing abilities were extremely rare—rarer even than the four unique abilities my guys had. There were only a couple of dozen healers in the world, and half of them could only handle minor injuries. The more powerful ones—the ones with Vitals—were in high demand.

"I'm sure this is the best thing for him, then." Tyler frowned.

"I think we all just feel helpless." Josh nailed it. All four of my guys were proactive, and I hated having a problem I couldn't solve. Sitting in a waiting room, listening to someone scream in pain only feet away—it was beyond frustrating.

But maybe there *was* something we could try.

Chewing my bottom lip, I extracted my hand from Josh's iron grip and stood, taking the three steps necessary to move in front of Alec.

He saw what I was planning written all over my features. His face fell, worry and disappointment replacing the frustration. "I can't," he whispered, narrowing his eyes at me.

"So you have thought about it?"

"Of course I've thought about it," he huffed, throwing his arms up and letting them flow back down to his knees. "But now is not the time to test it."

"Why not? What's the worst that could happen?"

He stood, his hands in fists, but I didn't step back, so we ended up chest to chest. "Are you fucking serious? I could make it worse."

"You won't." I had to look up to meet his icy stare, but I held it, refusing to back down.

"You don't know that."

"Yes, I do, Alec." I placed my hands on his chest. "I've never met anyone with more control in all aspects of his life than you. You have more control of your ability than anyone I know. I don't for a second doubt that you'll be able to hold back that part of it. It's second nature to you. The worst that could happen is nothing."

He was breathing hard, his eyes searching mine.

"You can do this, man." Josh's voice was steady.

"What makes you think it's even possible?" Alec kept his gaze trained on me.

"Logic." I moved my hands to his shoulders. "With my Light, Tyler can tell not only that someone is lying but what they're lying about. With my Light, Josh can not only levitate a few books in his room but hold up an entire floor of a building, make himself fly. With my Light, Ethan can not only set fires but put them out. Alec, he can *put out* fires he didn't start. There's no reason you couldn't take away pain you didn't inflict."

"I've been waiting for a good time to raise this, Alec." Tyler sighed. "But she's right. The research supports it, study after study showing that with access to a Vital, the ability can be used far beyond what—"

Charlie screamed again, cutting Tyler off. Ethan stood and placed a big hand over mine on Alec's shoulder.

"Alec, please try." His voice was hoarse, tears threatening to spill over. I wanted to take him into my arms and comfort him, but in that moment, Alec needed me more.

"You can do this." I injected as much confidence and intensity into the statement as I could.

Alec wrapped his arms around my waist, drawing me to him so tightly my feet almost lifted off the ground. I circled my arms around his neck and held on. I would hold on for as long as he needed, prove to him I was there—

that I was in this with him.

He'd told me hours before I wasn't alone, that I didn't need to do everything myself. Now it was my turn to show him the same thing.

"I'm so fucking scared, Evie," he whispered into my dirty hair, too low for the others to hear.

"I know, but I'll be there with you. You're not alone." He released me, and I pulled back to look at him. "You can do this, Alec. I know you can."

He took a deep breath, rubbed his hands over his cropped hair, and nodded.

I didn't wait for him to change his mind. I grabbed his hand and pulled him in the direction of the screams.

Inside the room, three nurses hovered over Charlie, moving quickly but efficiently, piles of bloody bandages in a heap next to the bed.

Olivia sat next to Charlie's head, holding his unburned hand, tears streaking her cheeks even as she murmured soothing things into her son's ear. In the opposite corner, Henry cradled Dot with one arm, her face turned into his chest.

"Stop!" I may have yelled a little too loudly, but I didn't want to waste another second.

"You not permitted to be here," one of the nurses said sternly in heavily accented English, pointing harshly to the door.

"We're family." Alec stepped in front of me, his voice hard and even despite the level of emotion it had trembled with only moments before. Charlie needed him to be strong. "And we can help."

He stepped forward and explained his ability to the nurses.

"I don't know about this." Olivia stood, her brows creased, one hand still on Charlie's forehead. "What if you just hurt him more?"

"We should let him try, Mom!" Dot piped up, her hoarse voice breaking on every second word.

Everyone started talking over each other, arguing for or against the plan, while the nurses continued to try to get us to leave.

I kept my eyes trained on Charlie. He was breathing hard, his teeth gritted, his eyes drooping, but he was meeting my gaze. After a few moments, he nodded and squeezed his mother's hand, cutting off whatever it was she'd been saying.

She looked down at him, and the whole room quieted.

"I want to try," Charlie breathed, his voice weak and strained.

Olivia closed her eyes, pushing more tears down her cheeks, and took a deep breath. Then she nodded, kissed Charlie tenderly on the forehead, and went to stand with the rest of her family.

Alec and I took her place. He rubbed his palms on his pants, blowing out a breath—the first signs of nervousness he'd shown since we'd walked into the room.

Charlie lifted his hand in invitation, and Alec took it. I threaded my fingers through Alec's other hand and waited for him to take the lead.

"Just give me a little to start with," Alec murmured, and I obeyed, letting the warm, tingly feeling in our hands take over. I released just a little Light, then shut it down and waited.

Alec closed his eyes, a look of intense concentration on his face. He bent over Charlie, gripping his hand just a little tighter.

"More," he whispered, and I gave him more—the same amount as before. As I was about to stop the flow, he spoke again. "Keep going. I'll tell you when to stop."

I let a steady, controlled stream of Light course through my hand and into his, briefly marveling at how effortless it was. The closer I got to my Bond—not just physically but on all levels—the easier it was to not only control the Light but understand it. Knowing exactly how much I needed to transfer and when and who needed it most was becoming second nature.

"OK." Alec squeezed my hand but didn't let go. I cut the flow.

For a few moments, everyone held their breath, the whirs and beeps of the machines in the room the only things penetrating the silence.

Then, Charlie sighed. Olivia sprang forward, looking poised to tackle the Master of Pain himself to the ground, but she stopped in her tracks when she saw the look of serenity on Charlie's face.

Pride swelled in my chest, as if I'd just done the impossible and not Alec. I grinned, rejoicing in the little twitch of his lips that indicated he was pleased too.

"How does that feel, Charlie?" Alec spoke low, caressing his cousin's hand with his thumb. Charlie loosened his grip, but Alec was holding firm.

"Like . . . nothing."

Finally, the smile broke out on Alec's face.

"Not like a pleasant sensation or anything, just . . . nothing." Wonder filled Charlie's voice, and his eyes closed; his body visibly relaxed. "The pain is just gone."

"You think you can keep it going?" one of the nurses recovered enough from her shock to ask.

Alec and I both nodded, and they sprang back to work.

We didn't speak, but we worked perfectly together—me pushing more Light at him as soon as I registered he needed it, him focusing fully on keeping the pain at bay.

The process wasn't flawless. A few times Alec's hold on the pain slipped, or I didn't push more Light in time, and Charlie would wince or cry out. But we quickly adjusted, and the nurses worked fast. They soon finished changing the dressings, and as they cleaned up, Alec finally released Charlie's hand. He was asleep.

Olivia pulled Alec down into a hug.

His face froze in an expression of shock. As much as people avoided him because of his ability, Alec had pushed people away too. It may have come as a surprise to him that his aunt was hugging him, but it was not a surprise to me. His family loved him.

Dot wrapped her delicate arms around his waist straight after, holding on to him for a long time, then turned and hugged me too. Over her shoulder, I watched Henry pull Alec in for a third hug, relief palpable in his red-rimmed eyes.

As we stepped back into the hallway, the others looked up expectantly.

"Well?" Ethan asked, his hands on his hips.

Instead of answering, Alec swept me up in his arms and kissed me. His arms banded tight around my back, he lifted me off the ground, and I twined my legs around his waist.

Kissing Alec was always intense, usually a surprise, and never failed to satisfy. This was no different, yet it had a new energy to it. He kissed me deeply, his tongue massaging mine in steady movements, his arms pressing me against his chest. I enthusiastically returned the embrace, still riding the high of what we'd been able to do for Charlie.

The kiss was everything it always was with him—all-consuming, making the rest of the world fall away—but it held none of the reluctance or restraint I'd felt from him in the past.

I felt giddy. Horny but giddy.

My surge of lust had me forgetting where we were, and I rolled my hips against the steadily growing bulge in Alec's pants. He had the presence of mind to break the kiss.

He pressed his forehead to mine and smiled in a way I'd only seen a handful of times—wide and genuine, his beautiful blue eyes sparkling with happiness. "Thank you." His warm breath washed over my face.

"What for? You did all the work." I chuckled as he set me back down.

He held my gaze, his eyes boring into mine with so much emotion, so much *hope*.

I had a feeling he wasn't thanking me for helping him take Charlie's pain away; he was thanking me for making him see it was possible. For showing him he was more than a monster, that he could use his ability for positive things.

"You're welcome." I smiled, hoping the look in my eyes conveyed my understanding.

"So it went well, then?" Josh chuckled.

"Knew you could do it." Tyler looked smug as Alec and I finally separated.

Ethan clapped a hand on Alec's shoulder and beamed, making his dimples appear.

But before we could explain to them exactly what happened, a doctor in scrubs came rushing down the hallway, one of the nurses from Charlie's room right behind him.

"Oh, shit." I pressed myself closer to Alec.

"Are you the man with the pain ability?" he demanded.

Alec nodded. "I am."

Without hesitation, the man held his hand out for Alec to shake, and after a pause, Alec took it.

My face nearly split open, I was smiling so wide. Someone casually touching Alec was an insignificant, everyday thing, but I knew how much it meant to him.

"Can you do it again? I have more burn victims than this facility is equipped to handle, and it would go much faster if patients weren't in pain." The doctor's face was wild with desperation and hope.

Alec looked at me, raising his brows.

"I'm up for it if you are." I shrugged. I was spent—absolutely exhausted, dirty, and sore in places I didn't want to think about, but I'd managed to have a nap on the plane, and I'd been sitting in the waiting room for hours letting the Light replenish. If there was anything we could do to help some of these people, I was on board.

"Lead the way, doctor." Alec's chest puffed out just a fraction as he threaded his fingers through mine and followed the doctor down the hall.

Tyler followed after us, heading for the exit. "I'll go try to deal with the press."

"I'll check in with Aunt Olivia." Ethan was already halfway through the door to Charlie's room.

"I'll get us all some food and coffee." Josh gathered his jacket from the plastic chair.

"Espresso!" I yelled over my shoulder. "Latte if you can get it."

He flashed me a grin and shook his head.

We all did better when we felt as though we had something to do—some way to contribute.

We had no idea if Lucian would make it through the night, Davis had escaped, Zara very likely had a dangerous new ability, and once again people had been maimed and killed. As soon as details made it to the public, I had no doubt tensions between Variants and humans would turn nuclear. We had one hell of a clusterfuck to deal with.

But in that moment, rushing down the hospital hallway hand in hand with Alec, at least I could take comfort in the fact that we would deal with it *together*. I finally felt as if I was part of my own Bond, and I knew they'd have my back no matter what.

EPILOGUE

"G'day, love. You right?" The trucker was about as cliché as you could imagine, standing between his rig and the back wall of the rest stop—potbelly, wifebeater, dirty red cap half covering his weathered, frowning face.

But what choice did Zara have? "Yeah, just tired."

"Strewth! American." He smiled, showing crooked teeth, but it seemed genuine. "Backpacker?"

Why did Australians insist on shortening everything? What was wrong with full sentences? She resisted the urge to roll her eyes and made herself stand up taller. "Yeah. Trying to get to Melbourne. Can I get a lift?"

"It's your lucky day!" The trucker pulled his shorts up, puffing his chest out. "Heading right through the city on me way to Geelong. Just gotta take a piss. Head off in fifteen."

He didn't wait for a response, walking around the block of toilets and leaving Zara alone in front of the semi-trailers. She let herself slump forward again, giving in to the shake in her arms.

She was somewhere just past Sydney. The couple in the minivan had dropped her off at the truck stop; they were heading into the center, and Zara needed to keep moving south.

It was a long way to Melbourne. Hopefully the trucker wouldn't want to do it in one long drive. Even though he didn't make the best first impression, she still didn't want to kill him. And she wasn't sure she could stay in control for that long.

She could feel the electricity now. It was always there, under her skin. Writhing, straining, demanding to be released. As if it knew it didn't belong there—that it wasn't Zara's to command.

Davis had a fucking contingency plan for everything, and it was almost laughable how easy it had been for them to slip away in Thailand. They'd been hiding out on a remote property in northern Australia, in another underground lab, as his scientists continued their work. But as Davis's plans moved forward, he had less and less interest in Zara and helping her bring her new ability under control. He'd all but given up trying to figure out why it was so unsettled—despite the fact she'd accidentally killed one of his men.

Even her own mother was paying her less and less attention. Zara was pretty sure she was fucking Davis, judging by the disgusting looks she threw his way any time they were in the same room. Apparently her father hadn't meant all that much to her, and neither did her daughter anymore.

"Right, let's get a move on." The trucker reappeared, climbing into the driver's side and not offering Zara any help with her backpack.

She'd packed only the essentials when she'd made a run for it. Not that she was entirely sure anyone gave a shit she was missing. But Davis was possessive of his creations, and he might come after her, which was why she was avoiding trains and airports. That and she was running out of money;

the odd plastic Australian bills were dwindling.

She threw her bag up and hefted herself into the passenger seat as the giant engine of the truck rumbled to life.

Zara couldn't see any other way out of the fucked-up situation. She needed to get to the one person who'd made it all possible—the one person whose very existence had given Davis what he'd needed to make Zara into an even bigger *freak* than she was before.

She needed to get to Evelyn Maynard.

There was only one way she could think to do that without getting caught by the police, the Melior Group, or worst of all, Davis Damari.

She only hoped Eve's ex Harvey wouldn't be too difficult to find.

THE END

ACKNOWLEDGEMENTS

First and foremost, to John – you are my partner in everything and this is no exception. Thank you for your unwavering support and faith in me.

To my loving friends and family, your genuine happiness and enthusiasm for this crazy thing I'm going means more than you know.

To Writer's Unite, your feedback is invaluable and your friendship treasured. Special mention for Julie – thank you for reading through the entire manuscript by my unreasonable deadline! You're a champ!

To my beta team, yes I know Americans don't put the letter 'u' in words like 'favourite' and 'colour'! Haha! Each and every one of you consistently provides valuable feedback along with reader reactions. Thank you for the time and effort you put in. Sam, you go above and beyond in your feedback. Thank you for your hard work but more importantly, thank you for your friendship.

Thank you to my ARC team. Your excited, ardent reactions make me excited to share my work with the rest of the world. Which is much better than the usual crippling self-doubt!

Thank you to my author friends, especially you bitches in the Sprint Team. The author world can be intense and crazy at times and I'm overjoyed to have such an amazing group of crown-fixing women in my circle.

To my readers – there are no words! You make it possible for me to do what I was born to do and there is no expressing the depth of gratitude I feel for that.

ABOUT THE AUTHOR

Kaydence Snow has lived all over the world but ended up settled in Melbourne, Australia. She lives near the beach with her husband and a beagle that has about as much attitude as her human.

She draws inspiration from her own overthinking, sometimes frightening imagination, and everything that makes life interesting – complicated relationships, unexpected twists, new experiences and good food and coffee. Life is not worth living without good food and coffee!

She believes sarcasm is the highest form of wit and has the vocabulary of a highly educated, well-read sailor. When she's not writing, thinking about writing, planning when she can write next, or reading other people's writing, she loves to travel and learn new things.

To keep up to date with Kaydence's latest news and releases sign up to her newsletter here: kaydencesnow.com

OR FOLLOW HER ON:

Facebook: @KaydenceSnowAuthor

Instagram: @kaydencesnowauthor

Twitter: @Kaydence_Snow

Goodreads: goodreads.com/author/show/18388923.Kaydence_Snow

Amazon: amazon.com/author/kaydencesnow

BookBub: www.bookbub.com/authors/kaydence-snow

NOTE FROM THE AUTHOR

Thank you so much for reading my book! It blows my mind that people are interested in reading what I wrote. I really hope you enjoyed Vital Found and you'll consider leaving a review. And if you didn't like it, that's OK too – I'm always open to feedback.

You can email me any time at hello@kaydencesnow.com